Swaying in defeat, Yattero cried out, "Dar Ell, kill him!"

Realizing too late, Landry glanced back as Jonathan Dar Ell opened the coach door to smite a gun barrel across the Marshal's skull. Landry collapsed as the woman screamed.

Ryke spun to his right and discharged a load into the guard primed on the roof. The impact blew the man back and down over the rear boot where he flailed into the mushy ruts. Swinging back, Ryke slammed the butt of his shotgun into the shocked driver, snapping his head and toppling him into the mud.

From the station, the keeper burst forth and pointed a long-barreled shotgun. But before he could aim, Ryke shot him.

"You damned fools," Dar Ell raged, stepping out of the stage.

"Kill the lawman. Kill the girl," Ryke throated. "Don't leave no witnesses."

Deliberately he punched three more bullets into the driver.

Also by Kenn Sherwood Roe:

MOONBLOOD
DUST DEVIL*
DEATHSTALK*

Published by Fawcett Books

COYOTE CRY

Kenn Sherwood Roe

FAWCETT GOLD MEDAL • NEW YORK

A Fawcett Gold Medal Book
Published by Ballantine Books
Copyright © 1993 by Kenn Sherwood Roe

Library of Congress Catalog Card Number: 93-90192

ISBN 0-449-14864-5

Manufactured in the United States of America

First Edition: August 1993

To
My wife, Dorey,
who suggested the ending;
and to her and my parents,
Vernon and Geraldine Roe,
who
proofread with unerring effort

Why the Coyote Cries

Long ago, from out of the swirly mists, E-sha the coyote and the first Indians emerged into the new world. Sun God looked upon coyote and the Indian as equal. He spread loving warmth over the land: the pinion harvest flourished; the rabbits multiplied; the deer and antelope grew fat; green grass and lush marsh drew flocks of wildfowl. Life was good. But coyote grew restless for he was dissatisfied. He lusted for more. "I will use my wit, I will steal all the harvest, and I will vanish into the wilderness," he said. And so, cleverly, he stole and hoarded all the bountiful things that Sun God had given them, leaving the Indian destitute to wander hungry as a scavenger.

When the angry Sun God confronted coyote, coyote taunted him and said, "I am not to blame. You have not given enough light. If you gave more light there would be plenty for everybody." Furious, Sun God fired the earth with his anger, turning it to molten rock and desert. Sun God caught Coyote and threw him against his hogan. Coyote hit so hard that some of his fur fell out. Sun God threw coyote three more times against a rock wall. Each time, patches of fur tore loose, leaving coyote with a shabby look. Fearing for his life, coyote fled.

Sun God picked up some fur and blew it to the east. "You, E-sha, will live in darkness," he said. Next he blew fur to the south. "You, E-sha, will roam the earth eternally, for your lost soul will drift with the wind, knowing no home." Then he blew fur to the west: "You, E-sha, will forever slink and steal and run." And finally, he blew fur to the north. "And those who befriend you will be doomed, abandoned in the wasteland to perish.'' Sun God lifted his eyes to the stars. ''All will fear the curse of E-sha,'' he proclaimed. And so it came to pass. Thus at twilight, the coyote cries.

Shoshonean Legend

(1)

In the top tier of the Nevada State Penitentiary, five convicts edged tensely against their locked doors. They waited. Downstairs in the warden's quarters a party was in progress, the lieutenant governor and his lady the honored guests. The sweet tones of stringed instruments flowed to them. Half of the guards remained off duty this quiet Sunday afternoon; a majority of those present remained stationed close to the dignitaries. The early dark of fall stretched purple shadows along the corridor. Outside, a strong wind hummed, whipping dust like fine shot against the stone walls to muffle any echo of footfalls. Guard Amos Biggs would be along shortly to trigger the plan. The prisoners, separated by rock walls, could not see each other, but their eyes held unseeing eastward, where their leader crouched in the last cell like an animal ready to spring.

Although at the age of thirteen Leander "Rattlesnake" Morton had disembowled a black man; at fourteen had sliced off the ear of an old Indian and had shortened the nose of a Chinese cook for fun; and at fifteen had raped and terrified two Mexican maidens, finding their screams and struggles most fulfilling; he had not gained recognition until nineteen, when he led five hooligans on a bank hit. "Swift, brilliantly executed," the Virginia City *Enterprise* had described it. The Morton gang made headlines the next four years, unexpectedly striking some banks, but mostly hitting Concord stages in the sweep between the Sierra escarpment and the rugged stretch of eastern desert. One-quarter Paiute, Morton had lived much of his life as a nomad, taking sustenance from the desolate land. An expert tracker, Morton was adept with a rifle or a six-shooter and particularly with a bowie knife, which he could throw with unerring accuracy and had dueled with successfully in numerous showdowns.

Medium in height, his enormous shoulders, muscled arms, and pine-sturdy legs intimidated men and struck panic in the weak. His long black hair accentuated a wide face and a flat nose; the beetling brows and droopy mustache framed thick lips that seemed frozen in a perpetual sneer. His piercing brown eyes revealed little emotion except as they burned with embers of consuming hate.

In those successful years, the Morton gang frustrated authorities, panicked stage officials, and terrorized a citizenry. So planned and efficient were the pillages that no one died in nearly two dozen robberies and holdups, until Tobias Johnson, eighteen, youngest gang member, tried to rip a jeweled brooch from a woman's bosom during a heist; as the woman shrieked and swooned, distracting Tobias, a teller pulled a hidden gun, only to be downed by the itchy-fingered youth. That evening in their mountain retreat, Morton pistol-whipped Tobias into a whimpering, senseless creature.

Despite the increased rewards, Morton had seemed to lead a charmed life with almost free rein, until a U.S. Marshal, Dirk Landry, appeared. Landry was something of a legend. As a lawman, he had cleaned up the tough towns of Panamint and Bodie, had broken up a notorious rustling ring as well as tracked down numerous killers, and had finished the rampage of one Moon, a crazed half-breed who had paralyzed the region for years.

Landry did not pursue Morton, rather, he decided it wiser to entice the desperado into a trap through a promise of fortune. Solid information indicated that Morton apparently sent his least-known members as spies to the various towns he planned to hit. Landry made certain that rumor established the sizable shipment of currency railroaded from the East to Carson City, and then shipped by wagon to the Coso Consolidated, a highly productive silver mine with a large work crew. The monthly payments included bonuses and dividends. Four heavily armed guards had accompanied a wagon and team to Benson Wells, a halfway station, where the strongbox was stashed in a small jail overnight, to be delivered the following morning. Of course, there was no currency, but Morton didn't know that. Two guards covered the jail, while the others slept in the upstairs of a nearby saloon to stand post at an appointed hour.

Under dark, six of the Morton gang converged from out of the desert. Morton was no fool; as a precautionary action he kidnapped the constable and his teenage son from their home and forced the "surprised guards" to surrender. Suddenly Morton's animal instincts warned him that the surprise was too successful, and he retreated, just as four of his gang members rushed the jail, into the guns of Landry and a select posse that had been stationed there several days prior. Landry's first shot had parted the eyes of a man threatening the constable and his son; the guns of the other lawmen exploded in greeting, spinning and sprawling the remaining four.

Rattlesnake Morton, not known for his loyalty or his courage under fire, had fled with the first barrage. He had reached the horses being held by young Tobias Johnson, the planted spy. But before the two could ride between protecting buildings, Landry had stepped from the jail with an aimed rifle to drop both their horses.

Despite public sentiment against Morton, and despite the prosecutor's plea for the death penalty, the defense attorney convinced the judge that Morton had not been directly responsible for the teller's death, and that Johnson was only a boy. Morton and Johnson had received life sentences in the state penitentiary.

As Morton watched guard Biggs approach, he thought about Marshal Landry. If the breakout succeeded, doubtless Landry would be on their trail again. He was the law's best in the Great Basin. Maybe fate would cross them again. Morton wanted that, but for now such wishes remained a distant dream. All that obsessed him was freedom from his hellhole: the isolation pens, the watery meals and moldy bread, the long hours of back-busting toil in a rock quarry, always in silence while guards spat and cursed. The march back to solitary cells at night, a worthless blanket to harbor one from the musty cold; in the ceiling, one narrow opening for light and air; a bucket for human waste to be emptied once each twenty-four hours. To be free, Morton would kill without hesitation, and he would die in a blazing exodus before ever returning, he had decided.

Bit by bit over the months, word by word, thought by thought, the scheme had evolved—the enticement, the monetary offer, the testing of Biggs until the appointed hour. The haunting sweet strains of a violin accompanied by a viola and a piano seemed to soften the harsh gray of blunt walls. According to plans, after Morton's taunting, Biggs would move too close. Morton would reach through the iron bars and pin Biggs, removing his small pistol and forcing the guard to unlock the brass lock, plus the leg chain and fifteen-pound ball. After trussing Biggs up with his own clothes and belt, he would release a half-dozen others, including his old partners, Tobias Johnson, Red, Weasel, and Slicer. One by one they would overwhelm the two guards or so below. Once they jumped the gate guard, they'd find the Mexican kid, Alvaro, waiting in the prison cemetery with the horses, guns, and ammunition. Biggs and the kid had collected some changes of clothing, but most of the escapees would have to forage their own along the way. Fortunately, the Sunday party and the break had correlated with a full moon that would allow night travel.

Morton had promised Biggs a six thousand dollar cache buried in a little town, Windy Flat, to the southwest. When they left the tier, he would reveal its exact whereabouts. But it all bothered him. Was Biggs so naive that he believed there could be honor amongst thieves? Was he so blindly gluttonous that he would agree verbally? As a kind of collateral, Morton had given Biggs the name and address of his only living relative—a half sister living in Austin. Biggs would verify that. But what Morton hadn't told Biggs was that the man could beat her near to death and he wouldn't care. They had never had much to do with each other—she was a religious convert who long ago had consigned her brother to hell. In fact, they hadn't exchanged words in over ten years. He knew her present address because it was on the official records in the prison office. What troubled Morton most: was Biggs up to something more, something bigger? A break of this significance would make national headlines, would attract the attention of every lawman and every citizen west of the Rockies. Biggs was not stupid, greedy certainly, but not a dupe. What else crouched in his devious little mind? Morton intended to find out. He studied the approaching guard. The man seemed to be chuckling to himself; perhaps it was nerves. Fool had better make it look convincing, Morton thought.

"Cold wind out there," said Biggs.

"It'll warm up before the night's over."

"Shut up." The words hissed disdain as Biggs moved closer. "There are two on the deck below," he commented softly; then loudly: "Close-up time. In your bunks."

"I don't feel so good," said Morton. "It's that hogwash we had for supper."

"Slop's good enough for a pig."

"I'd like to stuff that crap down your gullet, guard."

Biggs came close to the grill. "You're life ain't worth much now, but it's growing less day by day, Morton."

"Talk's big out there, ain't it, guard." Morton grinned through yellow teeth.

"You'll pay hell for that mouth, Morton." Biggs came too close.

Like a striking snake, Morton's hand shot through the bars, caught Biggs's lapels and slammed him against the door. With his left hand he grasped one of Biggs's forearms and pulled it through, twisting backward where the elbow lodged in the V of a cross link. "Not so goddammed hard," Biggs sizzled through his teeth.

Ignoring him, Morton reached under the guard's coat, withdrew the expected pistol and cocked it. "The keys, the keys, damn it." Painfully, Biggs snapped free the brass lock. Morton swung the door open. "Now for the shackles." Biggs produced a smaller key. Morton pushed Biggs away, held the gun at his chest and released leg irons that were linked to a ponderous lead ball.

Some prisoners began breathing heavily in an ecstasy of excitement. A few moaned like animals in anticipation. Morton snapped free a second brass lock and handed the shackle key to the prisoner. Then dragging Biggs with him, he proceeded to unlock more prisoners. "Unlock all their leg irons," he ordered the second escapee—a lion-maned individual called Red. "The gang members first."

"Tobias, Weasel, and Slicer?"

"Yes." And then Morton quickly freed the top tier of men, a total of fifteen hardened criminals, far more than Biggs had planned.

"What the hell you doing?" Biggs whispered, his voice rising.

"Shut up. The more we let out, the more confusing, and the better chance we got."

The prisoners scurried quietly about to bunch anxiously before Morton. "You was to leave me—leave me trussed up in the cell," said Biggs, his voice low but hesitant. He eyed the revolver pointed at his belly.

"Plans have changed." Clutching Biggs's shoulder, Morton marched the guard toward the stairwell.

"What do you mean?"

"You're my ticket out of here."

"You taking me as a hostage?"

"That's right."

"You double-crossing son of a bitch."

The music stopped. Apparently someone had heard the muffled movement of feet. Morton took his hand from Biggs and raised it in a gesture of silence. From the stairway below, a guard having heard a disturbance charged up two steps at a time, his handgun extended. As he pushed open the door to the third tier, Leander Morton stepped forward to kick his gun arm, discharging the weapon toward the ceiling. Another convict crushed a waste bucket across his skull. As the man sank against a wall, a half-dozen desperadoes rushed forth to kill. "Don't waste your time," Morton warned. "Let's get out of here." The words momentarily sobered the frenzied men. Several lifted the guard and flung him senseless into an open cell as one man picked up his gun. Then, as a menacing force, murderers, train robbers, hired killers, all dangerous criminals, they bolted down the stairway, dragging Biggs with them. From somewhere a woman screamed.

A second guard stepped bravely before them, his revolver pointing. "Halt," he cried, firing once below their feet, the bullet winging crazily twice before flattening into the wall. The prisoners ducked. But Rattlesnake Morton responded with two shots that spun the guard to roll lifeless, his head wedged over a step, his arms stretched downward. Now the convicts had three pistols. The escapees stepped out on a balcony overlooking the mess hall, where they surged toward the warden's quarters, an isolated two-story wing. The guards on the opposite balcony just outside his door rushed forward upon hearing the shots, only to be confronted by the first prisoners, all with guns blazing away. Carrying their rifles crossed at their chests, the guards proved easy victims. Before they could swing into position, the pistol lead had bored into them, flinging them around, to flop lifeless.

Unexpectedly, Warden Benteen opened the door, a lantern in hand, and met them as they swept toward the final stairwell. Defensively, Benteen discharged four bullets toward them, dropping the man in the lead, a wild-haired chap with crazed face and hysterical eyes, who rose and kept charging until a fourth shot split his protruding brow. The onslaught of prisoners suddenly turned toward the warden, parting their force to pincer around the balustrade toward him. They ran screaming and cursing, filled with the pent-up hostility of caged animals. Benteen fired his last shot, missing. Before he could slam and bolt the door, Red hurtled his two hundred pounds of mountainous flesh on the man, sending him back prostrate into his quarters. A woman screamed again, the piercing sound anguished. From the inner suite a trusty named Frank Denver, who was serving dinner, grabbed a chair and rushed into the confusion. As Big Red reached for the warden, Denver flattened him with a smash of the furniture across the shoulder blades. Swinging wildly, Denver knocked five more of the prisoners down; one of them, after twice hitting the floor, rose with a long, cell-made knife and charged. Denver gave him a blow of the chair that sent the man over the balustrade to the floor below.

"Let's get the hell out," Rattlesnake Morton roared. He stood far back, near the exit, well-shielded by the desperate men before him.

Momentarily countered, the prisoners pulled back and plunged on down the last stairwell, as Denver dragged the warden inside and bolted the door. The thirteen remaining prisoners, now pushing Biggs ahead of them, reached the outer door, where one of the few remaining guards on duty fired at them from the corner of an outer storage building with a carbine; its lead shattered away chunks of concrete. With such a superior weapon, the guard could hold them at bay, Morton knew, aborting their escape unless stopped somehow. While Morton considered their plight, a pistol in hand, the other two armed prisoners exchanged shots with the guard, shooting through the door and nearby window. Morton's reptilian eyes hardened as he focused them on the stone building to the left. "Tobias," he called, his voice hissing. "The armory. The armory. Ain't nobody there."

Tobias, handsome still, his leathery face horseshoed with a rich black mustache, and his full dark hair just beginning to tint gray, smiled knowingly. He pointed out three men and motioned them to follow. Recklessly, he broke out the side window with a bench and threw a blanket over the sill—a blanket that one of the men carried in anticipation of the need. The four poured through and sprinted their way to the nearby armory. Quickly, they broke off the lock with a rock and pushed inside to secure several rifles, revolvers, and ammunition for the remaining men. From the cramped tower above the east gate, a second guard started firing.

Morton leaned close to the front door. "We got one of your good friends here," he called. "His name—Amos Biggs." The shooting ceased. "Throw down your guns or he's dead," Morton threatened. For several minutes silence settled.

"More guards there," said Slicer, peering through the smashed window into the closing twilight. "I see 'em coming, barely see 'em now, moving toward us, quiet as coyotes."

Morton twisted Biggs's arm and pushed his head around the doorjamb, the pistol to his skull. "He's right, Hank," Biggs called. "They've got me."

The guard referred to as "Hank" stood up, partially concealed. "You know, Amos, that's part of the job. We don't spare nobody, no one, no guard, no one who's taken hostage. That's the rule. You know it, and they know it."

From the armory, the armed prisoners took positions. Tobias Johnson watched with satisfaction, listening, as he loaded a Winchester, took quick but careful aim, and squeezed. The bullet broke the kneecap of the guard called Hank. The three others followed suit to blast wildly. But Hank didn't go down. He remained unsteady but determined on one leg, shooting back until a second bullet broke his hip, dropping him.

Out of the dusk two more guards appeared, part of those closing in. They advanced in an explosion of shots, both falling incapacitated from the withering fire of those inside the armory, but not before their exchange wounded three of the prisoners, one seriously. A few shadowy guards behind disappeared.

Those escapees still imprisoned in the guard room edged out. But Hank in the tower kept them effectively pinned, his shots surprisingly unerring, so close that one convict wiped his skull and came up with a palm of greasy blood. "Everyone with guns," Morton throated. "Aim at that tower. Aim and fire, goddamn it. Fire, fire, fire."

All the confiscated weapons sounded in a barrage. The tower guard, hearing the order, ducked. But whining, ricocheting bullets riddled about him, one catching him in the throat. He came up clutching his neck, where blood squirmed between his fingers; swaying, he toppled over the wall.

Thirteen convicts and guard Biggs streamed out through the gates. Distant slugs nipped at their heels as those few remaining guards wormed reluctantly into view, trying vainly to stop the break. The night wind boiled sand across the expanse, pelting them, as the men in cotton stripes fled. At last, at Rattlesnake's signal, they stopped under the cloak of a giant cottonwood to check their bearings.

"It's up there on the slope—the graveyard," the felon called Slicer said. His hatchet-shaped face and narrow eyes gleamed in the moon glow. They plunged ahead and climbed through the tilted crosses and blunt stones. Under the umbrella of clustered trees they saw a slim form astride a horse. He was overlooking seven hobbled mounts, all with saddlebags filled with what staples and clothing could be secured. The Mexican boy trembled, hunching under the cold; he forced a smile, but his dark eyes dilated with fear.

"You, boy, we've arrived," Morton called.

"Not enough horses for you all," Biggs coughed. "What the hell you tryin'?"

"I want an army," said Rattlesnake Morton. "I want an army. Some of 'em will have to ride double till we pick up more horses. The boy's will add one more."

"Don't hurt the kid," Biggs said. "He done his best for you with a pittance for pay."

"You ain't got much to say about it, do you?" Morton rotated his hand, the small revolver scanning over Biggs's chest.

Biggs watched, his eyes protruding. "You're a fool. You can't get away—not with all of them here."

"Don't intend to."

"Meaning what?"

Morton pawed through the saddlebags one after another. "How many guns?"

"Six, sir—all I could get," said the boy.

"Hell, and no rifles. We'll have to pick more up along the way." In the cold, starlit darkness a waning moon rose in the east, whitewashing the sage; the prisoners took the horses. "Get those six guns and some shells," Morton ordered. "With what we got from the armory, that'll give some of us two pieces." A half-dozen men took the revolvers from the bags. From the prison to the northwest they could see men emerging, their lanterns casting shadowy glows as they searched for tracks. "Hurry," said Morton.

He stepped forward and clubbed the Mexican kid from his saddle. Deliberately, he barrel-whipped the boy again and then again across the youth's defenseless head until the boy lay quivering, uttering little animal sounds that ceased shortly.

"Why? Why?" Biggs cried.

"Needed his horse and clothes," Morton replied. Furiously, he tore the coat, shirt, and trousers from the body and tossed them to a smallish man with a flat, elongated head. "Here, Weasel, all yours." The man snapped them out of the air.

The escapees mounted and galloped away, Biggs in front of Morton, the saddle horn gouging his lower spine. Five others climbed on behind mounted riders, including Weasel, who was tugging his new clothes over the prison garb. They rode, then, into the moon darkness against the cold blister of sand, taking care to pick their way at a cautious trot, southwest through sage-covered hollows toward the black wall of Sierras.

An hour later, in the cleft of a sand bowl, they halted. All hugged their bodies, slapping their arms across chests in misery, the woolen uniforms of black and white insufficient for outdoor travel. Two men fussed with their uniforms where spots splotched a growing red—one man in the thigh, and the other along the left bicep where bullets had grazed. But a third escapee leaned precariously over the horse's mane, his body swaying, a crimson flow streaking down his left ribbing. Stoically the men watched. The moon, big still, made visibility good.

"We decide here," said Morton, reining tight, his horse prancing and twisting with impatience. Amos Biggs slumped forward slightly in discomfort. "We split here," Morton repeated.

"What do you mean?" Tobias Johnson demanded, his handsome features suspicious.

"We split three ways. It's the only way we can make it. We split, it'll terrorize from here to Utah. Nobody, no lawman, will know exactly where we are—'specially that damned Dirk Landry!"

"I'm not leaving you," said Tobias. "Me and you—we've been together too long."

"We split here," said Rattlesnake Morton, ignoring Tobias. "I figure one group toward the Amargosa, on into Arizona and maybe Mexico. Another east—before the snows—toward Austin or Eureka. You who go might have to hold out for the winter there, then in spring head north, best into Idaho or Wyoming. Law will never find you there."

"What the hell you plan?" Tobias leaned out from his horse and dropped a ropy splash of saliva.

"Me? I'll head over the Sierras into California."

"Well, for me, I ain't leaving you, either," said the bulky man with the shaggy red hair and beard.

"We ain't leaving you. We ain't leaving you no way," others chorused.

Morton's wide face hardened; his flat nose curled upward, the nostrils distending. "What the hell you mean?" His right hand swayed before the revolver in his belt.

Again Tobias Johnson ejected an elongated glob of saliva. "What they mean is, they suspect why you're haulin' that guard around for nothing'. Meanin' if you didn't want him for something we don't know of, you'd left him behind or blasted his brains out long back."

"You're full of it. You're crazy with imaginings," said Morton. "All of you are." He looked them over, then back at Tobias. "You. You're my best buddy and you think I'd double cross you?"

Tobias smiled and slowly spat again. "We're stickin' with you."

"All of you?"

"There's more than meets the eye, boss," Red called.

Morton studied the confiscated guns, all poised and readied in various positions. He replied calmly. "You're thinking's wrong—mighty wrong. If we don't split, we just might get killed, all of us real quick, 'cause there's going to be one hell of a lot of posse men behind us, combing the whole land, every damned inch." Morton's eyes avoided the guns, but settled over one after the other of those before him. "We move out as a body, we leave a trail like an invitation. They'll come on us from every side. I'll lay odds on your heathen souls that you'll all die before two sunsets."

"Ain't to my figurin'," said Red, scratching his grizzled beard. "For me, I'm stickin' with you, at least until you shoot that guard." Biggs wormed uncomfortably. A belt pinioned his arms behind him.

"My thinking too," said Tobias Johnson. As a unit all the others agreed.

"We're with you, Red, Tobias," a man said. The escapees rallied around Morton and his hostage.

"Fools," said Morton. "I sprung you all. Freed you. Got you a whole new chance. You asses. Don't you realize—all of us together will leave a trail as wide as a herd of cattle?"

"No use," said Red. "As I said, we split only if you shoot that guard. Otherwise we stick as close as the skin on a polecat."

"Biggs here, he's nothin' but coyote bait." Morton's horse sensed the tension and pivoted anxiously, swishing its tail and tossing its head, then pranced sideways and came back again.

"Prove it," said Tobias.

"How?"

"Blow him away. Here, right here and now," said Tobias icily.

Morton clutched Biggs, threaded his fingers around the man's biceps. "I keep him because somewhere down the way he may prove handy, especially if we cross some lawmen."

"Then let's go," Red growled, "time's wasting."

"Just one thing," said Morton. "You damned fools better understand that if things get rough, I don't owe you a thing."

"We'll chance that," said Tobias.

"We shore will," Weasel added.

"Lead the way." Red gestured.

Rattlesnake Morton rode into the lead toward high mountains that he had no intention of climbing.

Exhausted, in the frigid cold of early morning, the convicts took rest in the protected leave of a rocky cul-de-sac. They huddled together in miserable silence without adequate cover or ample food except for a cloth sack filled with salty slabs of beef jerky. As the wind blew relentlessly, they tore and munched greedily on leathcry meat. They watched the horses drink deeply from a steady seep at the base of an arrow-shaped outcrop. They removed the bits and waited impatiently while the animals cropped the marshy grass.

"Can't wait too damn long," said Red.

"Can't get too damn far with an exhausted or dead animal, either," Morton countered.

"Got to pick us up more grub and blankets," said Weasel, tearing at the jerky.

"And we got to get out of these damned prison duds, and soon," said Tobias.

"We will shortly," said Morton. "This moon's giving even more light than I'd hoped for. Take it slow, we should be able to get in some good miles yet."

"So where from here?" Tobias asked, pounding his body with crossed arms to stimulate circulation.

"Few miles ahead, there's an old camp, Windy Flat. Remember?" Morton said.

"Yeah, I remember. Just a water hole now. A saloon, a corral, even a store, I think."

"It's enough. We'll take what all we need there." Morton pulled Amos Biggs to him, cruelly, his thick fingers sinking deeply into the guard's flesh, and marched him out of hearing by the others. "You're our future," he said with relish. "You're going to get me—I mean all of us—out."

"What the hell you mean?"

"You know what I mean."

"No, I don't. Why are you kidnapping me?" Biggs's words had a thickness of fear in them. "I did my part. I got you out on a deal. Why didn't you leave me as planned? Why?"

Morton's wide face, flat nose, and beetling brows, all framed in the long black hair, shaped suddenly into a leering grin of triumph and certainty. "I been figuring all along— you ain't sellin' your future, your whole self, for a measly six thousand, which I'll take for myself anyway—when we get to Windy Flat."

"That's a lifetime of gold. I get fifty a month. You don't think six thousand is a fortune?"

"No."

"You're crazy."

"Six thousand ain't worth chancing one's life—at least in your case." Morton's piercing black eyes went deep into Biggs. "I smell a deal. I smell that you sprung us out for something bigger." Morton's eyes narrowed and his mouth pursed in consideration. "I have suspicion you ain't shared all your plans with us good friends. But if you treasure your life, you will talk—to me. And only to me."

Amos Biggs hesitated. He looked into the reptilian eyes and knew his life was as tenuous as the shifting sands around him, that he had no choice but to gamble and play for time. "Well, there is a bigger deal brewing," he said.

(2)

On the twilight desert where sagebrush hills rolled easily under the abrupt rise of Sierran thrust, a dozen coyotes circled the rimrock. Below, in a sloping recess, a squat hut slanted eastward, its gray blend of rock and adobe barely perceptible in the expanse. In front, six saddled horses stood patiently, their heads bowed, tails swishing lazily. Through the small windows where slits formed between the stone sills and the hung cloth, streams of lantern light haloed the ground about. The coyotes hunched and slunk erratically, their sensitive ears catching the sounds of a resonant, baritone voice— a man speaking with authority.

The animals watched. Sunset reflected in their opal eyes, gleamed eerily like those of some spectral forms, demon eyes in the gloom. The coyotes roamed restlessly; a few lifted their muzzles to yip and wail a high yodeling sound that trailed away mournfully. This lonely, forgotten spot remained their domain, abandoned for some five years now, since two prospectors had lost faith in the cramped mine on the back hill. But in the last days, man had intruded once more—three riders, an Indian, a youth, and a lean man graced with a flowing cloak, had ridden to the hut, had puttered and rearranged for a few hours while the coyotes had waited in seclusion, several low under an overhanging rock slab, another under the shade of a mahogany bush, one by her den. Their sleepy eyes had slanted and blinked, studying the encroachers until the three had left, the white men riding doggedly to the east, the Indian slipping away toward the Sierras.

But on this night, the man number had increased, their soft voices drifting up the swale, disturbing the perfect harmony of natural things. The coyotes separated and drew back. A pair of animals appeared on a rocky point due east of the pack. The swift rise of a full moon washed them in a mellow gold. Filled suddenly with a moon magic, they too raised their pointed snouts and sent eerie cries trembling into the night. The pack above the hut responded, chorusing with a cacophony of yips and barks and high waverings. First one voice and then another joined, often disjointed, sometimes harmonizing, sounds ending in long-drawn wails intended for the stars.

Former Shakespearean actor, stage director, elocutionist, and now manager of the Desert Globe, the finest theater and palace saloon in the territory, Jonathan Dar Ell looked out the window of the squat hut at the enclosing darkness. Amos Biggs, last of the participants, was late. Far in the desert, where a rising moon washed the sage land, forms moved like flittering shadows—coyotes. Their yipping wails echoed from behind Dar Ell. Outside the western window, where the pink of dying day silhouetted the High Sierras, more coyotes answered. A shiver ran through the man. Somehow the animals signaled something that could not be explained, only felt. "Something in the wind," he muttered, his eyes intent. "Let not my dreams become a comedy of errors." Tall, slender, with a thin, chiseled nose, slightly elevated at the crown, Dar Ell made a striking figure on a stage or behind a podium. The sleek black hair, the sensuous mouth, the strong jaw and high cheekbones, set him apart from other men; that and his penchant for wearing a cloak and a derby hat, and his seasoned baritone voice, so rich and mellifluous that those who heard his words never forgot.

But the coyotes. They filled him with tremors of foreboding. He guessed why. It was the old Paiute sitting cross-legged in the corner, rocking and humming some ancient chant to himself. His dark, decaying face, a wrinkled crunch of skin and flesh, stretched and hardened in the cheeks as if partially mummified. His stringy gray hair streaked his shoulders, to coil over his vest and soiled shirt. To look at the pathetic creature could give any white man misgivings, Dar Ell knew, but Nasa Tom had royal blood. His father and grandfather had been chieftains; and as a young man, he had guided John C. Fremont, and even assisted Kit Carson in crossing the Sierras. Probably not a man alive now knew the passes as intimately—ancient, untraveled, secret passes; Nasa Tom would lead his men to freedom and to a future afterward in California, maybe to Mexico if things didn't work out. The shrunken form was deceptive, Dar Ell knew. The old Indian could outclimb a mountain sheep, could eventually outpace a mule with time. Sinewy and solid, he could live on jerky, water, and tupa roots, and survive eternally. Dar Ell had checked all that out and had come by the old man through great effort and money. It was not Nasa Tom's appearance that so much disturbed him, but his words, the fantasies, his haunting allusions to coyotes. Yes, coyotes—those wild, primitive animals outside on the ridge.

Dar Ell was a reasonable man, an educated and intelligent man who had played before royalty in Europe and before the powerful and the wealthy in Boston, Philadelphia, and Charleston. That is, before things went wrong. Ignorance, superstition, myth repulsed him. But in the last days, while making plans in the hut, the final details for a heist that would leave him wealthy and set for life, the old Indian had talked crazily. Each time he had appeared for rendezvous in the Sierran desert, he had babbled incessantly about coyotes—wild things about a coyote god—something called E-sha, who had defied the Sun God and stolen all his goods, some great horde, and was consequently cursed forever, to wander the wilderness with no hope and no relief but death. Nasa Tom had grown progressively reluctant and withdrawn, claiming that all of them would suffer an inevitable curse. That some would die. His rambling had not been without effect on the other men, especially Yattero, who was unstable anyway. And now even Dar Ell was under the spell.

The old Paiute rocked back and forth still; his eyes had a distant, disconnected look. He sang to himself continuously, disconcertingly, his eyes rolling white, the musky scent of his earthy body permeating the room. "I'll pay you well, old Indian," Dar Ell had told him the day before. "You get my men across the mountains and you'll live the rest of your life like none of your people have ever lived." Could he be trusted? Dar Ell wondered. Not only was his state of mind suspect, but there had been stories that his family had been abused and demoralized by white men. And like so many of his people, he had been reduced to begging in a white man's world. Dar Ell could tolerate the Indian's eccentricities and irritable superstitions. But what hatreds might the old man harbor?

Lon Wiggins, the twenty-year-old sitting anxiously behind the battered mahogany table, had been instrumental in finding the necessary information on Nasa Tom. Dar Ell liked the youth. He had much promise—he had a burning ambition to be somebody, to be independent, to make money. Dar Ell admired that. Bright, clean-shaven, with long, curly blond hair and blue eyes, he was the kind of son any family would be proud of. The boy was much in love with a little Spanish beauty. His joy over her radiated in his face; and that sight warmed Dar Ell. Lon's mother had died giving him birth along the California Trail. The father, a prospector in the mother lode, had raised the child with the help of a Yana Indian woman and later a Mexican maid. The father had been a successful parent but a failing miner. After he had died from consumption, a broken man, Lon had wandered eastward over the Sierras, finding his way to the town of Limbo and to the Desert Globe. With fondness, Dar Ell recalled the boy, his clothes loose and ragged and his eyes exhausted but feverish with determination. Dar Ell had hired him for miscellaneous handiwork. Quickly he had proven himself a hard worker—sweeping, cleaning, repairing, ushering, sometimes bartending and cooking when necessary. Gradually, as confidence had grown between them, Lon had become a messenger, a private spy, really. Likable, disarming, he could infiltrate any group—miners, ranchers, engineers, speculators. Dar Ell had used him to find the best guide around who might know a little-traveled route across the Sierras, with Nasa Tom the result.

Lon had made contacts through a nephew of Nasa Tom—Johnny Wolfsong—a sulky, hard-eyed kid with athletic frame, who had worked for Dar Ell a few months, tending the animals and guarding the wagons for the evening patrons. Dar Ell had instinctively felt uncomfortable about the young Paiute and had dismissed him when he was caught stealing money from the bar, although Lon had protested, having struck up an unlikely friendship with Johnny. The two boys hung around a lot together, and sometimes went hunting in the foothills. Johnny had been a bounty hunter for predators and knew the land and its animals. Despite being handsome and intelligent, the Indian had a mean streak and was known for leaving animals in a trap longer than necessary.

Dar Ell could not explain his protective feelings toward Lon, but the boy was his concern and he didn't want him associating with the likes of Johnny Wolfsong. Last he had heard, the Indian had found work in California, although he had come back to visit Lon. Dar Ell wanted to give the youth a chance. That Lon would be labeled a criminal, that his moral being would be altered forever, weighed on Dar Ell. But the ultimate rewards, the art and beauty of a perfect crime, would give them all, especially Lon, a life of luxury and freedom from want. That fact alone overwhelmed his concern. What he had planned was right, he had decided.

To the side of Lon sat Miguel Yattero, squat, greasy-skinned, with faded brown eyes and a droopy mustache that overhung a wide, gap-toothed mouth. The Mexican took a deep gulp from the open whiskey bottle on the table. When amused, he had a habit of tipping his round, slouched hat back on his head, and when troubled, he would tip it far forward to glare out from under the rim. He wore a long-barreled .44 snug on his right hip under the flap of a corduroy coat, the heavy holster tight against breeches tucked in high boots.

Two years before, Yattero had drifted in from Arizona Territory to find work as a stagehand. He was relatively bright and could speak tolerable English. He seemed fascinated with the foreign world of show business. But he was strangely superstitious. Rumors had accompanied him—mostly whispers that he was wanted for robbery—but nothing ever materialized, no lawmen on the snoop or any wanted posters, although Dar Ell's intuition told him that Yattero did, in fact, have an unsavory past. Dar Ell had capitalized on his gifted sense to use the Mexican. Good with his hands and especially with horses, Yattero had taken a job (through Dar Ell's quiet efforts) as a stock tender for Wells Fargo at a swing station fifteen miles west of Limbo—a small stop called Willow Springs. There he unhooked the traces of six tired horses and hitched up a fresh team in a period of four minutes. He then greased the axles of the stages in preparation of the next haul. Yattero by now was well-established with the stage line. He proved little worry for Dar Ell, except for the unjustified fears that plagued the former actor. Would Yattero hold up under pressure? That was the one unknown factor that concerned Dar Ell.

Dar Ell scanned the room. Harrel Ryke leaned against the

sill of a far window, peering through the narrow opening of burlap. Nervously, he rolled the cylinder of his revolver again and again—an irritating habit that grated on Dar Ell. But he understood in this instance. A year of plans would be launched within five days, the heist of a lifetime, a two-year dream that had been his brainchild. Ryke had a nervous energy that marked his type: unpredictable and dangerous, the type that one never quite trusted but that was necessary in such undertakings. Slender in dark brown clothes, he had a hatchet-thin face that converged into a sharp nose. His narrow, brown eyes pierced rather than saw one. He was known in the trade as a shootist. When in the holster, his Colt hung low on his right thigh, strapped slightly forward with the butt at an outer angle.

Dar Ell had hired Ryke, one of seven applicants, as a bodyguard and an enforcer. In the adjoining saloon next to the theater, drunks, high-spirited miners, and cowboys congregated. And despite the rather elite reputation of the Desert Globe, liquor and crowds made for trouble. Husky bartenders and paid bouncers sufficed normally, but those few bolstered on whiskey or just downright mean demanded more than muscles to counter. Ryke had been recommended by Sheriff George Healy. Healy didn't know him personally. In fact, circulated rumors hinted that Ryke had a price on his head, but like Yattero, no one offered verification.

"Why'd you pick him?" Dar Ell had inquired, liking the new sheriff, an ambitious young man obviously hungering to prove himself.

"It's the way he carries that forty-five, low, tilted outward with the handle a bit forward. He moves like a cat, and it's his eyes. They nail you. If he just looks at some hoodlum, the fellow will think twice. That's what you want. My only concern, he's nervous, maybe too itchy. He might be easily goaded to shoot and think later," Healy had said.

The first proof of Healy's wisdom had come when the

seven applicants had competed outside of town to shoot at whiskey bottles, twenty feet, then forty feet, then sixty from them, the participants to draw upon command. In all tests, Ryke had won handily.

And then a week later, Ryke had proven himself completely. Three ruffians, quarrelsome and intimidating, had unsettled the crowd in the gambling palace. Swaggering and bulky in their sheepskin coats, they had bullied their way to the bar, forcing patrons to step aside. They had taken a bottle, had refused to pay, had deliberately broken glasses and forced themselves on a hostess, tearing her dress. When a hefty bouncer stepped in, one of the members had clubbed him unconscious from behind with a gun. Dar Ell had appeared then on the staircase, Ryke a step above and to his left.

Dar Ell's trained voice had rolled across the room, halting activity. "Get out. This place is off-limits. Get out and stay out," Dar Ell had ordered. In his hand under the full sleeve, tucked in the fold of his cloak, he had held a small cocked revolver. Surprised, the three had stood silently. Then the apparent leader, a wiry chap with low brows and a twisted face, had smiled expectantly, taking pleasure in what he saw.

He had grinned. "Well lookie, lookie. Ain't we somethin'—just pretty like somethin' out of a play." His partners had sidled in behind him, all judging Dar Ell and the gunman above him.

"You ain't got no choice now," Ryke had said softly, his words meant only for his boss. "They've already set their minds. Words ain't going to do no good now."

"They might," Dar Ell had said as the three lined threateningly at the foot of the stairs.

"Don't give them tramps an edge," Ryke had said through tight lips. "When I call it, you take that man in front. Shoot toward his gut, that way you'll get him higher where it counts."

"Now what you boys whisperin' about?" asked the leader.

Dar Ell remembered Ryke's snappy "Now!" As a dramatist, as an elocutionist, Dar Ell's mind had always remained clear. That was a professional commandment. But that moment was a hazy blur now. Vaguely he remembered raising his pistol and firing; remembered Ryke stepping to his left, his side arm flashing hot bursts next to his own arm. Dar Ell's two shots had taken the leader by surprise, the man's face blanching as he reached too late for his gun. The quick shots had sunk home, had knocked him in a crazy uncoordinated step back, his left arm flailing, his right fumbling across the holster. Ryke had followed with more shots in succession, the rhythm and sound merging as one. The two backup men never found their arms. Ryke's bullets had doubled one, had spun the second, his body convulsing brokenly as he nosed across a table, overturning it to sprawl loosely. Their leader, wobbly on his feet, his face stricken, had tugged free his gun. Simultaneously, Dar Ell and Ryke had pumped their remaining shots into the man, collapsing him in the roil of black smoke. Yes, Ryke was a strange one, a man filled with dark demons, who might fight or abandon one according to the changing winds; but he was indispensable in the present plans.

Dar Ell studied the others. He had cultivated them; they were tools for his dreams. "Are these then the halcyon days?" His rich voice, the words unexpected, turned the men to him. Outside, the coyotes had ceased momentarily. Dar Ell sensed movement. He lifted the window flap. A horse and rider moved into the funnels of light. At last, Amos Biggs. Relieved, Dar Ell took a silver flask from his coat and drew deeply, coughing as the brandy cut warmly. Biggs reined his horse close to the door and slid off. A paunchy man with full, flushed cheeks and slender mustache, he appeared in a government military coat and gray flannel pants and shirt. He's learning some sense, Dar Ell thought, for he half expected the man to ride into the desert dressed in his prison guard uniform.

Amos Biggs was Dar Ell's nephew by a long-deceased sister. No one knew that—a sacred secret that hopefully would bear fruit. Nearly four years earlier, shortly after Dar Ell had assumed managership of the Desert Globe, Biggs had sought him out, had given verifiable proof of his relationship, and then had asked for a loan to see him through until his new job as a state guard paid off. Dar Ell had loaned the money, not out of family compassion, but because the position interested him. The men had become casual acquaintances, Biggs visiting on days off to drink in the saloon and to talk of childhood recollections. Surprisingly, he had repaid his loan regularly. Then one day he had confided that the most noted prisoner, Leander "Rattlesnake" Morton, had approached him with an offer—if Amos assisted in a prison break, he would be guaranteed six thousand dollars in a hidden cache nearby, enough, certainly, to set Biggs up handsomely for a time. Biggs's confidences had been the core to an elaborate plan, a year of effort, detail, and meticulous planning.

Dar Ell wedged open the door; the fall wind gushed coldly ahead of the guard, to flicker the oil lantern and blaze higher the small fire that burned steadily in the hearth. "You're late." Dar Ell licked his lips.

"Didn't want to ride direct from the prison. I waited a time, then swung north and come down the valley."

Dar Ell softened. "Probably best you did. But you could have planned better. Started earlier."

Biggs nodded at the men in the room, who regarded him coolly. He looked curiously at Ryke, playing anxiously with the cylinder still, once again staring fiercely out a window.

"Sit down," Dar Ell ordered. "All of you. You listen hard once more and you listen carefully." Biggs picked up the whiskey bottle on the table and took a long draft, eyes closed until he sputtered, spewing saliva and bourbon across the room. Lon looked at him with disgust. "You, Biggs." Dar Ell pointed. "We start with you. You tell me what's to happen."

Biggs wiped his mouth with a backhand; his small brown eyes darted back and forth to Yattero and to Lon, around to Ryke, who had reluctantly taken a seat, and back to Dar Ell. He paused and took another swig.

Strangely, then, Dar Ell remembered his sister, a frail, sensitive woman. He recalled his last time home, comforting her, for their mother was dying in a nearby room. He had returned to their Boston mansion on an infrequent visit. He had been playing the lead in Royall Tyler's *The Contrast* in New York. His return had proven to be a mistake. His father had been critical and indifferent, as always, maintaining with a certainty unshakable as a granite mountain that acting and art held no substance. Business, investment, enterprise, that was the American future, the American way. In his aging eyes, son Jonathan was and would always remain a failure. Angered, Dar Ell had kissed his mother good-bye—she was to die shortly afterward—and had started to walk out, his sister begging him to reconsider. There had been a young man present, a business associate of his father's, an assured young entrepreneur who had been eyeing her during those emotional last minutes.

Dar Ell sensed the man had more than a casual interest in his sister. "I'm Jackson Biggs, your father's guest," the young man had said, stepping forward. Dar Ell and Biggs had nodded and had shook hands politely, but had felt in one another a distance impossible to bridge. Hefty, but debonaire, with thick dark hair, a pencil mustache, and long sideburns, the man had seemed too perfect, too polished in his striped suit and vest with the fancy watch, chain, and gold rings embellishing manicured fingers. Perhaps most significant had been the man's eyes—emotionless and distant with little threads of red from dissipation.

Both men had weighed and assessed one another. And Dar Ell's blue-white eyes had mocked and laughed and hated, knowing that his sister would be the ultimate victim. Dar Ell had felt the handshake go limp and withdraw as the man had stiffened in tall defense.

Years later, without surprise, Dar Ell had learned that Jackson Biggs had turned gambler on a Mississippi paddle wheeler; he had married the sister, had squandered her inheritance before abandoning her. And this sometimes amiable oaf before him was the result. Yes, Amos Biggs carried the Dar Ell blood, the Dar Ell genes, however weak and pathetic they might be. Well, he thought, dear nephew would fulfill a purpose in the plan; the man now was a necessary cog in the wheel of destiny, and, after all, that was all that really mattered.

Biggs shuddered, set down the bottle and pushed it aside, then waited for the procedure.

"Tell me, what happens now?" Dar Ell barked.

Biggs blinked slowly, his eyes blood-streaked and tired. "It's all arranged. Some clothes, arms, ammunition, and horses. A Mexican kid named Alvaro will be holding the horses in a graveyard south of town."

"What if the authorities get to him afterward?"

"It's all arranged." Biggs sat down on a crude bench.

Murder repulsed Dar Ell. He didn't want blood of any sort to flow from this operation. But this, in ways, was out of his hands. Much depended on whims of the escapees, and any killing would be blamed on them and in no way traceable to him and his crew. "Go on, Biggs, time's wasting."

"Seems stupid to go through this again."

"Why the hell do you think we're here, then? After a year of planning, we're here to see that nothing goes wrong, that nothing is misunderstood. There'll be no slip-ups."

Biggs nodded with resignation. "Sunday the warden and his wife is giving a dinner for the lieutenant governor and his wife; because it's Sunday, most guards are off duty," Biggs spoke mechanically. "I'm scheduled to check lockup, but I get jumped by Rattlesnake Morton; he takes my key and gun. He and maybe five of his buddies leave me trussed up and he breaks out from the top tier. Before anyone knows, they take out the guard on the main gate and they're out."

"You sure they can make it now? If their break fails, our plans are threatened."

"Ain't that many guards in the yard."

"Even with the lieutenant governor visiting?"

"Don't make no difference. There's never been an attempted break for years. Things have gotten lax. No worry."

"I hope not," said Dar Ell.

"The boy with the horses and guns will be waiting in the graveyard. The fugitives disappear, figuring I'll pick up the six thousand, assuming it's for real. Then I look you up later for my cut of the big take."

"Exactly," Dar Ell said. "Don't count too much on that six thousand—once Morton's out, he probably won't keep his word, because he knows you aren't about to complain."

Biggs looked at the whiskey bottle, grasped it and took a long draw. "It don't matter, it's the big take that counts. Just don't you cross me, Dar Ell, and skip out with my share."

Dar Ell regarded Biggs incredulously. "Do you think I would do that to my nephew?"

"Uncle, when it comes to money, people do strange things."

"You're a fool, my young nephew. Do you think I'd run out—away from a respected position? I'm a respected citizen. Do you think I'd purposely choose to be a wanted man when I can have it all?"

"I'm meanin' if something goes wrong. What if you have to run for it? Where's that leave me?"

"That's precisely why we're here," said Dar Ell, looking down his nose. "To make certain that nothing does go wrong." He turned to the boy. "You, Lon."

"Nasa Tom and me stay here the night before," the youth said carefully, his eyes riveted to Dar Ell's. "Little before four in the afternoon, we'll be waiting at the wooded swale next to the road two miles west of Willow Springs stage stop. We'll have horses and supplies for me, Yattero, and Ryke here. We wait for all of you. Send the stage on and force you to walk back to Limbo 'cause you're just an innocent passenger." Lon giggled.

Like a correcting tutor, Dar Ell raised a pointed finger. "But you don't send me back until what?"

"Not until we split up the take."

"And then what?"

"Then Nasa Tom takes us over the Sierras, along an old Paiute route into California."

Dar Ell nodded in appreciation and pointed at Yattero. "You."

The man gulped noticeably and tipped his wide-brimmed hat forward. "When the stage is ready to head out, me and Ryke pull down on everybody, I exchange with the driver and we're off."

"Let Ryke set the pace," Dar Ell cautioned. "Don't get hurried. We don't want anything to go wrong—not at this point."

"It ain't going to, boss."

"It sure as hell better not. And what's your role, Mr. Ryke?"

Ryke had returned his revolver to the low holster. He was rolling a cigarette. Deliberately, without replying, he sauntered to the hearth, lifted a glowing ember free with some tongs, and lit the roll. He drew deeply and expelled the smoke to watch a slow curl. "Nothin' more than I always do riding shotgun, except this time when we're ready to head out, I knock the driver from his seat and hold down on anybody in the swing station or anybody in the stage who might have notions of getting out and interferin'."

"And what's Yattero's job?"

"He whips the horses away and drives like hell."

Dar Ell smiled with satisfaction. "There shouldn't be many passengers—me and one or two others, probably someone on official business, maybe a mine superintendent. I've studied these monthly payroll deliveries. Wells Fargo takes care not to overload with passengers. Precautionary measures, I'm sure."

"That's true," said Ryke.

"And, of course, none of you know me. I'm just an innocent passenger, as Lon explained." Dar Ell looked solemnly at his men. "The only way I enter the fray is if something goes wrong. Do you all understand?"

The men nodded. Dar Ell looked down at the Indian, who sat silently, staring ahead. "Remember now, if we have passengers other than me, you drop them one by one along the way, with me last at where Lon and Nasa Tom will be waiting with your horses. And Biggs . . ." Dar Ell looked earnestly at the guard. "I'll take your and my share. We've discussed this. Stay afterward and we'll finalize it." Biggs shifted uncomfortably, his eyes darting over the other men.

Dar Ell had a calculating look. "The prison break, as you know, is planned for Sunday. It should draw every lawman in the territory away. Around four-thirty, Tuesday the seventeenth, I'll be coming from Placerville on the last stage. You all know this. But I expect all of you to have it memorized. That's why I wanted one final run-through." He regarded the bored expressions. "Any final questions?"

"Tuesday a bad day," said Yattero, "always a bad day, like your Friday the thirteenth."

Dar Ell ignored him.

Lon raised a hand. "My girl, Terena, I insist she goes with us."

A slight flush tinted Dar Ell's throat. "We've been through this before, my boy. There is no further talk."

"But I have to take her. I can't leave her behind." The youth's eyes flamed defiance.

Dar Ell said firmly, "There is no further talk. I do not want another person, especially a female, impeding us. After you make it to California, when things calm down, send for her." Dar Ell studied Lon. There was a fire of disobedience in the young man, which he secretly enjoyed. But also, he observed a self-centered side that had emerged of recent, a side that he wanted to slap out of the kid. "I want to hear again exactly what you'll be doing, boy."

Lon averted his eyes and narrowed his lips. "I told you, I bring the horses for Yattero and Ryke, with enough grub for three days, back here to this hut."

"And nothing more. Then what?"

The boy arched his back. "The day you take the stage—me and Nasa Tom here will be waiting west of Willow Springs."

Dar Ell nodded. "Good." He then scanned the men with slow, appraising eyes. "After resting, when you leave before dawn, go separately. We want no one to smell anything suspicious—or see any more connection amongst us—any more than we have at this point." Dar Ell had figured that authorities might remember that the principals had once worked for him, but nothing could be proven, he figured, as long as he returned home as a "released hostage."

Nasa Tom rose and looked at Dar Ell with glazed eyes. "I leave now. The moon and stars, they be enough light." Dar Ell dipped his head in acknowledgment.

"Good," said Ryke, "maybe I can sleep now without the stink." The Indian opened the door and hesitated. A gust of cold wind pelted them with fine sand. A staccato of coyote yelps greeted them as the old man slipped into the darkness.

Dar Ell gestured to Biggs to follow him. They walked outside into the brisk night as the Indian vanished.

"Make me feel better if you spell out every detail about my share. You know, in case something goes wrong," said Biggs.

Dar Ell looked contemptuously at his nephew, the man's features distinct in the pale light. "I told you, there's a cairn of rocks above the road there to the east." He pointed. "It appears to be an old Indian trail marker of some sort. I'll bury your and my share there. When we ride out at dawn, I'll show you it."

"What if the others follow you, see you bury it? They could circle back and take both our shares," Biggs suggested. "I'm risking too damn much to take that chance."

"From that ridge I can see a hundred miles. They'll be long gone. Give it a week. Make it around three in the afternoon, the twenty-fourth. We'll meet at the cairn—you and I."

"Guess I got no other choice," Biggs said, and turned back into the hut. Shivering, Dar Ell wrapped his cloak tightly around his shoulders and peered into the purple dark toward a ridge where the lonely wails echoed. He listened intently. "Misery acquaints a man with strange bedfellows," he mused.

Marshal Dirk Landry reined the chestnut up to a water trough next to the swing station. The station's copper plate could be reached through his front face through a telescope...

(3)

Marshal Dirk Landry reined the chestnut up to a water trough next to the swing station. Golden plumes of poplars and a few shaggy cottonwoods enclosed the squat adobe buildings, their leaves fluttering in the early evening breeze. Landry dismounted and looked back toward the Sierras, which towered to the east. Although the pale blue sky stretched eternally, dark clouds had been humping across their peaks, threatening storm. Landry watched the big animal nose into the cold water and gulp thirstily; the rivulets slapped playfully against the mossy plankings. Six-foot-three with broad shoulders, Landry had a lanky frame, well-proportioned in the sheepskin coat and corduroy pants. His face was narrow, with a wide forehead and a generous mouth that mocked more than smiled. His strong, angled nose revealed a break remnant of a brawling youth. The quiet gray eyes moved constantly, observing, assessing, recording. There was purpose in his every move, and an overbearing presence that made strangers aware of him and a little uneasy, for they sensed that he could be dangerous if provoked.

He caressed the horse, rubbed vigorously around the ears, then pulled the animal away. "Enough for now," he said, eyeing the rich red coat, sweat-bright, shimmering in the late sun. "Give you a little time, then you can have some more, just before we go on." Thirty-six hours earlier he had received a telegram about the prison break. Fifteen convicts escaped, two killed, one apparently wounded, with guards killed and one taken hostage. The region's biggest concern, of course, would be Leander "Rattlesnake" Morton. Ruthless, cunning, diabolical, he had earned his nickname. According to the telegram, Morton and his cutthroats had pushed south, with Sheriff George Healy and a sizable posse after him—a posse growing more infuriated as fearful citizens joined.

The authorities had asked Landry to ride north to Limbo, county center of the action, to coordinate further procedures with state and federal officials. He did so reluctantly, knowing that ultimately Morton would lead the escapees west, toward the concealing ramparts of the Sierras. Because only through a bulwark of forest and peaks could Morton confuse the posses and militia that would all be on his trail. Only in that magnificent uplift of granite could the convicts find refuge or protection. And with a concerted effort they could work their way over the hump, into California, where unlimited possibilities waited—good wine, mellow weather, and women with mellower eyes. A land of cattle and space to be purchased with solid money. But if things went sour, if authorities traced them, there remained always the easy access into Mexico. That would be Morton's direction ultimately, Landry figured, first over the summit and then into Mexico, if necessary. Time was precious. But authority was authority, and at this point he had little choice but to meet with officials in a time-consuming conference.

Dust swirls played recklessly across the shattered expanse, lifting fine sand and whipping violently the leafy strands of sage and bitterbrush. Landry pulled his Stetson tighter. By late night, with the help of a full moon, he would be in Limbo; but he wanted to defy authorities and move into the foothills. Having scoured the land for years in search of the wanted, he knew every pass, every isolated route, intimately; and if there were routes he had never traversed, he knew what to expect through the confidences of old mountain men and local Paiutes. Morton could try to force his way over the popular Luther or Johnson passes, but the traffic was too great; an army of lawmen would be waiting in ambush. Rattlesnake Morton was no fool. Most likely he would try one of the seldom-traveled Indian routes—nothing more than sheep and deer trails now, treacherous in places, but a sure bet if one remained cautious and determined. Landry had telegraphed back that he wanted to proceed on his own, to follow hunches and to cover the base of those little known passes where Morton would surely head. Federal and state authorities, respecting Landry's judgment and his record, had replied with unanimous agreement to give him free rein, but only after he'd conferred with them. The damned big-wigs had to feel important, Landry thought, scuffing his boot in the crunchy soil.

After watering the chestnut and filling his canteen, he would head due west. To hell with them, he decided. He would find an excuse later, and besides, they had no way of contacting him now, or he them, in this godforsaken country. The horse pushed again into the trough, gulping noisily until satisfied, then spraying water with a toss of the head as it pulled back—a fine, strong, spirited animal, Landry's favorite. He then led the chestnut around the front to check out the place, a professional habit now firmly ingrained. Wells Fargo had built swing stations every fifteen miles for the exchanging of fresh horses. The four minute stopover provided no meals or accommodations. A storekeeper and his tender cared for the animals and maintained the grubby buildings. The sod-roofed quarters had an adjoining stable housing less than a dozen animals, the warmth of their bodies adding precious heat to the cramped rooms during frigid winters.

Curious, the keeper came to the door—a stocky man with receding hair and grizzled beard that shimmered blackly in the angled light. He filled the doorway, his stout arms resting on the frames. "Ain't too often we see a U.S. Marshal snoopin' around." He smiled through gray teeth. "Figure you must be here because of that big break."

Landry looked at the man with quiet, amused eyes. "You're exactly right."

The keeper grinned broadly. He stood huge, his gut hanging over a rawhide belt, his black vest snug over his grimy long johns. "Doubt if they come this way. Too much traffic here. Lots of people moving through."

"You never know." Suddenly, the stock tender appeared, leading a team of horses in readiness for an arriving stage. The Mexican, under a saggy sombrero, hesitated, his eyes averting; then he proceeded in jerky steps. Mexicans were not common in the area; few felt comfortable in the inhospitable cold. The man seemed evasive and withdrawn, maybe too much so, Landry thought, watching him work the horses into their traces. The Mexican wore a low gun, Landry noted, a habit not common among tenders, especially when working around harnesses and reins, where the stooping and bending could entangle one easily with the possibility of loosening the gun or of striking the hammer. One mistake and a man could be disabled for life. Of course, he probably had the hammer resting on an empty cartridge. But a gun was impractical, and one so low raised questions.

Landry dropped the reins, immobilizing the trained animal. He crossed his arms and leaned back against an adobe wall to wait and watch. To the west, a streamer of dust and the creaking thunder of wood, harness, and animals signaled the approach of the afternoon stage.

The Concord rattled toward the swing station, the six tired horses galloping in even strides, their bodies caked with muddy sweat. The driver leaned forward, "talking" to the animals, with three pairs of reins in the fingers of his left hand, his right free for the whip. He huffed and barked his sometimes gruff, sometimes coaxing, commands. Beside him sat Harrel Ryke atop the box seat: a leather boot for tools, mail pouches, buffalo robes, water buckets, and the strongbox. Ryke and a second guard on the roof held sawed-off, double-barrel shotguns.

The brightly varnished coach swayed as the big spiked wheels winked in the sunlight; the body nesting on shock absorbers—thorough braces of ox-hide strips—seemed to float as if separate from the chassis. Inside, Jonathan Dar Ell, returning from Placerville, had been admiring the woman passenger on the leather bench opposite him, the only other traveler now, for which he was grateful. There had been eight others when they left, but each had disembarked along the way, and several had exchanged coaches for Carson and Virginia City to the north. As expected, Wells Fargo had restricted ticket sales. People inhibited guards from shooting, and encouraged highwaymen who knew that to take rash chances.

The young woman had regarded Dar Ell curiously with scrutinizing green eyes that had made him feel uneasy. Strong, pretty of face, her brown hair was piled high under a flat little hat with white feathers that tilted snappily forward; her high-necked blouse and feminine vest matched the green of a long, pleated skirt. She had lowered the leather curtain on the small window next to her to keep out the insidious dust that seemed always present despite the moist air that sometimes settled things. Dar Ell liked her classic features, the slightly upturned nose and the soft heart-shaped mouth. He appreciated, respected, and admired quality. Most women west of the Mississippi fell into simple classifications: those who entertained men—the prostitutes and hurdy-gurdy girls—and those durable kind, plain and simple usually, but faithful and devoted to their men and their dreams. Women who would bear children and struggle against harsh elements to create some semblance of civilization.

Then there were the prima donnas, the talented beauties brought to entertain a populace hungry to feast their eyes and indulge with their pay. Dar Ell had had a lifetime familiarity with that kind—vain, pampered women who worked tirelessly, feeding their own self-image.

And then there came that rare breed, women of sensitivity and cultivation, often schooled in the East. The woman before him was curiously different. Striking, composed, and quite self-assured, Dar Ell judged, not really classifiable but certainly closer to the latter. Although not a word had passed between them, they had been studying each other since boarding at Placerville. Her assessing face disturbed Dar Ell now that they approached the swing station. What if something went wrong? Surely she could recall him in every detail. His stomach had a queasy feeling, much like he had always experienced before going on stage.

Dar Ell sat up and pulled his cloak tighter. Suddenly he saw a law officer leaning tall against an adobe wall, the badge glinting in the sun, the big chestnut standing to the side, restlessly pawing. My God, what's he doing here? Dar Ell said to himself, aware of the observant woman before him. She, too, seemed tense, unaware of any reason, of course, except that she sensed his tightness. If ever I walked onto a stage, if ever I performed, it must be now, Dar Ell told himself.

Landry noted the double guards and saw the woman, and a man in a high derby. Payroll's aboard this one, he thought. He watched the sombreroed stock tender steadying the hitched team. The Mexican flashed dark eyes toward the marshal, then set to pulling the fresh animals into readiness. The stage rolled to a stop as the driver pulled rein and slowed with a push of his right foot on the brake. Swiftly, the Mexican set to unhooking the traces of the six tired horses, while the driver remained seated as the exchange progressed. The keeper stepped from the building, wiped his hands on his trousers and inquired about passengers and mail.

"Ain't no one for here," the driver called after spitting a length of tobacco juice, "just a fancy man and a woman headed for Limbo."

Landry's eyes settled on the messenger guard next to the driver. His thin features and burning dark eyes had a familiar look, possibly out of some wanted posters or perhaps just in fleeting recollection. Landry's trained mind recorded and classified such things. He straightened from the wall, moved the lower flap of his sheepskin coat behind the holstered colt, and stepped clear. He saw the derbied man in the coach watching intently, saw the woman follow the look and turn to Landry. He saw the stock tender peer up from under his sombrero, saw the messenger guard narrow his eyes in anticipation.

"Afternoon," Landry opened, sauntering easily, watching the front guard, studying the facial expression, particularly the dark eyes and the tense hands and arms that cradled the shotgun.

"Afternoon." Ryke's response had the tone of a tapped icicle.

"Just curious. Can't quite place where we met."

"We haven't, Marshal. I ain't ever seen you before."

Landry's mouth had a mocking smile. "Oh, I think we have. In fact, seems you may have drifted through Panamint a few years back. You know where—a couple of big valleys south of here." The marshal saw Ryke's chest rise, his arms loosen. From the side he was aware of the shotgun guard on the roof shifting and looking at Ryke with sudden interest.

"I told you, Marshal, I ain't ever seen you and I ain't ever been to Pana—what?"

"What's your name, mister?"

The guard hesitated. "What difference does it make?"

"Tell him, for God's sake," said the driver, chewing his tobacco furiously.

"Driver's got wise judgment," said Landry.

The guard worked his mouth in angered reluctance. "Harrel Ryke's the name."

"Don't recognize it. But slowly, I'm placing the face. The name don't matter. But your face—I'll put it all together shortly." With a flip of a forefinger, Landry tipped his wide-brimmed hat slightly and considered his words, his eyes narrowing. "South of Panamint, down near Rhyolite, spring of 'seventy-two."

"Don't know what you're talking about." Ryke rose slightly, his shotgun tipping somewhat toward Landry.

"It's coming to me. You were riding through from Arizona."

Ryke's thumb moved toward a hammer on the shotgun. But before the marshal could respond, a spiking force struck him in the side, knocking him hard against the coach. Yattero flung his sombrero aside and bolted from the hitched animals, his head down like a charging bull. The gut-wrenching impact stunned Landry, so that he almost blacked out. Shaking his head to clear it, he vaguely heard the woman cry out. Then the Mexican was upon him, grappling his arms and shoulders with a desperate but strong clutch.

Landry braced his legs apart, his bullet-battered leg holding firm as he leaned against the stage and forced the Mexican's arms apart, pivoting then, driving a chopping left-right to the chin. The Mexican's head snapped; his eyes rolled up, but he lunged back, holding tight, trying to pin Landry. They struggled, grunting, the Mexican almost whining in effort against the strength of a bigger man. Instinctively Landry straightened up and drove a right uppercut into the man's chin, buckling him; then Landry drove a countering knee into the groin; the Mexican doubled up and retched and started to go down, but Landry held him, flung the man's arms wide and crossed a massive right, twisting his fist to land flatly, perfectly, on the back jaw. As if hit by a gun blast, the Mexican flew back, landing on his back to somersault over. He came up on his knees and his left hand as he tried dazedly to reach his sidearm. Much faster, Landry drew his gun, directing it low at the man's midsection.

Swaying in stunned defeat, Yattero cried out, "Dar Ell. Mr. Dar Ell, kill him!"

Realizing too late, Landry glanced back as Jonathan Dar Ell opened the coach door to smite a gun barrel across the marshal's skull below the Stetson. Landry collapsed as the woman's piercing scream ignited the moment.

Harrel Ryke spun to his right and discharged a load into his partner, the guard primed on the roof. The impact blew the man back over the top and down over the rear boot, where he flailed into the mushy ruts, a lifeless carcass torn nearly in half. Swinging back, Ryke slammed the butt of his shotgun into the shocked driver, snapping his head and toppling him loosely to plop in a splattering of mud.

From the station the keeper burst forth, took a stance and pointed a long-barreled shotgun. But before he could aim, Ryke's second explosion blew him backward, crazily, his legs bobbling like a puppet's on strings. The keeper slapped backward into the siding, then pitched forth and rolled over, his arms outstretched, his sweat-stained front a mass of plastered pink.

"You damned fools," Dar Ell raged, stepping out of the stage.

"Kill the lawman. Kill the girl," Ryke throated. "Don't leave no one—no witnesses." Deliberately, he whipped out his sidearm and punched three bullets into the prostrate form of the driver.

Unsteadily, Yattero climbed up a front wheel into the driver's seat. "I take it now. I take it." He grasped the reins of the new team.

"You stupid asses, move out," Dar Ell shouted.

Ryke looked back, leering. "Kill the lawman, goddamn it. Kill the lawman and the girl or I will."

The horses pulled wildly, frightened but fresh with oated energy. Yattero held tightly, tugging the bits. "Can't hold much longer," he screamed.

Ryke pushed two more loads into his mountainous gun. "If you can't kill the badgeman, I will. Stand aside." He came back with a pointed thrust.

Momentarily, Dar Ell looked at the girl; her face had drained white; her green eyes watched him in horrified disbelief. She embraced her rounded luggage bag as if for protection. "Out," Dar Ell ordered. "You, young lady, get out." He grasped her arm, jerking her through the door and down the steps, where she fell, rolling slightly.

"Shoot," Ryke shouted.

Dar Ell hesitated, saw the girl's terror and fired two shots to the side of the unconscious marshal. "Rein 'em out," he commanded forcefully, knowing that he could never return to his respected world, that now he was a fugitive outside the law. He bounded into the coach as Yattero cracked a whip and sent the team into a jolting start. Creaking and rumbling, the stage rolled into the desert.

(4)

Dawn lit the horizon and the moon slid away. Sheriff George Healy, from the town of Limbo, rode several lengths ahead of the twenty-seven member posse that was growing hourly as frightened, angered volunteers joined: farmers, miners, teamsters, cowhands, many concerned about their families and indignant that such an element was swarming over their land, terrorizing and possibly killing. Healy, a newly elected sheriff, had won the respect and admiration of his constituents as a deputy, especially the day the two Donaldson brothers held a teller hostage when they learned Healy had arrested a third member on watch outside and had confiscated their horses. The then-sheriff, smelling of liquor, had declined action, claiming it would be bloody as hell if he tried anything. He did distract the Donaldsons long enough while they tried to bargain their way free so that Healy could climb a fire escape, lower himself into a hatchway, and approach the brothers from behind. Healy so effectively surprised the outlaws that he arrested them without a shot and freed the teller unharmed, a daring act that won the respect of citizens far and wide.

Healy, a sandy-haired man with a boyishly handsome face, sat his horse easily, flowing with the animal's natural rhythm. He spurred his horse an extra length ahead. Smallish, bandy-legged, he made up for his lack of commanding stature by sinewy toughness and an aggressive determination that rallied men behind him. And now he was the most determined of his life. Outside the prison, in the cemetery under golden cottonwoods, the guards had found the kid, naked, his skull caved in, a prison uniform beside him caked with absorbed blood. Healy had never seen such a brutal beating. The killers had headed southwest, their tracks evident. Rather than attempting to elude, they had deliberately chosen to outrun pursuers by following the steady valley route between the wall of Sierras and the block of desert mountains to the east. If they continued in that direction, Healy would telegram ahead from the first sizable town. The militia and other posses to the south might intercept.

But for now, a hostility born of outrage had been building in Healy. He would follow the killers into Mexico if need be. With the possible exception of Rattlesnake Morton, few of the escapees knew this wildly beautiful land as he did. As a boy raised in a Nevada mining camp, Healy had been tempered by the big-fisted worlds of timbering, cattle driving, and mining, where he had made a name for himself as a tough brawler against men much bigger. For a time he had ridden shotgun guard for a private staging firm. He had taken easily and naturally to guns, becoming an expert rifleman; quickly he had discovered that his dexterous hands could manipulate a revolver almost magically. Most men on a frontier had no real hankering for guns—no natural abilities. Many could master the demands of a lasso, a miner's pick, or an axe. But only a few had the sensitivity of control, of balance. Only a few had an intuitive feel for the shape of a side arm. Healy possessed those assets. Time, practice, and a gargantuan ego of self-assurance were needed additions.

Healy had learned the perfect forward tilt, exactly where the holster rested best, always within comfortable reach and adjusted perfectly to the natural swing of his arm and the roll of his thigh. He had learned the gunman's crouch, the hunched lean with knees bent, straddled steadily but not too tense; the hand near his gun butt, fingers spread, bent like bird claws; his body keenly alert, his senses alive, every muscle ready. He had learned to draw swiftly; but more important, he had learned that success lay not in speed nor in total execution, but in attitude and in accuracy. A gunfighter might fire first, but if he didn't hit his mark, if he didn't puncture a vital spot, the downed enemy with a slower but more cautious aim could kill and ultimately triumph.

George Healy had spent much time practicing, learning always to direct his Colt like a pointed finger, until he could splash ten out of ten whiskey bottles at fifteen paces, the most extended distance that a lawman could expect, for most shootouts occurred within less than ten feet. He had learned from some of the best, especially from Marshal Dirk Landry, that total awareness and a cool grace under pressure were the marks of a great lawman. But perhaps most significant was mastery of an implacable, intimidating stare.

While riding shotgun guard, he had jumped at an opening for deputy. The rest was history. He reveled in the heady position of sheriff. The power and respect, the challenge, and often, the hatred that it elicited, mingled his emotions. But more important, he had grown, experiencing more each day the weightiness of responsibility and of expectations. Healy felt good. He had a strong moral conviction about right and wrong. And now at last he could do something that could give him recognition.

He wanted to succeed, to build a reputation. He had known a few legends in the region, men who commanded respect from citizens, from fellow lawmen, and from desperadoes alike. Dirk Landry rated tops maybe, a veteran who knew the land and its people intimately, who possessed that rare capability, that inborn instinct, to sense when to act and when to hold back. Healy had conversed professionally a few times with the man, and the impression remained indelible: of a solid lawman, self-assured, knowledgeable, and always reserved. Yes, Healy had decided, Landry was his ideal, his model.

Now, too, there was a woman figuring in his life, adding a new and exciting dimension—Mollie Rose Tyndale, the lovely reporter from Placerville. She had interviewed him shortly after his stunning win for sheriff. Her penetrating eyes, meadow-green, had assessed him skeptically at first, as if expecting him to be nothing more than a straw figure, like a scarecrow in some field, puffed into a shirt and pants but without substance. However, they had ended having coffee and talking late into the night at the Pilgrim, Limbo's fanciest hotel. Things had moved quickly after that; she had taken more assignments to Limbo and throughout Healy's territory. He had made it over the hump numerous times to Placerville and to her home, there to meet her uncle—an impressive and influential man. The two had liked each other; and so, he had found reasons for frequent business trips into California to the old gold town. He and Mollie had wined and dined and carriaged into the spring green of foothills where the red bud blossomed riotously. There had been rail rides to Truckee, then a stage south to the north shore of Tahoe, that heavenly body of lake that Mark Twain had described as "surely the fairest picture the whole world affords." Once they had cruised by moonlight on a small steamer around the silvery waters, the surrounding mountains shimmering above them.

Healy thought about Mollie now. Knowing her, he guessed that she would be heading toward Limbo to cover the story of the prison break. He thought about her and about their possible future, although it worried him, for a lawman did not make the securest of husbands. But for now it was the fugitives that preoccupied him. The whole western basin would be vulnerable, paralyzed with terror as stories, facts, and rumors mingled and spread. Healy hoped to correct all that if he could bring them in, especially Morton. Rattlesnake Morton, the name sent shivers through him, for taking Morton or any of his gang would not be easy. Healy doubted if most could be taken alive. More desperate than ever, their killings would doubtless increase as they brutalized their way along.

Doubtless somewhere ahead the escapees would split, probably into three or four groups, to vanish into the vastness where authorities and pursuers would be fractured and splintered into a chaos of groups, inevitably losing communication.

So far, to Healy's relief, they had held together in a band that for the present headed steadily southwest like locusts across a rich grain field. Perhaps Morton didn't care that he could be tracked easily. Perhaps he wanted force. Three or four men could move swiftly, cover most of their tracks, and evade detection, but a small army of desperate, almost suicidal riders could overwhelm any citizenry in their way; they could lie in ambush and wipe out a pursuing posse. Of course, it was impossible to second guess what Morton had in mind.

Why had they taken the guard, Amos Biggs, beyond the cemetery? Certainly he was important as a bargaining card before the escape. But once they had cleared the walls, why take him farther? Of what value was he to them? That question perplexed Healy, who raked his pinto's side, urging the animal another length ahead. As the flush of desert red burned gold, the posse approached a small ranch, the rock and adobe buildings squat, blending with the setting. The cedar fences in sparse, rectangular designs reached eastward below the house and storage sheds. A few mottled cattle stood hoof deep in the slush of one enclosure, their heads swaying discontentedly. And farther out, several dozen sheep bumped and crossed restlessly against one side, where they awaited feeding.

The posse strung loosely around the ranch, reined their mounts under some golden cottonwoods where the horses could gulp fully from a mossy water tub. Healy dismounted, cocked his long-barreled Colt and called, ''Anybody here?'' At the sound of his voice, a few chickens scratching in the mud waltzed away, clucking in protest. Healy approached the plank door and gestured to his men to enclose, backing him. With a booted thrust, he broke the door open. Inside, a child whimpered. Healy looked down at the frightened features of three cowering children—a boy of perhaps four, another of possibly seven, and a girl around nine years. Much of the crude furniture had been overturned, the place obviously ransacked. ''What happened? Where's your parents?'' Healy asked, his voice thick with emotion. In fearful silence, the children stared at him, animal-eyed. ''You're all right. You're safe. We're the law.'' Healy pushed his badge toward them.

''They was lots of them,'' the girl said, her words barely audible. ''They come here.'' She puckered her face with hateful distaste.

Healy squatted before them, his holstered gun looking big and authoritative. ''It's okay, child. Tell me. Just tell me.''

The little girl put her arms around both brothers and pulled them protectively to her. She stood staunchly in pigtails and gingham dress. ''When they rode in, Daddy took a gun off the wall. And Mommy hid us down there.'' She pointed to a trapdoor, apparently concealed by a Navajo rug, leading to a tiny basement.

''And what happened, hon?''

''We just hid.''

''And?''

''We heard shots and then Mommy screamed.''

''Then what happened?''

''Men, lots of them come in. We heard them walking around and moving things.''

Healy looked around at the home, obviously stripped of food, clothing, anything of value. ''Who brought you out?''

"Nobody. We waited and waited until we got hungry."

"Healy," a deputy called. "Come out here." The officer, named Nelson, shifted from one foot to the other.

"Stay here, kids," Healy said, walking out into the open. The strained faces addressing him told him what he expected.

"We found the parents." The deputy spat a ropy chew of tobacco. He was a lanky, rawboned man with a red, weathered face.

"Where?"

"The man was dumped outside the corrals over there." He motioned eastward. "He's been shot all to hell."

"And the woman?"

The deputy shifted his feet again, looked down and pumped his cheeks. Healy knew before he spoke that it was bad. "They done her in with a bullet, but not before—" He swallowed with difficulty, fighting back anger.

"But not before they had their way with her?"

"Yes, sir."

Healy walked out a few paces to breathe of the aromatic sage. The forlorn desert, rose and purple in the early morn, flowed on rhythmic rolls of hillocks and depressions like a high sea. Somewhere in the distance between the patterned sage, of wooded arroyas and blunt-timbered rises, the killers fled, heading southwest still, through the natural route of valleys toward the Owens, maybe onto Death Valley and the Amargosa toward Arizona. Perhaps toward Mexico. But surely by now authorities had telegraphed every law enforcement agency between Carson City and the Mexican border. Again Healy mulled the fact that they persisted in leaving a trail any amateur could follow. Why? Something more, something unexpected and unfigured, played importantly in the scheme. Well, hell, he'd find out. He'd push the devils all the way to Hell if need be. But unfortunately, time and the land and the element of surprise lay in the escapees' grimy hands.

The deputy approached. "Best we bury them poor folks quickly. Before the kids see."

Healy acknowledged the suggestion and brought himself back. "Yes, Nelson, yes, take some men and bury them. I'll say a few words over the graves."

"What about the children?"

"We'll ask for a volunteer to take them back to Limbo. No other way. Surely somebody there will take responsibility."

"Poor little kids."

"That's why we're out here, Nelson, to be sure this thing don't happen again."

"But how can we prevent it?" The deputy tugged at a long, curving mustache; his face had bloated red.

"No assurance, Nelson, no assurance except that we can ride their tail, push 'em so hard they don't have time to raise hell, until we can run them down."

"I know the men are tired. But best we head on."

"Yes, soon as we take care of the parents and find a volunteer for the kids. Time's precious."

An older posse member, his bulky body topped with thatched gray hair, offered immediately to take the children back. His crusty but amiable face weakened possible resistance, so that the children submitted to being lifted aboard, the two little boys in front, the girl straddling behind the cantle, her arms clutching the man's round belly.

"Maude Abrams the old gal that runs the boardinghouse, might be a place to start," Healy suggested.

"Don't worry, Sheriff," said the man; the children squirmed for a comfortable position. "I'll find someone. Them's good people in Limbo. They don't let their kind down, 'specially little ones."

Healy slapped the horse's rump, and the animal with its

tragic cargo thundered north through the slush. When the children were out of sight, the men buried the dead, marking the mounds with simple stake crosses. Then, with sullen determination, they pushed on, the wind peppering them with a stinging cold. The land opened evenly—sage stretches touching big mountains, their peaks tipped with ponderous clouds. Healy judged that the fugitives would not attempt that formidable thrust of mountain but would drive on south. Yet, again, they might swing west and try to cross the Sierran rise before any winter snow commenced. But then only the most capable and knowledgeable would try such a venture, dangerous as it always was, especially if they tried to forge their own way. They dared not use an established route, as every major pass now would be blockaded.

Healy figured that Rattlesnake Morton very likely had the know-how to get across the mountains, but the smartest move would be to split up. He kept expecting to find evidence of small splintering groups. Did Morton believe he could out-fight any confronting or trailing force? And apparently they still held the guard hostage. Healy searched the sky ahead, expecting soaring vultures, for he anticipated finding the man murdered along the way.

By midday they rested the horses in a protected wash. But an impatient Healy pushed them on. In the next two hours they passed two small mines; in both cases the tiny shacks had been broken into, but there were no signs of the inhab-itants or any indication of violence.

The trail kept angling southwest down the wide valley that paralleled the mountain escarpment, straight toward the re-mains of an old camp called Windy Flat. As the riders came over a mounded rise, they saw six horsemen stringing across a far sink. Healy signaled a halt. One posse member squinted through a small scope. "Ain't any of the convicts. Some hard-ridin' gunmen, looks like." He rode up and handed the scope to Healy, who focused in on the six.

"They've seen us. They're looking us over good."

"They friendly, you think?" a man asked.

"Guess they don't pose no threat. They're turning our way," said Healy.

The two groups met at the edge of a white salt marsh. A curly-bearded man heading five heavily armed men introduced himself as Allen. A self-appointed posse, they had started out in hopes of cutting off the criminals or of turning them back toward the law that was surely not far behind.

"You know they outnumber you two to one—'course, we don't know yet how many guns or how much ammunition they got," said Healy.

"Don't matter," said Allen. "Matters like that don't bother us. We just came across their tracks when we seen you top of the ridge."

"Much obliged at your courage," said Healy.

"But I must admit you gave us a start." Allen grinned through tobacco-stained teeth. "When first seein' you, we thought maybe you was them convicts on our tail. But now we'll join forces."

Minus the man carrying the children back to Limbo, the posse now numbered thirty-three determined men. By dusk they glimpsed plumes of smoke beyond the horizon. They goaded their tired horses through serrated washland. "Windy Flat is just about where that smoke's pouring," Healy yelled. At last they emerged from the fan of a dry bed and rounded a low bluff. They saw tongues of fire engulfing the small town, spewing dark smoke into the cold air. "Come on," Healy urged. Hooves thrashing through sage, leather creaking, horses wheezing and blowing wind, the posse hurried forward.

Too late, the horsemen reined outside town, guiltily enjoying the engulfing heat. They watched the faded gold camp disintegrate as their mounts stomped and shifted restlessly; the rosy glow flowed over them, lighting the setting like a rising sun. Windy Flat had once been promising in both gold and silver a decade before, but had petered out suddenly. Now less than a dozen people remained to run a saloon, a general store, and a stable-blacksmith complex that served ranchers and miners in the hinterland, and served also as a way station for teamsters.

"Someone torched the place," Allen shouted.

"You know who," Healy called back.

The posse rode to the west, where a few outbuildings remained, saved by the wind that dropped strongly from the high mountains to push the flames back. There they unsaddled their horses and made a hasty camp. Outside the saloon, blazing out of control, they found the proprietor sprawled facedown in the wide front street, his body rent by random shots. The slopped tracks hardening in the heat revealed that he had been running away. Doubtless they had toyed with him, had allowed him a chance, then had gunned him down unmercifully. "Depraved devils," said Allen, spitting on the hoof-smudged ground. "We'll find 'em and we'll make 'em pay hell."

They tried to approach the general store, as someone claimed they saw what looked like a prostrate form inside the door, but the inferno forced them back. The stable and corral stood empty; either the convicts had taken all the horses, or had selected what they wanted and had sent the rest off, except for a swayback and a lame that crowded fearfully on the outer edge of the fencing.

Healy spoke bitterly. "That Rattlesnake Morton—he's mean and smart. He won't be taken easily. He'll go down hard, taking a lot of good men with him, I'm afraid."

"They couldn't have been here too long ago," Allen said.

"Not too long ago," Healy agreed. "But they have to be tired, too, unless they got all new mounts here."

The men moved outside of town as the flames reddened the sky, sucking and strangling noisily throughout the frail structures, crumbling them one by one. In a deafening roar they tumbled in upon themselves to shoot flames again higher, which arched sparks and globs of burning debris out over the desert. Stoically, the men watched; nervously, the animals sidestepped awkwardly in their hobbles, their heads flinging, the inferno frightening but warmly pleasant.

"When the flames settle some, we'll feed the animals and ourselves and try to get some rest," said Healy. "May as well take advantage. Nothin' we can do now except take in the heat until morning, then look for anyone who might have survived this."

"Think anyone did?" Allen said.

"Hard to tell in the dark."

The men camped a comfortable distance from the flames. From a rivulet formed by an early snowmelt, they watered the animals and fed them oats from nose bags. The men laid out saddles and unrolled their tarpaulins and blankets, making certain they were far enough away not to be silhouetted, in case Morton and his cutthroats should return to ambush any pursuers. Morosely, the men chewed on jerky and hard biscuits while watching the holocaust explode skyward. One man began raking embers into a circle with a board, and started a steady fire using the dried brush of gnarled manzanita limbs. Then he split the board, set the two parts upright in the sand, and fashioned a couple of slats across by niching out a depression that braced firmly. Soon others joined him, to string coffeepots that boiled quickly. A couple of others fried flapjacks and bacon. But most just settled for sipping scalding coffee from their tin cups. With time, they rolled into a restless sleep, as the night winds fanned an eerie glow that reddened the desert, burning lower in the long hours.

Before dawn, Healy woke the tired, stiff members. Slowly, they circled the smoldering remains of the old town, to learn if other citizens besides the saloon proprietor had been murdered or had perished. But the heat prohibited any possibility of a thorough search. "Won't know what happened here for days," Healy concluded. "Don't pay for now to wait around any longer."

"Sheriff," a man called. "Come here!"

"We found somebody," another responded.

The men encircled one of the few remaining outbuildings. "We got several here, Sheriff."

Healy marched ahead and pushed past those who had called him. He stared into the moldy cavern of a toolshed. Two boys and an old Indian woman awaited him, fear and uncertainty in their faces. Healy and the nearest posse members disengaged the three from a mess of old mining equipment.

"You talk English?" Healy asked the woman.

She shook her ancient head. *"Nada, nada,"* she said, and cowered lower against a spool of dank, decaying rope.

Healy looked to the children, both shrunken, impossible to judge in age. "You know English?" Both nodded vigorously. He looked at the larger boy. "What happened here?"

The youth, sweet-faced, his black hair straight and tight about a rounded face, looked back with lustrous eyes. "Men . . ." he began slowly.

"Yes, men, lots of men. Some in striped outfits," Healy assisted.

"Lots of men," the youth joined. "Lots of 'em come riding in." He hesitated and looked down.

"And then what?"

"It was bad, mister, awful bad."

"How?"

"They shot people up. Shot 'em up all over."

"Just came riding in shooting?"

"They pushed people into the street, some of them. Me and my brother and aunt"—he gestured toward the old woman sitting, her ankles crossed, rocking in pained silence—"we watched them from near here."

"What else? Did you see them take anything? Anything from the store?"

"Oh, yes," he said solemnly.

"What?"

"They brought out bottles from the saloon and all kinds of things from the store."

"What's all kinds of things?"

The boy shrugged. "I don't know—bags of stuff and rifles. I seen them bring rifles. They took some horses, the rest they slapped off, sent 'em kickin' away, except for them two bad ones you see over there." He motioned at a swayback and a lane, standing quietly, their heads low.

Healy looked back at his men, many hunched in the shoulders, their faces deep-lined. "Well, they got blankets, ammunition, just about everything they'll ever need for the time being." Healy inquired of the boy, "Then they fired the place?"

The boy shuddered. "Yes."

Healy rose and slapped a thigh. He looked off into the desert, his mouth working angrily. Before him the old woman kept rocking. The two boys stood glumly, the smallest sucking a thumb. "And then they took off south?"

"No, sir."

"What?"

"They headed someplace out there." The boy pointed toward the northwest. The smaller child nodded in agreement.

An audible reaction rippled over the man. "You must be confused, son," Healy pursued, "there's no sound reason they should be heading that direction. Now reconsider. It was down that way, south, southwest between all those big mountains. Right?"

"No, sir," the boy said firmly. "We seen 'em, all of them

headed that way.'' His sweeping arm settled in a northwest point.

"What's it mean?" said Deputy Nelson.

Healy tipped his hat back and rolled a cigarette. "It means we got tracks to make, that trouble's brewin'. They didn't change directions on a whim."

"What about me and my brother and aunt?" said the boy.

Healy smiled. "You boys and the old lady here, we're going to give you some goods and send you all back to Limbo."

"Yes, sir."

"Can you make it? It'll be up to you, you know."

"Yes, sir."

The men fashioned a rope bridle, then helped the old lady onto the swayback and swung the boys aloft, handing the reins to the oldest. They roped the lame and strapped it, with the threesome's few personal belongings, plus food and blankets, to the swayback. "With these two animals, it's going to take you a spell."

"We'll make it, sir."

Healy grinned broadly and saluted. "Tell them, there, that we're on the trail and closing in."

"Sure will, mister." The men watched the trio plod into the desert.

Outside the vanquished camp, the posse found the convicts had indeed made a decided swing northwest. "What the hell happened here to change their minds?" Healy lamented as they swung their horses toward the Sierras.

"Maybe they just wanted supplies," Allen called. "Maybe they just went to Windy Flat for what they needed, and all the time they was planning to head wherever they're going now."

"Maybe."

By mid-morning members began noting an increase of soaring vultures over a wash where the tracks suddenly looped. A half hour later they stared at the body of the prison guard, tossed over an embankment, like some discarded carcass, his legs spread, one arm twisted under him, the other stretched outwardly at an odd angle. Healy, Allen, and several deputies dismounted and worked their way down. The man's face had been blown away, they discovered, apparently by a shotgun blast.

"They killed him—didn't give him a chance," said Allen, noting another wound in the man's side.

"But why did they bring him this far before doing it?" a deputy asked.

Healy shook his head. "Don't know, unless they thought they could use him somehow." Healy looked curiously at the somewhat bulky uniform and tugged a little at the jacket.

"Something wrong?" Allen asked.

"I don't know." They found tags and papers on the body that identified Amos Biggs. Because of the distance and the needed manpower, Healy decided to bury the corpse and to ask for sworn affidavits later.

Efficiently, they buried Biggs in a shallow grave that they heaped with rocks to keep coyotes out. "Poor bastard," said Allen. "I hope the good Lord understands we're hurrying to bring his killers to justice."

"We'll get them," said Healy, his gaze holding on the citadel of mountains. "By God, I swear on high, we'll get them."

(5)

At the swing station, Mollie Rose Tyndale leaned over
Landry. Tenderly, she bathed his head with a wet towel, dab-
bing his forehead. Delicately, she worked around his swollen
skull through the thick flowing hair where blood coagulated.
Anxiously, she rinsed the warm rag and plunged it into a pan
of cool water, wringing it tightly with strong, feminine hands.
When the man revived, she would warm some water on the
wood stove, then bathe the broken skin properly. The marshal responded, groaning and shifting slightly, his eyes opening momentarily to flutter and close again. Mollie studied
the strong face, rugged with full brows, thrusting nose,
slightly hooked, and the granitic jaw. Appealing dimples dotted his chin and cleaved his cheeks. His wide mouth had
slackened, the lips full and sensuous. She ran the rag around
his neck and lifted his head to pack the wetness against the
back of his head. His big chest rose and fell evenly. He would
not die, she knew, but he might remain comatose or certainly
disoriented for a time. The sun lanced low, backlighting
darkly the Sierran rise. The russet glow played across the
adobe and stone building and played over the rolling sage.
Night would be on them soon. Mollie shivered.

An independent and self-possessed young woman, she had
become somewhat of an enigma in Placerville, California.
The niece of Henry P. Tyndale, influential editor of the
Mountain Herald, she had worked as a reporter for the past

two years, using the byline M. R. Tyndale because of the dismissive attitude and the prejudices against women in the profession. Many who had read her lively reports had accepted their authority and accuracy without question. Some doubts arose, however, when interviewees found themselves questioned by a pretty woman that tradition should have placed in fineries and surrounded by opulence, rather than in the competitive world of men. But that decision had been Mollie's choice, for she was ambitious. And people liked her, especially the young and wayward for whom she gave assistance and found work.

Mollie had never known her father, a mining engineer killed in an underground blast that someone had ineptly set. Following her mother's death from pneumonia, when Mollie was ten, Henry P. had assumed a fatherly role, allowing his niece freedom to develop her mind and talents and to will her own life. And she had done just that. Fellow reporters who had at first viewed her skeptically or had taken her presence lightly, changed attitude quickly. As a cub reporter she had ranged far afield, unruffled by torrential rivers, hairpin turns, and hostile people who often resented their intrusions on privacy. Many of her reports made front-page headings, not because of her uncle, but because of exhaustive reports and her sparkling style. She had written local color features with a refreshing slant that had lain waiting under the very noses of the other reporters. In Placerville she had unearthed some political shenanigans, had exposed political corruption in a mining operation that eventually included several of California's leading citizens. And now she had been on the way to Limbo to cover the big prison break—an exciting scoop about cutthroat fugitives who were sending tremors of terror throughout the whole of western Nevada and eastern California. Well, at least now, she decided, she had a firsthand account of robbery and murder. She trembled with relief that the dignified gentleman, apparently the leader, had spared her life and apparently the marshal's. It had been fate, for she had wanted an earlier stage.

Landry opened swollen eyes that regarded her with confusion and disorientation. Mollie smiled. "You're going to be fine, Mr. Marshal." The big man tried to sit up. "No," she said, pushing her slender fingers against his chest. "You just rest now." She dabbed the water once more and padded the cloth across his forehead. But Landry pushed himself up on his elbows.

"Look, lady, time's wasting." He rolled over and shook his head, trying to clear it; then he looked at her curiously. "You—You were the woman on the stage?"

"Yes."

Landry surveyed the three prostrate forms crumpled on the ground. "And they killed and killed."

Mollie shuddered. "It was horrible."

"And they pulled out fast—southwest on the road, I imagine?"

"Yes."

Painfully, Landry looked into her green eyes. "The question is, why are we still alive? Or at least, why did they spare me?"

"The fancy man opposite me—the one with the cloak—he pushed me and my luggage out and shot at you."

"How did he miss?" Landry said sardonically, hunched and a little woozy still.

"He missed you deliberately—I'm certain."

"Deliberately?"

"It was obvious he couldn't kill you."

Landry forced himself to his knees and tried to rise, when he lurched unsteadily and reached for the ground.

Mollie clutched him. "You're moving too fast. You need rest. You'll start bleeding again."

Landry laughed, smiling to himself, a silly, boyish smile

that seemed delightful across his strong face. "Maybe I do need a minute or two."

Mollie broke into a relieved giggle. "Yes, big man, you're not as springy as you think."

They sat for a time after the marshal allowed the young woman to patch his head with a crude bandage that she had found in a back drawer. She showed matronly concern as the side of his head blotched red through the cloth. Landry knew that the woman was comforting him, purposely talking in order to minimize his movements while the blood coagulated and until he gained his strength. So he waited impatiently; his mind swirled at the sight of so many unfortunate dead. The cooling shadows lanced beyond the building and corrals, knifing across the sage and through the hillocks. But Landry found that his eyes were not focusing well. The surroundings danced fuzzily and time was an eternal void. Landry tried to grope mentally through a throbbing dark that enclosed his skull like bands of shrinking rawhide. He felt the woman's touch, small, firm hands that steadied him. "Given time, you'll be fine," she assured, her voice like the coo of a dove.

Landry nodded, closed his eyes and shook his head, trying to clear it. The moments passed. Then, with effort, his jaw set, he flattened his hands against the cool ground and pushed himself to his feet. Mollie rose with him and steadied him for a time, her slight form ridiculous against his bulk; but she braced him for the first faltering steps. The blood stirring, strength came back into him quickly. He even managed to pick up his Stetson and the Colt. "We must get you inside," said Mollie, walking beside him, an arm around his waist for support. They worked toward the swing station, past the body of the station keeper; the man lay on his back, staring sightlessly, his arms outstretched, his barrel chest spattered blood-brown. Mollie turned her head away.

"Don't look at any of it," said Landry. Inside, he found a bench and sat heavily, his head bowed.

"The bleeding's started again," said Mollie.

"Don't worry, it'll stop, I been this way before."

"We're going to have to stay here tonight. There's no stage through until the morning." Mollie looked around at the accommodations, not certain she welcomed the stay. The place smelled of stale tobacco, of horses and old leather, of sage, cedar, and wood smoke.

"We'll have to get you on it—maybe there's one later this evening. I can't remember."

"No," she said, pointing to a schedule on the wall. "Mine was the last today."

As Landry's mind cleared, he figured that he should be pursuing the killers as quickly as possible. They would be several miles ahead now, southwest, but surely they would abandon the stage and head out with the loot. The anger and the frustration commenced building. "Damn," he erupted. Mollie looked at him curiously, sympathetically. Landry had been assigned to Limbo, following facts and general information about the prison break. A battery of telegrams, each with additional information, had informed him that young Sheriff George Healy had spearheaded a growing posse in pursuit. Healy was good—had promises of greatness even, if he lived. Landry had met the young man several times in Carson City at a number of lawmen councils, abortive attempts usually to unite all the enforcement agencies somehow.

Landry, long a respected veteran, a growing legend in the region, had been impressed by the new sheriff. In ways, Healy mirrored an early Landry, an idealistic, ambitious, talented, and determined Landry, but inexperienced. Inexperience, that was the roadblock, the curse. For all the physical vigor, the unlimited confidence, the capabilities, one brash judgment, one stupid miscalculation, and a man lay dead. Landry had witnessed the death of too many young lawmen. He had lowered his head and fought back inner tears over coffins of too many vain but inexperienced officers. Caution, keen perception, sound judgment, and the resolve to act decisively and with finality when the moment of truth arrived—those were immutable laws. Healy, he sensed, bordered on greatness, if only he survived. Healy had a pride, a gutsiness, that might push him into a trap. And now as Landry's mind shook loose the cobwebs of confusion, he fervently hoped that Healy succeeded.

Landry had a gentleman's obligation to be certain Mollie got on the morning's stage, and he had to officially report the incident. But he didn't want to continue on to Limbo. He wanted to pursue the killers; but his orders were to proceed to Carson City. Intuitively, he felt the region between the swing station and the mountains would be the natural direction for both the robbers and the convicts. The Sierras offered cover, an ambush advantage over pursuers, plus a good possibility of escape if any of them knew the country, especially a little-traveled route across the summits.

Mollie sat on a hard bench opposite. "Did you recognize any of them, Marshal?"

Landry nodded slowly with growing assurance. "Yes, the shotgun guard. I recall him." He pushed his hand across a thick mat of curly hair and thought seriously. "Don't remember his name, but his face—a face burns into my mind like a brand onto a calf."

"What do you remember?"

"He's a hired gun, a hired killer, I think. Made a hard reputation somewhere in the southwest: Laredo, Roscoe, Tombstone—can't place it now. Seems to me he killed a woman in one of those places."

"Killed a woman?"

"It was bad as I recall."

Mollie shuddered. "Bad?"

"Nothing I'd confide to a woman."

"I understand."

"That man in the coach, the fancy one with the cloak—the one you claim couldn't kill me—that's the one that interests me."

"He was furious, you know, enraged at the shootings."

"Behind every major robbery is a mastermind."

"And you suspect he's the one?"

"It's a reasonable guess. He rides anonymously along as a passenger to oversee things."

"You know him?"

"No, I simply recall him. He has the mark of a man you don't forget."

"Distinguished, proper," Mollie added.

Landry's eyes looked afar. "Once in Limbo, some years back, I attended a play. Afterward a man of—well, of culture—came out on stage and thanked us all. He promised better things to come. He was tall, memorable, a remarkable type, if you know what I mean. He had a polish and deep rolling voice—not the type you ever see in this land. Later I strolled into a gambling palace that was connected to the theater. He entered from some rooms above and came partway down the stairs to watch us. He had an unforgettable stature. Women kept looking up, smiling at him. There was a gunman beside him, a man in brown, remindful of that killer riding shotgun, the hired gun."

"I see the man vaguely."

Landry said, "But, of course, I couldn't prove it." He brushed his eyes and said groggily, "I'm not sure of anything right now."

"Well, I'm sure you need rest." Mollie touched his hand, her slender fingers soft and assuring. Landry smiled at her. But behind his pleasantry raged an inner battle, a compulsion to follow the culprits into the desert; but once again he resisted, for he had been assigned to meet state authorities in Carson City. That was foolish. While he traveled northeast, the escapees were moving in the opposite direction. His trained instincts told him to stay, that somehow events would converge in the flats between the basin towns and the high mountains. Well, he decided, he would remain long enough to get the girl safely on the stage to Limbo in the morning, assuming the stage arrived. Under the circumstances, nothing was certain.

"In Limbo, is somebody expecting you?"

Mollie smiled coyly with a superior glow. "Yes, I'm on assignment."

"On assignment?"

"I know who you are and I know why you're here. You're involved in the big break, and that's why I'm here, too."

"You are?"

"I'm a newspaper reporter." She pursed her mouth proudly, anticipating a reaction.

"You?" Landry questioned increduously. "You're a woman reporter?"

She giggled with delight. "Why not?"

Landry recoiled some. "Guess I'm not used to such things."

"My name is Mollie Rose Tyndale, and I work for the Placerville *Mountain Herald*. Maybe you've seen my byline—M. R. Tyndale. I use the initials because of people like you who might be shocked or maybe not so receptive to a newspaper woman."

"Tyndale, Tyndale," Landry pondered. "Your father is editor or owner?"

"My uncle—my father is dead."

"Sorry, but I just didn't expect a woman reporter."

"Few do. But I've worked hard. Certainly my uncle allowed me through the door, but believe me, I've had to prove myself from then on."

Landry smiled. "Think I've read your byline, and you're good."

"Today I've gotten my most important story. An on-the-spot heist, and I'm . . ." She hesitated. "I'm sorry that there had to be killings. It was horrible." She coughed and controlled herself from gagging.

"Death—murder, one never quite rises above it. I guess to save your sanity you grow harder, colder," Landry said, his words introspective. Grave, unblinking eyes reflected Landry's return to the realities ahead. "I must find out who the dead are. Make a report. We'll get the remains to Limbo on the morning stage." Landry rose, his stance relatively solid.

"Won't the authorities send someone when the stage doesn't arrive?"

"Wells Fargo will, I'm sure. But the next stop is another little lice den, fifteen miles southwest of here. Like here, they'll be limited with hands. But they'll send someone out. Trouble is, with lanterns in the dark—they'll have to wait until morning." Landry rolled back the top of a desk and fumbled through some invoices and schedules. "Should be in here somewhere, the name of that Mexican that was in cahoots."

Mollie watched him. "If it helps, I know there are posses afield since the prison break. And my friend, Sheriff George Healy, is afield. Someone may meet them and inform them. Those killers may not get far."

Landry assessed the girl. She was beautiful, talented, obviously bright, but incredibly naive.

"I'm sorry, ma'am," Landry said gently, "but such odds happening in this big country are practically nil. The killers will probably hide the stage, divide the loot, and head out on fast horses for some planned destination." Landry rubbed his eyes. "You know George Healy?"

Mollie's high cheeks pinkened. "Yes, we know each other quite well. In fact, he's asked me to marry him."

Landry looked up, his eyes red-rimmed but interested. "George Healy—that young scout. Will you accept?"

"I'm considering it very seriously," Mollie said coquettishly.

Landry nodded teasingly. "Now I know why the sheriff has been taking so many business trips to Placerville."

"I met him on an assignment to Limbo. I was to interview him." The woman grew solemn, as if needing to confide and to explain. "He asked me to coffee and a local café, and we got along quite well."

Landry studied her, his eyes less dilated. "He's a fine man. Capable, ambitious. He just needs some experience under his belt."

As if not hearing him, Mollie continued. "I knew I wouldn't see him this trip. I knew he and every able-bodied man would be after those fugitives."

"It's getting late." Landry rose, set his flat-brimmed hat on his head carefully above the bandage, and moved toward the door. "I've got to see if I can identify the dead. I suggest you remain here. It's a grisly job."

Mollie closed her eyes and lowered her face in understanding. Then she addressed him with a serene, resigned attitude. "Looks like we inherited each other for a time."

Landry tipped the edge of his Stetson toward her. "Could be. Could be interesting. You're somewhat different, ma'am."

(6)

The horses, pulling and bunching in their rhythmic pace, hauled the muddy stage down the slope toward the cluster of cottonwoods where pink-stemmed willows thrust thick fingers of growth up the watery draws. Yattero guided the reins, his accent thick and chafing. "Slow, slow, gringos, whoa." He applied the brakes slowly as the horses turned from the stage road and plunged unevenly into a grassy swale. Fresh and confused, they tugged and shifted, their heads shaking in frustration and confusion until they fell into an even trot. Yattero steadied them and pointed the leads into a narrow flanked by low cottonwoods, where he halted them.

The boy, Lon, rode alone out of the woods, leading two horses, their saddles laden with blanket rolls, slickers, coats, feed bags, and thick saddlebags. A furious Dar Ell stepped from the stage, intent upon raging at the fools who had fouled nearly two years of well-laid plans. But he stopped short at sight of the lone figure. "Where's Nasa Tom?"

"He abandoned us! Left us high and dry."

"He what?"

"When I brung the horses and grub and stuff to the shack, he was looking wide-eyed and talking nonsense. You know, wild things about a coyote god and how we was cursed. Before dawn, I heard him ride out."

"He gave no reason?"

"Just that coyote crud."

"Exactly what?"

"I told you. You know, how the coyote stole all that goods. Crazy Paiute. He called it the curse of E-sha, whatever that means." With a dismissing gesture, Lon drew his arm across his face to wipe out the sand. "He claims you're cursed, Mr. Dar Ell—that we're all cursed. 'Course, I don't much believe in such things. I figure that old man is just plain tetched in the head."

Dar Ell belched a sardonic laugh.

"If ever I see that worthless redskin, I'll kill him," Ryke interjected, climbing down.

"Maybe he knew something we don't," Yattero said, his eyes narrow slits. "This is Tuesday the thirteenth—this is a very bad day. Tuesday the thirteenth is always a bad day."

"Ah, shut up."

Lon said, "The Indian told me there are some men headin' this way—a dozen or more a half day's ride—and that was yesterday."

Ryke and Yattero looked at Dar Ell. Purposely, he avoided their searching eyes. "A dozen men?" he questioned. "Must be a posse, one of them after the convicts."

"Got to get out of here and fast, now," Yattero exclaimed. "Already, Tuesday the thirteenth is bad."

"Shut up and help me get the money," Ryke ordered. He and Yattero unlatched the leather boot, ignoring the mail pouch. They pulled free a sizable strongbox, the lock large and secure. Both grunted, lowering it to the ground. Ryke reached back and removed a buffalo robe. "Might come in handy on the high slopes," he said, more to himself.

Lon continued, slowly, as if trying to sift the facts in his mind. "The Indian said it wasn't lawmen, Mr. Dar Ell."

Dar Ell ran a quick tongue over dry lips. "Well, who was it? Some local citizens or some cowboys out looking?"

"He claims he saw a prison uniform. I think that's what spooked him," Lon said nervously.

"He's crazy. He couldn't have. He's imagining things. Rattlesnake Morton would never flee this way—with twelve thousand feet of mountain in front of him?"

"Best we take our shares and split it now," said Ryke. He aimed at the lock; the resounding shot echoed across the wooded swale as the well-placed lead shattered the metal hold. The startled horses shifted, tossed their heads and snorted in protest. Behind Lon and the saddled mounts, where a narrow break extended into the cottonwoods, a movement blurred, followed by the whinny of an unmastered horse. Ryke swirled around and extended his revolver toward the woody break. Wind played through the speckle of leaf gold. "What the hell?"

"Don't, Ryke," Lon cried, twisting around in his saddle to look back where a bay horse broke free, the girl astride.

Dar Ell froze, his strong jaw slackened. He stared at the girl: Spanish, full-bodied, her hair lustrous black. She tugged at the reins, forcing the animal to lift slightly, paw, then spin in confused but slowing revolutions, its hooves hammering the rounded stones of a dry creek bed. "Lon Wiggins, you double-crossing little devil," Dar Ell barked.

The youth looked down at the actor, his smooth face set in defiance. "I told you, Mr. Dar Ell—Terena and me, we're going together. Me and her, we ain't being separated."

"I told you explicitly, no females."

"Too late now, sir, but she goes with me." Lon's horse sensed the tension of its rider, for it began sidestepping and bowing slightly in a hitching prance.

Dar Ell looked into the youth's blue eyes, seeing someone now for the first time, someone that he did not know. In the upper glade, the girl watched, her face filled with apprehension. A man's sheepskin coat made her squat and bulky; the long flowered skirt had hiked above her booted legs, revealing fleshy white knees and thighs.

"Ain't no time to panic," Ryke said, blowing the lock

away with a second shot, the sound seeming louder this time, blasting across the desert and echoing back from the stony ridges.

"My God, man," Dar Ell raged, "anyone within ten miles must be hearing."

"No choice now." Ryke lifted the lid. A silence fell over them all; animosities, fears, doubts suddenly slipped away as if on the cool rising breeze. Yattero squatted before the box and Ryke leaned over; Dar Ell strode beside it and Lon dismounted. Their eyes gleaming, their faces lusting, they stared. Yattero drooled slightly; Ryke took on a leering, haughty look of one who felt power over his fate.

"Whooo-eeee," Lon exulted, removing his hat. They beheld stacks of paper currency, sausage-shaped sacks of gold dust, and fat bags of gold and silver coins. "Never knew there was that much money in the world," Lon gushed, running a hand through his thick hair.

"But what do we do with it?" Yattero asked. "Without the Paiute, we ain't got a guide."

"We divide it here and now," said Ryke. "Then if need be, we can split our ways."

"No," said Dar Ell. "Time's wasting; pack the money and gold in our saddlebags for now. We'll split it later."

"We got no choice," Ryke argued. "We've got to run for it now. Each to his own."

"We go on as planned."

"And how do we make it across without a guide?"

"We'll have to take the Carson or the Luther Pass."

"Too many people," Ryke insisted.

"Listen," Dar Ell exploded. "You gun-happy bastards fouled us up. I should be getting off someplace here to walk back. But now we've got to continue. I've lost everything now, my name, my reputation, my cover-up, just about all my life, because I trusted you two."

"Wouldn't have really mattered if you'd killed that girl

back there," said Ryke, unloading the take. "You should have killed her along with that marshal. You could have faked it. You could have walked back from here—claimed you escaped or something. Now she'll remember us and describe us. That could pay hell in the future."

"I'm not a killer of women," said Dar Ell. All the members separated the currency and gold at random and packed it in the various saddlebags draped across the mounts, and into money belts that they wore. Dar Ell stuffed some into his baggage. The girl, Terena, sat her horse apart and watched uneasily. When finished, they drove the stage deep into the trees and unhitched the horses, slapping them away into the desert, all except one. "You Lon, you Yattero, hide the strongbox; put it into that thick brush there and hurry." He pointed to a tight mesh of willows. The men dismounted, grasped the empty container and carried it away into the thickness.

"You think them convicts won't find it and know?" Ryke challenged.

"It will help for the time being."

Yattero fashioned a crude bridle from a riata he located amongst the small tools in the boot. They hoisted Dar Ell aboard the saddleless animal and handed him the rope.

"Ain't much of a creature for ridin'," said Yattero to Dar Ell, "but it beats walking."

Quietly but with haste, they left the flat and worked westward along a brushy draw where water crinkled and purled from the rise ahead. A half mile beyond where they could look down on the stage road but see clearly across the ridge of an upper plateau, Lon cried out and pointed. "Look. Men and horses." On the slope between them and the Sierras, a dozen or so men fanned slowly down a route between the rendezvous shack and the road leading to the swing station. Instinctively the Dar Ell gang bunched their horses close in the thick trees. Momentarily concealed, Lon removed a pair of small field glasses from his saddlebags.

"A posse, probably," said Ryke, squinting with concern. His animal caught his nervousness and began prancing and shifting.

"Ten, twelve, thirteen of them," Lon announced. He paused, sucking his breath audibly in the wind. "Mr. Dar Ell, you better look." Lon handed the glasses to the showman.

Dar Ell adjusted the lenses. He could not make out any features in the distance, but he noted the peculiar motley appearance of their dress, and then he glimpsed the trousers on one rider—the unmistakable woolen pattern of black and white stripes. "My God, the escapees!" he exclaimed.

"The what?" said Ryke. Terena stifled a cry.

"The convicts." Dar Ell passed the glasses to Ryke.

"They're like a pack of wild animals—they'll get us like the Paiute said," Yattero cried.

"Shut up," Ryke snapped, focusing in.

"They're coming right at us," said Lon. "They're following Terena's and my tracks."

"We don't know that," said Dar Ell.

"Sure as hell seems like it," said Ryke, studying them still. "Those in front are looking at the ground, it looks like."

"I can't understand it," said Dar Ell, his voice sliding high with emotion. "They should be a hundred miles south of here or east of here. I don't understand why they're here. And so many? Biggs must have released a small army."

"It's the curse," Yattero voiced.

"Oh, shut up," Ryke barked. "Quick, split our share now and run for it."

"I don't think they've seen us yet," said Lon.

"Well, it won't be long now," Ryke said, lowering the glasses and handing them to Dar Ell. The gunman backed his horse away. "We got to run for it now. Shoot our way free if need be."

"But where do we go?" Lon asked with fear. "They've cut us off."

"I want my share now," Ryke demanded. "I'm clearing out."

"Don't be a damned fool," said Dar Ell, "we're outnumbered more than three to one, and we have a woman with us." He glared at Lon. "We can't outrun them and we can't outfight them. I'm certain they've armed themselves heavily by now. We can't get to the Sierras and we can't return to Limbo. And we can't hide in the desert. We'd be sitting ducks."

"What we do?" Yattero had a wild-eyed expression.

"Wonder if that Biggs put them onto us?" Ryke snarled.

"It'll be dark shortly," Lon said. "What do you suggest?"

"I don't like it, but our only chance for now may be to hole up in the swing station."

"The swing station—you crazy," Ryke shouted.

"It's our only chance. We can fortify ourselves there and split the money up. We know there's no stage coming through; no one to find us. And even if those jailbirds are following Lon and the girl's tracks, they don't dare stick around on our account."

"We'll be trapped; if them convicts follow us, they'll pin us down," said Ryke. "Then if a posse or the militia rides by, what then?"

"They'll be after the escapees."

"But there's some dead men back there, and the girl— assuming you killed that marshal, which I question, seein' the way you shot at him. If you didn't kill him, he'll be there, smartin' with a headache."

"No, I didn't kill him," Dar Ell admitted. "I'm not a murderer—not of women and lawmen."

"That's just great, a marshal alive and waiting. Of course, there's one advantage, we could kill 'em both this time. Do it right. Leave no witnesses." Ryke's words had the ring of finality.

"What are you proposing?" Lon asked Dar Ell anxiously. "We got to do something, and fast."

"We could work our way up this wooded draw, slip on over across the ridge there." He pointed to the headwater where the tree-lined cut ended and the next divide began. "Chances are they won't see us. With dark coming on, we could sneak into the swing station unseen, assess the situation there and fortify ourselves if need be."

"Sounds reasonable," Lon chimed.

"You are a fool, Dar Ell," Ryke said bitterly, his horse twisting, sensing his building frustration.

Dar Ell guided his horse through the trees and upward, managing surprisingly well, despite the rope halter and the lack of saddle. Before vanishing through slumps of half-leafed willows, their bark a cranberry-red, he looked at Ryke. "Tell me, what better do you suggest? And your answer better be fast and damn good." A sullen Ryke had no answer.

They climbed intently, each peering back continuously toward the advancing fugitives as they appeared to be following the route of Lon and his girl. "They ain't seen us yet," Ryke throated. The horses clopped noisily where the rocks interlaced in the muddy base along the thinning willows.

"Hell, let's get going." Yattero spurred his horse, springing it ahead to shoulder against Terena's mount, which shied to the side. Terena squealed and tugged the reins, further confusing the animal.

"What the hell you doing, you stupid greaser," Lon mouthed. Dar Ell looked startled and saw still another side emerging from the boy.

"Who you call greaser?" The Mexican stood up in his stirrups.

"Drop it, you fools, drop it," Dar Ell stormed. "Our lives are at stake and you two fools bicker." Both men eased. "Damn, if I but had a decent horse and saddle. Get us going, kid," the showman commanded. Lon increased the pace, leading his horse ahead. For twenty minutes they snaked their way higher toward the crotch of the summit, where the shrunken willows squatted and the aspen grew skimpier and farther apart.

"They'll see us shortly," said Ryke.

"We got to get to the swing station, and fast," Lon said. "With my woman here—I can't chance it."

"We'll slip in carefully, and take over. I'll send you in, Ryke. There's low brush around the station, and it will be dark. If the marshal's about, take him prisoner, but I don't want him killed. 'The better part of valor is discretion.' "

"What?"

"He could be our salvation."

"What does that mean?" Ryke called forward.

"Nothing. Just keep him alive."

"Hurry," urged Lon, pulling at his girl's horse.

She watched, frightened, her lips trembling. "Please. I'm so scared," she uttered.

"That woman's going to be an anchor on us all the way," Ryke growled.

"Let's go," said Lon, ignoring the gunman and pushing his horse.

Yattero reined his mount and parted some branches. "I see them pretty clear, still following the trail toward the stage road."

"Look." Lon pointed through the filmy brush. "They're turning down the slope back toward where the stage is. They must have spied it."

"Or maybe they see one of the horses," Dar Ell added. They pulled their animals to a momentary rest while observing nervously through the matting of limbs. The thirteen riders a half mile below galloped their horses toward the flat. Briefly they vanished into the trees. "Now," Dar Ell ordered, snapping his arm in a forward point toward the rounded summit just above. "We ride like the devil now."

Lon bolted his horse into the lead. The five riders broke free of cover, and for several endless minutes they crossed an open dome of belly-high sage, blotched here and there with juniper. Dar Ell bounced unsteadily, fearful he might tumble off. The hefty stage horse followed easily, however, big-boned and sturdy, its muscles taut as the showman's long legs clutched it almost desperately. At the summit, Dar Ell tried to focus Lon's glasses as the boy pointed to the flat. A rider, then another, emerged. But with the bouncing horse, Dar Ell could not see clearly. Did the riders see them? At last they rode over the rounded ridge, hopefully undetected, and turned their animals back down, eastward, toward the swing station barely discernible in the distance, the last rays of sunlight stabbing through the purpling valley. Again they rested their horses momentarily, after the climb, regrouping.

"If that marshal is who I think he is, this could be our lucky break," Dar Ell said.

"If the convicts are fleeing, why are they on our trail?" Lon wondered.

"They must know something," Dar Ell answered. "Something connected with Biggs."

"And they'll soon figure that someone's heisted that stage back there," Ryke added.

"Time's wasting," Yattero yelled. They moved out, steadying their animals into an easy rolling gait.

Dar Ell wondered if the marshal would be at the station armed. With the Paiute vanished, with Biggs having failed or double crossed them, and with the fugitives pursuing, forcing them to return to the scene of murder, his elaborate plans were in shambles—unless he could use the marshal. And he knew just how. But for now, with the uncertainty, as they approached, his whole body felt exceedingly heavy. He looked back toward the fading sun glow. " 'The best laid plans of mice and men,' " he cried out. But the richness of his baritone voice was lost in the wind.

At the swing station, Marshal Dirk Landry washed in a shallow basin, a combination of drainboard and sink bolted to an outside wall. Stripped to the waist, he worked the lye soap around his neck and ears, then down over the tapered V of his chest and shoulders and along his muscled arms, scrubbing vigorously, cleaning away the trail dust. He whooped once, shivering as the cold water spewed over him, the remaining droplets glimmering in the faint light. He crossed his arms and rubbed his body and sloshed the water over him again. He grinned. "I'm alive at last." But when he worked his fingers through the thick, curly hair, he took care, for his head still throbbed with each pulse. At last he dabbed soap from his eyes with an old towel and worked the ragged cloth over his torso.

Watching from the frame of the swing station door, Mollie smiled. "You're feeling better and I'm happy. Maybe I should have been a nurse." But her actions were more bravado than real, considering the blanketed forms of the dead not far away.

"Safer, maybe, than being a reporter."

"But not as interesting or as exciting."

Landry finished his toiletry and pulled on a new shirt from his saddlebags. He adjusted the vest and smoothed his hair, examining himself in a cracked mirror above the basin. The right side of his skull had lumped painfully where the broken tissue, red still, had begun to darken under the cloth. "A real love tap," Landry said to himself. He would not forget the man who had delivered it.

Observing him, Mollie said, "I know you're anxious to be on their trail."

"Can't do a thing until tomorrow—until after I get you on the stage and the dead taken care of." Landry had learned their identities: the station keeper from random papers in a drawer behind the counter; the guard and the driver from official identification forms in their vest pockets.

"But I don't intend to continue on to Limbo now," said Mollie. She crossed her arms, leaned against the jamb and studied the marshal.

"Meaning what?" Landry did not look at her.

"Meaning I'm a reporter and I want to go with you. I want the story. Don't you realize this is the break of a lifetime? I've been involved with a holdup, maybe the biggest of recent years. I've witnessed killings firsthand. All because I took a late stage and because of a lawman who appeared unexpectedly. I can't turn back now—I'm too involved and there's too much at stake."

"And what about the prison break?"

"That's somewhere out there." She nodded eastward. "I'm here and now. Had it not been for the momentary compassion of that dignified man in the stage, they probably would have killed me. No, I'm too involved now, personally and professionally."

Landry stiffened slightly. "And you are a witness, Miss Tyndale. Did you forget that fact? Your life is in jeopardy as long as you're out here running amuck."

Mollie looked at him knowingly. "I realize that." Landry sensed that his words stung. Weak still, he felt woozy suddenly. Swaying, he grasped the drain basin and steadied himself, his head bowed.

Mollie rushed to him, carrying an oil lantern. "What's the matter? Are you all right?" She set the lantern down and clutched him, trying to steady his big frame.

"I'll be fine," he said, his eyes closed.

"You've done too much, too fast. Here, let me get a wet cloth." She dabbed a towel in the remaining water, turned to bathe his forehead and screamed. Her piercing voice shattered the desert dark as she looked up into the leering face of Harrel Ryke, aglow in the lamplight as he leveled his Colt at Landry.

"No," came a voice from the night. "No. We need him."

In one swinging motion Ryke dropped his revolver into his holster, stepped forward, and landed a left hook flush on the jaw of the disoriented marshal.

Landry awoke hearing the wind pelting the walls and the dull murmur of male voices. He did not react immediately. From years of professional work and of harrowing episodes where a sudden or false move could mean instant death, he knew how imperative was his quiet. He lay in a swirling daze, trying to clear his mind, remembering first the fight at the stage, the girl named Mollie bathing his swollen head, and later his sponging at the wash basin—then the girl's scream, his half pivoting, the shadow bulk of a man—and nothing more. His cramped forearms felt tight and restricted. Slowly, he realized that his arms had been bound in front. He squeezed his eyes, trying to push out the compounding mists that clogged his mind. His head pulsed dully. And when he opened his mouth, ever so slowly, for easier breathing, his left jaw pained and he didn't know why, because his head rested comfortably on some folded blankets; long, slender fingers swathed a water-cool cloth across his forehead, back again, and carefully over a painful puff of his skull.

Landry then recalled the swing station, the reporter Mollie and his mission. Calculatingly, he opened his eyes; through a film of lashes, he saw vague figures, heard them talking—bickering, their voices sharp with emotion. He saw the curved form of a woman kneeling over him, and he felt fully, titillatingly, the gentle touch of feminine, caring hands. Mollie! He and Mollie, he realized with a jolt that wrenched through him, which triggered a reaction in the woman. She clutched him, pressed him down and looked fearfully about; but the others did not see, so engrossed were they in their personal confab. Landry knew then, clearly, painfully, that he and Mollie had been taken hostage by the very gang that had robbed and killed. But why had they returned?

"I knew you were gutless," said Ryke to Dar Ell. "You couldn't kill a lawman. You couldn't kill a badgeman, a man who could hang us all." Ryke looked at Dar Ell, his face distorted with cold fury, the narrow features like a razor-sharp hatchet. He continued deliberately, "You got brains, Dar Ell. You got the smarts to plan all this, but you don't have the guts." He spoke each word deliberately, hissingly, explosively. "We're back where we begun, with that girl there, and that marshal still breathing. We should be riding."

"First of all, who panicked?" Dar Ell fired.

"Ain't my fault that the lawman showed up," said Ryke defensively. "It was Yattero who panicked."

"You didn't have to kill—no justification whatever. Like now with the marshal, you didn't have to hit him."

Ryke blinked. "What the hell you mean?" His fingers fumbled unconsciously over the butt of his revolver.

Dar Ell saw but continued. "I'm here because of you and Yattero. I should be in Limbo now, a free man."

"It was Yattero who lost his cool. I had no choice." Ryke's face whitened.

"You react. You don't think."

Ryke grimmaced. His fingers curled. "I take care of myself."

"Is that why you needed to knock the marshal out? You had a gun on him. Why knock him senseless? Now he's out and we need him, desperately."

Ryke curled his lips contemptuously. "We don't need him or anybody. And I don't need any of you."

Dar Ell, who had paced away, turned back, swirling his cloak. "You talk big. Your horse is saddled, count out what's yours and leave. Now."

"Yes, leave," said Yattero. Edged by a west window, he was staring into the dark, a gun in hand. But the dull lantern light made it difficult to see out.

"Me and Terena, we're staying here with you, Mr. Dar Ell. I wouldn't chance it yet," said Lon.

"Maybe you can make it out of here, Ryke," Dar Ell said matter-of-factly.

"I'll make it plenty far. Just count my share." Ryke smirked, but his eyes grew distrustful.

"All right, we'll count out your share right now. No strings attached. You just take your horse, your money, and ride out." The slender, cloaked man pointed at Lon. "Spread the money out."

"What you tryin'?" said Ryke, backing away an arm and finger-pointing accusingly. He tilted his head and cocked his hat back, also with a flip of his left hand. "You're pullin' something I don't like. Why you want me out suddenly?"

"I'm just offering you everything you want."

"No," said Ryke, glancing around, his ferreting eyes defensive. "You ain't getting me out there. Those jailbirds out there'll gun me down and take what's mine." His face grew conniving. "Or they'll shoot me down just outside, and you people will sneak out like coyotes and take what's mine."

"Your choice," Dar Ell commented.

"Everything's crazy. Everything's gone crazy here. Nothin' makes sense." Ryke spun about, his head wagging, his eyes extended. He looked at Yattero, at Lon and at his girl, and back at Dar Ell. "Stuck here with them cutthroats behind, and that marshal who should have been done in. Hell." He removed his revolver, whirled the cylinder, then absently whirled it once more.

Dar Ell regarded Ryke with the superiority of a commanding officer. "You still cannot understand that this lawman here, disabled as he may be now, is our ticket to freedom, our way out."

"I don't follow you, sir," said Lon.

"I don't expect any of you do."

Mollie felt the easier, rhythmic breathing in Landry, and knew that he was conscious. In the bleak light, she could see his eyes flutter slightly and hold narrowly as he observed. In an almost motherly way, she stroked an arm assuringly. Dar Ell had lit two lanterns, turning both very low, one on the floor where he and Ryke now worked with the guns, the other in a second room that had a combination of bunks and storage shelves but had no windows, only high vents. A bruising wind showered sand against the walls and windows; the willowing sound rose and fell and wavered strangely at times, like the cry of a coyote.

Lon and Yattero had taken up guard positions by the small windows both front and back. Under Dar Ell's orders, Terena had begun packing extra goods that could supplement their supplies. "We got enough food, probably," said Dar Ell. "What we need is as much ammunition as we can carry, and blankets. It will be cold up there."

"You're sure as hell confident we're going to get out of this hole," Ryke said.

"For now, here, we can hold them off. Time is on our side if we can hold them off until morning. 'Time is of the essence.' "

Ryke looked skeptically at his leader. "Don't see how you figure that. Even if them jailbirds pass on. Even if we get out before some posses come snooping about, how we going to get over the Sierras with that crazy Indian running out on us?"

"The marshal there."

"The marshal?"

"That's Dirk Landry. No man knows those mountains better," said Dar Ell.

Ryke pursed his lips. "He seemed familiar. Dirk Landry! Maybe we can douse him with water. There's enough moonlight. We could pick our way, start now."

Dar Ell squared his jaw. "Unfortunately, I'm afraid you have put him out of commission for a while. Besides, with the women here slowing us, and out there those cutthroats to overwhelm us with no protection . . ." He shook his head. "No, we have no choice except to take advantage of what we have—a temporary fortress here, and time."

Terena moved methodically, her mouth puckering with increasing nervousness. She kept glancing curiously at Mollie. Dar Ell and Lon had searched the premises. They had taken the marshal's rifle, his side arm, and a smaller revolver tucked in his belt back of his left hip. In addition they had gathered the shotgun used by the station keeper, a rifle and revolver from the guard, and a pistol off the driver. In the station, they had uncovered a Colt revolver from a front drawer, and two Winchesters on a rack, a total of ten pieces. They found numerous boxes of ammunition plus several bags of shotgun shells. The two men laid the bounty on the floor.

"One can't travel too fast with weight like that," Ryke said.

"Don't have too much choice," Dar Ell countered.

Ryke studied Dar Ell. "I want my split now," he said, bristling. "I work for you, but there's a limit. Things just ain't going well. And I'm not going to be trapped like some coyote in a snare."

"Don't use that word," Yattero said.

Ryke said to Dar Ell, "You know them jailbirds must have seen us. They're going to be on us like so many vultures, and they'll surround us." Ryke's face narrowed with a tightness of determination. "I want my share. I want it now. Because when this place explodes, we may not have no choice except to break for it, each on our own, with our own share."

Dar Ell listened patiently, staring uneasily through a cramped window toward the last westward flush. "You don't know if they saw us."

"They'll trail us."

"Maybe not. They're on the run. I don't think they can afford to tarry."

Ryke stiffened. "They'll find the strongbox. They'll know somebody's got money."

"But I doubt if they'll attack a Wells Fargo stationed with armed people. They'd be fools."

Ryke regarded Dar Ell scornfully. "But if they do hole us up, we could be left facing a posse with three dead men stretched out there. I want my share now."

Dar Ell nodded in surrender. "Sounds reasonable. We will count out everybody's share."

"That's all I ask for." Ryke loosened some. "I'll start dividing it." He strode to the first saddlebag, unbuckled it and pulled out some gold. "I'm afraid time's running out on you, Dar Ell. You got nothing going for you anymore."

"He's got me!" said Landry. His words so startled the gang members that Terena cried out sharply and dropped a canteen that bobbled across the thinly boarded floor.

"What the hell," Lon mouthed. Yattero slapped his thick fingers across his holster, his eyes shining darkly. Both Ryke and Dar Ell twisted around to center on the prostrate form. Even Mollie flinched.

"Well, well," said Ryke, "our big marshal is alive and well."

"Shut up," Dar Ell said simply. "He may be talking solid sense."

Ryke looked at Dar Ell coolly. "You'd trust a lawman?"

"I'm asking the marshal to explain himself."

Landry rolled over and sat up. He looked pale, unsteady, but professional. "You don't stand a chance. Not one. Even if you luck out with the Morton gang—that's who's out there. Even if they push on without your hides and the lady's and my scalps, you don't know where or how to get across these mountains, except by a main route." All eyes were upon him. "You need someone who knows this country, knows every rock and bush and pass."

"You can't trust him."

Dar Ell thrust a silencing arm toward Ryke. "Listen to the marshal."

Landry assessed the situation. "Lying here, I picked up that your guide ran out on you and that you need to get over the hump, but not by ordinary means."

"He'll bargain with you and trick you," Ryke warned.

"Let him speak. The marshal is a wise and perceptive man." Dar Ell leaned closer with great interest.

"Your old Indian guide was named Nasa Tom; he was to lead you over the E-sha Trail—an ancient but little-known Indian route."

"You're most acute, Marshal. Tell us more."

"Not hard to piece together. You picked a guide that was once good. But that was long ago. He's old and sick, if you know what I mean."

"No I don't, exactly."

Landry appraised the people listening. A total quiet had settled over all. "He's frightened. Like most of the Paiute elders, he believes in the legends and the omens of his people and his past."

"Don't you see?" Ryke growled. "Don't you see what he's leading up to?"

"Shut up," said Dar Ell, "and listen. Continue."

"This is the land of E-sha. E-sha is Paiute for coyote."

"Baaah," Ryke scoffed, and turned away.

Landry smiled to himself. "There is a legend that a conniving coyote stole the Sun God's harvest from all his fellow creatures. Took all their earthly goods. And a curse was set upon him. Any man or woman that steals or kills and flees into the desert, is subject to death. The omen is the same for man or beast."

"Don't listen to him," Ryke hissed, cocking, closing, re-cocking his side arm.

Dar Ell stood straight and looked skeptically. "Come, come, Mr. Landry. Surely you don't believe such fantasy."

"I didn't say I did. I said Nasa Tom and elder Paiutes do. This is the land of E-sha. Accordingly, anyone who takes from others, kills or destroys, as did you folks, is condemned."

Dar Ell grinned. "What do we expect now? A rabid coyote to rush up and bite us?"

"Considering the situation you're in," said Landry simply, "I'd say you've already been pretty well bitten."

Dar Ell sobered and stared at the lawman and did not reply. But Ryke said, "Can't you see he wants us to listen to that crap?"

"Oh, no, he tells it as it is," said Yattero, full-eyed. "It is the curse."

"That those who take and flee into the desert will be cursed. According to the Paiutes, the Sun God set loose a Demon Coyote to do his bidding." Landry had a conclusive look as he addressed Dar Ell. "So you see, apparently there is a kind of rabid animal somewhere out there waiting."

"You want me to shut him up again?" Ryke offered.

"No, no!" Dar Ell shouted, pushing Ryke aside. "Don't you realize the overriding reason I came back here?"

Landry sat higher. "You had no choice, with Morton's gang on your tail. Eventually I'll learn why. They may have just chanced on the stage and an empty strongbox and smelled a good thing. But I think it's more than that. There's some connection."

"You think you have it figured."

Landry said matter-of-factly, "Not much to figure. You and I know that behind Morton are posses; surely George Healy is not far away, and maybe the state militia."

Confident, Dar Ell listened patiently. "A few moments ago you hinted at some cooperation. That's precisely why I came back. You have a reputation for knowing this land—the mountains to the west—as well as any living white man, maybe even better than that old Indian. You could lead us over—to freedom.''

"I could."

"We will need the marshal if we are to escape the coyote curse," said Yattero. .

"I listened, but I still don't understand this coyote curse. This E-sha thing," Mollie said.

"It's an ancient Shoshonean legend," said Landry.

"It's nonsense," Dar Ell interrupted. "It's an old wives' tale. All foolishness."

"On the contrary, the Paiutes—they're an offshoot of the Shoshones—have built much of their entire culture and belief around Old Man Coyote."

"The curse intrigues me," said Mollie boldly.

"Fools, if anyone's outside, they'll hear our voices," Dar Ell warned.

Mollie continued, her words low. "Sounds familiar, ungrateful thieves steal the harvest planted and grown for all the Indians and all the animals."

"Well, the Sun God fixed Mr. Coyote," said Landry. "Laid a curse that ostracized him, forcing him to wander forever, hated and scorned. The Devil walks behind you. Isn't that what the Sun God told him, Yattero?"

"I don't want to think about it," the Mexican protested.

"Anyone who takes from others, who hurts and kills—the curse of E-sha is laid upon him. Isn't that how it goes, Yattero?"

"Leave me alone."

"The shoe—or the story—fits so far," said Mollie.

"Don't push him," said Ryke. "The Mex here gets a little crazier each minute without you."

"You shut up," Yattero raged.

"You telling me to shut up?"

"You damn fools." Crouching, Dar Ell moved between them. "The marshal's got you at each other's throats. For God's sake, keep your attention outside."

"I'm just telling her like it is," said Landry.

"And I wanted to hear it," Mollie confirmed.

"The Paiute believes that man is just as subject to the curse as was the coyote. And apparently it's so," said Landry. "That's why he's so ratty looking and an outsider. That's why at night the coyote cries."

Mollie clasped her hands. "I love it. It's perfect. I must remember it."

"Yes, young lady, remember it," Dar Ell said, "and someday entertain your children with it."

"If we get out." Ryke peered into the outer dark. "Don't see nothing yet."

Landry grinned wryly. "It's interesting that you're figuring the same deal that I was going to offer you."

Dar Ell had a superior smile. "Except you really don't have much of a choice, with the girl here." He looked at Mollie as if she were a prize possession; the girl glared back.

"The marshal's too weak to travel," she said.

Dar Ell ignored her and glanced westward out the window where Ryke hid to the side. "You're going to take us now— into the night—there's still enough moonlight. Those cutthroats probably have cleared out and moved on by now." Dar Ell motioned the marshal up.

"I'll take you over, but without the girl. I want her on the morning stage to Limbo."

"The girl stays with us."

"No deal."

"You have no choice, besides, she's my trump, my security that you won't abandon us or double cross us."

"Time's wasting," said Ryke. "Don't seem like they're following."

"They'd be smart not to. Let's go." Dar Ell waved his gun toward Landry.

"I said no deal. Unless you agree the girl goes free."

"There's cutthroat convicts out there somewhere," Dar Ell blurted, jerking his thumb over his shoulder. "Do you want that girl left here alone, or out there wandering about with them?"

"Please be concerned, I do feel so safe with you people here," Mollie interjected.

"Yes, you should be concerned," said Landry to Dar Ell. "They're headed by a man named Rattlesnake Morton . . . Leander Morton. If you ever heard the history of that man, you'd be heading for the nearest fort now, or praying for a posse to chance on us just to keep your head on your shoulders."

Dar Ell looked curiously at the lawman.

"Damn it," said Ryke. "Time's wasting if you're thinking of breaking for it."

"All right," said Dar Ell to Landry. "The girl goes with us for now; when you figure it's safe to release her, we'll release her."

Landry rose stiffly. "The moon may not be bright enough to avoid badger holes. The horses may break their necks and ours."

"Hurry," said Dar Ell, "grab the goods and the guns, we'll chance it."

"The marshal's not strong enough yet," Mollie protested angrily.

"Morton and his gang will probably hole up until dawn," said Dar Ell, hustling them along, "because they have no way of knowing what exactly happened here, how many are dead or alive. He'll want to size up things, I figure."

"Don't try to second-guess Morton," Landry warned.

"If we ain't got time to split up the take now, then we damn well better do it at the first rest," said Ryke. "If we split up or get separated, I want my fair share."

"We will, but for now let's move."

"Good," said Yattero. "There ain't no future this side of the mountains."

"Yes, please, let's hurry," Lon urged. "If the marshal knows a way over, let's try it now."

"Get some good horses for me and the woman here. Get all our horses and gear out there and the goods here on them. Hurry." Dar Ell pushed Landry toward the stable.

"I tell you, he'll pass out on you," Mollie cried. "Then what good will he be?"

"We'll tie him to his saddle and douse him off and on with water if need be," Dar Ell replied. "When that stage doesn't arrive, you can bet somebody will be out looking. And with the posses out there, and the Morton crew breathing down our necks, this is our break now that we got a guide." Dar Ell took the reporter by the arm and pulled her with him.

"Wait," said Yattero, "I think I see something out there. Something moved. The lanterns, cut the light."

"Turn off the lanterns," Dar Ell ordered. Lon, who had carried one into the stable, snuffed it out, and Ryke twisted the second one off. Curious eyes all peered out at the silvery sage, shadowed and blotched in the weak moonlight. The sage bowed and flagged in a cold wind. "Maybe it's just the night," Dar Ell said, clutching Landry's arm, his fingers gouging the flesh. Terena crushed her fat little hands to her mouth and cheeks. She whimpered like some tormented animal.

"Gag that woman," Ryke snorted.

"Greetings in there," came the voice, clear and penetrating over the buffeting wind. "I am Leander Morton. Some call me Rattlesnake Morton. We are here to make a bargain—your gold and your money in exchange for your lives."

(7)

Sheriff George Healy and the man named Allen walked from the adobe hut into the twilight. Around them the posse men had built three hot fires from the dried sage and twisted deadwood strewn about, three to keep their forces separated and not subject to night ambush or sudden sniping. The men talked softly while preparing their meals, tired but determined men. On the ridge behind, a pack of coyotes yapped, and from above to the west, others chorused in answer to their echoing cries.

Allen rubbed his bushy beard in dismay. "Them convicts was looking for something damn hard."

George Healy shook his head. "I don't understand it. I would have staked my next month's pay on them splitting up. That's the only thing that makes sense, split up individually or at least into small groups, that would break up our forces. Two or three men together could slip through this land with hardly a notice. Instead they hold together, leave a trail my grandmother could follow, and circle back nearly one hundred and eighty degrees from the direction they started."

"They're on to something, or certainly looking for something."

"Might be a take from Morton's earlier days. Lot of it has never been recovered, and some of his cronies are loose with him," Healy suggested.

"But why wouldn't Morton and his cronies stick together

and dig it up on their own? Why drag eight or ten others along?''

''Unless those others smell something and won't leave until they get a share.''

The posse had found the hut where Dar Ell and his gang had met before the prison break. It was dismantled, the fireplace broken apart, the cobbled flooring torn up, especially in the corners; the ground outside near the base had been upturned where the earth looked loose and possibly tampered with. The convicts had used picks and shovels left by some former miners. Their effort had been thorough. Healy squatted and sifted the moist sand through his fingers. ''I judge this was done only a few hours ago. They're not more than a half day ahead of us.''

''I figure that, too. We're closing in; maybe we should pack up and keep going. The moon's not as full, but it's still pretty light.''

''No,'' said Healy. ''It'd be too dangerous. Someone or one of their animals would see or hear us. We could walk into an ambush. Besides, the men and horses are tired.''

Allen nodded in consent. ''For sure, we have been pushing 'em.''

''We'll ride out early before dawn. Maybe you and I can scout ahead.''

''Sounds sensible. Where do you think they're heading?''

''Depends on what they're up to.''

''Sure feel sorry for anybody in their path,'' said Allen, tearing a chaw of tobacco.

''There's a few mining operations and a couple of isolated ranches up ahead; then, of course, there's the Wells Fargo swing station at Willow Springs. But that's off to the east, almost a complete circle away from the prison.''

''Don't see why they'd bother a station. They can't be in need of supplies yet. And a station like that could serve as an armed camp. Morton's dangerous, but he's no fool.''

"Yeah, I agree." But Healy wondered if he were trying to convince himself. Earlier in the day a heavily armed stage had passed carrying gold and coins. He recalled one of his confidential memos, that a sizable shipment of mining pay was headed for Limbo on this day. The big escape, however, had taken priority. Could that stage have something to do with the bizarre actions and erratic route the criminals had taken? But the shipment would have passed through earlier. It should be in Limbo by nightfall.

Healy was grateful that his girl, Mollie, would not be involved in the mess. She had telegraphed earlier that she might be traveling to Limbo on general business and to see him. Surely, upon hearing of the big break, she would not try to cover it? Or would she? Damn, he thought, why did she have to play at a man's job? Sure, she was a good reporter. But people got killed snooping about where they didn't belong. Surely her uncle had enough sense, and enough clout, to keep her from attempting such a foolish venture. If she had telegrammed him again, tried to reach him, he had missed it, having set out almost immediately following the escape.

Although supremely confident in himself, George Healy halfheartedly wished that Dirk Landry were in the area; the marshal would add an incomparable dimension; the two of them teamed, backed by a sizable posse, would make a formidable force. Unfortunately, by now Landry would be in Limbo, being briefed, miles from the action. The marshal had uncanny insights to such strange doings, and he had dealt with the Morton gang before, having brought Morton originally to justice. But Healy dismissed the possibility and began thinking himself fortunate. With the likes of Allen and the men beside him, they could take Morton. Only hours ahead lay the chance of a lifetime, the chance to be a legend, to capture the most dreaded killer in the basin country. Healy welcomed that chance the more he thought about it. In a matter of time, with a little bit of luck, Morton and all the fugitives would be his. He drew deeply on a rolled cigarette, taking pleasure before flipping it onto the turf to watch it die out.

"Can you see any of them?" Dar Ell demanded. They all waited, stricken in the chilling darkness. From the stable the horses stomped and nickered nervously.

"Don't see nobody," Yattero voiced. He ducked beneath a windowsill.

Ryke cocked the hammer of his revolver. "They got us surrounded."

"Be calm," said Dar Ell. "We've got to feel our way on this one."

Landry edged close to Mollie and pulled her back against the wall. "Get down," he said. Terena's whimpering continued.

"Why don't you shut that female up, lover boy?" said Ryke.

"I'll take care of her, Ryke. She's not your concern." Lon put his arms around the trembling girl and pulled her to the floor.

"All of you, shut up," Dar Ell ordered. "Listen. Somebody's calling out there."

At the outside drift of human words, they all quieted. "Do you hear me?" came the voice again. "I'm talking to you, Mr. Dar Ell. I am Leander Morton. Perhaps you have heard of me. Some call me Rattlesnake Morton." A blast of wind splattered fine sand against the station, punishing the windows. "You hear me, Dar Ell?"

"He knows me!" Dar Ell said incredulously. "He got my name out of Biggs."

"Better answer him," Landry suggested, "before he sends a barrage of bullets through here."

Dar Ell hesitated and sighed deeply. " 'When sorrows come, they come not single spies but in battalions.' " He pushed the front door ajar. "I hear you, Morton. We got nothing that concerns you."

"Oh, but I think you have. I know you have."

"Speak your mind."

"You got much to share, my good friend." Another whip of wind pelted the station. The girl, Terena, cried out.

"Shut that woman up," Ryke growled.

"Get off our back, Ryke," Lon spat.

"Don't push me, little boy." Ryke's voice raked harshly.

"Quiet, you fools," Dar Ell cautioned. His deep voice then rolled through the door, over the desert. "Talk. Speak your peace, but we don't have anything to share and we're not your friends."

"You best keep me a friend, my good man."

"Go your way and leave us alone."

"No, not until you share your good fortune."

"I told you we don't have anything to share except bullets in your gut if you try to come in here."

"Yes, you do. A guard friend of yours—Amos Biggs— told me so shortly before he departed."

"You're crazy. I don't know what you're talking about." A slight catch warbled in Dar Ell's throat. His always-modulated voice rose slightly.

"No—you all are the crazy ones, unless you cooperate."

"Go to hell."

"Give us your take—the gold and the money from the stage—and we will let you live."

"I have heard about you. I know who you are," Dar Ell called back. "The law is behind you. You have no time. Flee."

"Your time. My time. Those who hunt me will find you. Though the coyote be after the rabbit, he will eat the tortoise along the way. That is a wise old Paiute saying."

"We have nothing more to say."

"We follow you. We know how many there are of you.

Give us your take and we will let you live. We arrange a truce. One of my men—one of your men.''

"I told you, go to hell.''

"It is a pity. But we have ways. We will get you one by one.''

"You'd be smart to offer him half, or at least what he'll agree to as half, and maybe get him off your back,'' Landry said.

Dar Ell eyed the lawman. "It's not your business. You're alive because we need you. When I want your advice, I'll ask for it.''

"If the girl's life and my hide are at stake, you'll hear from me whether you want to or not,'' Landry retorted.

Dar Ell glared. "I've dreamed and planned and schemed too long to hand over a lifetime take to a bunch of worthless mavericks that chance by. I'll gamble and fight first.''

Fifty yards to the west, at the apex of where the thirteen men had encircled the swing station, Rattlesnake Morton lay belly flat in the sage, grinning, taking exquisite pleasure in every word. He sported an expensive white Stetson he had taken in Windy Flat. He lifted himself on his left elbow and motioned to the man on his right, who in turn signaled the next to his right, their gestures visible in the fading moonlight. Morton then rolled to his right side and signaled the man on his left, who in turn signaled the man beyond him. Slowly they began squirming through the sage-bound hillocks, all but Morton, who held back, his rifle readied. The fugitives cradled rifles across their arms as the biting wind buffeted them, forcing them to cower their heads and take refuge where available; but gradually they worked closer, until they could hear the unsettled squeal of animals in the stable.

Morton adjusted his fancy white hat and continued. "You and your men need not die.''

"Come and get us," Dar Ell shouted. He pointed a small revolver that he had removed, hidden somewhere under his cloak, and fired twice through an open window into the night, the flames belching bright orange. Everyone else in the station dropped low or took refuge behind whatever crude furniture was available. Yattero cursed in Spanish as he struck a knee, and Terena stifled a sob as Lon pushed her flat to the floor. But the expected response did not follow, only the bombarding wind and sand clattering the doors and windows. They waited. Terena's muffled sobs continued. Ryke mumbled something unintelligible about hysterical women. They waited, guns pointed at the front and back windows and at the main door, bolted shut. A second door led to the stable, a common arrangement in cold country, with the animals stationed next to the dwelling, where they could be fed or watered without the tender needing to step out into the winter cold; in return, the animals would afford necessary body heat to supplement the meager warmth from a squat hearth and a battered stove. Besides a locked sliding door, the only openings in the stable were high vents like those in the storage room.

Tensely, they crouched or lay, until finally a curious Ryke stood up, parted the burlap, and looked outside.

"What do you see?" Dar Ell asked, rising.

"Nothing. Not a damn thing. What are they waiting for?"

"I doubt if they're foolish enough to rush us."

"They got something up their sleeves, and I'll bet Biggs has got something to do with this," Ryke hissed.

" 'Misery acquaints a man with strange bedfellows,' " said Dar Ell, his words coming from afar.

In the desert, Rattlesnake Morton and the fugitives lay cold and miserable, pelted by a relentless wind; but Morton insisted on waiting, knowing that the quiet and inaction would unnerve those inside. But he could not wait too long—problem was, he didn't know how many men protected the swing station. Where were the workers and the stagehands? Some, he knew, were in on the heist. He had given strict orders not to fire until he sent the first lead slamming into the building. The moon rose rapidly, blending the landscapes and indenting patterns of light and dark; the hypnotic sway of sage and bitterbrush made human movement difficult to discern. "Ready now." Rattlesnake signaled toward Tobias Johnson, closest to his right. "Weasel, send in Weasel, and then Slicer."

Tobias Johnson squinted against the peppering of sand. Faintly he saw their leader gesturing furiously and heard the blasting voice. He rose to his knees so that the Weasel— nobody knew his real name—could see him clearly. Weasel waved back in acknowledgment, checked his Colt, and crawled easily, weaving through the mesh of sage ahead, his pinched little head extended, his black eyes ferreting out a natural route through the washouts and dry waterways that pointed toward the swing station in the flat slightly below. Weasel had built a solid reputation before his arrest and sentencing as a slippery creature, a shadowy little sneak, instrumental in setting up a number of robberies and back-shootings through his observations. An informant known to some as a squealer, he had built additional reputations for picking locks and for blowing safes. "Wish we had some dynamite," Morton called to him. "We'd save ourselves lots of time." Unhearing, Weasel grinned through narrow, pointed teeth and continued slinking toward the station.

The wind whimpered about the building, spewing sand that crackled and plundered incessantly. The Dar Ell gang and their hostages huddled, shivering in the darkness.

"My girl, she's freezin', can't we fire somethin' up?" said Lon. He referred to the hearth on the south wall, dormant with old ashes moldering. A small potbellied stove stood in one corner.

"No," said Dar Ell with difficulty. "We can't permit any light, not one spark. We have to be in the dark."

"But I'm cold," Terena complained.

"I'm cold, too," Dar Ell said.

"There's some kindling; I saw some wood, too," Lon insisted. "Just enough to break the cold. I'll set it, light it. None of us have to go near it after that."

"No! We remain in the dark. Those cutthroats out there are in moonlight now. If they come in on us, they'll be at a disadvantage."

"I warn you, Dar Ell," said Lon, "if something happens to my woman . . ."

With incredulous dismay, Dar Ell said, "You, Lon, are you warning me? What the hell are you saying?"

"I'm saying my woman is hurting."

"Damn it," Dar Ell roared. "You brought her along. She's here because of you, because you flaunted my orders."

"She's hurtin'."

"Then get close to her—any way. Wrap blankets around you. We got plenty of them here. Your woman was gathering them up a minute ago."

"Just remember she's my woman—nothing's going to happen to her, not now. Just all of you remember that." Lon's voice was more assertive than Dar Ell could ever remember.

"Christ!" Ryke hissed the word.

"Your boss is right," said Landry. "Our only chance is to remain in total darkness. Leave them exposed in the moonlight. Morton's already hinted about what he plans."

From a window, the moonbeams streamed inside the room, softly over Dar Ell's features, making a tracery across his beaked nose. He was looking at Landry with curious but appreciative eyes. All the gang members looked at the lawman. Terena came up slowly from her humped enclosure behind the desk, her face drawn. "I warned you," said Dar Ell, "but now I ask you to speak, to explain yourself."

"What the hell you mean?" Ryke asked.

"The marshal's telling us truth. Truth, you hear? How maybe to get the devil out of here alive." He turned to Landry. "What are you telling us?"

"I'm telling you exactly what Morton told us. They'll come in, one by one, from all angles, probably try to fill us full of holes. They could have the means to try and burn us out." In the faint light, Landry rotated his swollen wrists, trying to relieve them from the binding thongs. Mollie watched, her face pained. "You best push anything flammable into a corner and cover it . . . like that kindling near the hearth, and that cloth around the windows."

"I like you, Marshal. In different circumstances I might have liked you very much." Dar Ell had an enigmatic smile. He sighed. "Of course, ultimately, somewhere, someplace, I expect. You and me. You and I know that."

"Yes," said Landry simply. "You know it and I know it. But for now, all of you need me. You, especially."

"Ryke, Yattero, Lon, all of us, let's move the furniture back, anything that could burn." Dar Ell rose, slapped his cloak around him, and pressed next to the window first to look outside.

"You're inviting a bullet right up the center of your scalp," said Ryke.

But the dark of the station interior contrasted dramatically with the soft touch of mellow light outside. The high moon and the liquid flow of stars dappled the big land with indistinct patterns. "Don't see anything yet," said Dar Ell.

After clearing the room as best they could, the men settled into a cautious watch. The wind continued, pummeling the building, humming over the flat roof and around the blunted corners. Once, when a gust exploded sand against the east door, the gunmen jumped and pointed weapons. From the stable the animals stomped and whinnied in discontent.

"Wish somebody would try something," said Ryke at last, "just to break the boredom."

"They will—that's why you best take more precautions," Landry warned.

"Meaning what?" Dar Ell asked.

"Meaning we better damn well protect those animals out there. That's a logical break-in. If they can release or injure those horses out there, consider this place our tomb."

"You're right. Lon, check out the stable and take watch there," Dar Ell ordered.

"Why him?" said Terena emotionally.

"Why me?" Lon demanded.

"Damn it, kid, that's orders. All you have to do is take a position in there. Keep the door open between us and the stalls. She can go with you."

"No," said Terena.

"I'll go," said Lon softly. "You, hon, you fix us something to eat. You can feel your way around." He swatted her buttocks, the slap resounding. The others listened as he fingered the cylinder of his revolver, checked it in the feeble light, then cautiously opened the door to the stable and disappeared.

The animals beyond shifted and snorted. A few stomped and kicked the sidings. A rush of animal flesh, fresh manure, and dry hay filled the swing station.

"Can you find your way, girl?" Dar Ell asked.

"No, it's too dark," said Terena. "There is a sack of hard bread and jerky, and I saw some cold beans in a bowl when we came in."

"Are there utensils?"

"Yes, but I can't see them. If you could get me a candle."

"Maybe. We need food. What do you think, Landry?"

"Too dangerous if someone's sneaking around out there. But try it. The only way they can hurt us is to shoot through a window. So let them try."

Dar Ell said to Ryke and Yattero, "Keep your eyes open." The tall, slender man dropped to his knees and removed several long matches from his personal pack. He struck one against the siding. The quick blue spurt lit the room, making distorted shadows. Dar Ell hunched over and cupped the flame in an attempt to diminish the light. "Hurry," he said, deciding to light a small candle he found next to a bunk.

The girl busied herself. Landry looked at Mollie. She returned his glance and concealed an understanding.

Deftly, Terena found a long knife in the storage room and sliced the bread into narrow slices; she wedged hunks of dried beef and rolled the bread around each, making chunky sandwiches. Ryke shifted, smelling the goodness. Yattero squirmed and licked his dry lips. Almost in delight, Terena garnished the sandwiches with some flakes of dried peppers that she removed from her own sack. She scooped the cold chili beans across each creation, and arranged them with pride on a platter, taking deliberate pleasure. Ryke and Yattero watched greedily. With happy determination, the girl crawled dutifully forward, delivering each a sandwich. They all munched hungrily. "I take some to my love," she said musically.

"You do that." Dar Ell smiled at her for the first time. With childlike enthusiasm, crouching, she carried the food into the stable area.

"I have food, hon," she said.

"Good," came the youth's voice, "I'm starved."

"If we get out of here, and if you plan to make it over the mountain," Landry told Dar Ell, "you better make sure those horses have feed and water and oat bags to take along. There's nothing but lichen in that upper country."

"We have some oats already, but we could carry more." Dar Ell took the candle and pushed in behind the girl. The flare revealed Terena crouching against some grain sacks near

Lon. The flame trembled, then flickered in the swirling of drafts, and steadied, again thrusting yellow probes of light through the snug area, reflecting back in the uncertain eyes of the animals as they twisted and thumped nervously. He studied the windows, the high ventilation flues and the heavy sliding door that had been bolted from inside. "You, Lon, you see or hear anything out there?"

"No, sir, I been listening real good. Do you think maybe they moved on?"

"I don't know."

"I hear nothing but the wind. It's real spooky."

"I know. I want you to feed the animals. Be sure they have enough, and fill some of those oat bags we got. And you might saddle a couple more horses, one for the woman and one for me. That big chestnut there must be the marshal's"

"Yes, sir. If they're still out there? Do we try to ride through them?"

"My plan is to outwait them. If we hold them off until dawn, we have a chance."

"But there will be posses out there, looking for Morton, and for the stage," he protested. "The marshal told us that."

"That may be our chance. Our gamble. A posse will push Morton on."

Ryke appeared in the doorway. "While you got that light in here, I want our fair shares. You said we'd count it out. No tellin' what will happen."

"Bring me the saddlebags, your money belts, and my luggage." Dar Ell closed the door partially to keep the light from filling the main room. While Lon and Ryke watched and Yattero stood guard, he distributed equal shares as best he could, with a larger amount for himself. Then the other men recounted in turn, and stuffed their shares into their own belongings and back into their money belts. Dar Ell snuffed out the candlelight.

Then Ryke said, "I'm going to chance it now. I'm not going to stay."

"Your funeral," Dar Ell said. "I can't stop you." He watched the gunman sling his saddlebags over a shoulder.

Ryke took his saddled mount away from a long feed bin, where a number of animals were lined, held his hand over the muzzle for silence and led him to the large sliding door. He carefully unlatched it and removed his side arm.

"Do you think they're still out there—those killers?" Mollie whispered to Landry. They could not see directly into the stable area, but they could hear clearly.

"Of course; Morton's trying to unnerve us. He's just waiting for a stupid move on our part."

Ryke slid the heavy door aside, enough to permit his head, and peered out into the shadowy night; the door movement startled Slicer, who huddled on the lee side of a trough in the yard, his eyes heavy-lidded from lack of sleep. He jerked awake to see Ryke appear. At the same instant, Ryke saw the elfish form of Slicer bulging beside the water hold. Both men's guns sounded almost as one, the explosion and tongues of flame shattering the night. Both men missed. Ryke rolled back inside, flinging the big door closed as more bullets followed, winging through the planking and shaving splinters of wood away. Ryke's horse squealed and jerked back.

Everyone in the swing station was suddenly on the floor again. "Appears they're still out there," Lon added.

(8)

Dar Ell sat heavily on a crude chair. He sighed deeply and looked at Ryke and Yattero, each stationed patiently beside a window. "We must hold until dawn. But what are they waiting for?"

"It will be darkest at about two-thirty," said Landry. "The moon will be gone before dawn. That's what I think they're waiting for."

"A couple of hours, then."

"These bindings. Loosen them now." Landry held out his swollen hands.

Dar Ell nodded, approached and worked them free, only to retie them with greater give.

"You interest me," said Mollie.

Dar Ell looked skeptically at the woman, and then returned to his chair to wrap his cloak tightly over his shoulders.

With calculating exactness, Mollie asked, "What is your need? Why does a talented, capable man like you throw everything—all your future—away?"

Dar Ell's features registered no reaction, but his right hand flexed involuntarily.

"Why, Mr. Dar Ell? I want to know why?"

Dar Ell turned away, laughed slightly, his body shaking. Then he snorted in derision. "I sense 'the whips and scorns of time.' "

"Hamlet," said Mollie matter-of-factly.

Dar Ell looked at her in discovery. "Yes. How did you know?"

"I'm not an ignorant woman, Mr. Dar Ell."

"No, I don't believe you are."

Dar Ell leaned toward her intimately. Landry watched, detached but amused. "You are an unusual young lady. Miss. . . ?"

"Miss Mollie."

"Mollie is the last name?"

The self-assured woman hesitated and said softly. "Mollie Rose Tyndale."

Dar Ell pursued. "Tyndale. Tyndale." He touched his brow with long white fingers. "Ah—Tyndale. Power. Influence." The actor smiled in recognition. "Are you related to the newspaper man from Placerville?"

"I've had some association," said Mollie flippantly.

"Yes. And your clever little mind is recording everything that's happening here."

"Possibly."

Terena slipped back into the room, the candle aglow. "Blow that out or take that back into the stable," Dar Ell snapped. The girl blinked dully and retreated. The candle flame lifted, almost went dead, as wind through the open window buffeted it. "Best put it out for now," Dar Ell said. The girl blew out the flame, plunging the place into greater darkness, for the rising moon had lost much of its early penetration.

"At least those basturds out there are going to freeze their butts," Ryke said with satisfaction.

Mollie rolled up her long sleeves and unbuttoned the high bodice of her dress. She breathed easier, her bosom rising and settling rhythmically. "I'm still interested, Mr. Dar Ell. Why?"

Dar Ell also settled some, listening for a moment to the

restless wind. "Why were you caught in all this? What the hell is an attractive woman, alone, doing aboard a stage loaded with riches?"

"I was on assignment and I had intended to take an earlier stage."

"Assignment?"

"Yes, you've obviously heard about the big prison break."

Dar Ell smiled. "Yes, I did hear something." The actor tightened the cloak about him. The faces of those in the room were barely discernible now as the moon pulled farther into the night void and dropped. "Ryke, Yattero, you see or hear anything?"

"Nothing," they replied.

"You hear anything, Lon?"

"No, sir, but I need light to ready the animals. It's too dark."

"Here, girl." He handed some matches to Terena. "Take the candle to your man." He listened to the swish of her skirt. "I hope this is not madness."

"They're out there, that was just proven," said Landry.

"Then why haven't they rushed us, shot us up?" Dar Ell asked. "It must be miserable out there."

"It is. But time and discomfort mean nothing to their kind. They'll come in their own time, when they're ready, as I said, shortly when it's darkest."

Yattero said, "We got to bury the three dead out there. It's a curse on God to come back and not bury the dead."

"Hell," Ryke spat.

"There's no way now, not with those killers out there," Dar Ell said.

"I'm still waiting, Mr. Dar Ell," said Mollie.

The actor sighed. "You are a persistent young woman."

"My uncle is a good teacher and a good boss. So I'm waiting." The candlelight flickered weakly from the stalls, casting a dim fan of gold around the door Terena had left slightly ajar, enough light to reveal hazy outlines and features.

Dar Ell sat thoughtfully, aware of the night sounds, aware of eyes upon him, of Ryke's, of Yattero's, of Landry's bemusement, of Mollie's curiosity. He took a flask from his breast pocket and drank. "We are all mortals," he said, wiping his neck with a handkerchief from his coat. He held out the flask to Mollie. "The woman reporter, will she share? Imported brandy—*je suis élégant.*"

Mollie hesitated, then said, "Certainly." She took the flask, and without averting her eye hold on Dar Ell, swallowed. The liquor stung her throat, for she choked and coughed and a trace of moistness glittered her eyes. She handed the flask back. Dar Ell took it, a touch of amusement and respect in his eyes.

Mollie waited.

"I suppose if we survive this, you will expose me, or greater, attempt to immortalize me."

"I will do my best," said Mollie.

In the desert, Tobias Johnson, his face crusted with alkali and dirt, crawled next to Leander Morton. "We're freezin', damn it. How much longer? We ain't unnerved 'em, apparently. And it's near as dark as it's going to get."

"It's time. The men made them brush balls?"

"All ready."

"Have Slicer and Weasel lay low until after the shooting. Then start passing the brush. I'll let you know when. I'll give Dar Ell one last chance. Then we fire the place. They'll come pouring out, bringing the loot with them. We kill them all. Understand?"

"Good, this is it." Tobias Johnson began crawling away.

Dar Ell smiled to himself, a wisp of moonlight playing across his chiseled features. "Perhaps, young lady, I should

summarize it all in a favorite quote of mine: 'We are such
stuff as dreams are made on, and our little life is rounded
with a sleep.' "

"Shakespeare."

"*The Tempest*, to be exact."

"In other words, life is passing by, and before it ends you
want some satisfaction . . . maybe the good life. Certainly
in your profession you have seen that life."

"I saw it. I saw others with it. But I never had the wealth
to maintain it."

"And this is your chance?"

"Ah, a woman's reason."

"Am I not right?"

"There is another quote with which you may be familiar."
Dar Ell's rich voice filled the squat room. " 'There is a tide
in the affairs of men which taken at the flood, leads on to
fortune; omitted all the voyage of their life is bound in shallows and in miseries.' "

"*Julius Caesar*," said Mollie Rose without pretension.

"You are well-read."

"I've done my share of reading and watching."

"Need I say more?"

"This, then, was to be your tide; but at present aren't we
more bound in shallows and in miseries?"

Landry choked back an audible laugh. Dar Ell squirmed
slightly. Then composed, he replied, "I quote another: 'The
web of our life is a mingled yard, good and ill together.' That
is from *All's Well That Ends Well*."

"So you're confident that fate will eventually play your
way?"

"Yes, and you had better pray, lady, that it does with those
cutthroats out there." Dar Ell turned his back as if bored, to
sever the interview. He rose and walked to a window and
parted the burlap slightly.

From the stable, a horse squealed and drummed its hooves, sending a stir of discontent through the animals.

"What the hell?" Ryke inquired.

"What's happening, Lon?" Dar Ell pursued, hushing his voice.

"I don't know. I can't hear nothin' suspicious," came a restrained reply.

Yattero said quickly, "Jumpy animals, that's a sure sign of the Devil. Always a sure sign. He's looking over our shoulder. I feel it. They feel it."

"Oh, hell," Ryke blasted.

"They're out there," Terena wailed. She pushed the stable door open as if to escape. She had been helping Lon ready the animals, but now she was bunched in a fetal position.

"Blow that light out," Dar Ell ordered.

The girl did. "Please. I'm scared."

"Damn it, child, you wanted to be a part of us. You had to come with your lover. Well, you do your part. Be sure the food, blankets, extra clothes you found here are packed. That's your job. Now you'll just have to do whatever in the dark."

"We're going to die here," she said plaintively. "We are all going to die here."

"None of us are dead yet. And none of us will die if I have anything to do with it. Now you listen to me, child. Pull yourself together. And get back in there with Lon."

"Be sure you pack some sugar," said Landry.

"Sugar? Yes, I saw a box in the pantry," Terena added.

"Take it—If we make it out, we'll need it."

"Yes, sir." Her robust form crawled into the darkness. They waited then, in silence. The horses settled, stomping or wheezing occasionally. The early morning wind whined shrilly, rushing through windows to billow the burlap curtains. Mollie sneezed several times. "She's shivering something bad," said Landry.

Dar Ell brought her a blanket and draped it around her shoulders. "Nice if we could have a fire, but we can't."

"Don't envy those crazy bastards out there," said Ryke deliciously. He held his cocked .45 against the window edge as he peered around. "They got to be miserable and sufferin'." He laughed to himself. A short, mean chuckle.

"Doesn't seem to be discouraging them," said Dar Ell.

Their smugness was shattered as two pistol shots lanced thundering flames through a window near the front door, splintering glass over Landry and Mollie. The bullets ricocheted crazily, one angling off the plank flooring to ring an enormous frying pan hooked on a wall before sinking into the ceiling. The horizontal layer of rafters, brush, mud, and gravel poured loose particles over the room for several minutes. The second winged broadly, passing three inches from Yattero's cheek before splatting into the siding.

"Mother Mary," the Mexican hooted, ducking. Everyone in the room sprawled. Landry thrust his bound arms across Mollie, forcing her down as he wormed his broad chest across her. She stifled a cry and waited.

Ryke swung from his guard position and exploded three shots at the window sprinkling clear the remaining glass. From the stable, shots split the night, erupting squeals from stomping animals. Lon fired twice more.

"What the hell's happening?" Dar Ell called, rising slightly.

"Don't know," Lon called. "I think somebody was trying to get in the door."

"Did you get him?"

"I ain't going to open the door to find out." Cold silence clutched them all. Then Terena convulsed into a spasm of sobs.

"Damn it, shut that woman up," Ryke snarled.

Her anguish increased. Sympathetically, Mollie tried to reach her. But Landry pressed her back. "No," he whispered.

"The child's on the verge of hysteria."

"That's good. All the rift that grows amongst them is good. You understand?"

"Yes. Yes, I understand."

"You all right?" Lon called from the stable. "Terena, are you all right?"

"She's all right," Dar Ell answered. "Do you hear anything more?"

"Nothing. You all right, Terena?"

"I'm fine," she uttered in a sniffling voice, sitting up.

"Bitch." Ryke barked the word with disdain, loud enough for the girl to hear.

"Stay on your toes, all of you," Landry suggested dryly. "They're going to come in through those windows."

Dar Ell rose as Yattero cursed and fired twice, the sound loud in the tense room. "What was it?" Dar Ell flung himself against the wall, gun in hand.

"It's still too dark out. But I'll swear somethin' moved."

Dar Ell said to Terena, "Girl, hand us a rifle." Dutifully, she reacted by lifting a loaded Winchester from the piled arsenal. Dar Ell took it and handed it to the Mexican. "Here, you need something more accurate than a revolver."

Yattero leveled it. "Maybe it not a man out there. Maybe we need more than guns."

"What are you talking about?"

"Those Wells Fargo men we killed. If they not confessed, they come to haunt us."

"Shut up," said Ryke.

Yattero shook his head despairingly. "If you don't give a man time to repent his sins, his soul will haunt you forever. He's got to repent."

Ryke laughed. "You never prayed or confessed in your life."

"When I was a boy with my mama, I did. She taught me that. If we ain't getting out of here, you'll hear confessin'."

Yattero's dark eyes searched anxiously over the sage. He jerked the muzzle, pointed it, and then drew it back.

"You'll need no confessing," Dar Ell said. "The longer Morton stays, the more he's chancing a posse or the militia."

"But so are we," said Ryke bitterly.

"I disagree," said Dar Ell. "Anybody on Morton's trail will chase after them. They'll rightly conclude anyone defending this place are Wells Fargo personnel. They have no reason to believe otherwise. Oh, they could send somebody to investigate, but I believe if we hold, Morton will leave before dawn and then we can break for it. We have a guide now. A guide maybe more capable than that shriveled little monkey, Nasa Tom."

"Nasa Tom a wise man," said Yattero. "I know of the curse. He know what he say."

"Apparently, Jonathan Dar Ell, you know little of Rattlesnake Morton." Landry's words had a tone of perceptive finality. Silence fell over the gang. Even Lon edged to the stable door. "Nicknames aren't given randomly. Rattlesnake wasn't tagged because it sounded mean. He is a rattlesnake. He'll coil in waiting wherever you go. He'll wait along the trail you choose, silent and beady-eyed, and when you've passed him, he'll strike. You try to find him, and he'll slither into a hole. You climb those mountains, and he'll scent you out and crawl after you. You'll never get away."

"Your tactics won't work, Marshal," Dar Ell warned. "I know you're playing the devil's advocate. But I will not let you shake my men."

"No way am I playing a role," said Landry simply. "I'm just relating hard facts."

Dar Ell snorted derisively. "Besides, Mr. Marshal, it will be you, not me, who must outwit Mr. Morton. If you fail, then we may all perish. And this attractive woman here—I shiver to imagine her in the clutches of animals without scruples. Creatures who have been denied even the sight of flesh so lovely. No, Mr. Landry, I think for her and for yourself, you'll use every lore and wile at your disposal.''

"And are my chances with you any better?" Mollie inquired.

"My word, ma'am, is good."

Yattero had turned away from the window to watch Dar Ell. Ryke was glowering into the darkness when three rapid shots crashed through the west window, blowing shards of remaining glass across the room. One bullet grazed Yattero's leg and ripped away; the second and third ricocheted and flattened into the walls. Terena screamed as once again people ducked for cover. Landry flattened his big hulk over a startled Mollie.

All four armed men fired at the window. "Get back into the stable," Dar Ell shouted at Lon.

Ryke thrust his gun through the window; it bucked twice in his hand. "Three or four of them moving out there," he shrilled.

"Did you hit any?"

"Too dark to see anything."

"The darkest always before the dawn," Dar Ell muttered.

"You best untie my hands," Landry said.

"You must think me a total fool," Dar Ell called back, trying desperately to see something outside.

"I'm not asking for a gun. Only the opportunity to defend myself and the woman."

"We won't need you, believe me."

Suddenly Landry's voice had the dangerous rumble of a trapped lion. "The lady friend and I won't die like helpless animals, mister."

Dar Ell stiffened, felt the biting words shoot up his spine. "If we need you, I'll let you know."

Landry squirmed higher and pressed his back against the wall. His eyes narrowed, smoldering embers of anger burning deep within. There would be a time and a place. "If you

plan to do it on your own,'' Landry offered, ''you better
damn well assist that kid in there. That's where they'll hit.
You lose the horses, or they manage a fire, we're through.''

''You're right. I'll back Lon. You men hold your positions.''
Dar Ell moved carefully to the passage between the rooms and
the stable and swung the door wide. The fetid, musky odor of
manure suddenly permeated the station again. Mollie stirred
some but settled herself. And then the night exploded.

From outside, every member of the Morton gang opened
fire. The thunderous crackle of shots seemed almost one
sustained sound for a time. A fusillade of bullets rent the
doors, splintered the windowsills, and whizzed about overhead, forcing everyone to hug the floor in fear of their lives.
A crash of bullets lanced under the stable doors, nicking one
horse and dropping a second. The latter collapsed screaming
and kicking, its hooves beating the stanchions until it slowly
subsided with death. In the stable, both Dar Ell and Lon
Wiggins blasted back, their discharge splintering the door
bottoms to whistle away outside.

''Jesus Christ,'' Yattero screamed, and shot wildly toward
a window.

Dar Ell staggered out of the stable. Lon dove out head first
and did a somersault on the floor.

Landry whispered to Mollie, ''Stick beside me. Follow
me whatever I do.''

''I'm with you, whatever,'' she assured him.

And then the shooting subsided, the silence confounding
except for the eternal wind that had quieted appreciably before the dawn. They all waited. Expecting.

''You have no future, Mr. Dar Ell. You're all dead shortly,
unless you cooperate immediately.'' The words came out of
the desert black, like the voice of the Devil.

''Rattlesnake Morton,'' Landry droned, the sound riveting.

''God damn,'' Ryke spat.

''He is the curse of E-sha,'' Yattero explained.

(9)

"You hear me, Mr. Dar Ell? You hear me?" Morton's voice penetrated the building.

"What now, sir?" Lon asked. The youth kneeled next to the counter, his pistol pointed straight up.

"Nothing. Not a damned thing," Dar Ell said with resolve. "He needs us now. So we outwait him."

"Well, our moment of reckoning approaches," said Landry.

Again Dar Ell ignored him. But Ryke said, "I'm getting fed up with him by the minute."

Morton's taunting voice again dominated the moment. "I don't want to kill you and all your fine friends, those of you left. But shortly you give me no choice."

Dar Ell cautioned, "One of them will surely expose himself."

"After all, we're all opportunists," Morton continued, "and you have what we want. You are surrounded. We have men outside your doors and your windows. If any of you survive, we will get you in only a matter of time."

"Look for them—anywhere," Dar Ell said. "Blow 'em away."

But as Yattero leaned close to a window to see better, a gunshot from a few feet outside burst in his face so closely, black powder smoke rolled in. He screamed, covered his eyes with his hands, fell against the wall and slid down.

Another barrage from outside followed, centering through the same window, whistling lead around them.

"I'm hit," the Mexican wailed, digging his knuckles into his eyes. Dar Ell was beside him. Mollie started to move, but Landry again restrained her.

"Is he hurt?" Terena murmured.

"They got us pinned down. We ain't got a snowball's chance in Hell now," Ryke cried. "Should never have stopped here."

Dar Ell lit a match and spread his cloak over to contain the glow.

"Damn it, man, you'll kill us all," Ryke shouted.

In the sulfurish light, Dar Ell pulled Yattero's left hand away and examined the eye. "There's no blood. Where are you hit?"

Yattero gasped in near hysterical realization. "Bullets must have blown adobe into my eyes." Blindly he untied his neckerchief and wiped his tear-streaked face.

Dar Ell blew out the wavering flame.

"Now hear me clear," came Morton's voice. "Now hear me. We will leave you in peace. If you follow my orders. Do you hear me?"

"We hear you," Dar Ell shouted back.

"Then we are close to a deal." Everyone waited. "You lay all your take outside the front door. You can't cheat us because I figure pretty close how much a haul you have. Understand? My boys will come for it under truce. We count it out. If it seems reasonable, we leave you."

"You better take advantage," Landry suggested. "We've been damn lucky so far that we haven't all been killed—damn lucky."

"No! To die by inches because I have been pricked by the arrows of fate? No," Dar Ell shouted. "You, Landry. You and the girl think only of safety at any cost. But my life is purposeless; my being, my future, is nothing without this money. And two years of my life! For God's sake, no, I will not give it up.'' No sooner had he spoken when something or someone pushed on the stable doors. Lon reacted by punching four shots back. Terena shrieked. The horses shrilled and pawed. And a moment afterward something heavy hit the front door, a tossed rock possibly, but Yattero, whose eyesight had returned, pumped a bullet into the wooding.

"For Christ's sake, Dar Ell, you fool," Landry roared. "You're killing us all."

"Brace the door," Dar Ell demanded. Ryke and Yattero pushed a bench against the entrance, then backed it with a flour barrel and some boards wedged at a low angle.

Mollie began hacking, a deep wracking cough. "This girl is chilled," Landry said. "We need another blanket."

Terena suddenly crawled forth with a moldy, sour-smelling tarpaulin she had found on a back storage shelf. "Sorry," she offered brokenly. "It don't smell so good."

"Thank you. You are kind," said Mollie. Landry, with difficulty, tried to work the folds around the reporter's legs and up over her torso.

"I can manage from here," she said.

From outside, Morton called, "We're waiting. We'll give you a couple more minutes and that is all."

"Offer part of your take—a third, even half," Landry said. "For them out there, time is short. They just might accept and hightail away, leaving us a chance."

"He's right, boss," said Yattero. "Maybe we try to take too much. Steal everything. You heard the legend."

"It's too late to run for it now," said Ryke, "so I don't know."

"There are too many of them out there," Yattero added, his voice trembling. "Give 'em part, like the marshal said. The curse is for real, believe me. We will die if we take all. With part, maybe the gods will understand."

"Lord, what fools we mortals be. Two years of sweat and planning and work and dreams. I won't give it up. Besides," Dar Ell raved, "do you think Morton would really ever let us go? Give them half and they'll still want the rest. They're bluffing. They can last only until dawn, and that's not an hour away."

"But Morton doesn't know for certain how much your take was. Offer him half but give him a third," Landry said, measuring the man, knowing that one might push any of them too far. "But if you dig in here indefinitely, the greater the chance of them killing some of us, or the authorities finding us. And that's your end, Dar Ell. Offer them part. Chance it; then get the hell out."

"No."

"We'll ride out then, leave the girl here. She can't hurt you—not any more than you've hurt yourself already. You have me. I'll take you over the Sierras. I told you I know the secret way."

"No. No. We wait," Dar Ell fumed. "We wait it out."

"Wait for what? Death?"

"Let's give 'em something," Yattero begged. "We crazy to wait. Leave it outside. Even half of my share is a million more than I've ever had before."

"I've worked too hard to give it up now," said Dar Ell.

"You're not giving it up, only a part. Offer it and live," Landry tempted. "At dawn, if a posse appears, what will it all be for? What will you have gained?"

"I'll chance it. They'll be on Morton's tail. He's the one who can't chance it. He knows that. Besides, there may not be a posse for miles. But it's the fear, the unknown, that will cave Morton."

"You've been throwing fancy quotes about," said Landry. "Well, I'll give you one. 'A fool and his money are soon parted.' And you're a greedy fool, Dar Ell."

"I'm with you, Mr. Dar Ell," Lon called from the stable. "Whatever—I'm with you."

"And for once I vote with you, too, Dar Ell," said Ryke. "I refuse to give those bastards out there a pinch of gold for what we've went through."

"Well, that settles it," Dar Ell said, relishing his victory.

"You might be stage center in this instant, Mr. Showman," said Landry, "but the scenes change."

"Very excellent analogy, Mr. Lawman," said Dar Ell. "But may I suggest that though this is madness, there is method in it."

"Hamlet," said Mollie cynically.

"You're right, young lady."

"Well, I hope *you are* right, mister," Landry echoed.

Dar Ell rose and bellowed, "Morton, you hear me?"

"I hear you."

"Go to hell!"

Earlier the previous evening, Sheriff George Healy and the posse had settled in a broad ravine below the adobe hut, where the low ridges offered protection from the stinging winds. A few far rumbling clouds had warned them. Flash floods from sudden mountain downpours could sweep violently through the arteries of washes and cuts, overwhelming and sweeping men and horses away in a nightmarish deluge. But both Healy and Allen agreed that the distant sounds did not threaten yet, that the relative comfort and shelter afforded by the area were more important now. Bone-tired, both men and animals needed rest, for the pace had been strenuous and demanding.

A steady spring in a willow cleft above them spewed cool, refreshing water that funneled down conveniently for the men while pooling below for the animals. With a few on guard, the men settled drowsily, sharing words about their families and their work; Healy approached Allen. The hefty man stood barrel-chested, tugging at his curly beard in anticipation, his hat tilted jauntily. ''You want to join me for a short run?''

''Sure, where?''

''To the ridge yonder there.'' Healy motioned to a rise a half mile ahead.

''You want to consider what you think they're heading into.''

''Yes. There has to be some reason why they've swung this way—almost in a circle. And why they tore up that mining hut, like they was looking for something.''

Allen nodded in agreement. ''From them hoof cuts, they ain't all that far ahead of us now. You know that—less than a half day's ride, if that.''

''Can't figure it,'' said Healy. ''What I don't understand is why they don't give a hang about somebody being on their trail. They surely know somebody's closing in. And why aren't they splitting? That's the only tactic that would make sense—split seven ways to the wind and split up the troops following. And why aren't they attempting to hide their trail? And why, now, are they slowing, narrowing the gap between us?''

''I been thinking,'' said Allen. ''I been mulling this for some time. There's got to be something around here that Morton's looking for—holding out for—maybe some loot he hid a long time back. Obviously he was looking serious when he tore up that hut back there.''

''Yeah, after leaving Windy Flat, their actions seemed like they had something more important than escape, if you can figure that one.'' Healy had a questioning look. He stood contemplating the horizon. ''That's why I want to ride out a ways—not so far as to tire the horses, but far enough.''

''Let's tell the men and go,'' said Allen.

The two leaders nudged their horses into an easy trot and finally into a steady, long-pacing walk. As a white moon rose, they let their animals feel the way up the washed landscape. The men buttoned their coats, turned up the collars, and pulled down their hats as the temperature dropped suddenly. A sucking wind whirled around them to draw their long coats out, flapping them. The animals balked and minced their steps. Without communicating, yet sealed in a dual purpose, the two ascended the slope where shifting sand succumbed to broken rimrock; fractured curds of volcanic outcrops, gnarled and fanged from some ancient eruptions, had left the spot uninhabitable. "From up there we ought to be able to see." Healy pointed to the flat cap.

Progress grew more difficult. The two dismounted, both encouraging their mounts, then leading them with care through a rocky maze that ended on the ridge. Silently, both men squatted and looked as the animals nosed among the rocky outcrops for sustenance. The men glanced back on the splintered posse members, upon the small glowing fires that lit the sweep more dramatically than their size warranted.

The two men then looked northward in the direction the fugitives were fleeing. The veil of distance rolled on, indistinct until blending toward the next rise of foothills with the moon-blanched Sierras beyond. "Don't see nothing suspicious out there," said Allen. "If they're out there somewhere, they ain't burning any fires."

"Unless they're beyond that next rise," Healy speculated, "and I think they are, but not much further than that."

Allen grinned and bit into a tobacco plug; the wrinkles and blotches on his face arranged themselves into a pleasurable pattern. "I couldn't agree with you more, Sheriff. Them tracks we been following are just too fresh."

"How far ahead do you think?"

"If we pull out well before dawn, we just might give them a run for their money." Both men's attention was drawn to the distance, for it seemed they heard gunfire. They listened carefully, then dismissed the possibility, for the night air whipped and popped through the sage and over the broken land. But as they left, Healy looked back; something like sporadic shots sounded, carried on a continuous wind from afar. Both men looked searchingly at each other.

"You and me, we're hearin' things," said Healy, shrugging. They walked their horses down a volcanic wedge. The high curving moon made the way fairly easy, and the fires ahead were constant beacons.

"I just can't understand why they'd slow up," Allen questioned still. "It just don't make sense. Hell, if I was one of them jailbirds, I'd be pushin' my poor old horse right up the side of them mountains yonder."

"There's more than we've imagined—maybe something big," Healy responded. "They seem headed now toward the Wells Fargo swing station."

"Willow Springs?"

"Yes."

"They're not going to chance getting shot up or seen," Allen said, dismissing the suggestion. "Besides they got all the goods they can carry out of poor old Windy Flat."

"We'll sleep a spell. This moon's bright enough; we can pull out in a few hours and pick our way, follow their trail. We just might surprise the jailbirds—catch them off guard before dawn."

"We don't want to walk into an ambush."

"We'll play it by ear. If we can't keep on their trail, we'll just call a halt until it's light enough."

Allen tugged at his rich beard; he walked pigeon-toed, uncomfortable out of the saddle, his hefty belly protruding. He stared back into the milkish void. "What do you mean something big?"

Healy weighed his words. He, too, stopped. He tightened his coat around him. "Just something I feel. I listen to hunches when I get them."

"What do you feel?"

"Rattlesnake Morton and those skunks he's with are hated

and feared. There must be a thousand people in the West that would do him and his buddies in for less than a plug of tobacco. I can't imagine anyone who would protect or harbor him.''

"Then why in hell ain't he tailin' it out of here?'' Allen shouted, his words wavery against a swirly air rush.

"Because it's what we been suspecting. Something big is holding him.''

"Stolen loot!''

"It has to be,'' said Healy. "A sizable amount, or he wouldn't play foolish like he is. According to my telegram, a few of his old henchmen are out with him. Certainly there's money they took that's never been accounted for that's stashed somewhere.''

"What worries me, in the dark we could stumble onto the bastards, right into an ambush.'' Allen spat a length of tobacco juice.

"For the first three or four miles we'll pick our way in single file with Nelson in the lead. He's our best tracker. Then as it lightens, we can spread out to advance on them. They could gun down one or two of us—that's always possible—but we can hope to catch them in a cross fire maybe before the sun's up.''

"Think they'll try to make a standoff?''

"No, not unless we trap them. They'll run for it.''

"Hope you're right,'' said Allen, mounting his horse. "Best we get back and sleep. I'm spent.''

"Some coffee would hit the spot, too,'' Healy said.

In the black desert, at the coldest and darkest period in the hours before dawn, Rattlesnake Morton and his fellow prisoners huddled in misery as they ringed the swing station. They had bunched their horses in a partially tempered gully leeward of the prevailing winds; but the uncomfortable animals clumped, shifting and pressing for protection and warmth.

Rattlesnake Morton curled below a scraggly bitterbrush; his dark eyes glowed angrily. He worked his thick mouth in growing frustration, his curved mustache twitching. Throughout the night the gusts had pelted him, stinging his reddened eyes until they had watered and blinked unseeing.

Red came crawling to him. Even in the feeble light of a shrinking moon, his heavy, brutish face looked intimidating. His heavy-lidded right eye could not open completely because of a past knife fight. "The brush balls are ready and waiting, Morton," he said. "The horses are bag fed and rested some, and Weasel and Slicer are ready. We can't wait much longer."

Morton drew a long breath. "Now is as dark as it's going to be."

Red picked dried meat from his teeth with the point of a knife. "Hope we don't have to rush 'em. Weasel and Slicer are still next to the stable. They ain't done no good there, but at least we can pass them the brush balls. Slicer, he wants action."

Slicer was a square-faced little man, with narrow eyes and button nose and buck teeth that gave him a perpetual smirk. His overly large head appeared top heavy on a narrow, spidery frame. But he and Weasel had the prison's most infamous reputation as knife fighters.

"We took the kerosene from your bags," Red added. "The men are ready to douse 'em."

"All I could find in Windy Flat. Wanted dynamite. With dynamite, things would be different now." Morton sighed. "Warn the men, and make sure Weasel and Slicer stay low and by the stable. Like we planned, have Johnson and Kraft carry them balls of brush in. They can fire them. Weasel and Slicer can do the rest. At my first shot, I want the rest of us to fill them windows and that room with lead."

"It's done." Red grunted up to run, crouched toward where Tobias Johnson stretched.

Except for Mollie's hacking cough, no sound came from the bullet-shredded swing station. Ryke and Yattero continued studying the outside patterns of gray and black, the lay of the land less distinct now than at any time during the siege. The wind had quieted. A sense of expectancy gripped them all, for if Morton intended to fulfill his threat, it would be now or never.

Then Landry broke the silence. "It's a stalemate—seems to me you better make a bargain, and fast. You still can."

"We've taken everything they've thrown at us," Dar Ell countered.

"So far we've been lucky."

Dar Ell said mockingly, "No, discretion is the better part of valor."

His last words had hardly sounded when a bullet whiffed past his face, and the dark outside again exploded in gunfire. Ryke cursed, Yattero huffed something about a god, and they both dove for the floor. Terena squealed and Mollie cried out. And once again Landry tried to shield the woman reporter as bullets angled about, most splaying harmlessly, but others taking dangerous directions. For a seeming eternity the bombardment continued, the most intense of the long night. An enormous set of deer antlers and a decorative Cheyenne Indian shield came off the wall. A faded painting hanging askew, of a rounded stage drawn by rounded horses with slender legs, fell heavily, and a tin cup sitting on the ticket counter twanged away. No one in the room could engage the withering gunfire.

Immediately, the horses in the stable commenced shrilling and bucking, their hooves slamming high while others reared and pawed, knocking the wood supports apart as they tried desperately to mill and break away. One horse, hit, screamed piercingly, spun about and then dropped, shuddering. "Goddamn," Lon exclaimed, diving out of the stable to somersault into the main room again. Bravely, Dar Ell rose partially to fire back out of the nearest window in a futile gesture.

Suddenly, a flaming light haloed the western window, and then a second engulfed the eastern window beside the main door. The gunfire outside ceased; the brilliance lit the swing station as two more flaming spheres hurtled through. The crackling fires sprayed fragments of burning particles as they hit the floor and continued tumbling. Outside, the gunfire commenced sporadically.

Landry came to his feet, his bound hands managing to clutch Mollie and drag her to a corner as a fifth roll of flames came in, spewing lacy arcs of fire like a bursting rocket. The spiraling brush crashed into the counter and bounded up and back to the spot where Mollie and the marshall had huddled.

Burning embers dotted a Navajo rug in front of the door. Landry swept it up and began flailing at the burning fragments. The room was ablaze. Terena screamed, "My dress, my dress, it's on fire!"

"Oh, my God," Mollie cried out. The frantic girl was flapping and beating the side of her long skirt when Lon clutched her, threw her flat. Her breath went out in stunned pain. He and Landry rolled her over and over and then back as the blackened garment smoked out.

Dar Ell tore another decorative rug from the wall and began swatting and batting flames, some of which had spread to the paper and tickets on shelves behind the counter. "Don't let those flames reach the roof," Landry shouted. Although the building had been crudely constructed of adobe and stone, the roof was held by horizontal pinion rafters, covered with brush, mud, and gravel strewn across the hard pan. But the rafters and even the caked brush, if ignited, could turn the station into an inferno of death. Yattero picked up a smoldering blanket Terena had folded and he, too, battered away.

In the stable the horses bunched and parted, pawing at their constraints, some maiming each other in panic as the smoke rolled about them. Half blinded, the firefighters began choking and gasping for air.

Ryke stood back, a revolver in each hand, lobbing bullets out the windows, first to the west and then the east, in a desperate attempt to ward off the fire throwers.

Suddenly a sixth glow appeared at the western window; another sizzling ball of flame swelled up, about to explode in white heat. But Ryke daringly stepped in front of the window as someone outside poised the creation. He pointed his barrel just below and blasted three shots.

Outside, Weasel, who had carefully showered a woven clump of dry sage and wood with kerosene, had crawled under the window, and nurtured the fireball, forking it with a long stick, then had risen to heave the bomb inside. He caught the bullet impact straight on. The slugs flung him back and down, his arms and legs flapping wide as he hit the earth, the unheaved firebomb breaking over him, enclosing him. Slicer, seeing his partner consumed in flames, dropped the brush bundle he was preparing and fled. Morton stood up and called for another bombardment, but those in the swing station were already as low to the floor as possible, for air. Fortunately, most inflammable materials had been shifted to the pantry/storage room. Much of the sparks and tindering stems fell on a dirt floor or against the adobe and stone or solid planking. The sparks lapsed into smoldering ashes or weak embers that blinked out, but left an irritable smoke that smarted eyes, seared the throat and lungs, and left the possessors coughing and spitting.

Ryke wiped his arm across his face to clear the sweat and grime, blinked, and pointed a newly filled revolver out the western window, whamming three more shots into the desert. Unknown to him, several convicts ducked, nearly hit, turned tail and ran. Yattero pointed a Winchester out the east window and quickly sent two bullets screaming in Morton's direction.

"My God, we're alive," Dar Ell beamed through gritty teeth.

(10)

Well before dawn, the posse men, nearly forty members, stirred quietly, readying horses and snuffing out smoldering fires. When ready, they waited until Sheriff Healy took his horse and whistled to Allen and the rest. As a determined force they led their horses, an infectious excitement building, knowing that their purpose was nearly fulfilled, that the escaped murderers were not too far ahead.

Silently they fell behind in column as Nelson and Allen picked the way, for the tracks were only faintly visible under the waning moon. At the first streak of light, when dawn flecked the desert horizon, they would fan out to flank Healy as he pushed them to a steady trot. For now, most gave their horses free rein.

Anxiously they worked northward, across the rise and down into a corrugated space of washes, broken rises, and rivulets, an unwelcoming world of distorted volcanic forms where they tripped and stumbled, their animals pulling reluctantly. Allen moved his horse next to Healy, close enough to be out of hearing from the others. "They're holding together like fleas to a dog. That's strange." Allen leaned forward, his webbed face tired, his narrowed eyes contemplating the land. He frequently pawed at his curling beard, loosening the muddy droplets formed from mingled frost and dust. In the wan light, they could barely make out hoof chalks distinct in the gravelly depressions. "They ain't making any effort to evade us."

"It sure as heck is strange," said Healy. "Whatever's holding Morton has to be more important than the threat of us."

Allen considered his reply, finally drawling, "Well, Morton lived a charmed life until Marshal Dirk Landry nailed him. He just may be defying us and God, too."

Healy nodded stoically. They headed steadily along the lean of a rising plateau where juniper grew more frequent, stunted and fat, blue-black against the empty sweep. With the slow creep of weak light, they followed a spotty pattern of hoof marks that pointed to the ridgetop then dropped dramatically toward a wooded setting of cottonwoods and willows, nothing more than a dark splotch.

"They was hurrying their horses here," Allen announced excitedly. "See?" His plump finger pointed at the gouged earth, punctured from forced horses plunging their way, or where their hocks had scraped as they had descended stiff-legged like a dog sitting down. "They was hell-bent for that clump of trees. Must have been something important."

"Yes, I see," Healy said coolly, urging his horse ahead. "Send the message, hurry." The word rippled back.

By dawn's light they followed the trampled earth through a gold-leafed glade to the abandoned stage and the strongbox, empty, apparently dragged from the brush where someone had attempted to hide it earlier. "They've dang near turned in a complete circle," said Nelson. The posse men milled their animals, searching. Someone, exploring up the largest ravine where trees merged into brush to the top of the ridge, shouted his discovery of horse signs, perhaps the movement of a half-dozen riders who had recently pushed up the long draw.

"Maybe they split here," said Allen. But the discoverer's enthusiasm was quickly drowned by the clamor of posse members who were tracing a string of hoof imprints north-east and realized that some dozen riders had broken in the same direction of the half-dozen.

"Morton's after somebody," said Healy.

"And I bet that somebody has some loot," Allen added. The upturned earth glistened some from recent moistness. And it smelled fresh still. From several miles northeast came a popping and spattering of gunfire as if a battle raged.

"Come on," Healy called, rallying his men. "Somebody's found them, and we're almost on top of them."

The dying flame around and in the swing station cast streamers of fading light. Rattlesnake Morton spat a jet of saliva and angrily watched it ball and roll into a sandy depression. Time now was against him. Outside the swing station, Weasel lay dead, sprawled flat, his body strangely sunken, his brains crimson globules over the ground, his charred clothes smoldering.

"Chances of gettin' them and their take is over. They stood us off," said Red, awed, his russet beard nearly gray with blown alkali. "We damned well better get our asses moving."

Morton nodded a weighty acknowledgment. Hungrily, he looked at the swing station. Within the battered walls lay enough wealth, he figured; enough to give him his freedom from want forever, enough certainly to assure worlds of sensuous pleasure in distant lands. But with the dawn not far away, and with the posse they had spied several times doggedly pursuing them, he had no choice but to push on. The posse was too large to confront, and with each hour of delay, the lawmen relentlessly tightened the gap. Morton wondered if that new sheriff, George Healy, led the badge pack. Through prison word, gossip had it that the young leader was a good gunhand, smart and ambitious, and at times even foolishly courageous. Well, Morton thought, the man's enthusiasm, his ambition, certainly his inexperience, might just work to an advantage.

"We got to get out," Tobias Johnson called, his fine features bloated and webbed with fatigue and cold. "We should have burned 'em out earlier. We stayed too long. The horses, they ain't grazed too good. To use them proper, we got to get them good feed somewhere."

Morton nodded in reluctant agreement. He squeezed the Winchester in his grasp with such frustration that his whole body shook. His wide, pan-flat face with the beetling brows, crushed nose, and dirt-crusted lips, froze in a momentary mask of fury. Then he relaxed some, smiled cunningly, his droopy mustache twitching. He owed nothing to those fellow fugitives with him. They were serving his purpose and would serve his full purpose yet. With long, horny fingers, he scratched the whiskery growth that had prickled his face. He worked his tongue over broken teeth and tasted a sour bitterness of wind-blasted alkali. His puffy red-rimmed eyes regarded the swing station with a calculating exactness. He stared at Weasel's body, at the little ringlets of slow smoke. He looked south at the silhouette of low-rising foothills beyond which a posse surely approached. He saw the shadowy figures of restive men in the back sand swales, their rifles still pointing, but their heads up, their eyes roving toward one another. He took a swig of water from a stolen canteen, washed the liquid around in his mouth and spat it away, and then drank deeply, trying to clear his throat. Tired, he squirmed to his elbows to arch his back and lift his head above the bulwark of a sand mound. Some son of a bitch in the station might try to snipe him, he knew, but his message had to be delivered. "Hear me in there," he shouted, his voice echoing, so effective that he repeated the salutation. "Hear me. You won this round. But you have not won. When you run, we will follow you. When you hide, we will smell you out. If you split, we will find each of you one at a time."

He paused. With delicious delight he added with a taunting, arrogant ring, "Take care, because soon your gold is our gold."

Scurrying like quail in the dark, the twelve escapees took their tossing horses, adjusted the bits and cinches on the crazed animals and pulled them northwest behind Morton. Relieved to be free of the cramped confinement, the animals attempted to plunge away. "Where we headed?" Tobias shouted.

"East toward the hills." Morton answered. "There's timber and big rocks enough to hide a regiment. We can hole out there, or stand off an army if need be."

"What about the gold?"

"There's not a man alive that can hide his trail from me." Morton led them slowly through a desert dark-flecked with eastern light.

"See anything?" Dar Ell asked.

"Nothing," said Ryke.

"Are they leaving?" Yattero asked.

"Why?" Lon wondered.

"I told you, they had no other choice." Dar Ell smiled with superiority.

"It could be a trick to decoy us out," Ryke said, pushing his revolver barrel out a window. They listened. Nothing but a lazy wind hummed. They waited. Almost without warning the eastern horizon sent prongs of white-gold skyward, diffusing and then giving detail to the hillocks and hollows of sage where Morton and his men had found concealment.

"It's dawn," Dar Ell cried gleefully. "And now it's our moment. We have horses, food, and a guide."

"My God, look," said Ryke. Far out on the western ridge crinkled and laced with sunlight, came horsemen; they thundered across the stage road, heading north. "There must be thirty-five or forty."

"They're going on. They're after Morton and his bunch," Dar Ell sang with elation. "Come on, now." He gestured Lon and his girl up. "Get the horses and the grub and be sure we have plenty of blankets." He motioned to Landry and Mollie. "Move, fast."

"Temporarily the luck breaks for you," said Landry.

"Ah, Marshal, did you not hear that there is a tide in the affairs of men which taken at the flood leads on to fortune? This is our current." Yattero, Lon, and the girl began scurrying about.

The posse plummeted down the southern ridge, crossed the stage road, and swept on past the swing station. As the posse members reached the opposite rise, the animals slowed to catch wind. Healy stood up in his stirrups and looked around in the pearly light, then shouted at the nearest riders behind Allen. "Wells, Blaisdell." He snapped his arm eastward. "Check out that swing station," he shouted, "on the double. Somebody could be hurt." Businesslike, they nosed their horses toward the station.

As the convicts climbed a rib of juniper and pinion, Red cried out, "Jesus Christ, look back." Across the southern elevation appeared a spread of oncoming riders several miles back, abreast, riding fast, their force overwhelming. The fugitives whipped and heeled their animals to greater effort, lengthening the distance momentarily. But as the rise steepened, the unwatered, skimpily fed beasts began floundering.

Ryke said, "Wait a minute, there's two horsemen, two posse members heading our way."

"The devil they are." Dar Ell looked out the window. In the lucent air, two riders approached.

"Of course," said Landry, "any good lawman worth his salt is going to send someone down to check us out, to see what happened and if anyone is hurt. There has to be a reason why Morton would lay siege on a way station.''

''Maybe Morton needed guns and supplies. They have no reason to suspect us,'' said Dar Ell, suddenly sobered.

''They may have found the stage. Doesn't matter, a lawman's going to check us out. He has to.''

Ryke picked up a rifle and levered a new bullet into the chamber.

''Wait,'' said Dar Ell. ''There's been enough killing. Maybe I can talk them away.''

Ryke answered impassively, ''What do you think is going to happen when they see those corpses out there under the blankets?''

Yattero picked up his rifle.

Dar Ell started to say something, but hesitated.

''Looks like your tide is receding,'' said Landry.

Ignoring the marshal, Ryke said to Yattero, ''The posse's out of sight now. You follow me. When they stop outside, I'll step out and take the one to the left, and you take the one to the right.'' The two posse members neared rapidly some quarter of a mile distant.

''What can we do?'' Mollie whispered desperately to Landry.

''Dar Ell,'' said Landry authoritatively. ''Cut these bonds. I'll talk to them. If you promise to let the girl go when we leave.''

''What about you?'' said Mollie.

''Don't trust him,'' Ryke warned. ''In a few minutes we'll have those buzzard baits in our sights.''

''What do you say?'' Landry looked hard at Dar Ell.

''I can't promise you anything about the girl there.''

''If you kill those lawmen, you'll be more than part of a robbery and a killing of Wells Fargo people, you will be a killer of lawmen. You know what that means. Besides, if those two don't show up as reinforcements, you don't think the others will be riding back to see what's wrong?''

"We'll be long gone," said Ryke, his eyes watching the oncoming riders like a cat studying its prey.

"The marshal's right," Dar Ell said with conviction. He withdrew a knife and severed the bonds. "But we'll have guns at your back, and the girl will remain with us.'

"Again, you're a damn fool," said Ryke.

"I need a Colt," said Landry. Dar Ell looked with disbelief at the man. "I need a gun," the marshal repeated. "Empty it. But I'd be suspect walking out there without it on my side.''

Dar Ell nodded in concurrence, speedily found a revolver, thumbed five bullets out and handed it butt first to Landry, who sunk it into his holster. Rubbing his wrists, he stepped outside to face the two posse men. They rode swiftly, their horses lathered. Upon seeing the marshal, they pulled up abruptly as both horses pivoted under the momentum, flinging sand. "Marshal, what happened?" one called. "We're posse members.''

"Some trouble." He nodded toward the covered bodies.

"You're Marshal Dirk Landry, aren't you?" the second inquired.

"Yes, I am."

"We been on the track of them convicts for three days. Guess you heard of the break?" said the first.

"That's why I'm up north."

"Found an empty coach back there. Then we heard the shooting here. None of us guessed we'd be so close behind them.''

Inside, Ryke moved up an inch and tipped the point of his rifle toward them. Yattero, watching, did likewise.

"Let him play it out," Dar Ell cautioned. "Don't panic now.''

"Your sheriff will need you. You go ahead," Landry suggested. "I'll clean up here. Patch people up. There's a stage in here a couple of hours from now."

"You certain everything's all right?"

"Everything, considering."

"I'm Wells," said the man addressing Landry. He was a handsome, dapper fellow with a pencil-line mustache. "This is Blaisdell." He angled his thumb toward a stout, jowly man with a mustache that curled like the horns of a Texan longhorn. The man sat his horse heavily. "Sheriff sent us down here to find out what happened and to help if possible."

"I'll handle it," said Landry.

"It don't make sense them attacking you," said Wells. "What were they after?"

"Food, clothing, I guess. Maybe ammunition."

"That's strange," said Wells. "They wiped out a little stopover called Windy Flat, burned it to the ground. We think they took everything they needed there." Both men sat ill at ease, their horses dancing as their eyes darted continuously over the premises.

"Sorry to hear about Windy Flat," said Landry.

"That stage back there, we think it was carrying a few passengers and lots of gold and coins," Wells continued.

"Yes, there were two people on it. They're inside, a little shaken, but all right. One's a woman. I want to get her on to Limbo."

"He's pushing it again," Ryke hissed slowly.

Wells said with sincerity, "Sure we can't give you a hand? Them bodies, you want to bury them or take them on in?"

"Take them on in. Thanks, nothing can be done here now. You're needed with your men. Those fugitives won't be taken easily, not if I know Leander Morton."

"One more thing," said Wells, "could that stage money be here somehow? Something had to hold Morton, even though he's desperate."

"Tell your sheriff it's all safe."

"What the hell?" said Ryke, looking at Dar Ell.

"Hold it. Hold it," Dar Ell murmured soothingly. "I told you, let him play it out."

"Morton and his gang chased the stage back here, shot up the driver, a guard, and the keeper here. I just happened along in time to get the passengers and the strongbox free before sending the stage back as a decoy; but of course, it didn't work. You wish to check things out here?"

Although holding a poised rifle, Ryke reached down and cocked his revolver. The metallic click sounded above the morning wind. The posse man, Blaisdell, stiffened in the saddle and looked toward the station.

"No," said Wells, "we're just pleased all is in your hands, Marshal. I just wonder how Morton knew there was so much value on that stage?"

"In prison there's always been an in-house line on everything of value. You know that."

"Guess you're right, Marshal. But that killer has to be brought in." The men turned their horses toward the direction the convicts and the pursuers had vanished. "They killed lots of people along the way, including women and a state guard."

Inside the station, Ryke, Yattero, and Lon all glanced at Dar Ell, his features drained and tired in the morning light.

"Incidentally, who's your sheriff?" Landry called.

"George Healy, a fine man."

Inside the station, Mollie Rose Tyndale cupped her mouth in a sting of emotion. Her trembling fingers pressed into the soft of her lips.

"Tell him we're mighty obliged for saving us, that he doesn't owe me that drink anymore," said Landry.

"He owes you a drink?"

"Last time we saw each other. Cut cards up in Lost Chance, California—mother lode region. I beat him so bad, he couldn't afford all the drinks. But after this we're even."

The posse men laughed. Both waved and headed off in a steady gallop, with Blaisdell looking back. Landry removed his revolver, stalked into the station and handed the weapon, butt first, to Dar Ell. He looked sympathetically into Mollie's wistful eyes.

"Your removing your side arm so sudden, that didn't look natural or professional," Dar Ell challenged suspiciously. "And that chatter about drinks and cards, what's that all about? And mentioning the girl on the stage. What did that prove?"

Landry said gruffly, "I removed the gun before you all in good faith. The talk—how better to distract and set at ease some lawmen about ready to investigate? I saved their hides and your hides. And as far as the woman here, Tyndale is a big name west of the mountains. To save your neck, I suggest you leave her here for that incoming stage. Case is closed."

"I can't leave her, not yet," said Dar Ell.

"I've warned you. Somewhere down the line you'll pay."

Dar Ell ordered an immediate abandonment. Yattero readied the horses and watered them; they were spooked still and kept shying and prancing. Landry demanded his chestnut. Terena gathered the blankets and bags of goods she had packed. Hastily, Lon and Ryke tied them to various saddles along with additional guns. The already cramped saddlebags were stuffed with extra ammunition. "Better put some horseshoes in and a hammer and some nails," Landry suggested, "it's rough country ahead."

Mollie, who had stepped into the storage/pantry area to change, emerged in a shirt and riding breeches. To Landry she looked boyish but decidedly feminine, drawing appreciative glances from the other men, including Lon. "On assignment, I travel prepared," she said, smiling at his curious stare.

Yattero fitted one of the stage horses, a balky mustang, with saddle and bridle for a skeptical Dar Ell. Landry chuckled but quickly sobered when the Mexican prepared a second, wide-eyed mount. "Damn it, Dar Ell," Landry interjected. "You take a lot for granted."

"Meaning what?" a sweating, impatient Dar Ell asked, his eyes blazing darkly.

"I'll take you over the mountain. But the young woman remains here. You use me, but the lady reporter waits. There will be stages in, probably a posse by."

Dar Ell swallowed with difficulty. His features fixed slowly with unremitting resolution. He stretched to his full height, his lean features pronounced in the slanting sun rays. "No, Miss Mollie is my assurance against you trying anything. Besides, she's a witness, and that's dangerous to me, at least on this side of the mountain."

"Then you might as well gun me here and now as later, 'cause I'm not budging."

"No, we need you," Dar Ell said flatly. "I give you my word—the girl goes free in California and so will you. Once over the hump, we all go our ways."

"And what is your word worth?"

"I'm not a killer of women or lawmen," said Dar Ell heatedly. "No matter what you think of me, I am not that."

"But strange things happen, don't they?"

"Yes, the best laid plans of mice and men," said Dar Ell. "We need your expertise, and that's why the girl goes with us. But you have my word." He pointed his pistol and motioned Landry to move out. "When you have us safe across, you two will go free."

Submitting temporarily, Landry said, "She rides my chestnut, not a damn mustang."

Dar Ell nodded and called to Yattero, "The big chestnut, get it for the lady." Within minutes they had headed cautiously into the desert, and at Dar Ell's wave, spurred their animals to a run, halting briefly in a spur of willows and squat alders.

"Didn't see nobody anywhere." Ryke's tight mouth split into a rare smile. "Nobody's spotted us. I guess we're clear so far."

"With that posse on the trail of Morton, I doubt if any of them will be back this way for a time," Dar Ell said with satisfaction. The seven horses tugged and swung their rumps, their tails flailing. They felt the excitement of their riders. Mollie and the outlaws turned to Landry. "Where from here, Marshal?"

Landry looked at Mollie and assessed the men in front of him, then shifted in the saddle to look at the mighty upthrust of mountains; his roan mustang, a knobby, gaunt animal, looked too small between his long legs. Landry said slowly, "As you wish, we'll avoid the main routes: Carson, Luther, Johnson passes. Along the same summit there's an old Indian route, narrow, tricky, dangerous in spots. But you won't meet much except a mountain sheep. We'll ride northwest." Landry pointed. "Up one of those long draws through the foothills and up the side. We'll camp under the first rim tonight." His arm encompassed a dark line of canyon that rose steeply out of the drab to the base of the timbered mountain that peaked with two juts. "We'll take shelter tonight in that break under the highest tips."

"How long to get over?"

"There's two crests—the second is higher. Three days from now we'll be over and then down the ridge above the South Fork in the American River." Landry studied the panorama; his roan mustang drummed the gravelly basin. "There's an isolated old gold town—Lost Chance, named for a man down on his luck and lost, who found a fortune there. You can get needed supplies there if you're splitting. That's as far as the girl and I go." Landry's and Dar Ell's eyes met and sealed a bargain for the moment. "Best we get moving."

"Lost Chance—you mentioned that name to those posse members."

As they headed away, Landry studied the land about him for signs of movement—Rattlesnake Morton could never be counted out. He just might elude Healy. He nudged the mustang clear of the willow enclosure. ''Been there on assignments a number of times,'' he explained dryly. ''Met young Healy there when he was a deputy hardly dry behind the ears.''

Dar Ell goaded his horse up beside the marshal. ''We're not riding into that town until checking it out first. I'm no fool, Landry. We both know there could be a setup—a trap. I'll send someone in first to check it out, maybe just that one person for supplies.''

''Up to you. The old town doesn't have much contact with this side of the mountain. Draws most of its goods from the valley. Except for a few freight wagons in and out, not much activity there. The stage has discontinued, as I recall.''

Dar Ell heeled the swing station animal in the ribs to keep it beside Landry. The horses remained restless in the wind. Apparently, they still felt the effects of the shooting and the fire. Despite being on a trail, progressing, they frequently wheeled and backed under the bridles and tossed their heads, so one could hear the clinking of the bits along with the muffled, uneasy thudding. In protest, Dar Ell's mustang shook its neck, flapping its mane wildly, then suddenly bowed its head and stiffened its front legs to lurch the showman forward and almost over its head. The animal next bolted ahead, snapping Dar Ell back, almost unseating him. Pale-faced and startle-eyed, he clung tightly, cursing under his breath as the mutinous beast took free rein.

Landry could not suppress a hearty laugh before sliding his horse beside the frisky animal to grab its bridle with bound hands, then directing. ''It's a joy to see you so amused, Marshal,'' Dar Ell snapped in piqued frustration. ''But damn it, I'm not a horseman.''

''I never would have guessed. It's going to be an education

watching you navigate this piece of flesh over the mountain.''
Landry grinned, cocking an eyebrow in amused anticipation.

For two hours they followed Landry's lead where he swung
into a watery flat, blue-brown, the shallows reflecting an
intense sky, and the bronze strands of cattails broken or angled. Beyond, the mountains beckoned. Gradually the riders
moved higher through cramped draws, keeping to the cottonwoods, gold fluttering, the limbs bright black; on into the
sage, thick, gray-green, and belly high, where the bitterbrush and the mahogany paralleled the folds of higher desert,
and more frequently the rounded juniper offered increasing
cover. In the sandy breaks and in the alkali reaches where
the hooves sunk and the animals struggled, Landry let them
set their pace. When they crossed the hardpan of a wash or
a gravelly patch of wind funnels, he upped the gait to a steady
trot and sometimes to an easy gallop that rocked the riders
pleasurably.

Terena, clutching the saddle horn, bounced uncomfortably
in the saddle, her horse led by Lon, the reins wrapped in a
gloved hand. Obviously not used to riding, she had a constant, anxious expression. Mollie seemed natural on Landry's chestnut; several hands higher than the others, the
gelding could outpace and outreach, his stride flowing. Mollie neck-reined him with confidence, and he responded; frequently she leaned forward to pat his neck and coax him. In
the bright sunlight, the red-brown hide had taken on an especially rich hue.

As the flora thickened in the alluvial lean toward the
mountains, the riders fell into a line snaking through the
brushy jumbles as Landry selected a route that seemed to
emerge from nowhere, his direction always toward the blunt
sawtooth of mountains ahead. He led, with Dar Ell slightly
behind and to the side, usually within conversing distance;
then Lon and the Mexican girl. Yattero, burdened with a
greater proportion of gear, followed on a sizable dapple gray,

and Ryke brought up the rear several lengths back, his Winchester loose in the scabbard. He kept watching behind and around while letting his horse pace with the others.

The air sweetened with pungent sage as the sun climbed. Landry turned in his saddle. "You may have planned everything in detail, Dar Ell, but you picked a month damn close to disaster. Did you ever hear of the Donner Party?"

"Yes."

Landry's eyes canvassed the mountain block. "Well, it was about this time of year that done them in!"

"Early winter, yes," Dar Ell replied, well-aware. "But it's pleasantly warm now."

"Doesn't mean a thing. In the Sierras after about late September, anything can happen." Landry's eyes lifted reverently toward the back-tilt of ramparts. "Up there a man can feel close to God or close to Hell, depending. See those clouds packing up behind the spires?"

"Get off it," Dar Ell scoffed. "At this point I don't need games. You know and I know that there's a member here who's already spooked. And we know, Marshal, that it won't take much for him to spook the others."

"Yes, I know." Landry smiled. "But let's keep our eye on them."

For another hour the marshal led them through a network of gullies, serrated by runoff. The horses snorted and blew air and plodded steadily, their hooves clicking on the exposed rocks; the leather creaked as if in protest.

"Have you been noticing those balls of clouds pushing up behind the peaks?" Landry tossed back. "See how dark they are already? Well, just keep your eye on them. See what comes by late afternoon."

Dar Ell looked up with discomfort, seeing fingery streamers extending from fists of blackness, ominous signs building. Along the edge, rainbow colors dabbed the peaks with pastels. "As luck would have it."

"Not luck—fact," said Landry.

"Then give the devil his due," Dar Ell chided cynically.

"Henry something," Mollie called from behind.

Dar Ell twisted about, looked at her with admiring eyes. *"Henry the Fourth*, to be exact. Miss Tyndale, you are a woman of refinement."

"Woman of refinement or not," Ryke called, "let's get the hell up that mountainside."

"No," Landry blasted. "We move steadily but not fast. These team animals aren't used to mountain climbing. We push them too hard, you'll be walking."

"We trust your judgment, Marshal." Dar Ell swung his arm in an exaggerated gesture of permission. "You lead."

"Sure as hell would make it easier with my hands free." Landry looked at his swollen wrists.

"I sympathize with you, Marshal," Dar Ell replied. "I promise you relief for a time, later on. But not now."

Sullenly, they rode steadily up the steepening incline, skirting a protective screen of alder and wind-stripped cottonwood. Dar Ell eyed Landry, studied him curiously, as well as absorbed the sweep of mountain uplift that they needed to assault. Ironically, their future and ultimately their success rested totally in the judgment and ability of a lawman. "The slings and arrows of outrageous fortune," Dar Ell said mockingly to himself.

Led unerringly, the small party wound through the scruffy bottoms between time-corroded foothills. The conical junipers and rangy pinion appeared dark blots against the exposed soil. Where volcanic lava plugs pushed up heaps of rubble, the first yellow pine appeared, strong and straight, and in the higher moraines, the candle flame of aspen traced creeksides that drained hanging valleys. From the distance, they could hear the rollicking cascade of water. Gradually, behind them, the corrugated landscape slid away as the trail undulated over arid tablelands and volcanic spurs. Shortly they came upon a little green marsh spotted with sheets of water that shimmered in the sun. The trickling sound of a spring played from the spongelike rocks. Blackbirds exploded away then settled again in the rushes to throat their vibrant cries. "We rest and water the animals here," Landry said.

"Time is short," Ryke spouted.

"We rest and water the animals here." Landry repeated each word deliberately. The animals gulped noisily and fully, their hooves sunk to the fetlocks in the rich muck. Landry swung from his saddle and helped Mollie down, his bound hands clutching her slender fingers. She held his longer than necessary. They all dismounted except for Ryke, who remained stiffly aloft but let his horse take its fill. Those walking anxiously about, stretched, took water above the drinking animals, and hurriedly returned to their mounts.

Landry's gray eyes interlocked with those of Dar Ell's, measuring him. "You realize, if Morton shakes that posse and returns to find our tracks, there's no way to cover our trail."

"The gods for a time have smiled upon us," Dar Ell replied. "To be free here in the open, away from that swing station, is miracle enough for the time being." He craned his head and looked up at the towering tilt of mountain that slowly commenced to break into buttresses, domes, upflung fractures, and slabs that created cleavages where a trail might burrow through if one knew the secret. But he smiled with confidence, knowing that Landry knew. "Show me the steep and thorny way," he said to himself almost joyfully.

(11)

Rattlesnake Morton knew the Sierran escarpment, knew the land from years of hiding there while ravaging the people and the isolated communities below. Beyond the shattered volcanic land through which they fled, the Sierras splintered into numberless canyons and secretive clefts that all penetrated the enormous front of the eastern block. In that magnificent wilderness lay a chaos of thickening forests and irregular granite spires, an intricate maze of landforms, a nightmare for anyone pursuing. The emerald lakes and succulent meadows offered unlimited feed and water for animals, plus plants and game for human consumption.

Problem was, much of the turreted land held high cirques— steep, hollow amphitheaters—impossible to scale, becoming nothing more than dead-end traps. Unless one kept to established routes, all heavily traveled, or knew of some ancient Indian trail, the only hope was to hide out if opportunity permitted—an impossibility now with the posse hotly behind. But with the twelve of them well-armed, they could ambush the lawmen, even leave snipers along the route while the remainder drew the pursuers into a devastating cross fire. Hopefully, they could work their way clear afterward. And if they didn't, a single man could always escape undetected. Morton smiled and goaded his animal as he screamed, "Ride like the devil. Ahead, we go deep, take positions. We'll shoot the hell out of 'em."

The men whooped agreement, their horses bounding toward the enclosing woods. But Morton knew in his dark heart that none of them really had much of a chance against determined adversaries unless eventually they split, each of them making his own way, all scattering, forcing the posse to fragment their members or to concentrate pursuit on two or three escapees. Some of his gang would surely die or be captured—perhaps most. But Morton was determined not to be one of those.

Morton felt the roll and pull of the mustang between his legs. He sunk his heels into its ribs and rapped the bunching rump with snaps of his extended reins. He squinted, studying the lay of land before them. His thick lips parted in a cunning sneer, revealing black gappy teeth. He would hold his men together long enough to harass the pursuers, relentless citizens who had clung tenaciously behind; although never had he attempted to conceal his advance, the promise of quick wealth had diminished any desire for precaution. Whoever led them was doubtless a good lawman, probably the young upstart he had heard about, Sheriff George Healy: ambitious, dangerous certainly, but determined enough that he might be sucked into a bloodbath. Rattlesnake Morton relished that possibility.

Another fleeting thought jolted him. What if that army of angry pursuers were led by Dirk Landry? A shiver convulsed through him, a coldness that had no connection with the morning chill. He hated the lawman, hated him with a simmering fire that had burned in his gut like molten metal through the eternal days and months in prison. If Landry were somehow out there, he welcomed the challenge. "To kill that bastard," he roared aloud. Those within hearing distance shot startled glances. But Morton doubted if Landry was out there yet. Eventually yes, but the pattern so far was not Landry's intimidating, tactical way.

Well, yes, he would give the posse his bloody worth, Morton thought as they reached the first layer of encircling pines. But eventually, quickly, everything would come down to individual survival. He owed nothing to those with him—nothing. Not even to Tobias Johnson. They were all expendable. All that Morton needed was some decisive action that might detract, might draw posse members toward others while he stole away, to track down the Dar Ell gang. He hungered for that chance to prey upon them each. The take—the gold coins and dust, even the currency—riches that would be his ultimately. Morton licked his lips greedily and experienced himself in a euphoric fantasy, a super being of his former self in control once more, powerful, annihilating, a terrorist once again, someone to be reckoned with.

They steered their way into an enfolding hollow of pinion and pines, while behind a few anxious posse members unloaded futile revolver shots, the sounds loud in the clean air, the blue smoke holding in slow, drifting puffs. But the jerky, often snapping pace of the animals, breaking to stiff-leg over precarious dips and humps, made accuracy impossible. Most of the shots punched dirt far behind the convicts or whined harmlessly overhead.

Morton pulled his bony but tough cayuse up a hump of sharded granite, shielded from the posse by two fat trunks of curved pine. The space between opened upon a flow of valley from where they had come. As the convicts pushed their horses deeper into cover, jumping over logs or flailing through clumps of tangling brush, Morton waited; something intuitively drew him to watch the flat far below. Then he saw movement, at first indistinct, then well-defined—seven figures making some dust in the moist-covered surface. They were moving northwest from the swing station. In the distance he could not make out details, except that the horses appeared bulked with goods. They're full-prepared and they got all the take, he mouthed to himself. Puzzling to him, at least one of the riders seemed to have long, floppy hair. An

Indian? A girl? Could they possibly have a girl amongst them? That might slow them down, he thought, although some gamy women could outride any man in rough country. But for definite they were moving into the Sierras. "They're going to try and cross 'em," he told himself. He fixed in his mind the approximation of their route. They would pass south of a volcanic wedge that slanted prominently above the tumble of blown rock, a decided landmark that he would return to again to find their tracks.

Directly underneath, he saw the posse advancing, slower, more cautiously now, up the saged grade. Briefly they were exposed in the open spread, vulnerable to sniping from the fugitives who were experiencing relief for a time, in some matted growth.

Morton swung his horse into action toward his fleeing associates, riding rapidly while cutting across a rise of low brush and downed limbs where a storm had played havoc years before. Closing the distance, he shouted, "Hold it. Hold it. Pull up."

"They's coming. We got to find positions," Red shouted back, his small brown eyes fiery.

Tobias Johnson in the lead reined his horse and whirled it around to face the approaching riders. "Listen to Morton," he cried. "He's tellin' us something."

Morton galloped his horse amongst them, rotating the stringy animal while eyeing each man in turn. "We're going to ambush them just ahead. A half mile up there is a small lake. We gather there, then circle it to the south on the upper side. Beyond the lake the ground kind of pushes into a draw. We'll try to suck them in there, then shoot the hell out of them."

"I see 'em coming through the trees," Tobias warned.

Morton removed the fancy high hat and waved it forward. "Get going," he howled.

For the next hour the Morton gang pushed higher, to where

the fir and Jeffrey pine grew, the latter smelling like vanilla in the warming sun. The animals grunted and blew, their hooves clacking and slipping on the gray sheaths of granite, until ahead a blue body of water shimmered invitingly. The horsemen clambered free to pad about in the coarse sand where the thirsty horses were permitted to drink sparingly of the sweet, chill water and the men filled canteens.

"You, Red. You and Slicer. I want you to take that ridge yonder. Hole down in them teeth of rocks." Morton pointed to a narrow terrace of spiny rocks just above the clumped pines and paralleling the curve of lake. "Wait till them badgemen are past you. We'll pull 'em into the canyon up there." He motioned toward a crumple of ruined cliff entwined with brush and twisted pines. "We'll make a stand on each side of the draw—before they expect us to. I figure they'll expect us to go further into the bowl. The cut up there continues another half mile."

Tobias jerked the bit, forcing his animal to toss its head and haunch under in momentary pain. "Hell, why will they go after us? They'll have us holed up, trapped. There's too damned many of them. We shouldn't have come back for the money—should have kept going."

Morton glowered at Tobias. Repeatedly, the young felon kept neck-reining his horse back and forth impatiently. "We'd been a fool to pass up the take of a lifetime. I think it's a new sheriff, George Healy. I hear through the inside line that he don't run from nothin', he just plows in. He's got ambition, and I know that kind from the past." Morton looked back at the wooded drop, then at Tobias Johnson. "We can cut 'em down, break 'em up, then slip through 'em, unless you're harborin' thoughts of sneaking out behind us—maybe leaving us to face them."

"You talk nonsense," said Tobias, "considering we was partners for years." He swung his horse ahead, gouging it with his heels through a covering of brush.

"They's coming," Red shouted, pointing back and whipping his horse ahead. He and Slicer headed toward the rocky terrace.

The posse had spread wide in an enclosing net. George Healy spearheaded the pursuit. Now, with a density of trees and the tangled slash of wind-downed branches and toppled boulders, all enmeshed in brush, their progress had slowed. The horses seesawed, humping their shoulders and rocking their heads with growing difficulty as the climb steepened. Healy pulled his horse to a stiff halt. The animal lifted and dipped its snout, its lips and nostrils fluttering intensely. He assayed the situation, bobbing in the saddle as his horse shifted footing. Healy was taking pleasure in the challenge, much as an army officer might welcome the affront of an enemy, readying and positioning his men against attack.

Allen rode up beside, his black gelding twisting and anxious to continue. "There's a lake above us and no way out; it's a dead end."

"I know," said Healy, "that's why from here we take it easy. That back country up there is like a fortress. Harder than hell to root anybody out once they're stationed in there."

Allen spat a jet of tobacco and considered his thoughts. "But why did Morton take this route? For sure an eventual trap. I shore can't figure him out."

"I don't know." Healy shrugged, doffing his Stetson. He sat his horse hunched, his curly hair compressed with perspiration and the tight hatband. In the bright sunlight his face had the boyish, pugnacious look of a young warrior, confident, knowing that the kill and the victory were imminent. "But for sure, Morton wanted something in that swing station. Anyone see Wells and Blaisdell yet?"

"They're coming, riding steadily," said Nelson, who had joined them, holding his horse a half length behind. "We just seen them coming. They'll be here in maybe twenty minutes or less.''

''We'll wait for them,'' said Healy. ''I want to know about that station.''

''But shouldn't we press Morton before he can position himself?'' Allen queried.

''They'll position themselves no matter what. Anywhere any of them stick, he's behind a natural parapet up there.''

''Then what do you suggest?''

''That we rest the animals. They need it. Eventually we may have to chase Morton hell-bent out of these hills.''

''In the meantime?''

''It appears like Morton's gang has swung around the south side of the lake. They're climbing toward that wall of snaggled rocks up there.''

Allen wagged his head. ''That could be hell to pay. They'll be waiting like soldiers in a fort. They'll pick us to pieces.''

Healy looked at the high sun overhead. ''We have a good number of hours before dark. We'll all rest a time, then split our forces into a three-pronged advance.''

''Split our forces?''

''We can ride just so far, but then we'll have to go by foot.'' Healy stared at the stream gushing from the lake.

''They'll still have a drop on us,'' Allen said, troubled.

''No, because I know this area. We can work part of our force above them. We'll have them in our sights—not us in their's. We'll give 'em a surprise, I'll wager.''

Laboriously, the horses pulled up a trail that seemed not there but appeared always, surprisingly, as Landry picked their way. Frequently they stopped at the marshal's command to give rest, the animals then snorting and blowing in relief, their hides commencing to coat wet with effort. ''Will be harder,'' said Landry, ''as we move into thinner air.'' Frequently he eyed Mollie with concern, but she had adapted for the time being, her hair tumbling across her shoulders to flow in the wind. She kept glancing around to take in the view. A remarkable woman, Landry thought. A victim, kidnapped by frightened and ruthless killers, her life in question, yet she could enjoy the view that grew progressively more spectacular with each rising switchback.

They could hear the musical singing of water ahead in the fractured recesses where the early fall rains had increased the runoff. The gusty air hollowed its way up the funneled granite. They rose steadily, the horses plodding through sparse trees toward the firm bosses and domes. They moved through a wedged valley walled by towering blocks of jointed granite, all riven with cracks and seamed with-breaks. The slabs of granite ledges went on up again toward a rock castle in the west and a high col to the north. The trail lay indistinct. Pine and green chaparral clung tenaciously where roots had found beginnings in zigzags of weathered cracks and columns. They continued, leaning over the slanted backs of their animals. Leather creaked, hooves clicked on stone, and occasionally a man sighed or grunted.

The sound of rushing water grew louder. When they rounded a shoulder of mountain and swung back for higher elevation, they could look down on a long, thin falls. The cascading water crinkled white and silver in the drops where mist rainbowed and water plunged on. Under a frowning peak they found the source; a little spring bubbled out from a rupture in the stone. They watered the horses and filled their canteens as the animals gulped in satisfaction. "Give them all they want," Landry suggested. "It's cold and arid up there in the passes, can't always rely on water there."

"This water is heavenly after that desert stuff," said Mollie, drawing from her canteen. She choked suddenly and coughed hard. Both Dar Ell and Landry studied her. "You took chill last night, didn't you?" asked the latter.

Her green eyes pained with concern. "Yes, I'm afraid so."

From the higher reaches of the Sierras thunder rumbled. "Can we make it up to the first summit before nightfall?" Dar Ell asked.

"We better damn well get that far," Landry said. "Those are snow clouds building."

They turned again up the faint remnants of an ancient trail. The horses yanked from side to side, then scrambled, dug, and got under way.

Deputies Wells and Blaisdell approached, their horses frothy, a whiteness dropping away from the bits. The waiting lawmen turned from checking cinches, guns, and ammunition to listen. Healy, now in the saddle, sat stoically, his hat tilted back, his forearms crossed, resting on the horn.

Wells led; he drew rein, removed his Stetson and wiped his moist hair. Blaisdell pulled next to him, the man's limp jowls quivering. "Dirk Landry was there in charge," Wells opened.

"Dirk Landry! What the hell happened?"

"Apparently that's what Morton was after—a big shipment off that stage. Guess he got wind of it somehow."

"Explain."

"The marshal got the money and the passengers into the swing station, then sent the stage on as a decoy, but it didn't work."

"Anybody hurt?"

"A few shot up."

"Who was the passengers? Did he say?" Healy's voice tensed.

"Just two, that's all he mentioned. One was a woman."

"A woman?" Healy was all eyes. "It wasn't Mollie Tyndale?"

"Don't know. Never saw her. Marshal wanted to get her on the stage to Limbo is all I know."

"Damn." Healy ran his tongue over cracked lips.

"He said he could handle things there, so we came on back."

"Strange," said Healy. "How did Landry get in on it?"

The morose Blaisdell said, "Don't understand, but he handled his gun strangelike for a marshal."

"What do you mean?"

"I don't know just what I mean."

"Oh, by the way, you don't owe him them drinks anymore," said Wells, grinning.

"What the hell you talking about?"

Wells frowned and looked at Blaisdell. "He said he beat you in a card draw up in Lost Chance, that you owed him drinks you no longer had to fork up since we drove Morton off."

"Cards and drinks in Lost Chance?"

"You know—that old gold town, upper reaches of the mother lode."

"Yeah, I know, except I never drew cards with Landry, never owed him drinks, and I have never been in Lost Chance."

"Best get moving," said Allen.

"Yeah," said the sheriff, looking skeptically at the perplexed deputies. He drew the men about him.

"You, Wells, Blaisdell," Healy began, studying the cirque of wooded granite puncturing the sky. "Rest your horses here. Take cover and be our backup. We're at the shank of a draw here that encircles the lake. Some of those polecats might try to squeeze back out after attempting to ambush us. Nelson, you got the hardest job."

"Figures," said the bony man; his weathered skin tightened, giving him the look of a skull enclosed in worn leather.

"You're my most experienced, most trusted," Healy soothed.

Nelson formed a thin smile. "Me and whoever attacks 'em straight on." His words held no illusion.

"That's just about it. I'm asking for maybe five volunteers to go directly after Morton, track him around the south or the left side of the lake. Yours will be a direct assault."

Nelson twisted his mouth. "They'll be up there like hawks waiting to swoop on us."

"Exactly. You're not to press them. You're to keep in cover and push them on, but keep their attention on you at all times."

"We're decoys, otherwise?"

"You're to distract them, best you can."

"Don't matter."

Three of Allen's men volunteered immediately. After one awkward minute and Healy's assessing eyes, two of his men nudged their horses forward.

Healy then said to Allen, "You and about half of us left swing around the north side of the lake." He pointed. "See that strip of woods that kind of follows around the bowl?"

"Yes."

"Move through that, carefully. It's high enough to give you an overview."

"What are you going to do?"

"Me and the other half, we're going to climb." Healy thrust his arm toward a rib of granite, brush-draped and spiked by scattered pine and fir. "We'll go first by horse, probably to that break up there." He noted a strata of washed-out sandstone where the crevices and shaggy rises had been parted by talus slides and slashes of metamorphosed rocks. "We'll leave the horses with the kid here." He referred to their youngest member, a Paiute boy called Salty Joe, who looked more half-breed than pure Indian. "Then we'll proceed on foot."

"Could be dangerous footing," Allen warned.

Healy shrugged. "We'll have to chance that. Once we're above them, we can circle behind them. Trap them in a cross fire."

"Sounds good," said Nelson, "except for us that have to draw fire. But we'll try."

"You got a watch, Nelson? Have any of you volunteers?" Healy pulled his chain watch from a vest pocket.

"Yes," said one of Allen's men, "it's twelve past nine."

"Okay, close enough. We'll set our time. Give us some forty-five minutes, Nelson, then head in."

"Into the mouth of Hell."

"Into the mouth of Hell. Let's go."

On the south side of the small lake where the first terrace made a decided loop toward the interior, Red and Slicer took their rifles and hid some twenty feet apart behind the veed bulwarks of some stone blocks. Red had grunted down like some primitive bear, wallowing and twisting for comfort, before resting the Winchester across the pulpy flesh of his pawlike palm. With his one good eye he surveyed the swath of wooded route below. The lake shimmered blue, then darkened with grays and greens as sudden cloud shadows slid by. Red bulked high despite the barrier. He looked over at Slicer for support.

Slicer grinned his perpetual bucktoothed look. His spidery body sat easily between the clefts. "Good drop on them from here," he said with satisfaction.

"Good drop on them, but what then?" Red twisted his lion-shaped head and looked out at the yellow desert. "Ever think if that posse passes us by, we got clear sailing out of here? We could track after them stage heisters. They's left by now for sure."

"Do that to Morton and he'd string us by the toes and skin us alive when he found us."

"Not if he's dead. That's a box canyon up there. There's no way out."

"Morton ain't dumb. He'll find a way out."

"Maybe. But that posse is loaded for blood."

A quarter of a mile west, Rattlesnake Morton dismounted and his nine followers did likewise. He led them along the lakeshore and then picked his way through an elevated abutment of scalloped lava until the horses balked. "I should never have listened to you, Morton," Tobias Johnson decried. Tired lines made unhappy grooves down his mouth. Despite a stubble, his powdery white complexion contrasted with dark hollow eyes. "You got us into this, Morton. I shouldn't of listened. We should of split up. Now we got no place to go. You're sending us to Hell, Morton."

"Ain't so," Morton bellowed without looking back. "Them lawmen will bleed bad storming us." He pointed to a rocky parapet. "Up there, we could hold off the whole U.S. cavalry."

"But for how long?"

"Till dark is all we need. After dark we can slip through their ranks, maybe kill a few—them that survive, they won't be able to follow at night. The moon won't help. You can't move through this country like you can on the descrt."

"Don't think you're right," said Tobias heavily. "They'll close us off. There's enough of them. We'll never get our horses through."

"There's an old trail to the north of the lake," Morton said softly. "One or two can circle back over 'em—get the hell out; then go after them highwaymen with all that good take."

Anxiously, Tobias tugged his mount up beside Morton. "You and me, you mean."

"Yeah." Morton's broad face took on a calculating leer. "Weasel's dead. Red and Slicer can't be counted on yet. You and me, we're all that's left of the old gang."

His blood jolting, George Healy led some fifteen deputies up a difficult incline where decomposed rock funneled noisily away. He motioned his men to ease back. Riding boots had not been fashioned for mountain climbing. The men continued, with greater caution. Frequently the sheriff glanced at his watch as the appointed time ticked closer. Far down, still in view, Salty Joe waited with the horses.

Sweating, they felt the warming sun rise high. The resinous Jeffrey pine smelled deliciously of vanilla, and the long-leafed mule ears turned pungent, almost intoxicating in the sunbathed grasslands. Gnats swarmed dizzily about them. Numerous times when their feet sank in the scrambled earth near a rotting log, big angry red ants scrambled up pant legs and down boots to bite. Curses exploded from the abused men. One volunteer fell, bruising a knee and cutting his arm as he rolled a half-dozen feet. At another point a Steller's jay screamed raucously, protesting the intrusion as it flashed away in a long swooping flight. "Damn it," Healy mumbled. "Damn bird could give us away."

But by the time Deputy Nelson commenced his direct advance, Healy and his men were stationed on an upper terrace with a grand view of the glacial cirque. Healy scanned the area with the scope. He could see none of Morton's gang, nor could he see any of Allen's men, which was good. His periphery skirted the desert to the north of the swing station, to the mountain base where the uptilt of the Sierras continued. Slight movements, tiny specks with a streamer of dust caught his attention. Riders so distant they merged into an indistinct dottiness. A half dozen or more, he judged. He wondered what Dirk Landry was attempting to relay with the cards, the drinks, the old town of Lost Chance. Not all was right at the swing station, he surmised. Landry was telling him something that he needed to mull over.

And Mollie, where was she? In Limbo, he supposed. Or if God had directed, in Placerville where she belonged. But what if she were somehow, somewhere, in between? Who was the woman at the swing station? With Landry she would be safe, if the marshal were in control. Something had seemed wrong, at least to Deputy Blaisdell. After they had settled accounts with Morton, they would return to the swing station. But for now, duty called. He adjusted the scope on the lake edge directly below. A plodding horse came into view and merged with the woods; another and then another. Deputy Nelson and the volunteers were under way, moving with utter care, doubtless tense, awaiting the slam of bullets at any time from any angle.

"Nelson and the others, they're leading in," said a posse man. "You can see them now with the naked eye."

"Yes, I see them, too," another man echoed.

Together they watched glimpses of the six interweaving through the trees. Then someone said excitedly, "Look, Sheriff, look." On the first terrace, slipping away in the opposite direction of Nelson and his men, came two convicts afoot carrying rifles—one a hefty man, the other wiry, almost scrawny. Healy raised a hand, silencing any talk while they waited. The two descended almost recklessly, slipping and sliding. A number of posse members grinned as the unsuspecting two veered toward them.

"Randall, Hollings, Emerson, take the big one on the left. Smith, Reveiro, Bandon, the small one on the right," Healy ordered softly. The six took aim as the pair approached down under. Healy raised his arm and then waved it down. "Fire." Six shots sounded as one while several men snap-shot additional bullets. The impact lifted Slicer off his feet and spun him sideways, where he rolled in a disjointed fashion over a round boulder to end sprawled in a bed of squaw mat, his body riddled. Red toppled forward, his arms out; he nosed over, somersaulted slowly and slid on his belly down a talus shoulder. He came to rest two-thirds of the way down. A sheet of dislodged dirt slowly covered his head. "Hurry," Healy shouted, almost bounding away along the upper shelf.

Upon hearing the shots, Deputy Nelson scattered his small force and steadied his approach. Above the north shore, Allen and his men heard the reverberations and knew that Healy had made contact. He hurried his men.

Meanwhile, Morton and the escapees had settled into the rimrock; but when Healy's guns sounded, they took alarm. "They're up higher." Tobias Johnson pointed, his mouth loose and his eyes wide. "They're behind Red and Slicer. They'll chop us to pieces. I ain't waiting." He scrambled out of the rocky hold and bolted down the steep incline toward the horses tied to the shrubbery. Seven other convicts panicked and followed him. Morton and one man beside him watched in dismay.

Healy and his posse men, running with effort, their breaths pulling hard in the high, thin air, traversed the stony spine in time to see Tobias slip and slide the last way to the horses. Tobias released one and swung onto it. The animal yanked and pivoted, then plunged toward the north shore as Tobias whipped it. "The horses," Healy shouted, "scatter them. Shoot them if necessary." Many of his men dropped to a knee, rifles pointed; a few sprawled on their bellies, bracing their barrels on logs or rocks. Their sudden barrage puffed dirt and splintered granite around the animals. Terrified, the beasts pulled free. One bay screamed, went down on its side, its neck crooked in pain. It slid helplessly down a rock shoot and plummeted, crashing in brush underneath.

Three of the convicts managed to catch horses, all bucking and twisting now. With difficulty they mounted and charged after Tobias. Four of them, still coming down, saw the futility as the remaining animals dispersed. Desperately, they climbed back toward their rock fortress.

Morton judged the situation, turned back into a glade and began moving down along a wooded spit. "You ain't leaving me," said the man beside him, tagging nearly on Morton's heals.

Healy and his men then rained lead on the four abandoned fugitives, forced now to hunker down without returning a shot. Quickly, like a serpent through grass, Morton snaked his way down a brushy draw with his comrade behind. They worked steadily to the lake basin on the south side and crawled into the hollow of a huge log, to lay frozen as Nelson and his five moved past. When the lawmen had vanished, Morton wriggled out, and the two retraced their steps to the foot of the lake.

Too late, Tobias Johnson realized he had raced himself into a trap—a wall of armed men. All exchanged fire. Tobias's horse shrilled and collapsed, throwing him, knocking him senseless and breaking a leg. One of the three convicts left his saddle and hit hard, a bullet through one lung. A second hurtled from the saddle, rolled, sprang up and ran a few yards before being splayed flat by a dozen bullets. The third threw up his hands while still astride. One volunteer received a flesh wound in his thigh.

The four fugitives in their fortress, besieged by accurate lobs from the Healy group above and from Nelson's men below, waved a flag made from torn clothing. They exited timidly and climbed slowly down, to be shackled by Nelson.

Fearing what might have occurred at the swing station, an untiring George Healy headed back toward the horses. "Give us a chance to rest, and then we'll join you," one posse member called.

"You can catch up with me later, on the way to the Wells Fargo station." Healy said, leaving the exhausted men.

As Morton and his companion headed toward the foot of the lake, they caught sight of Salty Joe, the half-breed boy, waiting patiently with a group of horses. Morton reached back and grasped the man behind him, who was completely oblivious. Morton pointed toward the boy and his charges while withdrawing a bowie knife.

* * *

As Sheriff Healy dropped down a deer trail into the open flat, he saw the horses milling and pulling. He cocked his rifle and looked about. Then he saw the Paiute boy, Salty Joe, lying facedown. Without approaching, he knew the youth lay dead. Something, a flash or movement in the rocks to his left, caught his attention. Keeping close to wooded cover, he slipped toward the sight. He wound through a narrow maze of high rocks, peering here and there down the volcanic corridors. He knew he should have waited, gotten backing from his posse members, but the killer or killers had escaped their dragnet and were probably close by. Besides, it wasn't his nature to wait. He wondered if the others had captured Morton. What a feather in the cap to get him! Healy hadn't heard any shots. He concluded the boy had been killed by a knife. Morton had a legendary reputation as an uncannily accurate knife thrower. A rare uneasiness clutched Healy. He and Morton, possibly. Here. Now.

Rattlesnake Morton stepped from behind a high, blockish rock and back-shot Healy with a rifle from his hip. The impact had the strange likeness to the icy sting of a hand-thrown snowball that numbed Healy's total being. He stiffened, arched back and came slowly around, trying to raise his barrel, only to see Morton fire again. Sheriff George Healy fell backward into a crevice where he dropped through a layer of willows to land on some soft, moist earth. A dull awareness came over him, a sadness of regret, an accute sense of business unfinished. He felt a draining, and touched a slippery wetness, then realized it was his own blood. He looked up through the wavery patterns of willow leaf haloed by afternoon sunlight and saw the blue above. He thought of Mollie, saw vividly her smile and caressing green eyes. From what seemed an incredible distance, he heard Morton say, "We'll take some horses and chase the rest away. Come on, Biggs, they're heading up the Sierras with all that loot." Then George Healy lapsed into darkness.

(12)

The horses clambered higher, steadily, in a choppy rhythm, their hooves clicking on the polished stone. From a snowfall the previous day, seepage muddied the trail in spots; but the wet crust was already stiffening in the early cold. Dar Ell had loosened Landry's bindings enough to relieve the pressure and permit comfortable flexibility, but not enough to free his hands. Landry saw Mollie shiver. Her windblown hair had tumbled loosely, framing a pretty but pale face. As they rounded an outer bench, Landry called a halt. "We rest here," he said. "The lady needs a blanket or two," he told Dar Ell.

"I'm all right," she said unconvincingly.

"No, you're not," said Landry.

Dar Ell gestured to Terena, who produced two army blankets taken from the swing station. The showman rode up beside Mollie and fanned the blankets out over the rump of the chestnut and around Mollie's shoulders. She acknowledged his act with a smile of appreciation.

"Got anything for your head?" Landry asked.

"A shawl."

"Put it on, please."

Mollie nodded and produced a lacy wrap from the bag that hung to her saddle horn. She wound it over her head and ears and tied it across her throat.

"Dismount. Give the horses a break," Landry com-

manded. They all climbed down; dutifully, Yattero looked
over his horse, Lon's and the girl's. The animals breathed
easier. A few nibbled at the shriveled grasses where shale-
tasting water had cupped from last winter's snow. The view
spread magnificently of Sierran escarpment north and south.
The burnt hills rolled east with green valleys between them
and the Carson River, meandering into the outer yellow of
desert. Dar Ell took the field glasses and studied the route
they had climbed. He searched the surrounding area and
seemed satisfied. Landry checked the shod hooves of his
mustang and those of the chestnut. The liver-colored animal
nibbled at his vest. "You going to make it?" he asked Mollie.

"Are you going to make it?" Her eyes rose from his to
the stained bandage below his Stetson.

"I'm fine. They're looking at us," he said. "But somewhere, somehow, I must talk with you."

"Yes?"

"There will come a time when we'll have to break for it,"
he said tightly, "and you'll have to know what to expect."

"You two don't need to talk," said Dar Ell.

"I was saying, eventually we men will lead our horses."
Landry checked the cinches. "With all this plunder tied on,
we're going to have tired and sore animals. Maybe invite an
accident."

"He's right, boss," said Yattero. He had loosened and
then tightened his own saddle after shifting the weight of the
bags. Lon was adjusting his and his girl's gear. "But these
money belts, they're going to be heavy, walking," Yattero
lamented.

"Mine will stay with me," Ryke announced.

"Every pause slows us," Dar Ell protested.

"Every pause eventually gets you there," Landry said.
"At this elevation, only a fool would push his horse."

Dar Ell looked up at the granite tilt, so dominating that

they no longer could see the peaks of the summit. Dar Ell removed his flask, but thought better of it and returned it to his coat. "How in the hell are you going to get us through that?"

"That's my problem."

"Here I am—here we are trusting, giving our blind faith to a lawman sworn ultimately to bring us in." Dar Ell smiled inwardly. "How's that for irony? We believe we are masters of our fate. Maybe that is but a fool's paradise."

"It's not so mysterious," said Landry. "We'll camp to-night just under the first pass, where we're protected some. Unless there is some melting snow, we won't be able to water the horses until morning on the other side. We pick our way over the first summit pretty easily; then we drop down into a wooded valley partway and up to the second pass; that one's around 9,700 feet, and that one's not so easy." Landry faced his mustang uphill, holding the reins snug, and grasped the saddle horn. Despite the hitch in his leg, he toed his boot into the stirrup and sprang lightly and gently into the saddle. Dar Ell, Lon, even the morose Ryke looked on with regard.

For an hour Landry filed them upward, until they streamed through a narrow of sheathed stone that opened onto a small but exquisite valley rent eons ago by a rift in a fault block. The hanging valley was a world unto its own, with bald walls so sheer that only the most tenacious shrubs and pines re-mained cemented to a few ledges and fissures. A constant seep carpeted the narrow meadow with a plush grass, span-gled still with larkspur, bluebell, honeysuckle, and paint-brush. Contrary to the fall, the sheltered enclave had its own season; vibrant summer. "We let the animals graze here, eat their fill," Landry announced.

They loosened the cinches. Some sprawled on the soft grass and breathed in the perfume of blossoms while the horses pulled the succulent strands and munched noisily, their legs slapping grass with leisurely steps. Lon and Terena, as well as Landry, pulled off their boots and dabbled their feet in the chill water. "We'll be walking shortly," said the marshal. Yattero removed his boots and aired stockinged feet that were soiled brown. Mollie tugged the blanket around her, closed her eyes and tried to absorb the last heavenly warmth of lower sun rays, which would soon leave the east slope in early dark. Terena then primped herself, combing her raven hair with a whalebone brush as Lon observed her every movement. Yattero rolled and lit a cigarette, his legs crossed. He drew the smoke between his lips and jetted it in two streams through his nostrils.

Ryke sat counting his take. Landry lay back, pulled his Stetson over his face and dozed. Impatiently, Dar Ell wandered some fifty yards from the group, hands on his hips. He kept looking up at the rugged, seemingly impassable and potentially hostile land. Somewhere through that intricate maze was a passage. He tried not to think of the anguishing twist of fate that had forced him into the uncompromising circumstances he now faced. His past forever severed; his future tenuous, based at best upon a man he feared and mistrusted. He kicked at the grass that looped his boots. He didn't see or scent the beauty of the flowers or notice the wild ruggedness of the spot. The mountains; the oncoming night; the pressing time; the law behind; the marshal; the reporter among them; the threatening clouds still forming; the growing edginess that gritted amongst the members—everything and everyone was his enemy now.

At Landry's urging, they walked the horses after feeding, then rode up the hidden valley until the ascent steepened, the trail becoming more a stone stepway than a path. They all dismounted, including Terena and Mollie, who insisted she be no exception, but Landry feared that her faltering steps would soon force her back into the saddle. Fortunately, the big chestnut had the strength to carry her, he knew. The big gelding could outclimb, outrun, outendure any horse in the region. And that eventually might be Mollie's chance and hope.

They breathed with difficulty in the rarefied air; even the horses commenced gulping, their sides heaving. Brutal winters, expanding ice and battering winds, had shattered the metamorphosed structure. Frequently the horses floundered and stumbled, knocking a rock free that bounced and whizzed past those behind. Several times Landry warned, "Look out below." Ryke cursed once as a fist-sized chunk narrowly missed his shoulder. He glanced up accusingly at the marshal as if it had been intentional. Fortunately, the wisdom of the wild prevailed; those animals and those native Americans that had used the route for centuries had instinctively chosen the most secure way; the impressive limestone cuts had a marbled appearance, which could beckon the inexperienced with a promise of an easier, more direct route; but in reality they were slick and dangerously weak, and had therefore been purposely avoided, as were the corroded sections of volcanic magma that could peel away under minimal weight or sometimes from the slightest jarring.

Continuously, Landry kept looking back, not only to judge the progress of each member and mount, but to note landmarks. Twice, narrow troughs, and once a meadowed swale, led to dead ends, forcing them to retrace their way, resulting in much grumbling. "Damn," Dar Ell wailed once. "Too many ups and down will exhaust the horses and kill us."

"Anytime you want to find the way, you're welcome," Landry offered. "This is an ancient pass, not used much anymore except for a sheep or a mountain lion, and they don't leave much sign."

"Why aren't we camping on the other side of the first pass?" Dar Ell demanded.

Landry cocked an eyebrow. Dar Ell talked tough, but his pale face had taken the color of chalk and his breath came unevenly. Each step was wooden and progressively more difficult. Brandy, rich foods, and the sedate good life of the show business world were hardly preparation for trekking in a mountain wilderness. Landry wanted to tell him, we're camping this side of the rim because you're not going to make it beyond. In fact, in your condition you won't make it at all. We'll bury you under some rock cairn on a desolate windswept bluff. Instead he said, "Sinking air on the west side turns cold at night as it slides back down. The east side is warmer. Friend of mine who has studied those things for the government claims the air coming west over the mountain compresses and dries out this side. I don't understand, but I know from experience it's true. So we camp up there yonder." He pointed north of some cathedral spires.

Physically conditioned, despite his bad leg, Landry could have set a pace that would have forced the women to ride and would have dropped the men, including the youngest, Lon Wiggins. He chose, however, to set a comfortable, deliberate pace, always detouring barriers while climbing steadily; never did he shortcut, which didn't really save in the long run, but simply expended more energy.

Landry set periodic rests of five to ten minutes; never too long to stiffen the muscles. The trail rose always at a natural angle, looping around contours to avoid losing elevation. The children of the wild are very wise, Landry thought, finding the route pleasantly challenging. He had a natural stride of the man born to the land. He placed each foot carefully, squarely, as he swung his weight smoothly. He used his bound hands when necessary to grasp a plant or to balance his weight even while leading the mustang. He kept his body center-out from the slope. Yattero, trying to hug the slope, fell face forward several times as his footing failed. Lon tumbled hard on his side one time. And Terena, impeded by her plumpness, whined and complained frequently.

Ryke, more seasoned, climbed doggedly, his face and mouth too set. The seething angers within him burned precious energy. Dar Ell wavered and swayed sometimes, as if he were going to faint, but he tried valiantly to cover the fact; his eyes darted over his companions to see if they noticed. Once he and Landry looked at each other knowingly and Landry detected a light of growing fear and uncertainty.

Molly stared ahead without seeing. The big chestnut followed her obediently, as if sensing her growing need of support. The white of her face had flushed pink from exertion. A growing numbness filled Landry. She had danger signs. He had seen the healthiest outdoorsmen succumb if exposed to a combination of cold, wind, and wetness. And the summits ahead rose boldly, windy and exposed, subject to sudden snow and rainfall. On the second pass, glaciers lowered nighttime temperatures to subarctic levels. Could Mollie survive those conditions? Weakened by a cold, lacking good food, and near total exhaustion, she was vulnerable. He had encouraged her to walk, hoping that the effort would stir her blood; but soon she would have to ride, a situation that would leave her heated system subject to the piercing cold that would soon strike them.

To everyone's relief, Landry called a halt once more. The sinking sun had left the east side in a shadowed chill. The overhead rays stretched into the foothills far out, and warmed the desert lands with tints of pink and brown. But the steady build of dark cumulous clouds threatened to cut the last sunlight early. "I suggest the women ride now," Landry said.

"What about the men?" Dar Ell's normally deep voice had a tremulous tone.

"Not yet, there's a leveling off some, a kind of benchlike rise up there, as I recall. We can ride then for a time. We'll camp up there in the last of the trees. Tomorrow morning we'll make the first pass. It's a short way above, but very steep." The onlookers stared up at ledge heaped on ledge, rock piled on rock, which culminated in peaks shrouded in clouds, discomforting in their blue-black heaviness.

"Doesn't seem like there's a way through that," Dar Ell commented.

"There is if it doesn't snow," said Landry. The wind was rising. At first it had hummed pleasantly through the trees, but now it made a whooshing sound that flagged the men's coats and pants and plumed the tails of the horses. Then from afar thunder crackled. Landry listened. A second boom rumbled its way along the battlements. He addressed Terena. "You're apparently in charge of food."

"I guess so."

"Get some jerky out, it's salty. We need that. And we have plenty of water. Distribute some sugar, too." Terena's enormous eyes fluttered toward Lon and back to Landry. She dug into the sack slung to her saddle, produced a fat slab of jerky and held it out. Dar Ell motioned to Yattero, who produced his knife and sliced the meat into bite-size chunks, which he proceeded to distribute. They all munched soberly, the salt and taste renewing them. Terena opened a small wood box, pinched some crude brown sugar into the palm of one hand. Each in turn did the same, licking and savoring the pure, invigorating sweetness.

Landry had the women mount. They wound higher; the horses plodded faithfully on, their halters jingling and the leather creaking in a steady rhythm. When they stopped again near a tight grove of lodgepole pine, Lon's horse protested, tossing and blowing as if something were wrong. It kept swinging its stern, its heels clopping. It reared and whirled. Lon grappled its head and held it. The other horses caught its uneasiness and strayed from the trail slightly.

Yattero and Ryke trained rifles on the dark trees. "Something's in there," said Ryke.

"Maybe a bear or a mountain lion," Landry observed. Ryke pumped three bullets into the grove, the sounds reverberating down the mountain. Startled, the horses nickered and pulled. But nothing emerged. They waited. More thunder cannonaded and the first laces of lightning whitened the sky. Landry directed them on.

The nearly nonexistent trail swung south around an imposing spine of granite into a high glacial cup under the bridge of some pyramidal spires, bare except for a few dwarfed pines and droopy-topped hemlocks. Patches of last year's snow, and shafts of bluish glaciers, clung to dark recesses. "Up there, that's the first pass," Landry noted. He then led them into a sheltered vale cloaked in shadow, where sizable red fir and golden aspen enclosed a meadowland; rivulets of melting snow dropped musically from rift to rift, playing through the rocky confines. "Didn't expect to find water here this time of year. But that's a blessing. Good to water the horses again before tomorrow's pull. Maybe your tide is at its full," Landry said to Dar Ell.

From somewhere a chickaree—the Sierran red squirrel—lashed out with a twirring of animal spits, sputters, and growls. Another took up the cause, raging.

"What's that?" Dar Ell asked, troubled.

"Those are squirrels cussing the hell out of you for intruding here," Landry said.

"He's the mountain's self-appointed reporter," Mollie said. Pale, adjusting mechanically to the rolling pace of the chestnut, she surprised everyone. Landry looked at her. Her eyes had a defiant twinkle. The spunk and determination still sustained her, he thought with relief.

Thunder ripped overhead, alarming the animals again, so that they broke from the columned procedure, their eyes rolling. "We'll camp just ahead," Landry announced. "There is a cave in that strip of limestone. It's rough footing, and with the lightning, it's best we all lead the horses." As he spoke, the first snowflakes flirted about them, and the dark clouds turned milky white and pressed down.

Near the south head of a glacial cup, they set up camp outside a five-foot-high hollow that extended some ten feet deep; a steady seepage moistened the far end, but the main area remained dry and relatively free from the pelting winds. "We best enjoy this place while we have it. I don't recall such a convenience for tomorrow night," Landry told them. From the pad marks in the soft flooring, and the tawny hair caught in some rocks, he knew that a mountain lion had shared the abode recently, but he avoided any mention.

"Oh, I'm so sore," Terena moaned, hobbling toward where they were laying goods. "And it's so cold."

"Hell, we going to listen to that two more days," Ryke growled.

"She's not used to riding," Lon said peevishly.

"Lon, get some wood," Dar Ell interposed quickly. "We need a fire right away. And Yattero, take care of the horses."

"Why don't Ryke do something?" Yattero mumbled.

"Because he has to watch our trail for a time to be sure nobody picked up on us."

Ryke, standing behind Dar Ell, smiled tauntingly at the Mexican. "And don't hobble the horses," he said.

"I would suggest you do hobble them," Landry offered.

"No," Ryke said emphatically, "a hobbled horse can move too far. I lost one to a mountain lion once. Had to lug a saddle over ten miles."

"What do you suggest, then?"

"I'd tie them to them skinny pines directly below us." He pointed. "We can keep an eye on 'em and have them all together."

"Sounds practical to me," Dar Ell agreed.

"That'll restrict them—especially in the cold," Landry said.

"I like the idea of keeping them together," Dar Ell concluded.

They built a blazing fire on the flat in front of the cave with dead branches and downed limbs. Before dark they piled additional wood to keep the fire throughout the night.

"The Mexican can take care of your horses," said Landry, "but I'm going to check out my chestnut and the mustang I'm on."

Dar Ell nodded. "It's okay."

"Horses tied up don't receive maximum good from their rest period," Landry said irritably. "They need to move some for warmth."

"But like Ryke said, they might drift."

In the enclosure of a lodgepole stand, Yattero had secured each of the seven animals to strong but limber trees with four-foot ropes, enough to permit the horses to lie down, but taut enough to prevent them from getting a leg tangled. The Mexican began fitting the grain bags.

With his bindings comfortably loose for the time, Landry could manipulate the equipment. He approached the chestnut first. "How you doing, fellow?" The horse nosed the marshal affectionately as the big man rubbed its muzzle. He said to the Mexican, "Tomorrow in the high valley beyond the hump, we'll have to graze them. Too much grain is going to founder them."

"I know. But the boss and Ryke, they won't want to stay too long. Probably not the hour or more needed."

"They won't move too fast if they have to carry their goods." Together they checked the shoes for looseness and for rocks or sticks, where a wedged particle, if allowed to remain, could cause serious lameness. "These Fargo horses haven't been ridden for a time—better check them," said Landry. They looked for signs of soreness where the hair had been slicked down, or for chafed spots. The chestnut, well cared for and in excellent condition, looked sleek and re- laxed, ready to continue if necessary.

Dar Ell joined them. "If the animals look good, Yattero can carry on. I want you back under my eye." In his fluted sleeve he held a small pistol. Landry climbed past the show- man without looking at him.

Misty clouds like streamers of fog draped the peaks, dropping lower to swirl about them. A steady streaking of wet snow commenced, melting on first contact but taking hold to feather the branches and the low shrubbery. Wrapped in layers of blankets, Terena and Mollie huddled before the fire. Landry extended his confined hands to absorb the warmth. Lon had constructed a forked stick, braced across a log and weighted with rocks, to which he hung a coffeepot. Except for a light stubble, the young man looked fresh and chipper for the ordeal, in contrast to the others, who had sunken, red-rimmed eyes. Mollie smiled feebly at Landry. She looked especially tired and withdrawn.

"Be damn glad when this is over," Ryke said, fanning his coat front in an attempt to force moist air out and receive heat.

Mollie coughed, the sound deeper; she shivered noticeably—a good and bad sign, Landry knew. Obviously the cold night in the station, the horrors of murder and assault, had taken their toll. But from years of experience, Landry had perceived that shivering was the body's normal method of resisting. Prolonged or violent shivering were grave warning signs. Or the lack of shivering could foreshadow death. Despite the cold of snow, the cloud cover would act as an insulating blanket, Landry hoped. For the time, the wind had eased; but the vagaries of mountain weather could produce a violent storm before morning, so severe that the pass could be blocked for the winter, forcing them back into the valley. Landry knew the others were keenly aware of that possibility, for they kept looking into the settling mists cloaking hidden peaks. Dar Ell's features had taken a pasty, shrunken look. From a coat pocket he produced a pair of soft buckskin gloves and tugged them on, his mind elsewhere. Mollie blew her nose on a frilly handkerchief. "Get some hot liquid in that woman," said Landry.

Lon poured two tin cups full and handed them to the two

women. Mollie lifted hers with shaky hands and breathed the steam. Her eyes closed and she sipped, taking pleasure.

"Ooh, so nice and warm," Terena bubbled, her face suddenly childlike.

Yattero returned to the fire. "All finished, boss." He poured himself some coffee. Dar Ell did not reply except to take a draw on his brandy flask.

"You'll have to check them before retiring," Landry said, enjoying the hot sear of coffee. "Boil some water, the reporter needs some broth. We could all use a broth of sorts. But first we need to eat something solid. It's important. If you keep the fire stoked throughout the night, it'll keep that cave cozy, long as people bundle down together."

"We're going to post a guard throughout the night," Dar Ell said. "The one on guard can keep the fire going."

"That include you, too, Dar Ell?" Ryke asked.

"That includes me, too." From the divide below, a coyote wailed. Another, somewhere beyond, yodeled and ended in a long, drawn-out reply. Yattero swallowed too much coffee and choked, spilling part of his contents. All of them turned and listened. No one spoke as darkness closed rapidly.

Lon fashioned a second stick, to which they hung a kettle filled with water low over glowing embers scraped from the fire. A cold and sluggish Terena pulled additional sandwiches from her sack and distributed them. To the slowly boiling water she added chunks of pork, some peppers, dried onions, and other odds and ends she had collected. It soon simmered into a hearty broth, the aroma appealing. All but Dar Ell and Ryke partook of the thin soup. "I suggest, Mr. Dar Ell, if you plan to make it across those big mountains, you better sup some of that stuff, too," Landry said. He turned to Terena and held up his cup. "A toast to the new Mrs. . . . ?"

"Wiggins," she said.

"You'll make a fine inventive cook, Mrs. Wiggins."

Dar Ell tossed his coffee out and dipped a cupful of broth from the kettle.

"It is good," said Lon.

"It warms, but I'm so miserable," said the Mexican girl. She rolled doe-brown eyes toward the youth.

"Don't worry, hon. Hang with me." He squatted beside her, put an arm around her and rocked her slightly. "Just keep thinking about our future. In California it's warm. We'll have money. We won't be like others starting out. I can buy you anything you want. All our dreams will come true." His face shone radiantly under the tightly pulled hat, its brim slouchy. His eyes focused afar.

The snowfall increased, making sizzling sounds as flakes hit the fire. An icy wind gusted suddenly, spraying the new fallen snow in a fine powder. It flapped the men's clothing and shot the fire higher. Mollie stood up unsteadily. "I must change your head bandage," she said to the marshal. "I brought along some extra cloth."

"Good idea," Dar Ell mused, "don't want him to pass out on us."

But Landry moved to her, supporting her shoulder with his coupled hands. "I'll be fine, you must not get chilled," he warned.

"I know," she said hoarsely. "I'm sorry to be any trouble."

"You hardly volunteered for this." He assisted her into the cave. "You must rest and bundle as close to the others as possible."

"They'll never leave witnesses," Mollie said wearily. "And you a marshal—they'd be fools to." She removed his hat. The bandage had caked where dried blood had oozed. "The boy and the girl—foolish, just young in love. Mr. Dar Ell seems honorable. But the other two, especially that Ryke . . ."

"Don't think about it."

She removed the bandage. Her face softened with concern at the pulpy bruise. "It is better. It might be better to leave it uncovered now." She took a handful of nearby snow and washed it over the swelling. Landry flinched.

The marshal's usually assertive voice was barely audible. "Tomorrow as we head toward the last pass, I'm going to try something."

"What?"

"Just keep your eyes on me. Before we get over, they're going to be very tired. Whatever happens, give my chestnut full rein. He's surefooted; none of their horses will ever catch you. Follow north, down the valley. The Johnson toll road crosses it. Somebody will help you."

"What about you?"

"Best not talk anymore, they're looking at us."

"Tell me," she whispered, "why have you been so helpful to them? Why not let them all fall flat on their faces?" Her curious green eyes had paled with fatigue.

"We may all need each other for a time—especially since I've seen something behind us that I don't think they've noticed yet."

"What did you see?"

"That's enough," Dar Ell called. "This is not a tea social. I get suspicious of too much talk."

Landry turned away.

"We all need rest," said Dar Ell. "Yattero, better check the horses once more. I'll take the first watch. Two hours. Then Lon, Ryke, and Yattero, and me again, in that order until daylight. The one on guard will keep the fire up. I propose we get in that cave where our bodies will help for warmth." As Yattero slipped toward the horses, a short torch in his hand, Dar Ell told Landry, "You're going to sleep on the outer edge of the cave, where we can watch you. Lie down." He tossed the marshal two blankets, then bound the man's hands tighter.

"You can give one of these to the lady, she needs it."
Landry held up a blanket.

"No, there's plenty for her. I want you in top condition."
Dar Ell squatted and bound the marshal's boots together. "I
know this is uncomfortable, but we can't take chances."

"I expected it." Landry stretched out and worked the
blankets around him while basking in the direct force of the
fire.

"Lon and Ryke, leave your guns outside by the fire," Dar
Ell said. Lon laid his down.

But Ryke said, "Me and my gun don't part."

"You in there asleep, even that frail, lovely lady might
manage to slip it away, all cuddled up together."

"I keep my gun."

"You want to blow somebody's head off in there? Leave
it."

Reluctantly, Ryke unbuckled his belt. Yattero snuffed the
flaming stick out in the snow and returned. "No problems,"
he said, dropping his gun near the fire and picking up a
bedroll. Within a few minutes they had settled inside the cave
under tarpaulins, all bunched. Yattero lapsed into an immediate snoring. Ryke checked his money bag thoroughly, then
lay awake somewhat to the side, his eyes open. Mollie dozed
self-consciously against the two lovers who had settled
tightly, giggling and mewing. At the rim, Landry pulled his
Stetson low and watched Dar Ell through squinted eyelids.
The showman tugged a heavy army blanket around him and
pulled the cloak up over his ears just under the derby—a
strange-looking figure against a desolate night.

The fire burned steadily, fanned frequently by gushes of
wind that soughed through the trees. Dar Ell closed his eyes,
jerked them open, nodded. A horse nickered. Then several
neighed, stirring. Dar Ell came to his feet. Ryke and Landry
sat up. "What the hell goes?" Dar Ell exclaimed.

"Something's out there," said Ryke, crawling out of his bedroll, a gun in hand—one he had hidden.

"Could be a mountain lion. I've seen signs of them around," said Landry. "Or a prowling bear. They haven't started hibernation yet."

Lon and the women came to their elbows. Dar Ell pointed his rifle toward the pines. "There is something out there."

"Don't shoot," said Landry, "you might hit the horses."

A sleepy Yattero said, "It's the coyote devil." He wormed himself back against the limestone wall.

They waited. A horse grunted, but the animals settled shortly, their breathing regular; a few shifted, their hooves clopping on stone. The night waned. Dar Ell awakened a drowsy Lon, who fed the fires and sat mesmerized by the crackling movement. The snow had ceased. A frigid air settled in the vale, followed by a deathly quiet. Ryke took the midnight watch. He, too, stirred the fire, then drank some coffee and listened to the horses breathe. Those in the cave lapsed into a fitful sleep.

Past midnight, just before Yattero's watch, the horses clattered about, shaking snow from the supple pines. One horse suddenly reared and squealed and then another shrilled. And then the night erupted in chaos, the horses heaving and jumping, wheeling insanely to break free of the hitching trees. There came the low, quavery sob of a moaning creature. The animals stampeded brokenly, hammering away in all directions. A bulky form materialized indistinctly, snarling in a crash of brush.

"Oh, God," Yattero moaned. Everybody was up.

Ryke yelled, "Get away." He shot overhead.

"Be careful of the horses," Landry cried. Suddenly Lon was beside Ryke with a rifle, aiming. He fired at the blurry object, and a horse screamed and fell heavily; it lay somewhere thrashing and gurgling. A strangulation of fear grasped the watchers. Terena thrust her hands to a contorted face and emitted an earth-rending screech that shimmied her whole body.

"Cut my bindings. My legs—cut the bindings, damn it," Landry roared. Dar Ell pulled a stubby knife and rolled across the partially prostrate Mollie, her mouth hanging aghast, and sliced the rope around the marshal's ankles. Free, Landry bounded up and headed toward the confusion of the unknown, toward the ghost marauder. A hundred feet below, a spooked horse whinnied and plunged noisily, its hooves racketing down the mountainside. It fell heavily, voiced throatily, and commenced thrashing to gain its feet. A wheeze of constricted terror sounded along with a pouring of rocks. After a moment of silence the animal crashed far down.

"Oh, God," Terena sobbed.

"Hurry, get some light down here," Landry called back. The men each picked up sticks, lit them in the fire and plunged through the snowy slush. One wild-eyed horse remained, still tugging its tie rope. Six had vanished.

Yattero grasped one of the several ropes and looked at the frayed strands in the burning glow. "Some animals chewed it apart, chomped it in two," he said. The men stared.

"Loosen these bindings," Landry demanded, holding out his hands. Dar Ell worked the thongs free. Landry examined another strand. "No," he said strongly, "this looks too cleanly cut. But we can't tell for sure until daylight. Looks like someone tried to mangle it like an animal would."

They moved around the mushed snow with their torches, looking for tracks or for human sign; but the frantic animals had destroyed any evidence, leaving mostly slush. Landry lifted his hands to his lips, curving his little fingers to his teeth, and blew sharply, his whistle penetrating far. He waited and tried again. From a rocky enclave above came an answering neigh and the steady clip-clop of an anxious horse. From the shadows, the big chestnut emerged to nudge his master fondly as Landry rubbed the gelding's ears and head vigorously.

"What do we do?" said Lon.

"You've done enough, kid," said Landry. "You killed at least one of the horses. We won't know for sure until dawn."

"We have to have animals," said Dar Ell woefully.

"We don't have much choice." Landry took the chestnut. "Bring the mustang. We're going to hobble these near camp like we should have in the first place. They'll serve the two women and be enough to carry some grub and goods."

"Best we get the hell out of here, and soon," said Ryke.

"We don't dare budge until dawn," Landry snapped. "Nothing we can do but get some rest."

As they returned to the cave, Dar Ell said mostly to himself, " 'Tis now the very watching time of night when Hell itself breathes out.' "

Ryke cursed and slammed himself down before the fire, crossed his legs and braced his rifle. Grimly he said, "Maybe whatever it is will return for our last two horses."

Terena sat transfixed, staring out into the dark, her face red and bloated, her eyes wet. Every so often an uncontrollable spasm would shudder her body so that she would gasp for breath. Lon did not comfort her this time, but stayed back, dazed.

Mollie sat waiting, her eyes addressing Landry. He simply shrugged evasively. Dar Ell looked at the hobbled horses in the outer circle of light, then around at the black void. "Maybe with light we'll find the other horses," he said with stubborn hope. "Surely whatever it was won't follow us."

Yattero, sitting, his head bowed, muttered, "It's the coyote devil. There is no escape."

Although it was Yattero's turn to stand watch, Ryke and Dar Ell accompanied him. The hours dragged by; no one slept except Terena, who sank into a torpor from emotional exhaustion. The heavy air of morning clung like viscous ice.

And then somewhere south across the chasm came a long reverberating howl, at first bass, rising tremulous and desolate. People listened in rapt silence. A series of throaty barks wavered high into a long, drawn-out wail—eerie, pervading, sending shivers down the listeners.

"A wolf," said Ryke. "Ain't heard one of them for years."

"Wolf, coyote, it's all the same—the sound of the Devil," Yattero managed.

"It's damn strange," said Landry, "different somehow from any wolf I ever heard."

The first tint of dawn across the bleak desert far below painted the backbone of the ridge across the way and blazed brightly on an island of twisted pine from where the howls had seemed to come. Ryke pointed his rifle at the sparse woods and fired as fast as he could cock the lever.

(13)

Against the bright glimmer of open snow, the party wound its way through the broken rubble of the high country, where a bland sun played through torn clouds. Landry looked back down the way they had come. His eyes registered concern. Determinedly he picked the way along an indistinct route toward a disjointed mass of domed buttes that marked the crest. The empty land, fractured and weathered from battering weather, subzero freeze, and icy blasts, lay gaunt and forbidding, the few trees squat and twisted, their branches feathered away from the prevailing winds. Yattero, Lon, and Ryke struggled along, fat-waisted with money belts, and their coats and trousers bulging with as much ammunition as they could hold. They and Dar Ell carried their weighty saddlebags, luggage, blankets, and guns. Lon led a buckskin with Terena astride. Yattero led the chestnut, the reins tucked behind to his belt. Grim-faced but determined, Mollie sat high in the saddle. Both horses had been laden with feed bags, food and necessary gear, but all else—the extra saddles, pots, pans, clothing, rope, and much food, especially canned goods—had been left behind in the cave. They had cached all extra guns under a nearby log.

The updraft of morning air blew the new snow into a stinging pelt like driven sand. But the night's storm clouds had moved out across the washboard of raw desert. Landry entered a cut between rocky columns. "Eye of the needle," he called back. Breathing hard in the rarefied air they entered, they leveled off and rounded the shoulder of a bend to look down into a valley, rich with timber on the western slope, bouldered mostly on the eastward side and rising once again to more towering, more formidable peaks. The second pass. Clouds building early for a new storm sailed aloft, making dark moving shadows along the ridges. Directly before them, where the dead prongs of a white-bark pine gnarled outward, a narrow trail threaded the side of a sheer granite wall that plunged dramatically away some one hundred feet.

"Good God," Dar Ell exclaimed.

"You ain't getting me on that," said Ryke tightly.

"This is why the E-sha Trail was popular with only those who dared use it," Landry said, a trace of smile creasing his face. "But first, I'm going ahead to see if the trail's all there. If we lead a horse out there and have to back up, we're in deep trouble."

"What if we can't make it?" Dar Ell asked.

"For your sake, just hope you can."

"Just come back," Dar Ell said dryly. Landry looked at him and laughed. They waited patiently in the wind as Landry disappeared along the wall. Mollie watched apprehensively, staring out at the high valley, at no time making eye contact with the others. Ryke grumbled about their rotten luck. Terena whined about her discomfort. They waited, eyes riveted on the precarious trail. At last Landry appeared. Mollie breathed a noticeable sigh. "We can make it, if we take it easy," he said. "There's a few washouts here and there." He motioned to the women. "Off, girls, we walk this one." He approached Dar Ell. "I need balance—and use of my hands. We all do. You'll have to free me for now."

"No," said Ryke.

But Dar Ell stepped forth and with his small knife loosened the knots and released the marshal.

A strong wind pummeled the cliffside, and countless rivulets of melting snow crickled noisily down every draw, thrashing loudly in the lower chasms.

"It's slippery. I'll lead my horse," Landry said, stepping off. Mollie stood concave, her face colorless. She held onto the saddle for support until the marshal said, "That won't work; take hold of his tail. He won't hurt you." Landry addressed the others. "Any weight you're carrying, keep on the inside." When he pulled the chestnut, the animal tugged against him for a moment, sniffed the trail and then reached out, surefooted. Mollie shrugged and grasped the flowing tail, to be jerked forward until she found her balance. Lon moved directly behind her, leading the buckskin, with a tense-faced Terena clutching his belt.

Dar Ell, Yattero, and Ryke fell in line, all attempting not to look down while encumbered with their baggage. The wind buffeted, swirled around them to gush downward with an echoing wail. It detained them, swayed them so that once, sickly, Yattero leaned against the rocky wall, unable to proceed. "Move, damn it," Ryke bellowed.

Landry proceeded cautiously, kicking loose rocks away that lay in their path. Seasonal runoff had gutted the route, narrowing it in spots, crumbly material that sloughed easily away, giving each member a queasy uncertainty.

The chestnut faltered once or twice but pushed on with Landry's coaxing. But at one washout the buckskin balked. Lon tugged and cursed, but the swollen-eyed animal lifted its head and set its front hooves. "Push him, somebody, whip him," Lon cried.

"I won't ever get that close to the rear of any horse," Dar Ell said, fidgety. With trepidation, Yattero slipped around Dar Ell, laid his saddlebags down and approached the animal on the inside. He talked to it softly, most of his words lost in the wind. He reached across the rump and struck a smart slap. The horse whistled and bolted, crossing the wash but knocking Lon back and bowling Terena over, to nearly trample her. She screamed in terror, further confusing the animal, which drew back, shuffled, and almost lost balance. Those observing paled, fearing the buckskin might go over, but a desperate Lon hung on, steadying the creature, keeping it from rearing as Terena crawled free. Mollie dropped beside the girl to cradle her in her arms as everyone calmed.

"You hurt, hon?" Lon asked.

Terena looked painfully down and pressed her left ankle. "Help get her up," Landry called. "Once we're off this nightmare, we'll check her out." Both Mollie and Lon lifted Terena to her feet, where she limped ahead, whimpering, her fingers clutching at the stone wall for some security. Tediously, they reached a widening plateau that bridged the dizzy drop, then swung along the western crest.

"Please let us rest. Oh, please, I'm so tired and my ankle hurts," Terena pleaded.

Without protest, they all sprawled in relief. Dar Ell removed his hat, leaned back and closed his eyes.

Lon worked Terena's boot free. "It's swelling."

The girl rubbed vigorously. "I don't know how far I can walk."

" 'Least it's not broken," said Lon.

"Get some snow on it," Landry suggested, "then get that boot back on before the swelling makes it impossible."

Terena pouted. "It'll hurt."

"No, it will give your ankle support."

Lon scooped up a handful of slush from the trailside and packed it over the length of the foot and lower leg as the girl winced.

Yattero flopped down. "I left my blankets back there. And I'll be damned if I'll go back after them."

"I stepped over 'em," Ryke said. "They ain't my responsibility."

"We're really our brother's keepers here," said Landry.

"What the hell does that mean?"

Dar Ell interrupted. "It means we're going to kill each other unless we start working as the team I once thought we were."

"We're going to make it," Lon said buoyantly, his arm tight around his girl. He was beaming, his face boyish. He tucked Terena's head into the cup of his shoulder and rocked her, looking down at her. "You and me, Ter, we're going to make it big, once we get to California."

"You are in California," said Landry.

Mollie's eyes danced with mirth momentarily; then she broke into a spasm of coughs. Landry patted her back. Terena came up from the comfort of her lover's shoulder and touched the reporter's arm.

"Try breathing through your nose rather than your mouth, if you can," Landry told Mollie.

"Better get the marshal's hands strapped again," said Ryke.

Dar Ell sat up wearily. "Yes, I'm sorry, Marshal, we can't take chances."

"Sure," said Landry deeply, holding out his pressed wrists. Dar Ell bound them loosely again, his face somewhat apologetic. His fingers trembled.

Landry studied the showman. The precarious trail and the exhausting climb, the pressures were telling slowly. "She's ill, you know. Getting worse by the hour."

"I know, but in one day you said we'll be to Lost Chance. We can get her help there."

"One day is a long time. And you, a wanted man, are going to help a damsel in distress. Come, come, Dar Ell."

"The food," Yattero said, "maybe we shouldn't have left so much grub."

"If need be, we can eat some off the land, even at this level," said Landry. "Anyway, you'll have to get some supplies in Lost Chance if you hope to make it down the foothills to Sacramento."

"I promise you, the woman goes free in this Lost Chance," Dar Ell said softly.

"And me?" The lawman looked cynically at Dar Ell.

"I don't know for sure where. It depends. If we split there, I will try to give you your life, but I will not lay down my life for you."

"You sound as if you're already there."

"I do feel good," said Dar Ell, for all to hear. "The big pass may be ahead, but I feel good. I see the light at the end of the tunnel, so to speak." He smiled to himself. " 'Oh brave new world, I have immortal longings in me.' "

"I feel great, too," said Lon. "It's all behind us. We have the money, and it's only a matter of time now."

"Well, before you all pat yourselves to death, you best keep your eyes open. We're being followed."

A stunned silence immobilized the group. The wind willowed musically around the naked crannies. "What do you mean?" Dar Ell challenged. "I've been watching our back trail steadily, all the time, and at every stop. You've seen me using the glasses."

"I ain't seen nothin', either," said Ryke indignantly, sitting up stiffly.

"You people have been too involved with yourselves," said Landry. "You can't see beyond your feet."

"He's trying to put us on," said Ryke, grinning meanly. "He's just trying to get us all shook up."

"Think of it this way. It's to my advantage not to tell you—except I'm thinking of the ladies' and my necks. We just may all need each other to get out of these heights alive."

"What did you see?" Dar Ell burst.

"Two or three of them on horses. Could be more."

"Where? When?"

"Yesterday afternoon in the wooded breaks below us."

Dar Ell contemplated the mountain flow beyond, his eyes

narrowing. "Why the hell didn't you say something?" Dar Ell's pallid face had pinkened.

"Wasn't sure they are after us. Could be some hunters."

"How do you know they aren't?"

"Saw them this morning again, dogging us."

"Morton! Could it be Morton?" Dar Ell's deep-set eyes had hollowed deeper; his voice had a chill.

"No telling."

"A posse maybe," said Ryke, getting up. "They're on horseback. We ain't. They'll catch us. It's only a matter of time." He was looking back at the hanging trail above the drop.

All of them except Terena and Landry were on their feet now. "Could be bounty hunters," said Yattero. "The word could be out by now."

"You deliberately withheld what you saw, hoping they would kill some of us," Dar Ell said angrily, pointing a bony finger.

"I told you, I wasn't sure until this morning."

"Get on your feet. You're going to take us the hell out of here."

Landry rose slowly and stretched to his full height. "We're going straight down through those trees and boulders below," he explained. "But not all the way down. It'd be too hard to climb out the other side. So we're going to follow one of those old terraces over there. The one that's thick with alder and fir—good cover. It'll take us around to where we start up again. Looks like another snow night." Already the clouds had blued the peaks, piling and flattening.

"Dar Ell," said Ryke. "Someone with a rifle could pick 'em off easy on that skimpy trail over there. Just wait in them broken rocks above us."

"Ambush them." Dar Ell licked his lips in anticipation. "You, Ryke, you're the best shot here. You can do it. If you can't get them, get their horses."

"And you folks go on without me."

"We'll wait along that south terrace. From there we can pretty well watch you, I would think," said Dar Ell. "Besides, you have your share—your money belt and your saddlebags with you."

Ryke said calculatingly, "I'll do it if you leave me one of the horses."

"I can't walk," Terena cried. "My ankle's sprained."

"Put both females on the marshal's horse—just leave me the mustang. That's not asking too much if I'm to do the dirty work."

With difficulty, Dar Ell pondered for a moment and glanced at Landry—his eyes implacable, waiting. The showman swallowed. "No," he said. "With your cut and a horse, what's to stop you from heading out and just leaving them on our tail?"

"Not a damn thing," Ryke said icily. "Except I don't want them buzzards screwin' up my chances any more than you do."

"Besides, without Landry, I don't think you could find your way out," said Dar Ell. "You can have the mustang, but I think you're limiting your chances. If you don't stop them, they're going to pick you off. Seems to me you got a hell of a lot better chance alone on foot than trying to haul a scared horse through that mess down there."

The logic rocked the gunman. Ryke chewed on the thought.

"Make up your mind," said Dar Ell. "We got to move, and fast."

"All right, I'll chance it. Your word as partner, you'll wait on that middle terrace down there."

"We'll wait."

As they moved out with the two women in the saddles, Ryke took a position in some rock heaps, backed by seams

of ancient rocks, where he could view the trail and the prec-
ipice.

The others dropped steadily into the basin and through a
heavily wooded band. "What would you have done with
Ryke?" Dar Ell shouted to Landry.

"Exactly what you did."

Mist from melting snow moistened their faces with a fresh
softness as they dropped quickly through dwarfed trees into
a mid-zone of red fir, lodgepole, and silver pine, where aspen gleamed golden in the grassy breaks. The boulders and
give-away rocks forced the horses back on their hocks at
times, so that they humped and turned their rumps under, descending stiff-legged like dogs sitting down. Several
times the women had to climb off to wait red-eyed in misery.
At last Landry turned south along a wooded terrain where
they could look up at the high summit toward Ryke's hide-
away.

"Why do we have to climb again?" Dar Ell asked. "Why
can't we just travel down the valley?"

"Because the valley would take us into the Tahoe Basin
and the Johnson Pass," said Landry, "with more stages,
freighters, travelers, and lawmen than you could shake a finger at."

They took refuge in some willows where a spring purled,
letting the horses cool before watering them. Dar Ell adjusted
the glasses on the summit. Mollie lay back, closed her eyes
and turned her face to the warming sun. Her breathing
sounded raspy.

As the two horses munched vigorously in the wiry grass,
Landry sloshed through a wet meadow to where moist em-
bankments rose. The others watched curiously. He called
Lon to join him, and then began pulling dead stems from the
earth, drawing forth tuberous clusters of roots. The two
worked industriously. Landry gathered as much as his bound
hands permitted, then washed them in the clear water.

"What you got there?" Dar Ell inquired.

"Indians called it apah. Early pioneers named it caraway." Landry directed Lon to cut the roots away, peel and store them in one of the marshal's saddlebags. "The roots have a sweet, nutty flavor if you eat them raw. Cooked, they taste like carrots. Might come in handy; at least supplement our dwindling food supply."

"I see them. I see them," Dar Ell exclaimed. Everyone gazed at the pass they had crossed. The showman could not contain his ecstasy. "They're heading right down Ryke's barrel. The one in the lead is stocky. The one behind is heavier." He handed the glasses to Landry.

After a moment the marshal said, "Rattlesnake Morton always was one hell of a good tracker."

"Morton?"

"That's who's on our tails—no other than Morton. I could pick out his walk and looks as far as I can see him."

Under the crest of the Sierras with the hazardous trail before him, Ryke waited, his narrow eyes squinting down the barrel of the Winchester braced across a flat rock. Suddenly he jerked alert. Higher up in the rocky fortress he saw fleeting glimpses of two men leading horses, both hugging the landforms. He smiled with sullen satisfaction. A good clean kill brought fulfillment always. To see a man buckle under the pump of his gun; to feel the God power gave him meaning—a total exhilaration, a high that sometimes lasted for days. Whiskey wasn't all that great. A jackpot didn't do much either. Women—he could love 'em or leave 'em—mostly leave 'em. Even those he had taken against their wills had not gratified that much. But a clean, sharp kill—that was something else. Ryke swayed the barrel on his palm, rotated the muzzle in anticipation until settling on the trail curve where they would appear.

* * *

Leander Morton studied the mushed trail before him discerning the tracks of two horses and several people. Vaguely he saw the bowled valley in front of him as his attention centered where the bearers of wealth had passed. Within hours, before the sunset, he would overtake them, despite that oaf Biggs floundering at his heels, for they were now down to two horses . . . and with women. Here and there he had seen the flop of long hair, the slender shape of apparent females. Fools, he thought. Why take a magnificent haul and then drag females along? Well, he chuckled inwardly, they would all pay for it shortly, and the women would be his. The thought made him liquidy inside. The long-dried responses of his body throbbed with awakening anticipation. Morton looked down into the high valley. He could not see the pursued, but they moved somewhere in the trees, he judged. He edged onto the perilous trail, a dangerous section, he knew, exposed to any ambusher who lay along the way. An uncanny instinct, born to him, which had served him well, warned him suddenly. His keen eyes scoured the rocky prongs ahead. Had he seen a glint of light or a movement? Morton recoiled and worked his horse back, away from the ledge. They would wait. He would climb above the trail, sneak ahead to look down.

"What's the matter?" said Biggs, puffing from exertion.

Morton narrowed his eyes, his concave face and flat nose hardening with resistance. "Something's wrong. I don't know yet."

Ryke grinned tightly, cruelly, his finger on the trigger. He saw a squat man appear, long-haired, his face dark with heavy brow and mustache. He squinted the barrel sight into the V, lowered it to the man's midsection, and saw him step back and disappear. Ryke sat up nervously. Then farther up he saw a second heavier man appear, familiar somehow, his horse trudging listlessly. The heavier man then withdrew, apparently warned by the first, but his horse remained visible. Frustrated, Ryke waited, wanting to gun something. When he saw the black being step back, he shot five quick bursts—two bullets grazing the black, which bucked wildly, went off the upper trail and slid squealing some fifteen feet into a crevasse, where it lay thrashing, one of its legs broken.

Morton's horse, a bay, confused by the commotion behind, bolted forward, breaking free to gallop tenuously along the high, narrow trail. Ryke watched it coming, expecting it to lose footing, but it maintained balance to clamor past him and on down the rock-strewn drop into some woods to the south. As the horse passed, Morton leaned out up above, from behind boulders, and snapped several pistol shots that whiffed past Ryke to splash rocky splinters around him. For several minutes they exchanged gunfire, until Morton departed. A quiet fell.

Assured that Morton and his partner had either given up momentarily and retreated or were attempting to bypass him, Ryke left his position and worked stealthily down the mountain, keeping to the trees or in the embrace of mammoth blocks. He lightened his saddlebags along the way, tossing out all food, currying brushes, tools, and a horseshoe.

From the terrace, those waiting stared up the heights and listened to the sound of battle. Dar Ell and Landry took turns with the glasses. "If it wasn't an animal, then they must be the ones that cut our horses loose," Dar Ell speculated.

"Can't say for sure," said Landry. "If Morton had gotten in that close, he'd have killed us all."

"Then who or what?"

"I don't know."

"Least Ryke's slowed them up. Without horses, they'll remain about even-paced." They saw Ryke cross an opening. Bullets from the crest wanged by his feet, spitting dirt. He dodged into a thicket of willows. Morton and his partner had circled above Ryke's ambush spot. "He's lucky he got the hell out of there,'' said Dar Ell. ''They would have killed him.''

''Don't seem like they have rifles,'' said Landry. ''Those were pistol shots.''

''Guess we can count our lucky stars on that fact.''

''It helps, but Morton has a habit of shortening the odds.'' They saw the two men stand up, dark silhouettes against the sky.

By the time a foot-weary Ryke reached them, Lon and Yattero were urging they move on. ''Son of a bitches damn near got me,'' Ryke moaned, dropping into the moist grass to drink gulps of crystal water and splash it over his face and neck. His knuckles were still white from clinging to his coat and saddlebags. He sat back, the fat money bags bulging under his brown vest, his eyes shining feverously. ''They don't have rifles. They'd be damn dangerous if they did.''

''They do the Devil's work,'' said Yattero, his eyes blazing queerly, his voice mechanical and distant.

Ryke wiped his face with a neckerchief. ''Sure as hell warmed up.''

''It will cool soon enough.'' Landry looked up at the soiled clouds, bigger, more ominous, than those of the night before. They hung darkly about the peaks, slowly shifting and coupling.

''You were lucky, Ryke,'' Dar Ell said heartily. ''They damn near got you.''

Ryke's narrow eyes regarded Dar Ell piercingly. ''I saved your ass for a time.''

''The E-sha Pass up there, it's going to pack in with snow tonight,'' Landry said, assisting Mollie, then Terena onto the horses. ''We got just so many hours now.''

Two sleepless nights, constant tension, and a second day of climbing were taking its toll. With each jerk or misstep in the mustang's gait, Terena moaned or emitted a childlike mew. Skittish about Morton in pursuit, most members kept peering back frequently, except Yattero, who churned regular steps, his face set stoically ahead. Lon led the mustang but kept close to Landry, curious and observant as the marshal sought a way, always moving toward an array of domes and spires. Ryke sometimes turned around and walked backward, as if expecting a rear attack or a slam of bullets in his back. Dar Ell grew pasty-faced, his breathing more labored. Once when they paused, Mollie asked Dar Ell, "Is it worth it? Is this an ill-fated venture?"

" 'For in that sleep of death that dreams may come.' *Hamlet*, my dear." Dar Ell had a forced smile.

"You're not going to make it, Dar Ell," said Ryke. "We'll bury you somewhere along the trail."

"Your compassion warms my being," Dar Ell replied wearily. "I shall make it over the pass and to Lost Chance— not that I much like that foreboding name."

Landry saw Mollie shiver again. She looked frail, more thin and drawn. They all took water, some jerky, and dried fruit. A low string of clouds came over, blotting out the sun for a time. Lon sat close to Landry. "Whereabouts is this Lost Chance? I hear tell of it when I lived in the mother lode, but I never been there."

Landry looked curiously at the young man. "If I told you, you wouldn't need me, now would you?"

Lon grinned.

"I'll tell you one thing, if you ever try the E-sha Trail yourself, keep to the crest once you're over. Don't ever try to take a horse straight down."

"This Lost Chance. A big town?" Lon continued, not fazed.

"Not any longer. Probably less than a thousand citizens. One or two old mines keep the place alive."

"With luck we'll be there tomorrow."

"With luck. Just how did you get into this, kid?"

"With open eyes," said Lon.

Landry smiled to himself and said quietly, "Well, you best try to keep your woman held together."

Lon rose, cupped a hand under Terena's arm and assisted her to rise. She limped toward the dozing mustang. "I'm tired. I need more rest," she lamented.

"Son of a bitch, look!" Ryke pointed at the forested slope north, which connected with the middle terrace. Two figures on foot darted along a natural corridor in the manzanita. Dar Ell snapped the field glasses to his cheek and looked, but the men had vanished. The showman took a drink of brandy.

"My God, they're still coming," Ryke remarked, his normally set features registering apprehension.

"Morton's gaining on us," Landry added calmly. As they hurried on, Dar Ell stumbled and lost his footing, rose immediately, embarrassed, to shuffle on.

"They are the Devil," said Yattero.

Ryke looked back where they'd last seen Morton, drew his revolver and stared at empty vastness.

For three hours they climbed, resting more frequently, but reluctantly, knowing Morton was ever behind. Landry found switchbacks that added distance but eased the strenuous pull. Despite his disabled leg, he kept a constant stride that ate away the miles. Only Lon kept even. The women pitched and swayed monotonously as their mounts maneuvered through the rugged land. A cold wind came off the mountains, blurring everyone's vision.

"I'm getting cold," Terena complained.

"It'll get a sight colder," said Landry. "This pass has year-round glaciers."

Yattero clumped weighty step after weighty step, his head straight ahead like a soldier under marching orders. Ryke climbed erratically, perspiration beading his forehead. His eyes had taken a peculiar hollow look. Frequently he picked up gobs of melting snow to slush it across his face and neck, while scanning the land sweep for the expected trackers. Dar Ell now was the slowing one. The once fine derby had wilted, its rim warped and the crown permanently stained with sweat and caked mud. The showman would take several painful steps, as if each boot had been molded in lead. He would stop then, teeter, and gasp deeply, as though the thin air could not fill him satisfactorily. But when he saw Landry observing once, he countered with, "Oh, my kingdom for a horse."

With time they reached a plateau where the trail confronted a shoulder of mountain and seemed to diverge, one left into a cirque of cathedral spires that embraced a blue glacier, the right toward a cut where peaks disappeared in clouds. Landry stopped at the base of a needlelike shaft. The women nearly tumbled from the horses in dismounting, and the men collapsed in exhaustion. "I'm not sure," Landry droned.

But Ryke picked up his words. "What the hell you mean you're not sure?"

"There's a natural break in here somewhere."

"Hell, that's easy," said Ryke, "it's up there." He pointed to the right trail, toward the cut.

"Nothing up here is certain. Seems to me it's to the left, but let's look the right over." Dark thunderous clouds swept down, congesting about them, bringing a strong wind that flattened the chaparral and made the horses grunt and turn their rumps into it. The blast flagged the women's blankets and snapped the men's clothing. A squirming mist blotted out the amphitheater of parapets and domes. "Doubt if we get over before nightfall. We'll have to make camp up here somewhere," Landry said.

"You better damn well know what you're doing," Ryke warned. "With snow, the food low, and those bastards behind—maybe we just better keep going."

"With new snow, it's slippery up there, and dangerous.

It's hard enough now to see a trail in bright sun. Besides, it's easy to shake loose an avalanche with all that bare rock.'' Lightning made incandescent threads along the summit. The horses protested. ''It would be best to hole up in a canyon up here and set up guards.''

''Can we make it after a storm?'' Dar Ell sat expended, his arms loose to the sides.

''For now I want to rest the horses. It's going to be rough. We need a fire, but a fire will make us a target for Morton.''

''We're going to have to set up a damn sound guard plan,'' Dar Ell said. ''Maybe two men at the same time.''

''Don't want no repeat of last night,'' Ryke added.

''Why didn't you kill them two when you had a chance?'' Yattero asked.

Ryke screamed, ''You smart Mexican greaser, why didn't you volunteer?''

''We'll check out the trail to the right, toward the notch up there.'' Landry cinched the chestnut tight again and helped Mollie astride. She clenched the reins more than needed. She looked at the marshal with haggard but resolute eyes. ''Can you make it?'' he asked, deeply concerned.

''Yes,'' she murmured shakily.

''Keep an eye on me. They're tired,'' he muttered. ''We might just have a chance.''

''What will you do?''

''If the chance comes; if you see me go for one of them, drive your horse into someone. Yattero's closest. Quick as you can, throw off the saddlebags, anything with money. Ride back down the mountain and north toward the basin.''

''And you?''

He ignored her. ''They can't catch you on this horse. They won't shoot you. And Morton won't bother you without the money. Take the lariat and tie yourself on, so that you can't fall no matter what. You have blankets and some food. Find shelter tonight. Tomorrow the big fellow here will find civilization. He'll take you through. You can't miss the Johnson toll road.''

"What are you two talking about?'' Dar Ell's voice cracked.

Landry waved them out, sluggishly. A wobbly Dar Ell came last, his face a doughy gray. They worked across a flank of splintered shale toward the cut, appearing and disappearing in strangling mist. A murky chill fell over them. The area smelled damp of recent electricity. Landry ordered the girls off the horses again in case of close lightning. "Be our luck to get hit,'' Ryke grumbled.

Milky clouds came down and swirled about them, so that they could hardly see fifty feet ahead. "At least Morton can't snipe us,'' Landry consoled, leading them toward what they hoped was the pass.

They progressed slowly, the horses lathering, the men staggering and lurching, burdened with the ponderous bags, although it was cold enough now to put on their coats. The mist lifted some as they came to a notch near the summit. Heavy globs of snow commenced. Terena, half mesmerized by the bumpy movement of the mustang, looked vacantly ahead. Something visible, odd, made her come alert. Her eyes hardened, then expanded. The men, including Landry, were looking at the ground for footing. Terena thrust both tight fists to her face and screamed, the prolonged sound vibrating down the mountainside. From the top of a long stake in the center of the trail, the severed head of a coyote stared at them through glazed eyes; its swollen tongue hung long between toothy jaws, the snout curled in a snarl of death.

(14)

Far below in an aspen grove, Morton and Biggs leaned against straight white trunks. Morton cut strips of soft inner bark that he had gouged from the tree backing him. He chomped hungrily on the stringy fibers. Biggs gnawed his strips, spitting them out. "Tasteless crap. We shouldn't have lost the horses. Now we'll freeze or starve to death."

"Didn't see you helping much." After shooting the black with the broken leg, they had attempted to reach the carcass for the blankets, the tarp, and the saddlebags, which contained both food from the posse members and some abandoned by the Dar Ell gang. But the slippery siding and the crevasse proved impossible to descend. And Morton's bay had disappeared in the mountain fastness. "Wasn't for you, Biggs, I'd be closing in now."

"I ain't in condition for climbing high country."

"You got too much of a gut."

"They're on to us now. They'll try to ambush us again, so what now?"

Morton picked his teeth with a knife. "If I had a rifle, I'd have cleaned 'em out long before now."

"But we don't."

"We'll keep dogging them. On foot, carrying all that money and with little grub, they'll be hurtin'. They already are. They'll head for the nearest settlement—that's Lost

Chance. They'll send somebody in for supplies there. If we don't get them along the way, we'll get them there.''

"They're sure doing good without that Indian guide, Nasa Tom," said Biggs. "Don't understand whatever happened there. He was kind of spooky. Maybe he just run out on 'em.''

Morton said seriously, "Whoever that man is leading them—he knows this country better 'n most Indians do. He knows his way. He's big. From a distance he reminds me of Dirk Landry. But that don't make no sense—Landry leading heisters. And with women. Unless they're hostages. The way he leads them, sometimes it looks like he don't have use of his hands. And that horse, the one the second woman's on, Landry used to ride flesh like that. Makes me wonder.''

"The first girl, that's Lon Wiggins's woman. Don't know how Dar Ell allowed that," Biggs said, looking at the fringed border of forest. "I'd like to see my uncle's face when he finds out who's really threatening him.''

"You'll probably have your chance." On his hands and knees, Morton slurped some water from a trickle and rose. "Can't see the peaks anymore. It's snowing up there.''

"My uncle, he was cultured. Thought himself somebody—better than my side of the family.''

"We get his money—you can exchange places with him." Morton started along the narrow terrace.

Biggs grunted up. " 'Course, maybe I don't want to see nobody. I'm considered dead. Probably buried now near Windy Flat. I should keep it that way." Biggs referred to the badly wounded convict who had died near Windy Flat. They had slipped on Biggs's rather oversized uniform before blowing the man's features away. "I'm clear unless some of your pals sing—them they captured.''

"Come on," said Morton. "Since they lost them horses of theirs, and with them women, they're slowing something fierce.''

"Can't figure that," said Biggs, starting to pant, his belly bobbling. "What spooked their horses? And all that shooting last night. Was it some big animal?"

Engulfing snow angled wetly—a steady fall that stuck and made visibility nearly impossible. After hurling the coyote head into the brush, Landry dropped back, retreating to the fork of the trails, and swung to the left into the cathedral. Shaken by the coyote omen, the members seemed readily inclined to attempt another route. "It is a death warning," Yattero whined.

"Who the hell did that? Who's ahead of us? It's not Morton?" Ryke questioned.

"I have no idea," said a very sincere Landry.

They worked into a chaos of iron-dark ramparts, seamed and scarred with trenches and arroyos all padded softly from the previous night's snowfall; spindly-leafed alder and stunted chaparral matted the breaks. The foglike streamers parted some to reveal serrated ridges, then squirmed back around them. Quick-eyed, Landry marked the positions of those following; Lon close, leading Terena's horse, then Mollie on the chestnut, led by Yattero, then a suspicious-looking Ryke, with Dar Ell closing the rear. The showman's face had no color; his lips and fingernails had tinged bluish. His breathing had grown progressively more difficult as he faltered, dropping farther back.

"You know what the hell you're doing, Landry?" Ryke blurted. "This don't look like no way out. Besides, we're going to have to bury Dar Ell somewhere," he taunted.

"I'll climb my way out of Hades before you will," Dar Ell retorted.

Landry caught the waiting eye of Mollie. Yattero was stumbling, giving under the effort. Lon and Terena had started bickering, preoccupied with their problems. Ahead lay a cul-de-sac—a dead end, Landry knew. But to the side of the path that he had purposely forged, a chute of swirled rocks, broken and striated, dropped straight away, a plush slide of ice and snow protected on each side by thick brush.

"What the hell are you doing?" Ryke called angrily. He drew his revolver and charged double-step toward the marshal. "I don't see no pass; nothing up there."

"We have to look," said Landry.

"Maybe you're pulling something on us. And if we find a pass, maybe you figure we don't need you no longer."

"Maybe."

Ryke pivoted slightly back toward the others. "Hurry up. We're going to talk this over."

"Ride!" cried Landry. The word erupted from his toes upward as he swung his clenched hands backward in a powerful sweep, catching Ryke in the face to spin him around. The outlaw staggered but remained on his feet. Landry lunged, caught Ryke's gun hand and twisted the wrist inside as he brought a knee up hard, into the man's groin. Ryke gagged and doubled over. Clutching Ryke's forearm, Landry whirled his two hundred pounds to wrench the arm back, dislocating the limb at the shoulder joint. Ryke screamed in agony and hit the ground, his dark hat spinning away like a tiddlywink. The revolver sailed free and disappeared in a puff of snow. Landry kicked the heel of his boot into Ryke's head, knocking him senseless. The marshal ran then and dove, somersaulting into the snowy ravine to roll over and over, his body shooting down the icy chute.

At the command, "Ride," Mollie whirled the chestnut around, slapped its shoulders with the reins while heeling it in the ribs and driving the beast into Yattero, who tried to get out of the way but was knocked sideways to fall heavily, the breath going out of him.

Stunned, Dar Ell drew his short-barreled gun and dropped belly down in the snow. He saw Ryke scream out, saw the chestnut come plunging by, splattering mud and rock splinters that forced him to shield his face. He looked up to see Landry dive over the edge and disappear. "Halt," Dar Ell shouted, firing into the air. He yelled at Lon, "Get that girl. Bring her back and get the loot."

The youth pulled Terena from the mustang. "My ankle. My ankle," she bawled. Ignoring her, he launched into the saddle, spun the animal around, and thundered down the slick rise again, forcing Dar Ell to duck. Both riders vanished.

Landry continued his rolling slide down through the cottony snow until he reached bottom. He pushed to his feet and sprinted into an enclosure of high chaparral where he crawled through parapets of tumbled rocks, taking care not to shake or ripple the shrubbery and give away his position.

Coming to his senses, Ryke flopped about on the snow, searching for his gun; his right arm hung useless. Painfully, he dragged himself to an indentation, stuck his good hand in and removed his revolver, then crawled quickly to the funnel edge and peered through the dreary snowfall. Desperately, left-handed, he emptied his gun at the brush strip below. He fell back on the snow then and attempted to reload with one hand, but passed out in shock. Dar Ell and Terena sat dumbfounded.

Weak, but momentarily exhilarated, Mollie slapped the great horse faster down the rocky waste toward stands of hemlock. She threw off the money bags. The chestnut slipped once, nearly going down on the wet sheets of granite, the clothing and food bags flopping against it. She saw Lon on the mustang, falling behind. He had stopped for the money. He's not going to catch us, she thought, excited. She ducked a low branch and decided to let the horse pick its way. The chestnut sloshed into some wet snow, cut across a switchback and whinnied in fright as its hind hooves skidded. The animal dipped and swung its rump to maintain balance. But

Mollie, weak and inexperienced, pulled rein, confusing the gelding, so that it hunched back and reared slightly; the rocking twists snapped the girl forward and flung her sideways. She emitted a sharp, feminine screech before landing in a bed of fluffy snow. She lay dazed, trying to reorient herself as the chestnut clopped over to her, sniffing, checking her out.

Before she could struggle onto her horse, Lon arrived, rolled from the mustang and tackled her. His arm encircling her waist, he threw her back into the snow and twisted on top of her, his strong young arms pinning hers. "Oh no, you don't. You've gone far enough." He giggled, relishing the moment.

She squirmed under him, her tight fists pummeling his thighs. "Let me go," she spat.

He tightened his grip and let her struggle against him. "Oh, a real she-cat." The shawl fell from her, and golden hair tumbled loose, cascading around her throat and over her shoulders.

She squared her jaw, her lips curled in spite. Her green eyes glared at him. And then she ceased. Mollie looked not into the face of a youth, but at a leering man, excited by her struggling, by her flush of anger, by her helplessness in his grasp. The way he looked at her suddenly, his handsome face twisted in a lurid grin, frightened her. Her heart pounded. Alone, isolated, who would hear her screams or care? His eyes devoured her face, assessing her body. He attempted to nuzzle her as one hand slid to cup a breast. She turned her face aside. "Your girl is waiting for you," she said as nastily as she could. "She apparently wants you, sonny. I don't."

Lon withdrew. He looked at her, befuddled, wounded. Then anger filled him. He grabbed her shoulders, lifted her and slammed her back into the snow, then hauled her roughly to her feet. "Damn bitch; you're going back now."

* * *

For the next twenty minutes, with darkness closing fast, the snow unremitting, they climbed deeper into the cirque, Ryke leading, cringing with each step; he cradled his right arm with his left. The throbbing had dulled, and a paralyzing numbness settled partially through his body, making travel excruciating. Twice feeling faint, he had considered tearing one of the women from a horse and taking it for himself. He would do that in the morning, he decided. For now, any more internal conflict would be stupid, with Morton behind and Landry on the loose. But he needed medical attention, desperately, he knew.

Holding both reins, Lon guided the women on the horses; they could not chance Mollie attempting another run. A sullen Dar Ell had taken hold of the chestnut's tail. He tripped and stumbled often, for he did not watch his feet, but tilted his head back for air, his mouth hanging open. A highly nervous Yattero brought up the rear, his rifle angled across his chest. Every few steps he would rotate around, looking behind, to the sides, above, always expecting something or someone.

At last, directly ahead, the crumbled stretch of broken rocks ended under a barren rise of minarets and towers, an impassable wall—a fortress of stone. "You damn fool," Dar Ell gurgled. "There's no pass. Landry tricked us into a dead end."

"You've killed us," Terena shrilled.

"Must be the other trail—the one with the coyote head—the one I figured all along."

"All trails are cursed," Yattero moaned. "We can't get away. None of us."

"That bastard marshal," Ryke sputtered. "But he ain't going too far with his lady friend still here."

"He'll die in the cold," Lon said prophetically.

"Don't bet on it," Dar Ell scoffed. "But we will if we don't get a fire soon."

They struggled their way back down in hasty retreat to the

fork once more. The snow continued unabating, cloaking everything now. The wind wailed cruelly through the twisted heights, and the temperature plunged as darkness encroached. Where the trails diverged, Lon led them to the right up the north one, past the stake, stained dark with dried coyote blood. "We can't go on. We have to camp for the night," a fatigued Dar Ell called.

"We ain't camping close to that coyote place," Yattero objected, his face constricted with fear.

During the descent, Mollie had clutched the chestnut's mane while hunched far forward over the arched neck. "She's going to fall off. She's going to," Terena exhorted. Lon tugged the horses next to a high rock bulge and lifted the reporter from her horse. Her knees buckled, collapsing her in his arms. He half carried, half dragged her to the rock and propped her up. Dar Ell reached the rock with an extended, groping hand. He leaned against the stone and slid his body along the roughage until sinking beside Mollie. Ryke struggled up behind them, mumbling to himself, his face contorted with pain.

"Got to make a sling," Ryke grumbled. "Got to get to that Lost Chance for a sawbone. Can't stand this—that bastard Landry, he'll pay." The gunman had rotated his gun belt so that the revolver swayed next to his left hand, backward but reachable. Painstakingly, he removed his coat, unbuttoned his shirt, and pulled it and his vest open.

"Oh, God," Terena gushed, seeing the abnormal knot of shoulder joint, the injured ligaments and tissue swelling. Ryke rubbed snow over the injury, gasping in shock and some relief, but the cold penetrated him so, he worked his clothing and coat back on with the help of Lon, who then fashioned a sling from a blanket that lifted and secured the arm but did not help the pain much.

The horses nosed about, nibbling at the lichen. "Only a little grain and water left for them," said Dar Ell, his eyes feverish. "Best feed 'em now, Lon. Maybe tomorrow we can find them graze."

"Ain't got much grub for ourselves—some of that root crap—that the marshal packed for us. It's in his saddlebag on the chestnut."

Dar Ell looked at Mollie. She had lain to the side, her eyes closed, her body sunken. He shivered and turned his head away. "She's going into a coma, I think."

Terena beheld her through soft, fawn-brown eyes. "We can't leave her. But how do we take her along?"

"We got to get heat," said Lon, bustling about. "We'll all die without heat." They had double-wrapped themselves in every available blanket. The saddlebags, heavy with precious metal and currency, lay tossed askew, forgotten in the moment.

Below the timberline, Landry had hidden in a thicket of tobacco brush that gave good cover. One of Ryke's wild shots had splashed near him while fleeing, but now with the closing darkness and the cold, he knew they would not search for him. Ryke, the tormentor, the stalking panther, might have organized them and led them, but not now, with his shoulder painfully ruined, as Landry suspected. In a narrow but deeply gutted canyon, he found further refuge under an overhang. Much polished rock, deposited from a retreating glacier of long ago, and a pile of shale from some recent avalanche afforded varied building material. Landry set to sawing his bindings across a razor-edged slab. The effort warmed and revived his senses; the threads parted immediately. He removed his gloves and massaged the bruised wrists.

Methodically, he set to finding some Indian food—first some black, stringy lichen along the north fissures, hardly savory, but palatable. Then he located a hand-sized flat rock, one edge almost knife-sharp. In a wash, he chose some smooth-barked willows; he sawed the outer bark free and cut deftly into the soft inner core, stripping away tender cuts. He gnawed industriously on the bitter fibers until he noticed a small grove of lodgepole pines thirty yards below him. He tossed the willow aside and chose a young sapling. Although cutting to the inner bark proved difficult, the sugary strands had a pleasant, satisfying taste. He saved the sharp hand rock. The snowfall intensified. In a rocky cleavage, Landry searched, smiling knowingly as he uncovered some twigs and dry materials, the nest of a pack rat or a pika. He carried the crumbling structure back to the overhang.

In near darkness, Landry built a buttress of shale, packing flat rocks thickly with snow to form a semicircle around him. For a roof he pulled over him a broken fir bough that he found nearby. He wished he had a carbine so that he could rub oil over the dried grasses and twigs. He took a handful of sulfur matches, congealed in paraffin, from a coat pocket. Anxiously, he lit one and blew the flame into a growing life. The material sizzled and commenced licking around the dry branches, to send off heat. Landry lay back and removed his Stetson. His head throbbed some where the puffiness remained. He sucked on a handful of snow, then plastered it against the swelling. He thought of Mollie. She had played her part well by trying to ride. But she was so weak now. Had one of them stopped her? If not, she would ride until dark, when she would seek shelter. If she had not tied herself on, she might pass out and tumble from the big horse to perish in the cold. He wished he knew. Damn, he wished he knew. Doubt claimed him. He wished he had not encouraged her to flee. To have remained with the fugitives might have been better than to have braved the elements. At least he would know where she was now. But for the time being there was nothing he could do until just before dawn. At least he was free now to strike at Dar Ell when and where he chose. What he needed most was sleep.

* * *

Near the timberline where the fugitives had settled, Yattero tethered the two horses, giving them the last of the salvaged oats. He let them feed as best they could on some green shrubbery close by, the leaves leathery and heavy from bombarding snow. Lon had collected dead limbs and debris, but the wet made them frustratingly difficult to light. At last he managed a low, smoldering fire. Terena set a kettle of water over the weak flame, hopeful it would boil. She distributed what little food remained plus Landry's apah roots, which, surprisingly, had a sweet, nutty flavor. "The lady reporter needs something. I don't even know if she can eat," Terena pronounced.

Ryke gritted his teeth and rocked back and forth, trying to ease the pain, his free hand fingering the distorted bones and swollen ligaments at the connection between his upper arm and shoulder. The pulsing flesh bulged under the coat. He lifted and settled the arm in a vain effort to seek relief.

Dar Ell's cough had gone deeper, a rattling wheeze that robbed him of all normal voice tones. "Fire and food," he uttered. "Fire and food. Survive the night and try to find the pass."

"I will find it," said Lon. "We don't need Landry now anyway. The pass is just above us. Then we follow the ridge for a couple of miles before working down. Stupid marshal told me that."

Dar Ell sighed. "You have been loyal. You defy me, yes, like with the girl here. But you've been a godsend so far."

"I ain't turning back or giving up," said Lon tightly. "Not with what I got planned ahead."

The water boiled. Terena hung her head over the pot and breathed in the steam. Then she helped Mollie to sit up. "You sniff in," she ordered. "It'll warm all through."

Mollie gasped in the curling vapors. "I'm so cold," she apologized. "Is the marshal dead?"

Terena twisted coyly. "Oh, that big man—he's tough. He'll get away."

Mollie smiled. "Thank you." she braced herself rigidly, her eyes dilated.

Terena bubbled, "We all eat now. Get strength back."

Coughing, sneezing, clearing his throat miserably, Dar Ell joined them. He, too, inhaled the steam. Everyone had labored breath; every move cost each something. They had chosen a campsite against a low granite wall directly below what appeared to be the pass. To the right of the trail the snow kept building in a narrow moraine where a bluish glacier receded. Over the centuries winter and spring avalanches had gouged clean a swath some quarter of a mile wide, carrying tons of debris and granite chunks down the mountainside to create a devastated area swept clear of all living vegetation. Dar Ell looked out on the scoured region where colliding snow and earth had plummeted with destructive ferocity. "I don't like being so close," he said feebly.

"I ain't moving another step," said Ryke. "We're almost to the pass."

Lon cut strips of pine and hemlock branches that he webbed in a flimsy lean-to against the granite. Although the weighty snow bent it inward, the interlacing formed a snug compacting that withstood the wind and held much of what little heat they could eke from the low fire. Terena and Lon commenced bickering again. Yattero continued rotating his head like a big owl, as if expecting something or someone to swoop in. He babbled to himself, talked incoherently at times. Dar Ell kept trying to get his lungs full. He refused food, claiming nausea, although he took a swig from his flask, draining what was left. Ceremoniously, he tossed the container over the edge into the slide area, then suddenly crossed his arms to hold his chest. His mouth opened roundly with pain; his eyes closed tight.

"What's the matter?" Lon said.

"A tightness in my chest." Dar Ell garbled his words.

Touching his upper right arm, Ryke watched Dar Ell without emotion. Then he studied Mollie. Apparently, she felt his eyes roving over her body. She opened her eyes and addressed him squarely. "What's wrong with you?"

"You're a good looker, lady. Spunky, too. Get across the Sierras and find a sawbones for my shoulder, then maybe me and you can get to know each other."

"I'm afraid I'm not your type." Mollie's eyes flashed. She raised her head. "That's right. Take me. Anytime. I can't stop you."

"If I didn't hurt so, lady, I would."

Dar Ell cut in. "While you gab, nobody's on guard. The marshal's out there somewhere. And I'll give you odds he's surviving. Morton's down there. And we don't know what or who that was last night."

"Well, I ain't obliging you tonight," Ryke said in pain. "You and the others will have to hold the fort."

As the women moved into the lean-to, some coyotes staccatoed down the trail. Startled, Yattero jumped up and spilled his coffee. His eyes darted suspiciously. "This elevation's too high for coyotes, unless they're following us."

Dar Ell doubled over in spasms of body-wrenching coughs. When the tremors had subsided, he fumbled into his luggage and withdrew a sack containing coins, bills, and bullion. He secreted some into his pockets and sleeves before lying back, expended. Shortly afterward, Ryke shuffled over to Dar Ell, removed the snub-nosed revolver, patted around the body of the defenseless actor for more weapons, and when satisfied, said, "You're not going to make it, Dar Ell. These mountains are your tombstone. So I'm taking over."

Landry jerked alert, his fire out, the embers so dull they gave no glow. Something or some things of size had passed by, had crossed the ravine thirty yards downwind, moving upward, almost flitting across in the semidark. Was it a big cat? Was Morton moving in the night? Only a fool would attempt that. With most of the remaining moonlight blotted by clouds, a man could break a leg in an instant or fall to his death. Perhaps he was imagining, Landry thought. His tired body ached. The pressures and drain from the past days might cause him to hallucinate. He dismissed the thought to listen. The snow had ceased. Then he thought he saw a second slower, more deliberate movement, but he could not tell. Must be seeing things, he decided. At last he leaned back, pulled his coat tighter, and settled his hat over his face. He waited the night out without rekindling the fire, but he could not sleep.

Because Ryke could barely manipulate his body, the responsibility of guarding fell first to a surprisingly self-possessed Lon. Ryke agonized his way into the lean-to and tried to find some comfort, but the excruciating hurt of a swollen arm and shoulder tortured him throughout the hours.

At midnight a restless Yattero took the watch, but because of some mysterious phobia, he refused to sit near the low-burning fire, believing he would be too exposed in the light to some force out there. He settled near a gnarled white-bark pine that leaned over the slide area. "You're crazy—you'll freeze to death," a watching Ryke called from the lean-to.

The snow eased. A wind came up, shifting the whiteness like fine-blown powder. In the arctic cold of early morning, Lon tossed about, disturbed, to talk in his sleep. But he did not wake. Ryke, who twisted slowly, trying to find relief, heard something. With great effort he sat up and pulled a gun from his blanket. He looked at Dar Ell, who lay as if drugged. Ryke listened. He decided it was the wind or a blowing horse. Then he heard the horses stomp noisily and whinny. He looked out. The fire was nothing more than fanned embers. Yattero appeared to be sitting asleep. Ryke thought of attempting to investigate, but the effort would be too great.

As the first thread of dawn laced the eastern dark, Lon awakened to Terena crying out, protesting, "Don't. No. No." He shook her, brought her awake, her eyes wide, alarmed. The act moved a sluggish Dar Ell to worm up, his filmy eyes not focusing at first. Mollie opened her eyes. The pretty hollows of her cheeks had sunken, giving her a gaunt appearance, as of delicate carved ivory. Ryke struggled up, gun in hand, his strained features white as the surroundings.

Lon emerged from the lean-to into the clear, frigid air to slosh around. He bawled, "Oh, my God."

Ryke struggled out, his hard face twisting with repulsion. Propped frozen against the white-bark pine, Yattero, his head back, stared sightlessly across the devastated area, his rifle embraced across his chest, a thin layer of snow coating his body and his blue-black features. A raggedly gashed line girded his throat, the oozing blood solid. On his lap curved the headless carcass of a coyote.

"Don't let the women out here," Lon warned, too late, as Terena hunched out, her steps unsteady. Her familiar shuddering scream brought an unsteady Dar Ell to his feet, and a crawling Mollie.

"Someone or something slit the greaser's throat," Ryke exclaimed fearfully.

Dar Ell staggered forth like a drunk man and dropped into a hump of snow. In the ghostly silence they all looked around. Ryke and Lon held readied guns. But the gold curve of sun, far east, caressed the peaks and ignited the glistening expanse, naked, shredded by erosions and ancient eruptions, devoid of visible life.

Again Ryke enfolded his arm and tried to support the distorted shoulder with his left hand. "There's some son of a bitch out there. Landry didn't do this—Morton did. He's on our tail. Hear he's good with a knife."

Dar Ell, recovering slowly, hacked, spat, and said through

a gummy voice, "If Morton got that close, we'd all be dead. Landry told us that."

"Well, at least we got more to split now," Ryke said thickly.

Dar Ell again spat into the snow.

"Get the horses," Ryke ordered Lon, waving his Colt. "Get the women; get any provisions worth taking. Let's move, and fast."

Lon moved anxiously. "The pass—not that much snow fell. Once on top, I think we stay on the crest for about two miles north before going down. Landry hinted that."

Ryke cringed with pain, but managed to roll a cigarette from his vest, and lit it shakily with one hand. "Don't matter, really. As long as we get to Lost Chance." He then walked over beside Dar Ell and picked up the man's luggage bag and his saddlebags, taken from the swing station. "Guess we'll take these. You ain't going to need them, old boss. You ain't going to make it over. You and Landry. You two can join up." His haughty mouth twisted crookedly. Despite his hurt shoulder, he took deep pleasure in the moment. "Let's go," he barked, and walked away.

From some deep recess in his cloak, from some intertwining folds, Dar Ell produced a silver derringer, polished, perfectly fit to his hand, the ultimate in concealed deadliness. Slightly dizzy, Dar Ell sat up and hugged his elbow to his side for support, swung his arm, the derringer extended like a pointed forefinger, and fired his one and only shot into the tapered back of Harrel Ryke. The bullet splashed to the outside of the right shoulder blade, near the distorted joint. Ryke lurched around, his face twisted in shocked disbelief. Dropping Dar Ell's goods, he pulled his revolver with his left hand, awkwardly, attempting to spiral smashing death into his former boss. His shot went wide of its mark and sang away.

Coolly, Lon drew and cracked two bullets, one missing,

one sinking into Ryke's lower gut. The gunman crunched his gun to his bowels as if to keep them from pouring forth, and pitched headlong over the ridge into the snowy swath of the rock flow. Like a gray old man, Dar Ell sat dazed, the empty derringer in his hand.

Lon moved the horses out from their hitching, both still saddled. "Get on, Terena, get on the mustang." The girl obeyed as if drugged. "And I'm taking you, Miss Reporter." He pulled Mollie to her feet. She stood unsteadily until the youth placed his arm around her. "I just can't leave a pretty lady out here to die." Terena watched dully as he hoisted the woman onto the chestnut. Stiffly, Mollie pulled a blanket tight about her and closed her eyes.

Below the ridge in the snow, Ryke, badly wounded, struggled quietly toward them with great effort, the Colt still gripped in his left hand. His sallow face had hardened with desperate determination. He wormed his way, leaving a trail of streaming blood, his right arm dragging helplessly.

Humped and gasping, Dar Ell tried to get his breath as Lon walked to him. The sun broke above the horizon, tinting the cold peaks with a soft pink. "Sorry, Mr. Dar Ell, but it's my one and only chance." He picked up Dar Ell's and Ryke's saddlebags, the luggage, and then Yattero's. Gingerly, with revulsion, he pulled the bags away from the frozen arms and from under the coyote carcass. Then he tore loose the rifle and revolver and heaved them far out into the rock plunge. Then, deftly, he cut the Mexican's money belt free.

Dar Ell had a look of primal gloom, of profound disappointment. "You, Lon? You?"

"You taught me. Seize the opportunity. Remember? That's what you taught me."

"You ungrateful little Judas," Dar Ell hissed. "There's small choice in rotten apples."

Lon looked at Dar Ell combatively. "I know where the

pass is now. I know I can find my way from here. And I have an old map of the region which will help.''

"And you'll just leave me to die?''

"Landry will find you.'' Lon climbed on the mustang behind Terena, clicked his tongue and goaded the horses into a brisk climb.

Dar Ell picked up a rock, rose, staggered toward the retreating animals and tried to heave it, but fell flat on his face in the slush. Ryke, who had managed to pull himself partway up, saw the horses with their hunched riders round the top of the slide area. He fired at them, futilely, the bullets wailing into the mountain. Above the riders at the head of the devastation area, a broad sheet of new-fallen snow, not yet congealed to the glacier, broke away to slide a few feet and stop.

"You, Dar Ell. You there,'' Ryke called weakly. "I'll get you if it's the last thing I do.''

Dar Ell grinned, sat up, tossed back his head and laughed, a high, mocking cackle. He plucked some printed money from his sleeves and coins from his pants. "Yours, Ryke.'' He threw the coins over the edge to sink in the wet crust. The paper bills fluttered about, and some drifted far down on the updrafts. "Too much of a good thing,'' he called, laughing uncontrollably. "An ill-favored thing, but mine own.''

"You're a damned fool, Dar Ell,'' Ryke shouted gutturally.

"Oh, I am fortune's fool. And by a sleep to say we end the heartaches and the thousand natural shocks.'' He gurgled in mirth. "For the rest is silence.''

Mired, draining blood, Ryke could move no farther. He shot once toward the sound of Dar Ell's voice; but the bullet merely flailed snow, its sound echoing and reechoing.

"That he is mad, 'tis true, 'tis pity.'' Before Dar Ell could emote another word, a force hit him from behind, sprawling him. Landry bent the actor's left arm back, knocked the derby away, and clutched the long black hair, forcing his head back. His eyes bulging, Dar Ell tried to twist around, but Landry easily overpowered him, then dragged him away from the chance of being hit by Ryke's wild shooting. From his coat pocket he produced the rope that had bound his hands, and with what remained, he secured the showman. The man lay back in resigned defeat. "You don't have much of a prisoner. You'll have to carry me back."

"I'm taking you on to Lost Chance. We're going after Mollie. Besides, a stage still comes through."

"You told me it didn't."

"I don't always tell the truth."

Ryke fired again.

"Don't shoot, you fool," Landry shouted. "This steep a slope, and new snow, you could start an avalanche."

Ryke gasped out, "Help me, Landry, I'm bleeding to death." Cunningly, methodically, every movement nearly unbearable, he reloaded his revolver.

"Throw out your gun and belt so I can see it," Landry ordered. "I'll see what can be done." He asked Dar Ell, "You got more loads for that derringer?"

Dar Ell wagged his head. "They're in my belongings on the horses. Look!" he cried. On a ridge below the pass, two men appeared. They stopped and looked back.

"It's Rattlesnake Morton. They must have shortcutted— gotten ahead of us," said Landry through gritted teeth.

"My God. My God, it's Amos Biggs—my nephew, the guard."

"Ah, now the pieces begin fitting."

Morton opened fire. Even at the great distance, the whining lead forced the marshal and his new prisoner behind a log. "He can't hit us this far away, can he?" Dar Ell wondered.

"He may be trying to make noise."

Morton and Biggs stood to the side of the glacier and above

the chute. Ryke answered Morton with his own volley. Both Morton and Biggs blasted back. As Landry had feared, a rumble sounded. An immense slab of new-fallen snow, wet and heavy, pulled away from the ancient glacier and humped up over a lower sheet that gave way to crumble and heave in a flowing torrent. The hissing rumble became an insistent, thunderous motion as cartwheels of snow came hurtling down faster, tumbling rocks and dirt, a wall of immense white.

(15)

After cutting through the narrow pass, Lon removed a map and studied it. "We keep to the ridge for a spell," he told Terena. "We had to get through the E-sha Pass. Now we follow the crest for about two miles. Then the trail drops down straight west along a divide between the headwaters of the Cosumnes and the American rivers. We hit an old pack train route, then the wagon road to Lost Chance," Lon gloated.

"How do you know?" Terena questioned.

"A friend told me."

"What friend? And where did you get that map?"

Mollie perked up.

Lon chuckled. "You're not marrying no dumb kid. I been a step ahead of Mr. Dar Ell for some time now."

They moved north two miles, paralleling the crest of the divide, keeping on the western side of the jagged rim where the snow spread thin, melting already, not piling in the high drifts so characteristic of the lee side. Streamers of sunlight flowed over the peaks and reflected gold off the misty foothills and the marshy fog of the Sacramento Valley. They looked down coalescing ridges, rounded and wooded, separated by muscular rivers that flexed dramatically, punching their way to the great valley and ultimately to the sea. "Down there, Terena, that's our new home." Lon motioned. But the girl seemed more interested in surviving the weary ride, for she gave the vast region but scant notice. Mollie hung on, faint at times, her lips tight, her body rigid in a posture of both defiance and determination.

Despite the two nights of light snow, strong winds had pushed most of the drifts across the exposed heights and on over, leaving the ancient trail readily visible. Those behind could easily follow their tracks, Lon realized, but his head start and the horses gave him a decided advantage.

"Can't we rest?" Terena wailed.

"Not yet." Lon looked back and saw Mollie leaning far to one side. He drew the buckskin up. "Don't fail us now, lady. I just can't stop for you if you give out." Both horses pawed, anxious to continue.

Mollie wiped her face and nose with another handkerchief. "Don't you worry. I look at this as one of my more difficult assignments."

Lon's stolid features cracked into a boyish chortle. "You're all right, lady." He heeled the mustang ahead. The sterile granite spikes gleamed dully in the steady light. Below, the forests and the dark, sunken canyons beckoned, yawning with the openness of promise and assured escape. When they rested, Lon exchanged horses. He tied all the gold, currency, and coins on the chestnut; the blankets, clothes, utensils, and remaining food on the mustang. He ordered the woman onto the buckskin and swung proudly onto the big gelding.

"What are you doing?" Terena implored. "Why all this?"

"'Cause I say so," Lon asserted. "We got big things ahead of us."

"Then how much farther? We gotta turn down soon, someplace ahead."

Lon's features shifted in forced judgment. "See that knob ahead—a tinker's knob—a half mile ahead?"

"Yes."

"I figure that's where we go down."

From the distance behind, something quaked, accompanied by a muffled roar. "Thunder? There's not that many clouds yet," Terena said, puzzled. Mollie twisted stiffly to look back.

"That ain't thunder," Lon said. "That's an avalanche."

Rumbling, the first wall of snow crashed by, spewing foamy whiteness, erupting, cannonading, tumbling, a tumultuous movement a quarter of a mile across, still streaming off the glacier. Landry grasped Dar Ell, lifted the lanky form and threw him away from the avalanche area, then dived on top of him, rolled over and flung the man again, twisted on top of him, rolled, and heaved him once more. The cascading force exploded past, swept by the ridge, and took a screaming Ryke with it, widened and curled over the shrunken form of Yattero and carried it away. The reverberations continued as the avalanche flushed on down the mountainside, but not before covering the route they had come, burying the E-sha Trail here and there in huge mounds. Landry dragged Dar Ell behind a refuge of volcanic knobs.

Under the break of the pass, Morton and Biggs observed with guns in hand. Morton smiled with amusement. Biggs stood awed at the fearful might of the avalanche. "Did it get them all?"

"Couldn't tell for sure. Think so. But it don't make no difference. It's the kid with them women that we want. Come on." He holstered his revolver and stepped out with vigor despite the impeding snow.

For some time Landry and Dar Ell lay waiting. "Wish to hell I could have gotten a gun," Landry lamented, peering up the slope. Nothing moved.

"Can't go back now. And it'll be hell to pay ahead," said Dar Ell.

"Oh, we're going on, just like I said." He hauled the showman to his feet. "Just get to the summit, then from there on it's level until we start down. We can make it to Lost Chance before nightfall if we try."

They climbed to the pass, a narrow cleft made by a shifting fault block. "Morton will be waiting in ambush," Dar Ell sputtered. He stumbled and staggered, but Landry held him steady, almost carrying him along.

"Don't think so," said Landry. "They're pushing ahead. Morton realizes the kid has the loot. He probably thinks we're dead." A half hour later they crossed the summit and let up for Dar Ell to get his breath. Wheezing, he sank into the snow, his knees buckling under him. Landry lifted him to a dry rock. Both men had wet trousers from wallowing in the snow. "We'll both be lucky if we don't catch our death of pneumonia," the marshal said. He gave the showman some fifteen minutes to recuperate, then lifted the protesting man to his feet, again half carrying him as they struggled along the Pacific crest, following the hoofprints and the later tracks of Morton and his partner. Mist curled around them, obscuring the more gradual westward drop, bare still, but promising thick forests in the timbered belt. Suddenly Landry stopped, jolting the swaying Dar Ell, whose heavy-lidded eyes attempted to focus. "Smoke."

"Smoke." Dar Ell repeated the words without fathoming anything.

"Yes, from behind those rocks up there." Landry pointed. Nothing seemed to appear, and then a frail, whitish vapor coiled above a ring of blunt rocks overlooking the trail. Holding Dar Ell back of him, Landry approached cautiously to peer inside the stone enclosure. Powdery embers had been fanned into life by the rising wind.

"Campfire?" Dar Ell asked.

Landry shook his head. "Indian death sign." A sizable fire had been built on an oblong mound. Removing the sharp rock from his coat, the marshal began digging and scraping, pushing the smoldering embers away where they sizzled and steamed upon touching the snow. A few inches deeper and Landry probed into the flesh of a blotched forearm crossed over a charred black vest and soiled shirt.

"God!" Dar Ell gulped. "What is it?"

Landry scratched around the puffy form of what had been a human with gray-streaked hair. He then excavated at what he judged the midpoint until he found a belt with sheath. He removed a battered hunting knife and tucked it in his belt Then, with care, he pushed the mushy covering back over the body.

"Who the hell is it?" Dar Ell pursued.

"Your friend, Nasa Tom." Landry tossed the sharp rock away and washed his hands in the snow.

"Murdered?"

Landry pulled his gloves on. "Can't tell for sure, but it looks like somebody parted his skull, then gave him a proper Paiute burial. Left him with some earthly remains and then burned the spot to keep away bad spirits."

Lon Wiggins, sitting confidently on the chestnut in the center of a wagon road, ran his hands gleefully over the stuffed saddlebags and sacks that draped from the straps and the horn to surround him. He entwined his fingers in the long mane and felt the magnificent animal under him, the head and neck bobbing with each rhythmic step. "Didn't figure on this bonus," he tossed smugly to Terena. Both women had dismounted temporarily, Terena sore and weary, Mollie faint and nauseated. "Never dreamed I'd have horseflesh like this."

Mollie walked from the trail into some trees and sat down on a rock to lower her head on her knees. Terena's moist eyes clouded. One tear slid down an olive cheek as she approached Lon to look up in condemnation. "You shouldn't have brought that woman,'' she blurted. ''She'll die on us. You should have left her for the marshal.''

''For all we know, Landry's dead.''

''Do you honestly believe that?''

''What the hell you want me to do? Take her to the nearest sheriff? I was trying to save her.''

''Were you, or did you want a hostage?''

''Do you honestly believe that?''

''I don't know what to believe anymore.''

''We'll try to get her to Lost Chance, but the truth is, she's slowing us.'' Lon studied the reporter. ''We're probably going to have to leave her.''

Terena's immense eyes beheld her lover in a new light. ''Where? Along the road here? Maybe there won't be any more people along.''

''There will be. I'd leave her if I thought she wouldn't talk. But we can't chance that. My friend told me there's a cabin not far from here, with food there, hopefully. He marked it on my map. If she doesn't get better, we can leave her there. Give us time to get away.''

''She can't fend for herself.''

''Somebody will find her.''

''Who? When?''

''I don't know, damn it,'' he snapped. ''She's just a burden. Besides, she's not our responsibility.''

''Then whose responsibility is she? You brought her.''

''Sometimes I wish to hell I'd brought only myself.'' Angrily, Lon tugged on the reins, backing the chestnut.

''You didn't tell me it was going to be like this,'' Terena wailed, injured, her back vigorously erect.

''Oh shut up,'' Lon said sharply. ''You're richer now than a queen. We're richer than a king and queen.''

''You didn't say it was going to be like this.''

Lon glared at her. ''Get that woman out of the trees and on the horse.'' Lon moved his horse down the road. Several times they had heard freighters approaching and had been forced to hide in the brush until the teams had passed. But as the day waned, the travelers became fewer. Gradually, they dropped into the upper mother lode country, into the yellow pine and the incense cedar, where stately sugar pines held long branches out like great arms at right angles. The dogwood leaves fluttered reddish purple in the wind. The sun, firm in the southern sky, backlighted the black oak leaves, golden-brown and topaz. The rose-pink of poison oak and wild grape, the burgundy of blueberry, contrasted dramatically with the evergreens. A thousand feet below, between great matronly hills, the South Fork of the American river droned westward through a sculptured gorge, a green glide of water laced with white foam, a stupendous boulder trough where a generation of miners had panned and sluiced for gold. But neither Lon nor Terena saw or cared. Mollie rode with her eyes closed.

As they rounded a dizzying curve, Lon pointed. Far down on a wooded benchland overlooking the canyon, the weathered buildings of Lost Chance appeared, the main street nearly empty except for a few wagons and some horses switching at a hitching rail. Beneath town the step roofs of a stamp mill receded. Lon pulled the chestnut to the roadside, turning it to yank from side to side.

"What now?" Terena asked, her voice tremulous. She had her arms around Mollie, supporting her. They stopped. Terena helped Mollie down once more, took her to a flat of squat manzanita and assisted her in bedding down for a few minutes. The damp banks of the mineralized earth gleamed russet-red.

"Pretty," Mollie said wistfully.

Terena returned to Lon and looked up at him expectantly. "She can't make it much further."

"The cabin's not far ahead, I figure. We get the lady there—let her rest, and hope there's some grub for her." Lon looked at his map. "Outside of town, up the hill a few miles, is an abandoned stamp mill and mine. It's right here." He held out his map and poked a finger to the spot. "We never have to go into town, we go to the old mine."

"How do you know all that?"

"I just know."

"What's happening, Lon? Please, what's happening?" Troubled, her face puckered.

"Nothing's happening. It's just that I'm in charge now."

"This isn't like you. Why didn't you tell me all this? What you are trying to do? You're hiding something."

"We're going to that abandoned mine. Somebody's waiting for us." Lon was not looking at her, but at the hill above Lost Chance.

"Who?"

"Somebody with all the supplies we'll need. A partner—somebody I wouldn't want to double cross. Now get the lady back on your horse."

For a time Landry and Dar Ell treaded behind the distant hoof marks of the horses, slushing deeply in wet ground. Here and there beside the tracks, sometimes smudging into them, were the booted imprints of two men. At last, south of a promontory like a tinker's knob, Landry said, "Ordinarily we'd go to that rocky point yonder and start down. Instead, hang on. We're going straight down from here. The kid may have the horses, but we can shortcut him maybe, and possibly catch him and Morton." He smiled. Wherever the horses led, Morton would be there. They dropped through a carpet of manzanita into the white-bark pine and hemlock.

"Without guns, what happens if we catch them?" Dar Ell mumbled, his face screwed up and anxious.

"That's my problem." The action carried them on down into a spine of red fir and silver pine, where they emerged onto a once trodden road now partially overgrown. "Old pack train route," Landry explained. "Goes by a line cabin once used by miners and teamsters for a storm shelter and for caching. Might be some grub there."

"You knew that all the time," Dar Ell fretted. "Then we didn't have to go into Lost Chance."

"Not necessarily. There might not be food there. And if there is, I'm sure it wouldn't have been enough for all of us."

Black clouds billowed behind them, forcing a wind to sing in the branches. A light rain began, and silver slivers of distant lightning played across the peaks. From the canopy of some red fir a pair of sooty grouse clattered away, sailed to an open limb, and stretched their necks, staring stupidly at the invaders. Landry could see one clearly. Even with a pistol, he could have killed it—delicious roasted. He licked his lips.

They proceeded through meadowlands where cascading water made green champagne in bubbly pools. The startled fat deer, migrating, eyed them within easy rifle range. Chunky red squirrels came down to the ends of the flouncy branches to scold and protest their presence. "Damn," said Landry. "I could almost club them with my hat. Good eating. Maybe the best."

Revolver in hand, Lon thrust Terena from the cabin. "Get on that horse, and fast." Crying, the girl floundered into the saddle, her skirts above her hips, revealing full fleshy legs. Lon attempted to bound onto the chestnut, misjudged the height and fell off. He caught the saddle horn and clambered aboard, cussing and spouting. He spun the horse and shot at Biggs, fifty yards away, skirting the edge of the clearing.

Terena kicked the buckskin into a spur of eastern woods that nearly touched the cabin. As Lon attempted to join her, Morton rounded the building, extended his gun and snap shot, triggering it as fast as he could work the mechanism. Rusty from lack of practice, the bullets sprayed crazily—but one hit, splattering part of Lon's thigh away above the right knee.

The youth, low over the chestnut, his face drained with fear, felt the impact, felt himself float for an instant, almost leaving the horse as it lunged into the embracing underbrush, his blood splashing about the enclosing lilacs. The girl and the boy rode recklessly, the horses bolting without direction somewhere northeast, on and on, over logs, down bushy aisles, under limbs that nearly unseated them, on until emotionally depleted. Terena reined her courageous mount into a glade; sobbing, she looked back to see the big chestnut thunder up, rear, spewing lather as Lon tumbled away to land flat on his back in the soft needles. He sat up, touched his leg and felt a warm wetness. His hand came away dripping crimson. "Oh, my God," he cried. Terena dropped to his side.

"What do we do?" Her hands reddened as she attempted to stem the blood flow.

Lon tore his neckerchief free and wrapped it above his knee. "We have to find the mine. Find my friend."

"No," she protested. "We have to get you help."

He shook his head. "No. No. Cut some blankets up; hold me in."

"I do what I can," Terena jabbered, "but we got to get help. A doctor in that town."

"No," Lon said fiercely. He looked up into her face; his eyes had a sick sheen. "You got to get me on the big horse. We can't lose now what's ours."

Back near the cabin, Morton stood watching, frustrated. Biggs reeled toward him across the opening. "You got him. You got him."

"You horse's ass," Morton raged. "We could have gotten 'em, trapped 'em, killed 'em in the cabin. But you, you stupid idiot, you showed yourself. I told you to wait, to cover me.''

"The Mex girl, she seen me. I heard her scream. She seen me," Biggs bellowed defensively. "I had to rush 'em."

"Damn near. Damn near got them." Morton grumbled, replacing his gun.

"Where now?" Biggs asked meekly.

"We go on to Lost Chance and wait."

"Lost Chance?"

"Them two don't have much food that I know of, and that kid is hurting bad. They don't have no choice but to find help."

Ahead, Landry and Dar Ell heard a loud battery of exchanged gunfire. "Hurry up," Landry barked, swinging Dar Ell in front of him with such force that the showman almost pitched over.

"What are you doing?" Dar Ell demanded. "We don't have guns."

After fifteen minutes of effort, the old shelter cabin appeared, blended in cool shadows and golden sunlight, a crude structure of pine logs and shakes, with a stone fireplace at one end and a few outbuildings, the barn and corral all in decay and broken disarray. Cautiously, Landry hunkered down in the brush, Dar Ell beside him. Landry untied Dar Ell's hands.

"What the hell you doing?"

"Temporary change of plans." His hands free, Dar Ell faced the marshal, his eyes darting with temptation. "Don't try it," Landry warned, "you wouldn't get two steps." He then sat the showman against a sapling, but not before knifing off any low branches that might interfere or poke into the man's back. He tied Dar Ell's hands behind him around the base. "Just to keep you put till I get back."

"What if you don't get back?"

"Just pray to the coyote god that I do." Landry swung right into the thick foliage that bordered the eastern end of the cabin. By the trampled ground he could see that horses had been tethered for a time in front and that they had headed off in great bounds toward the east. He looked about. Nothing moved. Knife in hand, he stole close. Afternoon light filled much of the cabin. He rolled by a partially boarded window and saw something, a form on a bunk. Despite the old wound in his leg, Landry rounded the cabin like a young Indian buck in athletic competition. He kicked the door open, to see Mollie wrapped in blankets on a bed of pine needles. He approached, his bruised head pounding from effort. Her eyes closed, she did not appear to be breathing. He touched the woman. She shook involuntarily, her eyes opening wide, startled, absorbing the surroundings and then him, momentarily without recognition. Quickly they registered elation.

"Dirk Landry," she whispered, turning her head, trying to sit up.

He restrained her. "You frightened me. You were so quiet."

"Thank God you're here. I was so scared they'd killed you. Your head, how is it?"

"Fine. The kid and his girl, they abandoned you here? Just left you?"

"I got so weak. The girl, Terena, she didn't want to leave me, but I slowed them. It took forever to get here." Tears welled in her eyes. "They stopped here to look for food, and the young man and girl started arguing over leaving me. Then she screamed. I thought he'd hurt her, but they ran out, frantic. That's when I heard shooting."

"Take it easy," Landry consoled.

"You need to know."

"All right. What happened?"

"I don't know, really. I passed out. When I came to, Morton and the other man were in here looking at me."

"In here?"

"I was petrified. I thought sure they would kill me. But they just looked at me and then ransacked the place, I guess for food."

Landry boiled inside. He nearly cursed bitterly, but said softly, "Lon will pay." He had never killed a man so young, except once, an ego-crazed twenty-year-old who had fantasized himself as a shootist of legendary proportions. Landry had tried to cool the swaggering gunslinger, had tried to back him down with sensible reasoning and intimidation. He had always regretted that killing, as unavoidable as it was. But this Lon Wiggins—an arrogant, greedy pup, too big for his britches, who could leave a sick woman to die alone or at the hands of Morton. Secretly, Landry welcomed a showdown.

"Was there any food in this place?" Landry looked over the shabby setting, the hearth missing some stones; a table and chairs, crude and broken; the shelves cobwebbed and empty, strewn with flour that whitened the walls and floor from crudely torn sacks.

"None," Mollie said, "not a thing. They still had a little of those roots you picked but that's about all."

"Looks like a marten's gotten in here—destructive little creatures. A terror with cabins and food. But it's good that he did, maybe. It means that that couple, or at least one of them, will have to go into Lost Chance for supplies." Landry tried to put her at ease. "I'm going to get you there for medical help right away."

Landry released Dar Ell. "We're heading to Lost Chance, promptly."

"You letting the kid get away?"

"Morton may have bought us some time. Right now we got the reporter to think about." He swung his head toward the cabin. "She's in there, in bad shape."

"What was all the shooting?"

"Morton and the kid. I don't know if anyone got hit, but he apparently sent the kid and his girl running like hell in a direction that's not toward the town."

"How did they all get here so fast?"

"I told you this would be a gamble, a race. At least we cut the distance and almost got here first." Landry marched Dar Ell toward the cabin. "I'll check around before clearing out."

"You'll lose them." Dar Ell grinned. "Morton will kill the kid and be long gone with the loot. Or maybe not. That kid is more capable than I ever gave him credit for."

Landry looked hard at his prisoner. "Right now I must get the woman help if she is to live. And I have a feeling Morton and the kid will be finding their way there, too. If we hurry, we might still beat them all. And, of course, there is a cell there waiting for you. Your part in this ordeal will be over."

In the cabin, Dar Ell and Mollie stared at one another in silence, their eyes holding, mingling with a bombardment of emotions. As if in explanation, Dar Ell said, "When sorrows come, they come not single spies but in battalions."

"I'm taking you to Lost Chance," Landry promised Mollie. "It's not too many miles down the road. Not much of a town anymore, but there will be people, food, and warmth, and when you're better, a stage to Placerville. I'll contact your uncle, since I'll be taking Dar Ell that way, once I've settled with the kid and Morton."

"You'll lose your felons because of me."

"You're more important for now."

"I appreciate that. I'll try to walk out," she said sluggishly but bravely, sitting up at an angle.

"I have an idea. I'm going to borrow that axe in the corner," Landry said, referring to a lumberjack's large double-edged tool. He knew that reaching Lost Chance would be difficult at best. He doubted she could walk far, even if supported in his arms. Her constant enemy: cold, had chilled and numbed her, tapped her energy. He had seen the warning signs in others: uncontrollable shivering, trembling hands, stumbling, drowsiness. The grave danger would be her lapsing into a coma. Good food, rest, heat, and attentive care could counter growing dangers. He had to get her to Lost Chance. And soon.

As for Dar Ell, Landry had dismissed him as next to useless in transporting Mollie. But he would push the man. Difficulties lay in Dar Ell's lack of conditioning, and perhaps most of all, the failure of his dream. His shortness of breath, the cough and tightness of chest, could be the beginning of pneumonia or simply a reaction to high altitude. Only time would tell.

Landry took Dar Ell outside. "We're going to look things over, and I want an eye on you." Landry studied the hoofprints that revealed dramatic twistings and turnings. They followed them into the spur of woods. Landry grew rigid, crouched suddenly, working his injured leg at an angle for support.

"What's the matter?" Dar Ell worked his bound wrists for relief.

"These lilac bushes." Landry motioned.

Dar Ell tightened. "Blood."

"Someone or something got hit in that shooting. See, they went like crazy into the woods, heading northeast."

"Probably hit a horse."

"Might have," Landry said dryly, hoping it was not the chestnut. But he noted the distance of the mighty strides and decided that the horses remained in good condition.

"You can't get to Lost Chance, not with that sick woman," Dar Ell said cheerfully.

"Oh, but we will. And I have a feeling Morton will be there waiting."

* * *

Landry's presence sparked life into Mollie. Her face took color and her voice had a lilt. Even Dar Ell seemed less sallow, his coughing less wracking at the lower elevation. Landry axed two eight-foot fir boughs, linking them with strips from the torn flour sacks and long-abandoned harnesses. He had Mollie lie in the cushioning fan of the boughs and secured her to them with Dar Ell's cloak, tying the sleeves around the limbs. "That's an expensive piece of cloth," Dar Ell complained.

Landry untied the showman's bindings. "You'll get your fancy cloth back, and you won't need it with the sweat you're going to work up." He ordered Dar Ell to take the base of one limb while he took the base of the second, the axe in his left hand. For a mile they dragged Mollie down the pack trail. She cried out frequently, as the bouncing and jolting wrenched her body and pinched her flesh. Landry looked back frequently to see her grit her teeth and wince.

Dar Ell's breathing seemed fuller and deeper, leading Landry to assume that the man's problems had been mostly altitude. But after another half mile the showman began tottering and reeling. Binding the man's hands again, Landry took the limbs up like traces and pulled Mollie by himself, forcing Dar Ell to stay ahead. Twice they had to stop and cut fresh boughs, restructuring them as the friction of the earth tore needles and smaller branches away.

Once as they rested, Landry appealed to Mollie to bear a little more, the stage road was not far. She assured him she could make it, but her timorous voice did not convince. On the next haul she passed out. When they reached a U in the trail, Landry decided to cut across, hopefully saving time and distance.

"It'll kill her," Dar Ell observed.

"Not with the two of us." The marshal once again released the man. "While she's out she won't feel it." Side by side they bumped and slid their way.

"I can't keep up," Dar Ell moaned.

"Take it easy, damn it," Landry warned, seeing the woman's head flop back and forth. "We could break her neck." The bobbing and jouncing was impossible to control over the rocks and fallen slash. He wondered if their hurrying was a mistake.

Compassionately, Landry looked back at the woman, and stepped on a rounded rock, which rolled. He lost his footing and fell; trying desperately to save Mollie, he tossed the double-bitted axe to the side and held the stretcher up, but landed on his back, the wind going out of him. Stunned, he shook his head, fighting the black fuzziness that flushed through him. He saw Dar Ell pick up a large rock in both hands, large enough to bash in a man's skull. His senses clearing, Landry pulled the knife from his belt and poised it. Dar Ell hesitated. Landry, lying cramped in some brushy snags, looked up at the imposing sight of the tall man, with the rock swaying overhead. "Try it," the marshal hissed. "If you miss, I'll cut your guts out and leave you for the buzzards."

"I got nothing to lose."

"Except the last of your pride and your self-respect. If you want the murder of a marshal and the death of a girl on your conscience, go ahead and try."

On the stage road to Lost Chance, a skinner wheeling a mule train of dry goods blinked in disbelief as two men appeared from the woods in front of him, hauling a stretcher of boughs holding an unconscious woman, her long hair cascading about her.

On Main Street above the Dry Diggins Saloon, Leander Morton and Amos Biggs waited in a corner room. The scrolled bureau, wrought-iron beds, chipped porcelain bowl and pitcher had seen better days, especially the peeling wallpaper with faded fronds and big cockatoos. Morton, grubby still from the trail, sat in a chair to the side of an open window and scanned the street. An autumn breeze billowed a lacy white curtain. A second side window offered a view through the alley toward the canyon, and an active stamp mill below. Beyond the buildings across the main street, a forested mountainside slanted away. Morton gnawed the cork from a whiskey bottle, spat it on the floor, and guzzled a long draw.

Amos Biggs, freshly shaved, with a new set of duds, sat at a squat table and forked a dinner delivered by a comely maid: fried steak smothered in onions, beans, stewed tomatoes with bacon rinds, and fluffy golden biscuits. He chewed and gulped, chewed and gulped. "Ain't you going to eat?"

"Plenty of time for that later."

"Tastes good, considering you paid with my money." Biggs referred to Morton's generosity. The room, the liquor and food had all been paid by him from the money cached at Windy Flat, money promised Biggs.

Morton gargled some whiskey, spat at a spittoon, and licked his lips greedily, his wolfish eyes roving over the street and buildings. "That six thousand ain't nothing compared to what the kid's carrying."

"Could be they won't come in."

"It'll be that Mexican girl who comes in. They ain't capable of livin' off the land, and that kid's hurtin'. If he don't need a doc, he'll need aid, bandages and things. And you, Biggs, you're going to get off your fat buns and hit the street out there to be damn sure when she comes in and where. You understand?"

Biggs choked on his steak. "Me? I don't know how to handle no little filly like that."

"You don't." Morton sucked a draft of liquor. "Just let me know. You report immediately. There ain't that many people in this camp. Shouldn't be that hard to see her or that kid. If it's the girl, we'll follow her out of town, right back to her beau. Meanwhile I'll cover from here.''

His mouth full, Biggs said, ''Them people was lookin' us over good when we come in.''

''This is a dying camp. They got nothin' better to do. Our only concern is that kid and his haul. He's got it all, and we're going to get it.''

A thought of relief brightened Biggs's puffy features. ''I'll be free, set for life. Authorities think I'm dead, all except my uncle.'' He grew serious, his face clouding. ''Dar Ell suspects me, I'm sure. He and that other man—the big one— saw us clearly.''

''They don't worry me—appeared like that avalanche got 'em anyway.''

''Sure hope it did.''

''If it did, I'll never know.''

''Know what?''

''Who that big fellow was that led them. Don't makc sense still, but he shore reminded me of that Landry fellow.''

(16)

"She going to make it?" Landry asked.

In a back room of the Long Tom Hotel before a sparkly fire, three men and an older woman crowded around Mollie, who lay bundled in layers of thick blankets, unconscious. Judah Mayberry, a crusty little man, his red face cross-hatched with creases—horse doctor and only medical source in town—replied slowly. "Don't know yet. All we can do is keep her warm."

"And pray," said the older woman.

"This is Mae Bingham, wife of the manager here. Nobody in town will give her better care."

"I'll be with her every minute, Marshal," said the chunky woman, rosy-cheeked with crinkly blue eyes and a pug of white hair. "I'm going to keep heated rocks in her bed. Maybe I'll give her a mustard plaster. I don't like that rattle in her chest."

"I appreciate it all," said Landry, removing his badge and tucking it in a vest pocket. Under an arm he carried Dar Ell's rolled-up cloak. "I'd also appreciate you people keepin' under your hats that I'm a marshal. I got business in this town. I can move better if no one suspects a lawman."

"Yes," said the third man, Lew Dutton, owner of the livery stable and the town constable—a gawky, rawboned chap, thin of neck, with a long nose and pointed ears. "We don't get many lawmen around here much anymore."

"We'll keep it under our hats, Marsh— I mean, mister," Mayberry said.

"I'll be in touch." Landry and Dutton strolled out back toward the livery stable, where the constable maintained an office that served both his business and the two connecting cells, one now occupied by Jonathan Dar Ell. "I still want to see the animals in your stable. You say you haven't seen a blond youth about twenty and a Mexican girl, pleasantly plump. They'd have a buckskin mustang and a big red Morgan—mine."

"No sir, I ain't had no visitors for the last two days, no new horses."

"They were ahead of us. Should have beat us here. They may have got lost or are afraid to come in. But they're short of supplies, and I think one of them is wounded. We've got to keep a lookout for them."

"I'll alert a few people in town we can trust. There's a few here who never miss a thing."

"Did you see two men on foot? One kind of heavy. He'll look somewhat dragged out. The other one's a hard looker— short, powerful, with long hair and a mustache. You'd remember him if you saw him, especially his eyes."

"Hope to hell he didn't show, don't need that type in town. 'Course, they could have walked in through a back alley and done their business. All types pass through here."

"Well, the big-bellied one is a former guard at the Nevada State Prison, who went in cahoots with some prisoners. His name is Amos Biggs."

Dutton swallowed; his Adam's apple skittered along his celery neck. "Not that big break in Carson?"

"That's the one."

"Driver on the stage through here this morning said they captured or killed most of them."

"Well, one of them they didn't get, the hard looker, is Rattlesnake Morton, their leader."

"God almighty. There's a second stage in shortly, one from Tahoe. We only get two through here anymore. The driver on that one may have heard something."

"I'm going to prowl around the saloons. Maybe you can set me up somewhere—not obvious, but where I can see the street, especially the general store or stores."

"Sure, we have one, Donnovan's General Store. In fact, there's an old abandoned newspaper office just above it with a side entrance. I could tell Donnovan there'll be somebody interested in the equipment, what's left. This camp hasn't had a newspaper in fifteen years, you know. From there you have a view of the front street, the alley, and out back."

"Also, I'd be much obliged if you'd check the registry at the hotel and wherever there's rooms available. Talk to the clerk. Morton and Biggs won't use their real names, of course, but someone just might remember them."

"There'd be only two places, the Long Tom Hotel and over the Dry Diggins Saloon. I'll check. Just who is this fancy man you brung in?"

"It's a long story, but he's involved with Morton and Biggs, so you'll have to keep an eye on him."

After walking through the backside of the old town, rustic and worn, smelling resinous in the pine-warm afternoon, they entered the spacious livery stable. "All the flesh in here are for rent or are owned by the townsmen," said Dutton.

Landry looked over the munching creatures, satisfied that he could not recognize any. "Not that I doubt your word, I just had to be sure."

"I understand. This boy and Mexican girl, what did they do?"

"Just say Morton and I are both looking for them. The boy, a Lon Wiggins, got away with a Wells Fargo heist. But I doubt if the kid appears. It'll be the girl, I figure, unless she was the one who was hurt. They'll have to get supplies before continuing."

"What else can I do?"

"I wanted a shave and bath and some new clothes, but I'll have to forego that luxury. But I'll need to borrow a couple of side arms, a belt, and some ammunition."

They went into the jail, where Dutton outfitted the marshal, who checked the revolvers for balance and feel while working the triggers. "Two more things."

"Sure."

"Could you sneak a rifle up there above the general store? It wouldn't look good for a stranger to walk up there carrying one, especially into an abandoned office. Might arouse suspicions."

"No sooner said than done."

"And could you round me up two or three trustworthy kids that I could pay to keep an eye out? I'll pay a bonus if they report seeing any of the wanted."

"No problem. Jake our barber has two boys. Do you need money?"

"No." Landry dug into his front pants pockets and withdrew some coins. "About the only thing I didn't lose. Those kids should work through you. Keep me out of it until you got something for sure."

Landry looked in on Dar Ell, who sat sulking in a corner. "You don't look so sick now."

Dar Ell peered up through the bars. "Men must endure."

"I can assure you the judge will give you many years to endure."

Disregarding him, Dar Ell asked, "Hear anything about that double-crossing little lout?"

"Not a thing, but I haven't prowled around yet."

"Or Morton and my trusty nephew?"

"Nothing."

"And you plan to go up against them, not knowing where any of them are? Ah, Landry, the joys of a lawman. 'But man, proud man, drest in a little brief authority.' It'll be too bad if they back-shoot you.''

"Don't worry, I'll give the constable here all the facts and details to make sure he gets you back for trial. Incidentally, I left your cloak on the constable's desk. Mollie won't be able to thank you personally."

"How is she?"

"We don't know yet."

"She's a fine lady."

Landry walked out back, stripped to the waist, and washed vigorously at a hand pump, feeling the water revitalize. He slicked his hair and cleaned his mouth; when time permitted, he would purchase clean clothes, get a hot bath, a shave, and good whiskey, he promised himself. He strapped on the gun and belt and practiced several dry gun pulls. The second gun he tucked back in his belt. With growing confidence he set out to check the saloons, but not before he looked in on Mollie. "Meet you here in about forty-five minutes," he told Dutton. "That should give you time to round up those kids and place a rifle above the store."

"Shouldn't be no problem. I'll check the hotel rosters."

Landry repeated a description of Terena and the outlaws. "The kid and the girl might try to trade in the horses or buy new ones; certainly they have money to do it. And Morton and Biggs are going to need mounts to get out of here."

With lengthening shadows caressing the building as a ruddy sun filtered rays through the high pines, Landry approached the Long Tom Hotel through the rear entrance. He liked Dutton—a humorous-looking individual, but certainly cooperative and conscientious. Landry sensed that the man might not be much of a fighter or a backup, however. But one never knew for sure until faced with the test.

Mae Bingham met him at the door. "Not much change," she told him, "but I think she is resting better." He could see Mollie still humped with blankets, the gold flicker of a crackling cedar fire dancing across the room.

"I'll be back," he said.

The hotel bar had some green gaming tables, a dark, battered mahogany bar, walls adorned with antlers, dear head, and some romanticized pictures depicting lofty mountains that had no resemblance to the Sierras. Smoking kerosene chandeliers glinted over the rows of bottles and glasses and reflected back from a long series of mirrors that gave the room an illusion of being much larger. Some nondescript people drank and played cards at a couple of tables. Others pressed against the bar. The place had a musty, demure feel. The California Gold Rush had ended its heyday fifteen years earlier. A sense of repose, of civil responsibility, of finality, had settled over those towns that had survived the decline in gold. Most of the men present were mining officials, local businessmen, and a few salesmen intent on pushing some enterprise. If any noticed Landry, it was with indifference.

Landry found his way to the Dry Diggins Saloon, the obvious life center of Lost Chance. Some saddled horses and a half-dozen paired teams with wagons waited outside. Boisterous laughter and talk from the men filled the street. A tinny piano tinkled out a medley of lively tunes. He looked over the bat-wing doors, assessing the casual patrons, most young and getting drunk. When a man pushed by, Landry followed to order a beer. He found his way to a murky corner. A narrow, rickety stairs led to a balcony and some halls connecting with second-story rooms. No one present whetted his curiosity. At a free lunch counter he ate some pickles and made a huge sandwich of rye bread, hogshead cheese, and thick ham.

Back at the jail, Dutton was waiting, sitting on his desk, one leg swung over a corner. "Learned something," he greeted. "There was two men that registered at the Dry Diggings— one was a big-gutted guy with a little string of a mustache. Said he and his partner wanted a room overlooking the street—listed their names as Thomas Thompson and Jackson Smythe."

"Unlikely names, but I'd bet a month's pay that's them."

"The clerk never did see the second man—probably went in from the outside stairs. They got a corner room. The southeast one."

"Can they see the general store?"

"The general store and just about everything. In fact, you'll be stationed just opposite them."

"Couldn't be better. Are there any men you could deputize?" Landry asked. "We could trap them in there, as long as we cleared possible hostages."

Dutton shook his head. "These are citizens and businessmen gone soft with the fat of civilization. I couldn't ask 'em to risk their lives against the likes of Morton. They'd probably get more in the way. Maybe Jake, our barber, might be a possibility as a backup. Of course, he sees himself more as a vigilante. Incidentally, I got his two boys for you. Quietly, they're going to keep a lookout for the youth and the girl and for Morton and his partner. Kids will probably see a dozen suspects and drive us crazy, but we'll just have to sift through what they see."

"Good." Landry dug out some additional coins. "Do they know there's a bonus?"

"Yes, they're in rivalry for it. I got a rifle up in the old newspaper office for you, and the Donnovans expect somebody to be prowling around up there."

"Wish all of my men were as capable as you," said Landry.

"I'm proud to work with the likes of you, Marshal."

Landry wound his way through a back alley and up the side entrance into the abandoned newspaper office, dusty with cobwebbed tables and handpresses. He barely parted the dirt-caked curtains. The place afforded a fine view of the street. He wiped off a stool and pulled it up, the rifle across his lap. He could see the front window open in the east corner of the second story over the Dry Diggins Saloon—Morton's room—the lace curtain billowing. Taking Morton and Biggs would be difficult; the responsibility rested upon him alone, with what little assistance Constable Dutton might provide. His wisest action now was a waiting game. Apparently Morton, like Landry, had concluded the probability of Terena or Lon arriving eventually. And for Landry, one or both of the young people would be unsuspecting decoys.

By mid-afternoon a weary and failing Lon Wiggins, with Terena close behind, guided the horses up to the best-looking building—the superintendent's shack in an abandoned mine on the side of the mountain just south of Lost Chance. Weighted by a money belt, he dropped heavily at the chestnut's feet. Terena hurried to him and tried to pull him to the shack. Painfully, Lon called, "Anyone in there?" His voice echoed. They waited.

"Don't see no other horses," said Terena.

"He don't use a horse. Doesn't need them," Lon explained. "Don't think I can get up to look inside." Terena had fashioned a crude bandage around the youth's thigh to stop the bleeding, but it had soaked red.

With apprehension, Terena squeaked the door open and looked inside. Except for a rough-hewn table and a few battered chairs, the place was empty. "It don't look like anybody's been here."

"That don't make sense." A shiver ran through Lon. Terena came back; she was shaking. They glanced around. A large, windowless building covered the shaft head and hoisting works, linking with several wings that had once harbored carpenters, blacksmiths, and machinists. Ghostly head flumes crumbling tramways, flumes, and broken water towers hulked over it all. The area was snaked with braided steel cable, piled with cylinders, rubbled with drums, giant spools, pulleys, flywheels, and pipes. An early wind played mournfully through gaunt structures, monotonously slamming some corrugated tin roofing.

"God, I don't like this place," Terena bawled.

"He was supposed to be here—this building. The one at the head of the road. He'll come. He'll be here."

She helped him inside. "Who?"

"My partner, he'll be here. I guaranteed him half the take."

"Please tell me."

"He'll be here. He knows I'd never double cross him. Besides, I'd never get away with it." Lon laughed begrudgingly. "He's the best tracker and outdoorsman either side of the Sierras. Who do you think spooked them horses? Haunted us? Slit Yattero's throat?"

"My God, who?"

Lon cried out and doubled with pain. "Christ, it hurts." Terena removed the bloody rag. Several inches above the knee the bullet hole throbbed, ragged and dark, but clean, for the lead had passed through. Purple tendrils of dried blood hung from the wound. Terena looked at it sickly, rose, gobbed up a handful of cobwebs, returned and planted the mess over the opening. "The money, the sacks, get those in here," Lon said faintly. Obligingly, she retrieved the precious cargo and piled it inside. The youth lay back on a bedding of wealth. "Wish to hell he'd come."

"There's no food, nothing," Terena lamented. "You said this friend would bring supplies."

"I don't understand."

An hour passed. Lon became progressively withdrawn and despondent. The shadows lengthened. Terena found some water in a nearby spring. She bathed Lon's forehead and then the wound, which had swollen, festering. He drank great gulps of water and coughed much of it back up. His eyes had a feverish shine.

"I'm going into that town," she said. "We need food and whiskey and tonic. We have to get you something."

"It's too dangerous," Lon said feebly. "He'll come yet and bring us what we need. After all, I have his share."

"No," she said. "I'll take the marshal's horse. I'll be careful. I can see the top of the town from here. Expect me back before dark."

"Morton—he could be waiting." Lon's voice wavered. "God, why?" he wailed. "Why the hell did this happen to me?"

"Whiskey or kerosene, that could stop the rotting," she said.

"Yes, whiskey. I want whiskey," Lon whined.

Terena took the chestnut, some money, and a gun. She shuddered at the oppressive eeriness of the setting and rode out. She had an unexplainable feeling, an intuitive feeling that she was being watched.

Back in the superintendent's cabin, Lon feared for Terena, and doubted she would be successful, but he knew he had little choice. The bleeding had stopped momentarily, but the swelling and the hurt intensified. He had seen a man die once of blood poisoning. He pushed the thought out of his mind, worked his way across the room and squirmed himself to a sitting position behind the door, with his revolver braced in two hands across his good leg. He left the money pile in full view.

Landry heard footsteps up the outside stairs and a light knock. "It's me, Dutton." Landry slipped his revolver back and opened the door. "The kid we hired, the one stationed in the loft of the livery stable?" The constable stepped in.

"Yes?"

"He just seen a girl on a big red horse following the south

edge of town. Apparently come down from the mountain back of us. I looked, and sure enough, she's waiting out there at the wood's edge, a little timid, but she'll be in.''

Landry looked out a back window.

''Can't see her from here. Incidentally, Judah Mayberry come looking for you. That sick girl you brung in, she was asking for you. Left a message with him.''

''She's conscious, then.''

''Yes.''

''How is she?''

''Not too good yet.''

''Damn,'' said Landry. ''I just can't go to her now.''

''Maybe later.''

''When the Mexican girl comes in, arrest her. I want to talk with her. Safest place after that is your jail. If Morton sees her, we may need some backup.''

''I've got a sawed-off shotgun,'' Dutton offered confidently.

''You may need everything you can get your hands on. I been thinking. In the army I learned the best defense is an offense. It may have to come to that with Morton.''

They waited some ten minutes, watching out the back window until they saw the girl appear out of the pines where the needles gleamed a greenish gold and the brick-red earth glowed in the late sun. She rode slowly up to an Indian cutting wood and stopped, apparently for directions, as he pointed to the building where they hid. The big gelding, anxious to keep moving, shifted and danced. The girl, unsure, clutched the saddle horn and stared ahead. Dutton left down the side stairs.

Less than ten minutes later he returned, accompanied by the girl; she was protesting softly. When she saw the marshal, she uttered a little animal cry. Landry said, ''We have much to talk about, Miss Terena, mainly about the whereabouts of your boyfriend.''

"I didn't think you'd made it."

"Well, Dar Ell and I did make it, but no thanks to your friend."

Her lips trembled, puckered, and tears flowed. She wiped her eyes and nose with a cloth. "He's bad wounded. In the leg."

"By Morton. At the old cabin where you left the lady reporter."

"Yes, but I'm so sorry about that lady. We panicked. I looked out the window and the fat man was coming at us."

"Where is Lon?"

She stiffened. "I can't tell you."

"You'll let him die alone? Bleed to death? Or just let the leg fester as poison streaks up it? That's one miserable death."

"Please."

"At the worst, with good behavior, he'll get off with five to ten years. That may be a long time to wait for him, but that's better than having his death on your soul."

"Oh, I've been thinking." Her face twisted with emotion. "He's changed so."

"Meaning?"

"I thought I knew him. But suddenly, he's changed. I even thought of leaving, not going back to him, but he's so hurt and alone out there," she confessed, looking at Landry directly.

"Let me know where he is and I'll help him. You realize, I can't allow you to go back to him anyway."

"Why?"

"Didn't the constable tell you—you're under arrest as an accomplice. And for your own protection. Rattlesnake Morton's looking for you, too."

She sighed. Her shoulders sank, almost in relief, as if a great weight had been lifted. "When I ran off with him, I knew he was part of something in the wrong, but I didn't expect all the greed and all the killing. Someone smarter or tougher than Lon will take that loot from him or kill him for it.''

"That's right. That's why you can help him. Now.''

"He may not need me anyway.''

"Why?'' Landry responded quickly. His face had an interrogative expression.

"He was expecting a friend with supplies. A partner.''

"A partner?''

"All I know, whoever it is, is the one who spooked our horses and killed that Yattero fellow. And he caused all the scare. But that's all I know.''

Landry looked at a curious Dutton. "The coyote haunter. Things are starting to slowly fit.''

"I don't understand any of it,'' Terena said.

Landry said gently, "You're Lon's girl. You're too close to see that he's a very confused young man who's got his values wrong; he's headed for death one way or the other. Do you think that partner will really share with him? The killer is unknown. Only your Lon knows who he is. And all that money for easy taking?''

Terena chewed her lips and said evenly, "He's in a mining building, a half hour ride from here. He called it the superintendent's office. Oh, God, I hope he'll forgive me,'' she blurted.

"That's the old Argonaut Mine,'' said Dutton. "Hasn't been active since the late fifties.''

"I was there once. Your beau still have the mustang?'' Landry asked Terena.

"Yes.''

"I'm going to bring him back. He'll forgive you eventually, because if it's not too late, you will have saved his life.''

"He's sick and bad off, but he won't give up,'' Terena pleaded. "Please don't kill him.''

"I'll bring him back, miss, I promise.'' He looked at the

constable. "I'll need a fresh horse. 'Least now my chestnut will have a square meal. Take good care of him, Dutton."

As Dutton led the horse and escorted Terena toward the livery stable and a cell, as inconspicuously as possible, Amos Biggs in the shadows beside the Long Tom Hotel saw and turned hurriedly toward the room where Morton sat armed.

(17)

Conflicting thoughts flooded Landry. He studied the room where Morton apparently watched. With Lon Wiggins armed and dangerous but maybe dying, protecting a treasure of wealth; and with someone out there, unknown, a specter, a slayer; with Morton threatening the well-being of the town, and the safety of Terena, and even the life of a fine and dedicated constable; and in that back room a woman who had asked to see him while still fighting for her life—he sat before the window, thinking. He really had no choice, he realized. He would steal into the rear of the hotel and see Mollie before heading out after Lon. Time was short, with the dark coming and with Morton in town. A side of him knew that he would have to take out Morton, and the sooner the better.

Stealthily, he sneaked his way to the Long Tom. Mae Bingham met him at the door following an insistent knock. "She's gone into a coma again," said Mae, her face haggard.

"My God, how come?" The rosy warmth of the room flowed into the chill hall.

"I don't know. All I can do is keep her warm and wait it out."

"Where's Mayberry?"

"Somebody's cow had a stillborn calf."

"And he left her?"

"He's dead tired. And there was nothing else he could do that I can't do."

Landry lowered his head. "Did she ever mention why she asked for me?"

"No."

"When she wakes, tell her I was here."

"You know I will."

Landry said impulsively but with growing conviction, "I must do what has to be done." His face set, he walked out the back door, checked his revolver in the holster, and the extra one he had borrowed from Dutton, snug in the belt in the flank of his backside, reachable under a flap of coat. He stalked determinedly to the fire exit of the Dry Diggins Saloon and stole into the upper hall and down to the east room, gun in hand. Landry listened. Nothing. Halfway up another hall a woman entertained a man, their voices a little thick and coarse with liquor.

As far as Landry could judge, Morton and Biggs did not expect a marshal in town. The element of surprise was all his. Landry booted the door with his heel, thrusting all his two-hundred-pound might; the latch parted, splintering the wood, smashing the door wide onto the room. In the instant of impact, he rolled to the side and dropped into a crouch, his Colt extended in both hands. Before him stood an unused bed, a table with dirty dishes, some chairs askew, one in front of an open window, the curtain ballooning. An empty whiskey bottle stood on the sill. All personal belongings were gone. Realizing he was too late, Landry rushed to the window to see some riders pulling out far down the street, disappearing around the livery stable. He hurried up the hall. A short man in a suit, accompanied by a bare-shouldered woman with high-piled hair, emerged from a neighboring room, inquisitive. "What's the ruckus?" the man called, stepping back as Landry bowled past, gun in hand, his face taut.

* * *

Dutton lay sprawled facedown on his office floor, the cell holding Dar Ell open, both he and the girl gone. South toward the mountain, Landry heard two distinct shots. He felt Dutton's scalp, saw the red lump rising, and thought of his own skull, puffed still. He turned the man over. Dutton twisted up, his head bobbing, his sharp features almost comical, like a puppet on uncoordinated strings. Landry took him in hand, steadied him. He dipped some water from a pitcher and sloshed it over the constable's head and face until his groggy eyes cleared. "The girl and Dar Ell, what happened? Morton?"

Dutton, his eyes rolling again, flopped his head up and down. "Not sure."

"But how?"

Dutton slurred his words and tried again. Landry helped him to a sitting position, a hand on each shoulder. "Just got the female in the holding cell when somebody, a man, called me. I come out, and wow! Someone got me from behind; that's all I remember."

Landry on a black mare, beside a slow blinking Dutton on a dapple-gray, headed into the slant of sunset rays. Less than a quarter of a mile out of town, they saw a horse standing, rippling in nervousness, the saddle empty; twenty yards behind lay the ruined form of a human. The two rearranged the man with care, stretched his legs for comfort, his arms to the sides, and arched his back for easier breathing, although the life flow had ebbed too long. Dar Ell could not see Landry clearly. The faded eyes saw inwardly without care. But the man of courtly dignity retained an awareness still in his once magnificent voice, deeper, richer than in the past days, a voice reflecting the awareness of ended time, of drained talent, of defeated dreams.

"Dar Ell," Landry said softly. "Who did this?"

"Morton. Morton and my nephew—" His words broke and trailed off. "Useless, useless, useless."

"Try to tell me."

"They forced her to talk."

"Go on."

"It's at a mill—her beau."

"I know."

"Girl confessed he has a partner." Dar Ell choked, spewed some bloody saliva, and cleared his throat.

"Who?" Landry demanded.

"Could only be Johnny Wolfsong." He uttered the name like a curse, which cost him energy.

"Johnny Wolfsong?"

"Nephew of Nasa Tom. A bitter, vindictive kid."

"How do you know him?"

"Used to work for me. Was a friend of that little traitor, Lon Wiggins." He choked again. "They remained friends even after he went to California."

"Take it easy. You have time."

"No. No time." His voice gurgled. Landry helped him to clear out a red foam. "Wolfsong used to be a hunter of predators." Dar Ell struggled and tried again. "Used to work for the cattlemen. Hell of a tracker, I guess. Knew his animals." His eyes fluttered—slowing.

"It figures."

"All for nothing now—lines I spoke but never heard." Dar Ell seemed to be talking more to himself, a soliloquy of sorts. Both Landry and Dutton leaned close.

"Don't fight it," said Landry.

Dar Ell turned his head toward the marshal's voice and tried to focus. "I did forget those most important lines." Suddenly, his voice was clear, steady: " 'To thine ownself be true—that the fault lies not in the stars but in ourselves that we are underlings.' " He gasped and coughed.

Landry wiped some sputum from his lips. "Which one shot you?"

Dar Ell tried to answer, couldn't, then managed, "Morton, I think. Was riding off. Begged them to give me a chance. Didn't want the damn money anymore." Again he coughed. His eyes constricted. "You know . . ."

Landry leaned low and waited.

" 'Tis all a tale told by an idiot signifying nothing." He convulsed. His eyes glazed. He spoke so low that only Landry could make out his far words, each distinctly pronounced: "Out, out brief candle."

Landry remained kneeling for a time, then tenderly closed the man's eyelids. "You know," he said to Dutton, "I was coming to like the man." He looked up at the dark rise ahead. A stolid calm came over him, chilling, inscrutable, the steeliness of a man consumed with intent.

In the purple of twilight they reached the mine. The mustang, still in front of the superintendent's building, raised its head and nickered, and above from somewhere amongst the crumbling buildings an unseen horse answered, revealing that Morton and others had arrived. Landry and Dutton left their mounts concealed, and both carrying rifles they had taken from the jail office, moved under cover in a close pincer movement. Dutton waited behind some broken barrels while Landry skirted a slag pile and took refuge next to a toolshed. He in turn signaled Dutton, who ran the partial length of an old tramway. Landry crouched, his rifle ready, for he expected some reaction. The black, glassless windows of the stamp mill gazed upon them like eyeless sockets.

Dutton approached from the left, Landry from the right. They met at the superintendent's shack, moving low, apparently undetected. Landry motioned Dutton to an end window. They listened and heard nothing. Much in the same manner that he had broken into Morton's hotel room, the marshal kicked the door, swinging it, but this one broke loose and fell to the floor, the noise snuffed by something underneath. Landry readied his rifle and stepped back as Dutton glanced quickly into the building and ducked. "Somebody's on the floor," Dutton called.

Landry looked and saw a small man's face in a smear of blood, one hand stretched above, holding a long knife with a wicked blade, the body under the door. Carefully, both men entered. There was no sign of Lon Wiggins or of the money. Removing the door, they bent over the form and turned him over—a handsome young Indian; a rawhide band held his long, straight hair. His sightless eyes and frozen face registered shocked surprise. His chest and belly and right backside had been riddled. While walking or sneaking in, he apparently had been gunned by someone behind him, had spun around to be met with bullets, and had kept spinning away, to be nailed in the side. "Has to be Johnny Wolfsong—maybe Dar Ell was right," Landry said. Searching for identification, Landry removed a folded note from a pocket over the heart. It was written in a beautiful and distinct scroll:

Johnny:
Just a final note to let you know that my thoughts will be with you. I know you will succeed. But as I told you, for both our sakes, I must never know details or names, only that we are sharing partners. You know where to contact me. Good luck. Be careful. Please destroy this.

"What's it mean?"

"I don't know." Landry tucked the paper in his vest.

From the building near the shaft head, underneath the remains of a towering head frame used to hoist cages of men, equipment, and ore from the bowels of the earth, came Morton's voice. Dutton poked Landry and jerked his head in the direction. Both craned their heads and moved to the east window.

* * *

Morton, gripping Terena's arm cruelly, smiled calculatingly and wetted his thick lips. He stared at an auxiliary shaft, a cluster of buildings connected to the main ship by a tramway, many of the boards having fallen away. "Hear me down there, kid?" There came no reply. Biggs crawled closer and rested his pistol across an overturned ore cart and waited. "I have your girl here." He turned to Terena. "Tell him." He sunk callused fingers into her arm, powerful fingers from prison rock work.

"Please," she whimpered.

"Tell him."

"Lon," she called, "he's going to hurt me." The evening wind hummed in the manzanita and sifted the fine dust.

"He's hurt. Maybe he's dead," she said in great distress.

"He's down there." Morton shouted again: "Throw out your take, all of it, kid, if you want your girl in one piece." He twisted her arm slightly. "You can have her. We'll let you both go free. But first throw out the bags one by one."

Fearfully, Terena looked into his menacing face, the ponderous overhang of forehead above small, cruel eyes. She forced herself higher and yelled with all her strength toward the cabins around the auxiliary mine. Upon arrival, they had seen something manlike moving erratically there, as if limping about, but they weren't certain it was Lon, and he had not been seen again. "He means it, Lon. Can you hear me?"

Morton bent her arm. "Scream."

"Help."

"Scream," he hissed viciously, wrenching her arm. Without further prompting, Terena, a searing anguish in her face, emptied her lungs, the sound piercing, echoing over the hill and canyon. No reaction issued from Lon.

In the superintendent's office, Dutton gritted his teeth and began moving in the direction of her voice, but Landry restrained him.

Morton let her arm go, placed both his mammoth hands on each side of her head and pressed. Terena rolled her eyes back and forth as the thick fingers curled over her forehead. "What are you doing?" she cried.

"Beg him. Go on. Beg him. Tell him I'm going to crush your brains out in my hands."

"Lon—for God's sake, are you down there, he's going to kill me." Morton extended his elbows, his biceps knotting, and enclosed her skull a little tighter. Terena squirmed. "Help," she wailed. "Lon, please, he means it."

"It's your choice, kid." Morton laughed maliciously. "Better deliver."

"He's hurt. You know that." Her voice wavered. "I told you. He may be dead."

"She could be right," Biggs said. "He might of passed out."

"We'll find out," said Morton. He yanked Terena up as a shield and moved into the dusk along the tramway, revealing himself for the first time. He approached steadily. Unexpectedly, Lon opened fire from the cluster. The lead sliced close to Terena, chopping out chunks of wood. The shots caught Morton off guard, knocking him and the girl back. He, Biggs, and Terena retreated in a run through the middle of the tramway, although the youth's bullets smashed around here and there. Abruptly, Morton pushed the girl away. "She ain't no good. It won't work with her. We've got to kill that kid without her." After exchanging a few more shots, the two men found their way to the main building with the shaft's head. The blasting sounds broke flimsy siding and roofing off, to slide noisily, and forty feet up on the scaffoldlike structure, a hoist gave way; loose boards sailed down to clatter and bounce, some fantailing crazily over the hillside.

Landry and Dutton watched Terena flee some twenty yards and hide beneath the remains of a water tower. "Come on," Landry urged. He and Dutton sprang anxiously up the rise, littered dangerously with holding bins, sheave wheels, pieces of track, and long-rusted debris. They came up behind a storage building. "Cover me," Landry called. He broke free to race the best he could on the crippled leg to Terena, cowering in a recession. She looked up with a start, her face then beaming with joy at sight of him. He embraced her shoulders. "Wait, then we're going to run like the devil," he said as they heard another exchange of gunfire. He drew a long breath and lifted her slightly, poising her. "Now." Holding her hand, he jerked her toward a wing of the main hoisting building.

Morton saw Landry tugging the girl and fanned his gun wildly until emptying the bullets, splaying the area but missing, spitting dirt behind Terena's heels. Landry drew the girl inside an empty room and held her against the swell of his big shoulders.

From the top of the tram Morton thumbed cartridges into his revolver. "Girl told me it was you, Landry." He let the words flow across the waste and echo around the dead building. He cupped his mouth like a megaphone. "Maybe at last we can finish what we started long ago." Then he clambered into the main building so that his voice would stream from another area. He leaned out a glass-shattered rim of a narrow window. "I'm going to kill you, Landry."

As darkness fell, Landry waved Dutton to him. They would have to work closely if they were to take Morton, Biggs, and the kid. In such a chaotic setting, they could easily shoot one another. For an hour they waited, listening. Time dragged. A standoff: Dutton, the girl, and Landry in an upper wing; Morton and Biggs somewhere near the main shaft in the hoisting building; and Lon wounded, below, in one of the cluster buildings, but dangerous always; all of them connected by tramways, bridges, and a nightmare of corridors, ladders, and conveyor belts; all of them separated by death traps of tangled junk and rubbish, hidden pits and concealed shafts, the flooring crumbling everywhere. Bats flitted darkly, and the wind spiraled through skeletal structures, making a cacophony of music. Some coyotes joined in a haunting aria of lonely cries.

For a short time Terena rested her head back on a wall and closed her eyes, but time and again she would shake alert to confide, "I just didn't know him. I thought I did."

"Money, especially big money, seduces men," Landry said, his voice soft. "I've seen it all my life."

The night plodded on. Landry and Dutton led Terena from the room to an angled foundation of a building long gone, the base forming a barricade that both fortified and offered a sweeping trajectory of the setting. The spot not only situated them between Morton and Lon Wiggins, but removed them from where Morton had last seen them.

"What you plan next, Marshal?" Dutton sniffed the air.

"With the first light, we'll go after the kid. As I keep saying, wherever the kid is, Morton won't be too far. But in the dark now, we stay right here. It's too dangerous crawling around out there." The slender moon cast a bland light that blended the landscape.

"Damn nice home for rattlesnakes," said Dutton. "They'll be swarming about."

"Oh, Lord, I didn't think about that," Terena said. "Now I am scared."

"We can hope they join their brother Morton up there," Landry said. Terena chuckled heartily. "You're okay," said Landry. "Your boyfriend doesn't deserve you."

"When we go after the kid, what do we do with the young lady here?" Dutton asked.

"We'll leave her here. She'll be fine. Nobody's going to hurt her now."

Before dawn a timorous voice reached them from the

building cluster. "Landry, help." The voice had an ethereal quality. "Landry, please save me. I'm dying."

"Help him," Terena cried out. "Oh, God, he's dying." She sat up to call out, when Landry clasped her mouth with a big hand. She struggled against him, her eyes blazing.

"No, Terena. No," he said firmly. "You'll draw him out to his death." She relaxed some, aware that he was not using her. "I want your beau alive, not a worthless carcass, although there's a side of me that would like to pack him back that way."

"You hear me, Landry? I know you hear me. I seen you ride up with my girl. Come help me. I can't hold out much longer."

From partway down the tramway, both Morton and Biggs punched shots at the region of Lon's voice, where he crouched waiting; flames stabbed into the black. In the dark they had attempted to sneak up on the youth. And Lon answered, pumping five shots back at them.

"That would have been our welcome." Landry whooped: "Now let's give Morton hell." Their rifles centered, Landry and Dutton levered a volley of sizzling bullets at Morton and Biggs that smacked and whined throughout the old wood and tin remains. As fast as the two could shoot they emptied their rifles; someone yelped. A second person withdrew, blasting back at them, moving toward the hoisting building again until disappearing.

Terena, chewing a clenched fist, pressed flat behind the two lawmen. Up near the main shaft came the resounding topple of wood and earth folding in upon itself, first rumbling, then crashing as earth and framework collided, smashing, to go under. A man screamed, his voice trailing; there followed a tinkle here, a clatter there, the funneling of slowing dirt, and finally, silence. "Someone fell," Dutton said curiously.

"Sure sounds like it." Landry reached back toward Terena. "You all right, girl?"

"Wow," she whispered, sitting high. "Wow."

"Nothing we can do until morning," said Landry, thinking about Mollie and wanting a shave and a bath.

At the first silver of dawn, Landry and Dutton circled uphill, cut above the stamp mill, then separated again in a pincer movement, with Dutton above along an east wing. Landry approached from a shack to a holding bin to a slag pile, keeping anything sizable between him and the cluster building where Lon had been, and between him and where Morton and Biggs had been last sighted—a dangerous undertaking, Landry knew. They could walk into sudden death, but a lawman sworn to his job had few alternatives than to confront a problem face on. Dutton reached the main building; the ghostly edifice of the head frame—the hoisting works like some monumental windmill—cast bleak shadows about him. He gestured to Landry that he was going inside.

Landry liked the constable. Dutton's gawky appearance was deceptive. He had proven himself far more professional than Landry had dared hope for. Landry held up a hand, the palm flat toward Dutton to delay him a moment. He then sidled along the tramway and ducked under a window next to a doorless opening.

Dutton picked up part of a broken pipe and tossed it through an opening. Landry heard a revolver cock on the other side of the wall. As Dutton slipped inside, Landry inched around the frame to see Biggs slumped back, his revolver slanted upward toward Dutton as he came down the tramway. "Hold it, Biggs, don't move." Landry stepped forward. "Move or breathe, you get it between the eyes." Biggs's mouth dropped open as he stiffened. "Now let it go." Biggs's revolver rolled off his trigger finger and clattered on the planking. "Where's Morton?"

"Sounded like he fell through something last night." Biggs tossed his head toward the upper tramway. The guard had twisted his leg in a fall during the night shooting. Dutton checked him for additional weapons and sat him up. They bound him.

"We couldn't stand to have you get away," said Dutton.

"Ain't going far with this knee."

"Did you shoot Dar Ell?" Landry asked.

"Morton did," he answered immediately.

"But you had more to gain."

"You can't prove nothin'," Biggs said acidly.

At the upper end of the tramway, near the head shaft, they found a splintered six-foot hole next to a broken car rail. Together the lawmen approached. Morton had apparently backed into an old winze or crosscut, a vertical tunnel used for ventilation and communication between levels, some twenty feet down. Through the dark they could see a pile of boards but nothing clearly, only another auxiliary shaft running north and south.

"The entrance is down the hill a ways. We can check it out," said Dutton.

"Yes, we'll have to find out whether Morton's dead or alive. But first, now, it's the kid down there. He may not have made it through the night."

Again apart, with vigilance, they labored parallel to the tramway toward the cluster of storage buildings, finding the first two empty. However, next to the third shack, Landry saw a trail of dried blood. Anger still seething in him, he rounded the building. Where a door tilted open, Lon lay facedown on the floor, one leg drawn up as if in a crawl, the gold sacks and saddlebags entangled and clotted over him. Doggedly, Landry came upon him; the youth twisted to his side and brought up his six-shooter. Landry hop-skipped and swung his right foot up with such a swift and solid kick that the gun sailed away.

Lon screamed. In terror he thrashed away, the throes of his body frenzied as Landry grasped his coat and lifted him into the air to shake him as a dog might shake a squirrel. "If you wasn't hurting so, I'd beat the hell out of you," he bellowed. "But I'm going to keep you alive just to see you sentenced."

"It was self-defense," Lon whimpered. "It was self-defense. Johnny tried to double cross me. He was trying to kill me."

"And what of Nasa Tom? Who killed him?"

The youth froze up. "I didn't know he was dead."

"We uncovered his body near the pass."

Lon frowned. "He somehow got wind of me and Johnny. He was going to try and stop Johnny. He was afraid for him—that coyote stuff. That's why he abandoned Dar Ell and took off."

"Probably Tom and his nephew had it out. We'll never know now."

Directed by rays of light streaming down the winze, Dutton and Landry traced a horizontal tunnel to where Morton had supposedly fallen. Along the murky side they found a fancy white hat. Hurriedly, they sorted through the piled ruins to uncover a side arm. But no sign of the man called Rattlesnake. They peered into the gloomy recession of the shaft. Overhead the wind fluttered some loose roofing. Edgy, Dutton swung his rifle up and fired, erupting a flowering of earth and wood that showered around them.

(18)

A few curious citizens stood in the doors as Landry led the troop into Lost Chance and up to the livery stable with Biggs tied to the saddle and Lon clinging to his saddle horn. He and Terena avoided each other's eyes. Dutton pulled two horses strapped with the bodies of Johnny Wolfsong and Jonathan Dar Ell, their arms swinging loosely.

As Landry climbed down, two men emerged from the jail office—Deputy Nelson and Sheriff George Healy. Healy moved stiffly, favoring his right side with the support of a cane, his left arm in a sling under his coat. He and Landry greeted one another. "Me and my deputy just got in on the stage by way of Tahoe," said the sheriff. He grinned wryly. "I come to buy that drink I owe you." He looked at the bodies and at the prisoners. He took special note of the Indian. "See you've been active since my deputies left you."

"It's a long story," said Landry. "This is what's left of the gang that robbed a stage at Willow Springs and killed some Wells Fargo personnel."

"I figure my fiancée, Mollie Tyndale, should have been with them," Healy inquired anxiously.

"She's here in a hotel. Last I knew, she was awful sick, but alive."

"Thank God."

"I'm heading to the Long Tom now to see about her," Landry said, not hiding his deep concern. "Come on."

"Oh, Marshal," Dutton called. "When the doc gets a chance, I'm going to need him for the young scalawag here and maybe for the others, too. And Marshal, it's been a pleasure working with you."

Landry smiled. "And the same for you, Dutton. I'll be taking the girl, Terena, back with me."

"The constable has a lot of work cut out for him, Nelson. You might help him," Healy told his deputy.

Landry and Healy headed down the street, one tall with a hitching stride, the other short and limping. "We got much to talk about," said the sheriff.

"Looks like you ran into some troubles," Landry said sympathetically.

"Leander Morton tried to do me in. Fortunately, prison time hasn't helped his aim. He grazed me in the arm and the backside. No bones or vitals hit, just a little blood loss that slowed me up some. Otherwise I would have been here sooner. We killed or caught all of them except Leander Morton and one other."

"The one other is that big-gutted fellow I just brought in— Amos Biggs; he's the guard they took at the state pen. He was in on the break and the stage heist."

"Biggs is not dead, then?" Healy exclaimed. "Then the guard we found must have been a prisoner in his uniform. I was suspicious, but I never knew what the guard looked like."

"Yes."

"It all starts to fit."

"Well, I tried to do Morton in for you. He fell down an air shaft."

"Dead?" Healy's voice rose with hope.

"We found what we're sure is his hat and the gun, but not a hide nor hair of him."

Healy grunted in disgust. "That Morton should have been

nicknamed Cat Morton. He always seems to have another life. If he's alive, we'll know it eventually.''

"How did you find me?"

"I picked up on your clue to my men—about this town which I'd never been to—especially when we went back to the swing station. I was pretty weak. My men wanted to take me on to Limbo, but I insisted we search out the station. Of course, we found the dead there and saw all the hell that had taken place. But most important, Mollie had left her bonnet and a dress she'd once worn when we went out once.''

"Didn't know she'd done that." Landry chuckled, obviously pleased.

"That's when I knew you were in trouble for sure. Then too, I knew you'd never leave those station people without a decent burial.''

"It turned out to be bigger than anyone dreamed—a clever plan that just went wrong. A planned prison escape was part of it.''

Healy looked dumbfounded. "I sure as hell do have a lot to talk over with you.''

"There have been some surprises for sure.''

"I recognized the kid you brought in. Kind of a drifter about Limbo who used to work at the theater there some.''

"Lon Wiggins. He turned out to be the biggest culprit of them all. He tried playing both ends against the middle.''

"No honor amongst thieves, I guess. One of those dead, he looked familiar, but I didn't take a close look.''

"That was Jonathan Dar Ell. Managed the Desert Globe.''

"My God, yes. But why him? The brains, I'll venture.''

"Greed, lust, ambition.''

"I thought he had everything to make people want to be like him. And so many hurt because of it.''

"It's the curse of E-sha,'' said Landry dryly. "We've all been the coyote damned.''

"What?"

"It doesn't matter."

"Mollie will be sorry to hear that Indian kid was involved."

"Johnny Wolfsong?"

"I just knew him by Johnny. He used to work for her paper. Did odd jobs. He worshiped the ground she walked on. Would have gone to the ends of the earth for her. Sometimes thought I had a rival there." He laughed self-consciously. "She claimed people underestimated him. He was no dumb Indian, I guess, 'cause she saw something in him."

Mae Bingham came running out of the hotel into the muddy street, her skirt swooping, her arms outstretched, her face glowing. "They just told Mollie and me you were back." She took a deep breath and burst out, "She's going to make it. She'll be just fine." Mae hugged the marshal. "Early this morning she sat up and asked for soup."

"Thanks, Mae. I'm so happy," Landry said. "And Mae, this is Sheriff George Healy."

Mae curtsied.

"George is Mollie's husband-to-be."

Mae's face drained of color. She could not contain her disappointment. "P-P-Pleased to meet you."

Landry said to Healy. "You'd best go in and see Mollie now, she's been worried."

"Not looking like this." He glanced down at himself and ran a hand over the thickening whiskers. "Give me a chance to clean up."

"She won't care." They walked into the hotel and toward the back room. "Where's Mayberry?" Landry asked Mae. "He's needed for our prisoners, especially one."

"He's in the saloon celebrating."

"I can't tell you how much I appreciate all your work—yours and the doc's," he told her, shaking her hand.

"It was my pleasure." She curtsied again.

"Tell Mollie there's somebody special to see her."

"I can't go in yet," Healy protested, holding back shyly. "I still smell of trail dust."

"She'll be pleased to see you, too, Marshal," Mae said, opening the door.

Landry declined with a curt wave of a hand. He could see her inside, propped up against an enormous pillow. She was combing out her long hair. "Get in there, Healy."

"In this garb and the wounds?"

"Yes, get the hell in there. Doesn't matter at this point." He placed a flat hand across Healy's back and pushed him in.

Replacing his badge, Landry sauntered into the saloon section and did not look back. Doc Mayberry, alone at the bar, downed a whiskey, his face blazing red, his nose purple-veined. Landry set his mind on soaking away the grit and having a barber scrape off his stubble. First he'd have some whiskey. Then he'd send a telegram to Henry P. Tyndale in Placerville, assuring him that Mollie was safe, and then several to authorities in Limbo and Carson City. In the evening he'd enjoy a thick steak and a long-needed sleep in a too soft bed. Come morning he'd put Terena on the Tahoe stage back to Limbo and would tag after on the chestnut. There would be a hearing on her as an accomplice, but little would come of it, he felt certain. Nelson and Healy could have the pleasure of taking Amos Biggs and Lon Wiggins in. "Constable Dutton's got some prisoners he wants you to check on. One man got a little shot up," Landry said to the doctor.

Mayberry put his glass down. "You lawmen are giving me good business."

"I told Mae and I'll tell you. I really appreciate whatever you did for Mollie."

"We got her blood flowing again, that's all. She's a healthy woman. A fine woman."

"Yes, I know. What do I owe you?"

"I'll bill your office."

"Do you know what Mollie wanted to tell me? I never found out. She had passed out again when I went to her room."

"Oh, yeah, she left a note for you." He fumbled a sealed envelope from his coat and handed it over, then shoved the bottle forward. "Here, have a drink on me."

Landry tore open the letter.

Dear Dirk:

Thanks to you, I am still alive. And I am beholding to you. Before you leave, I expect you will come see me. Please do. I must talk to you. I hope and pray that someday in your heart, you can forgive what I must confess.

Mollie

His hand trembling, Landry produced the note he had found on Johnny Wolfsong and saw the same beautiful and distinct scroll. Shocked, his mind reeling, he poured a tall glass full and started out the front window as Mayberry shuffled into the empty street.

RIDE INTO THE WILD WILD WEST WITH

FAWCETT WESTERNS